Mor
Summertide,
Book One of
The Heritage Universe

"Charles Sheffield has been called 'the new Arthur C. Clarke' so often that one expects someday to meet a teenage fan who knows Clarke only as 'the old Charles Sheffield.' . . . We should expect to find in a Sheffield novel thrilling and almost religious descriptions of galactic phenomena, both natural and artificial. . . . To no one's surprise, this is just what's delivered. And if anyone can do a better job of this sort, I'd like to know about him."

The Washington Post

"Like Arthur C. Clarke and Greg Bear . . . brilliantly balanced seesaw between enormous concept and lifesize characterization."

The London Times

". . . rich with the imagination of one who knows and loves science, and who communicates with it . . ."

Locus

By Charles Sheffield
Published by Ballantine Books:

PROTEUS UNBOUND

SIGHT OF PROTEUS

TRADER'S WORLD

THE WEB BETWEEN THE WORLDS

The Heritage Universe
Book One: SUMMERTIDE
Book Two: DIVERGENCE
Book Three: TRANSCENDENCE

DIVERGENCE

Book Two of
The Heritage Universe

Charles Sheffield

A Del Rey Book
BALLANTINE BOOKS • NEW YORK

A Del Rey Book
Published by Ballantine Books
Copyright © 1991 by Charles Sheffield

All rights reserved under International and Pan-American Copyright Conventions. Published in the United States of America by Ballantine Books, a division of Random House, Inc., New York, and simultaneously in Canada by Random House of Canada Limited, Toronto.

Library of Congress Catalog Card Number: 90-42422

ISBN 0-345-36938-6

Manufactured in the United States of America

First Hardcover Edition: February 1991
First Mass Market Edition: February 1992

Cover Art by Bruce Jensen

To the same Gang of Four, and
anyone else who has advanced to
the magical average age of seventeen.

CHAPTER 1

"BLINK YOUR LEFT eye. Very good. Now close your right eye, hold it closed until I say 'Ready,' and then open it and smile at the same time."

"May I speak?"

"In a moment. *Ready.*"

The bright-blue eye opened. Thin lips drew back to reveal even white teeth. Sue Ando studied the grinning face for a few seconds, then turned to her assistant. "Now *that* needs attention. It's enough to scare a Cecropian. We need an upward curve on it, make it look more friendly."

"I'll take care of it." The other woman made a note on her computer scratchpad.

"May I speak?"

Ando nodded to the naked male figure standing in front of her. "Go ahead. We want to test your speech patterns anyway. And stop smiling like that—you give me the shivers."

"I am sorry. But why are you going through all this again?

1

It is quite unnecessary. I was thoroughly checked before I left the Persephone facility, and I was found to be physically perfect."

"I should hope so. We don't take rejects. But that was a month ago, and I'm checking for changes. There's always a settling-in period for an embodied form. And you'll be going a long way, to a place where they've probably never even *seen* an embodiment. If you run into stability problems you won't be able to drop in to a shop for an adjustment the way you can around Sol. All right. One more test, then we have to get you to the briefing center. Look at me and lift one foot off the floor."

As the bare foot was raised, Sue Ando stabbed with her fist at the unprotected jaw. One hand began to move up in self-defense, but it was too slow. Ando's knuckles came into hard contact with the chin.

"Damnation!" She put her fist to her mouth and sucked at the bruised joints. "That *hurt*. Did you feel it?"

"Of course. I have excellent sensory equipment."

"Not to mention tough skin. But now do you see what I mean about settling in to that body? I should never have got within a hand's length of you. A month ago I wouldn't have. Your reflexes need to be turned up a notch. We'll take care of it later today, after your briefing. It will mean popping your brain out for a few minutes."

"If you insist. However, I should mention that my embodied design is intended for continuous sensory input."

"We can arrange that, too. I'll run a neural bundle from your brain to your spine, so you'll receive your sensory feeds for all but the few seconds it takes to plug in the bundle at both ends."

"That will be appreciated. May I speak again?"

"I'm not sure we can stop you. Go ahead, talk as much as you like. Talk is going to be your main mode of communication."

"That is exactly the point I wish to make. I do not understand why I am to be provided with information in such an inefficient manner. I am wholly plug-compatible. With the use of a neural bundle, I can in one second send and receive many millions of data items. Humans are painfully slow. It is truly ridiculous to dole information to me via such a medium, or force me to provide it to another entity at a similar meager rate."

Sue Ando smiled at her assistant's expression. "I know, Lee. You think I ought to tone down his asperity level. But you're wrong. Where he's going annoyance at inefficiency will be a survival trait." She turned to the expressionless male figure. "Sure, you can send and receive faster than we can—to another computer. But you're going to the Dobelle system. It's poor and it's primitive, and I doubt if anyone there has ever seen an embodied computer. They certainly can't afford the facilities for direct data dumps with you. Your sources of information are going to be *humans,* and maybe other Organics. We may be slow and stupid, but you're stuck with us. Get used to that as soon as you can."

She turned back to Lee Boro. "Anything else we need before the briefing?"

Lee consulted her checklist. "Body temperature is a couple of degrees below human normal, but we'll fix that. Ion balances are fine. A name. We ought to settle one before we go any further."

"May I speak?"

Sue Ando sighed. "If you must. We're running out of time."

"I will be brief. Another name is unnecessary. I already have a complete identification. I am Embodied Computer 194, Crimson Series Five, Tally Line, Limbic-Enhanced Design."

"We know that. And I have a complete identification, too. I'm Sue Xantippe Harbeson Ando, human female, Europa homeworld, Fourth Alliance Group, Earth clade. But I wouldn't dream of using that as my *name,* it's three times too long to be useful. Your name is going to be—" She paused. "Something nice and simple. Embodied Computer Tally. E. C. Tally. How's that sound, Lee? E. Crimson Tally, if he wants to get formal."

Lee checked her computer. "It's not taken. I'll make an isomorphism between E. Crimson Tally and the full identification." She entered the note. "E. C. Tally for short. And we'll call you just Tally. All right?"

"May I speak?"

Sue Ando sighed. "Not again. They're waiting for you at the briefing station. All right. What's your problem now? Don't you like that name?"

"The identification that you propose is quite satisfactory. However, I am puzzled by two other things. First, I perceive that I am without clothing, while both of you wear your bodies covered."

"My Lord. Are you telling us you feel *embarrassed?*"

"I do not think so. I lack an internal state corresponding to a condition labeled embarrassment. I merely wonder if I am to wear clothing when in the Dobelle system."

"Unless they don't wear any. You'll do what they do. The whole point of your embodiment is to make you as acceptable to them as possible. What's your other problem?"

"I have been embodied in male human form, and I wonder why."

"For the same reason. You'll mainly be interacting with humans, so we want you to look human. And it's a lot easier to grow your body from a human DNA template, rather than trying to make some inorganic form that comes close to it."

"You have only partially answered my question: namely, you have explained why I am in human form." E. C. Tally pointed down at his genitals. "But as you see, I have been embodied in the *male* figure. The female figure, the one that both you and Lee Boro wear, appears lighter in construction and needs less food as fuel. Since I will be obliged to eat, I wonder why I was provided with the larger and less efficient form."

Sue Ando stared at him. "Hmm. You know, Tally, I don't have any answer to that. I'm sure that the Council has a reason for it, and it's probably got something to do with where you're going. But you should ask during your briefing. One thing's sure, it's too late to change bodies now. You're supposed to get to the Bose Network and head for Dobelle in three days."

"May I speak?"

"Certainly." Ando smiled. "But not now, and not to me. You're overdue with the briefing group. Go on, E. C. Tally. When you get there you can bend their ears as much as you like."

Three standard days before departure: that was seventy-two hours—259 thousand seconds, 259 billion microseconds, 259 billion trillion attoseconds. The grapefruit-sized sphere of E. C. Tally's brain had a clock rate of eighteen attoseconds. Three days should have been enough time to ponder every thought that had ever been thought by every organic entity in the whole spiral arm.

And yet Tally was learning that those three days would be insufficient. The hours were flying by. It was not the *facts* that provided the problem, even though they came trickling in with painful slowness from the human intermediary. The difficulty came with their implications, and with the surges they produced in the unfamiliar query circuits added at the time of E. C. Tally's embodiment.

For example, he had been told that the choice of male form had been made because the government of Dobelle was predominantly male. But every analysis of human events suggested that in a male-dominated society the effects of a single female could be maximized. How did Organics manage to ignore the evidence of their own history?

Tally put such ineluctable mysteries to one side, pending the long trip out to his destination. For the moment he would concentrate on the simpler question of galactic power groups.

"Dobelle is a double-planet system, part of the Phemus Circle of worlds." The man providing the briefing was Legate Stancioff, brought in specially from Miranda. He also seemed to Tally to have been chosen specifically for his leaden vagueness in thought and speech. He was staring at Tally with furrowed brow. "Do you know anything about the Phemus Circle?"

Tally nodded. "Twenty-three stellar systems. Primitive and impoverished. Sixty-two habitable planets, some of them marginal. They form a loose federation of worlds, on the overlapping boundary of the territories of the Fourth Alliance, the Cecropia Federation, and the Zardalu Communion. They are roughly one hundred parsecs away from Sol. They contain one Builder artifact, the Umbilical. That artifact is to be found in the Dobelle system."

The machine-gun delivery ended. Those facts, and a million others about the suns and planets of the spiral arm, had been stored in Tally's memory long before he assumed the embodied form, and he had seen no reason to question them. What had just recently been added to his internal states, and what consumed trillions of cycles of introspection time to achieve even partial answers, was the need to examine *motivation*.

The Dobelle system was a planetary doublet, twin worlds known as Opal and Quake that spun furiously about their common center of mass. They were joined by the twelve-thousand-kilometer strand known as the Umbilical. The orbit of their mass center about the star Mandel was highly eccentric, and the time of closest approach to the stellar primary induced prodigious land and sea tides in Quake and Opal. That closest approach was known as Summertide. The most recent Summertide had been an exceptional one, because the approach of Mandel's binary partner, Amaranth, and a gas giant planet, Gargantua, had led to a lineup of bodies, the Grand Conjunction, that took place only once every 350,000 years.

Very good. Tally knew all that, and he understood it perfectly. Wild as the celestial motions might be, nothing stood in defiance of either logic or physics; to induce such a breakdown, apparently Organics were needed.

"You tell me that a group of humans and aliens converged on Quake and Opal for the last Summertide," he said to Legate Stancioff. "And they went there voluntarily. But *why?* Why would anyone go at that time, when the surfaces of the planets were at their most dangerous? They could have been destroyed."

"We have reason to believe that some of them were."

"But surely humans and Cecropians and Lo'tfians and Hymenopts don't want to die?"

"Of course not." Stancioff was in the human condition that

E. C. Tally was coming to recognize as senescence. He was probably no more than ten years away from lapsing to a nontransitional internal state. Already his hands shook slightly as they were talking, in what was clearly a nonfunctional oscillation. "But humans," Stancioff went on, "and aliens, too, I suppose, though I don't actually know many aliens—we take risks, when we feel we have adequate reasons. And they all had *different* interests. Professor Lang, of Sentinel Gate, went to Dobelle because of her scientific interest in Builder artifacts and in Summertide itself. Others, like the Cecropian Atvar H'sial and the augmented Karelian human Louis Nenda, went there, we suspect, for personal gain. The Lo'tfian, J'merlia, and the Hymenopt, Kallik, are slaves. They were present because their masters ordered them to be there. The only beings on Quake in line of official duties were three humans: Commander Maxwell Perry, who controlled all outside access to the Dobelle system at Summertide; Captain Hans Rebka, who is a Phemus Circle troubleshooter sent to Dobelle as Perry's superior; and Councilor Julius Graves, of our own Fourth Alliance, who was present on Council business. Don't you wish to make notes of all these names?"

"It is unnecessary. I do not forget."

"I suppose you don't." Stancioff stared at E. C. Tally. "That must be nice. Now, where was I? Well, never mind. There's a whole lot of information in the files about everyone who was on Quake at Summertide, much more than I know about it. Not one of them ever came back, that's the real mystery, even though Summertide was over weeks ago. We want you to find out why they all stayed. You should study each dossier while you are traveling to Dobelle, and form your own conclusions as to each person's needs and desires."

Needs and desires! Those were exactly what were missing in Tally's internal states; but if they decided so many human and alien actions, he must learn to simulate them.

"May I speak?"

"You've certainly shown no reluctance so far."

"I am perplexed by my suggested role in this matter. At the beginning I understood that I was to go to the Mandel system and assess the problems there on a logical basis. Now I learn that at least two other individuals are qualified to deal with the problem. Hans Rebka, according to your own words, is a 'troubleshooter,' and Julius Graves is actually a Council member. Given their presence, what do you expect me to accomplish?"

"I am glad that you asked that question. It is a good omen for the success of your mission." Legate Stancioff moved out of his chair and came to stand in front of Tally. His hands had stopped shaking, and the vagueness was gone from his manner. "It would be an even better sign if you were to answer the question yourself. Can you do so, if I tell you that on this assignment I am assuming that your weakness may also be your strength?"

After a millisecond of analysis, Tally nodded. "It can only be because I am not an Organic. My *weakness* is my lack of human emotions. Therefore my failure to share organic motivations and emotions is also my strength. You must believe that Graves and Rebka acted from emotion in deciding not to leave the Mandel system."

"Correct. We cannot prove that. But we suspect it." Legate Stancioff placed his hands on Tally's firm shoulders. "You will find out. Go to Dobelle. Learn what you can and report back to us. I do not want to risk another human in finding out what happened at Summertide."

Whereas you, as an embodied computer, are quite expendable.

E. C. Tally was learning. He was able to make that inference within a microsecond. It produced no reaction within him. It could not. If he had no human emotions, he lacked the internal state to resent the suggestion that his loss was acceptable, while a human loss was not. But he began structuring the first simulation circuits. There might be situations where an understanding of human emotions could be useful.

ENTRY 14: HUMAN.

Distribution: Humans, plus derived or augmented forms, can be found in three principal regions of the spiral arm: the *Fourth Alliance,* the *Zardalu Communion,* and the *Phemus Circle.* Of these, the Fourth Alliance is the biggest, the oldest, and the most populous. It includes the whole of *Crawlspace,* the Sol-centered, seventy-two-light-year sphere explored and colonized by humans in sublight-speed ships before the development of the Bose Drive and Bose Network. Almost eight hundred inhabited planets belong to the Fourth Alliance. They lie within an ellipsoid with Sol at one focus, stretching out seven hundred light-years in a direction roughly opposite to that of the galactic center. The supergiant star Rigel sits almost at the farthest boundary of Fourth Alliance territory. Humans are the dominant species of the Fourth Alliance and account for sixty percent of all intelligent beings there.

By contrast, the Phemus Circle consists of just a score of impoverished worlds, ninety percent human, nestled near the part of the Fourth Alliance closest to the center of the galaxy. The Phemus Circle shares a region where the Fourth Alliance, the Cecropia Federation, and the Zardalu Communion all have overlapping territories. It is a measure of the poverty of this group that none of the larger neighbors has shown interest in developing the Phemus Circle, although the Circle is nominally under the control of the Fourth Alliance and recognizes the authority of the Alliance's Council members.

The humans of the Zardalu Communion recognize no central authority. In consequence, their numbers and distribution are difficult to judge. Efrarezi and Camefil estimate that no more than twelve percent of all Zardalu intelligent forms are human. Of these, almost one half live close to the disputed borders with the Fourth Alliance and the Cecropia Federation. The number of worlds inhabited by humans in the region of the Zardalu Communion is unknown.

Physical Characteristics: Humans are land-dwelling vertebrate bisexual quadrupeds possessing bilateral symmetry and a well-marked head and torso. The extremities of the upper limb pair have been modified to permit grasping. All sensory apparatus has low performance and is especially poor for smell and taste. The grelatory organ is entirely absent.

The human form is receptive to modification and augmentation, with a high tolerance of alien tissues. The mutation rate is the highest of any known intelligent species, but this does not seem to be an evolutionary advantage.

History: The origin of the human clade is the planet Earth, which with its sun, Sol, marks the center of the reference-coordinate system employed in this catalog. Human history extends for approximately ten thousand years before the Expansion, with written records available for roughly half that time. Unfortunately, the human tendency for self-delusion, self-aggrandizement, and baseless faith in human superiority over all other intelligent life-forms renders much of the written record unreliable. Serious research workers are advised to seek alternative primary data sources concerning humans.

Culture: Human culture is built around four basic elements: sexual relationships, territorial rights, individual intellectual dominance, and desire for group acceptance. The H'sirin model using just these four traits as independent variables enables accurate prediction of human behavior patterns. On the basis of this, human culture is judged to be of Level Two, with few prospects for advancement to a higher level.

—From the *Universal Species Catalog*
(Subclass: Sapients).

CHAPTER 2

LIFE IS JUST one damned thing after another.

To Birdie Kelly, squelching through the juicy dark mud of the Sling with a food tray balanced in front of him and a message flimsy stuck between the grimy fingers of his right hand, that thought came with the force and freshness of revelation.

One damned thing after another! he repeated to himself. No sooner was his boss, Max Perry, shipped off to the hospital for a couple of weeks of rehab surgery than Birdie found himself nursemaiding an Alliance councilor, no less, from far-off Miranda. Perry had been hard to take, with his obsessive need to work and his fixation about visits to Quake, but Julius Graves was no easier. Worse, in some ways, sitting there talking to himself when he should have been on his way back to Miranda weeks before. There he remained, day after day, loafing about indoors and not lifting a finger to help with the reconstruction work, and all the while ignoring recall messages from his own superiors. He seemed ready to stay forever.

Even so . . .

Birdie paused at the entrance to the building and took a deep breath of damp sea air.

Even so, it was impossible to feel anything other than elated these days. Birdie stared up at the dappled blue sky with Mandel's golden disk showing through broken cloud, then around him at the torn vegetation pushing out new shoots from broken stems. A light breeze roamed in from the west, signaling a perfect day for sailing. He loved it all, and it all seemed too good to be true. Summertide was over, the surface of Opal was returning to its usual tranquility, and Birdie had *survived*. That was more than could be said for half the unfortunate population of the waterworld.

It was more than he had expected for himself. One week earlier, as Summertide reached its climax and the gravity fields of Mandel and Amaranth tore at Opal, Birdie had huddled alone in the prow of a small boat and watched the turbulent surface ahead of him veer from horizontal to near-vertical.

He was a goner and he knew it. Radio signals had warned that the monster was on the way. Tidal forces had created a great soliton, a solitary wave over a kilometer high that was sweeping around the whole girth of Opal. Sling after Sling had sent their last messages, reporting on wave speed and height before the huge but fragile rafts of mud and tangled vegetation were torn apart and fell silent.

There was no way to avoid it. Birdie had crouched in the bottom of the boat, clutching the bottom boards with white-knuckled hands.

The boat's prow tilted up. Thirty degrees, forty-five, sixty. Horizontal and vertical switched roles. Birdie found himself with his feet braced on the boat's stern, his hands holding tight to the centerboard and the little mast. He was lifted, with a two- or three-gee force on his body that went on and on, like a launch from Starside Port to orbit. Rushing water flew past, spray two feet from his nose. For half a minute he was carried up and up, a flyspeck on a wall of ocean, up into Opal's dark clouds. He poised there, forever, unable to see anything as the boat leveled off. At last came the fall, leaving his stomach behind on the downward plunge.

He had been permitted one breathtaking view as they dropped out of the clouds: Opal's seabed lay ahead, exposed by millennial tides, dotted with long-sunken ships and the vast green bodies of stranded Dowsers, unbuoyed by water and crushed by their own multimillion-ton weight. Then he was swooping down a long, foam-flecked slope, toward that muddy wasteland. He knew, even more certainly than before, that he was about to die.

A second, smaller wave, running crosswise to the first, saved him. Before he could be smashed onto the unforgiving seabed, there was a scream of wind and a harsh slap on the boat's rugged stern. He found himself being lifted again in a boiling torrent of warm spray, holding harder than ever, almost unable to breathe. But breathe he did, and held on, too, an hour longer than he would have believed humanly possible, until Summertide was past and the tough little boat had been tossed to calmer waters.

It was something to tell his grandchildren about—if he ever got around to having any.

He had not intended to, but now he might. Only weeks after Summertide, and the social pressure was already on. Every fertile woman would be pregnant within the next month, pushing Opal's population back toward survival level.

Birdie looked up at the calm blue sky and drew in another long, reassuring breath. Perhaps the real miracle was not that he had lived to tell the tale, but that his story seemed to have been repeated again and again across the entire surface of Opal. Some of the Slings, caught in contrary crosscurrents, had been held together by watery whirlpools when all logic suggested they should have been torn apart. Survivors told of flotsam that had come within reach just as their own strength was failing.

Or maybe they had it backward. Birdie had a new insight. Maybe they had hung on, like him, for exactly as long as was necessary until a means of self-preservation came to hand. People who lived in the Dobelle system did not give in easily. They could not afford to.

Birdie pushed the wicker door of the one-story building open with his knee, wiped his muddy shoes on the rush mat in the entrance, and walked through to the inside room.

"Same thing again, I'm afraid: boiled Dowser, grilled Dowser, and fried Dowser, with a bit of Dowser on the side." He placed the tray on a table of plaited reeds. "We'll be eating this stuff for a while, until we can get the fishing boats back into service." He removed the lid of the big dish, leaned forward, and sniffed. His nose wrinkled. "Unless it gets too rotten to eat. Not far to go, if you ask me. Come on, though, dig in. It tastes even worse cold."

The man sitting in the chair beyond the table was tall and bony, with a bald and bulging head burned purple-red by hard radiation. His eyes, a faded and misty blue beneath bushy eyebrows, gazed thoughtfully up at Birdie and right through him.

Birdie wriggled. He had not really expected his cheerful comments to elicit a matching reaction from Julius Graves— they never had in the past—but there was no reason for the other man to look so mournful. After all, only a week earlier Graves had survived an experience over on Opal's sister planet, Quake, that by the sound of it had been as harrowing as anything that Birdie had been through. The councilor ought to be filled with the same zest for life, the same satisfaction at being alive.

"Steven and I have been talking again," Graves said. "He has me almost persuaded."

Birdie laid down the message flimsy and helped himself to food. "Oh, yes? What's he been saying, then?"

Steven Graves was another thing that Birdie found hard to take. An interior mnemonic twin was no big deal; it was something employed by a number of other Council members, an added pair of cerebral hemispheres grown and housed within the human skull and coupled to the original brain hemispheres via a new corpus callosum. All it did was provide an extended and convenient organic memory, slower but less bulky than an inorganic mnemonic unit. What it was *not* supposed to do—what it had never done before, to Birdie Kelly's knowledge—was to develop *self-awareness.* But Julius Graves's mnemonic twin, Steven Graves, not only possessed independent consciousness; on occasion he seemed to take over. Birdie preferred him in many ways. Steven's personality was far more cheerful and jokey. But it was disconcerting not to know who you were talking to at any given time, and although Julius seemed to be in charge at the moment, in another second it might be Steven.

"For almost a week I have been summoning my energy to return to Miranda," Graves said, "to report on my experiences here."

And the sooner the better, matey, Birdie thought. But instead of speaking, he picked up the message flimsy that he had put down on the table, brushing off the dirt and dried black mud that had somehow found their way onto it.

"I had been oddly reluctant to do so," Graves went on, "and I suspect that my instincts knew something denied to my forebrain. But now I think Steven has put his finger—metaphorically speaking—on the reason. It concerns the Awakening, and the ones who went off to Gargantua."

Birdie held out the grimy message. "Speaking of Miranda, this came in about an hour ago. I didn't read it," he said, in an unconvincing afterthought.

Graves scanned the sheet, held it out between finger and thumb, and allowed it to flutter to the floor.

"According to reports I have had since Summertide," he continued, "the awakening of the artifacts ended with that event. For years, Builder artifacts across the spiral arm had been showing signs of increased activity. But now all that stirring has come to an end, and the spiral arm is quiet again. Why? We do not know, but as Steven points out, Darya Lang insisted that the events of this Summertide have an influence beyond this planet, or even this stellar system. The Grand Conjunction of stellar and planetary positions here takes place only once every three hundred and fifty thousand years. Lang did not want humanity to be forced to wait that long for another awakening, and I agreed with her. When she and

Hans Rebka decided to follow the sphere that emerged at Summertide from the interior of Quake, I did not oppose it. When J'merlia and Kallik requested permission to go to Gargantua also, to learn whether their former masters were living or dead, I *encouraged* them and took their side, although I felt in my heart that this was scarcely my business. My task was to return to Miranda and report on the case that brought me here in the first place. But—"

"That's what the message is all about." Birdie dropped the pretense of ignorance. "They want to know why you're still here. They ask when you'll be leaving. You could be in a lot of trouble if you don't reply."

Julius Graves ignored him. "But what could be assigned to me on Miranda half as important as what may be happening out near Gargantua? To quote Steven again, if we return to Miranda we will surely be assigned to another case of interspecies conflict and ethical dilemma. But if the Builders *are* waiting out at Gargantua, as Darya Lang insists they must be, then the greatest interspecies meeting in the history of the spiral arm is waiting with them. The ethical issues could be vast and unprecedented, and all these events may be triggered by the arrival of Darya Lang, Hans Rebka, and the two slaves—unless they have already been precipitated by the earlier arrival of Atvar H'sial and Louis Nenda. In either case, my own future action is at last clear. I must requisition a starship and follow the others to Gargantua. I do not say this immodestly, but their interactions could be disastrous without the mediating influence of a Council member. I therefore ask your assistance in finding me such a starship, and in outfitting it suitably for the journey to Gargantua . . ."

Graves was maundering on, but Birdie was hardly listening. At last, they were going to be rid of a useless drone—for that's what Julius Graves was proving to be, even if he did happen to be a Council member. If he wanted a ship, Birdie could not stop him, though Lord knows where they would find one, with everything in such a mess. Birdie would have to do it somehow, because a councilor could commandeer any local resources that he or she deemed necessary. Anyway, the temporary loss of a ship was a small price to pay to get rid of the distracting and the time-wasting influence of Julius and Steven Graves.

". . . Mr. Kelly, as soon as possible."

The mention of Birdie's own last name jerked his attention back to the other man. "Yes, Councilor? I'm sorry, I missed that."

"I was saying, Mr. Kelly, that I appreciate this to be a time of considerable stress for everyone on Opal. With Starside Port out of action, finding a working spaceship may call for considerable improvisation. At the same time, I hope that you and I can be on our way to Gargantua fairly soon—shall we say, in one standard week?"

"Me?" Birdie had not been listening right; he must have missed a key part of what Graves had been saying. "Did you say me? You didn't say me, did you?"

"Certainly. I know that Gargantua and its satellites are already fifty million kilometers away and getting farther every minute, but they still form part of the Mandel system. I discussed the matter with Commander Perry, and although his own duties on Opal prevent him from traveling, he believes a presence from this planet's government is important. He is issuing orders for you to accompany me on his behalf to Gargantua."

Gargantua.

Week-dead Dowser did not taste great at the best of times. Birdie pushed the plate away from him and tried to hold on to what he had already eaten. He stood up. He must have said something to Julius Graves before he found himself once more walking outside the building, but under torture he could not have recalled what it was.

Gargantua! Birdie peered upward, into Opal's blue sky. Mandel was rapidly sinking toward sunset, as Opal and Quake performed their dizzying eight-hour whirl about each other. Somewhere out there, beyond the pleasant blue sky, out where Mandel was diminished to a squinty little point of light, there rolled the gas-giant planet surrounded by its frosty retinue of satellites. They were stark, frozen, lifeless, and dark. Even the best-prepared expeditions to Gargantua, led by the Dobelle system's most experienced space travelers, had suffered considerable casualties. The outer system was simply too remote, too cold, too inhospitable to human life. Compared with that, Opal during a Level Five storm felt safe and welcoming.

Birdie stared around him. He knew it all, from the sticky familiarity of warm black mud underfoot and the thicketed tangle of vines that began just a few meters from the building, to the heavy backs of the huge, lumbering tortoises, making their unhurried way inland through the undergrowth after surviving Summertide at sea. Birdie recognized them all; and he loved them all.

Earlier in the day this whole pleasant prospect had seemed too good to be true. He had just learned that it was.

CHAPTER 3

THE *SUMMER DREAMBOAT* had started life as a plaything, a teenager's runabout intended for within-system planetary hops. Everything aboard the ship had been designed with that in mind, from the compact galley, sanitation, and disposal facilities, to the single pair of narrow berths. The addition of a full-fledged Bose Drive had provided the *Dreamboat* with a far-ranging interstellar capability, while whittling the internal space down even further.

Its occupants—or at least the human ones—were cursing that addition now as wasted space. The passage from Dobelle to Gargantua had to be done using the cold-catalyzed fusion drive, which could make no use at all of the Bose interstellar network.

During the second day of the journey Darya Lang and Hans Rebka had retreated to the berths, where they lay side by side.

"Too many legs," Rebka said softly.

Darya Lang nodded. She did not say it, but they both knew the cramped quarters were harder on her. He had grown up on Teufel, one of the poorest and most backward worlds of the Phemus Circle. Hardship and discomfort were to him so natural and so familiar that he did not even recognize their presence. She had been spoiled—though she had never known it, until the past couple of months—by the luxury and abundance of Sentinel Gate, one of the spiral arm's garden planets.

"For me, too many legs," she repeated. "Sixteen too many. And too many eyes for *you.*"

He understood at once and touched her arm apologetically. The Lo'tfian, J'merlia, seemed mostly legs and eyes. Eight black articulated limbs were attached to the long, pipestem torso, and J'merlia's narrow head was dominated by big, lemon-colored compound eyes on short eyestalks. Kallik was just as well-endowed. The Hymenopt's body was short, stubby, and black-furred, but eight wiry legs sprang from the rotund torso, and the small, smooth head was entirely surrounded by multiple pairs of bright, black eyes. Kallik and J'merlia did not mean to get in the way, but when they were both awake and active it was impossible to move around the ship's little cabin without tripping over the odd outstretched appendage.

Darya Lang and Hans Rebka had retreated to the berths as the only place left. But even there they found little privacy—or too little, Darya thought, for Hans Rebka.

The two months since she had left her quiet life as a research scientist on Sentinel Gate had been full of surprises; not least of them was the discovery that many "facts" about life on the backward and impoverished worlds of the Perimeter were just not so. Everyone on Shasta knew that the urge to reproduce dominated everything on the underpopulated planets of the Phemus Circle, where both men and women were obsessed with sex. The rich worlds of the Fourth Alliance "knew" that people on Teufel and Scaldworld and Quake and Opal did it whenever and wherever they could.

Perhaps so, in principle; but there was a curious primness

in border planet society when it came to practice. Men and women might show immediate interest in each other, from bold eye contact to open invitation. But let the time arrive for *doing* something, in public or even in private, and Darya suspected they were oddly puritanical.

She had obtained positive and annoying proof of that idea when the *Summer Dreamboat* embarked on the long journey to Gargantua. On the first night the two aliens had stretched out on the floor, leaving the berths to Darya and Hans. She lay in her bunk and waited. When nothing happened, she took the initiative.

He rebuffed her, though in an oddly indirect way. "Of course I'd like to—but what about your foot?" he whispered. "You'll hurt it too much. I mean—we can't. Your foot . . ."

Darya's foot had been burned during the retreat from Quake at Summertide. It was healing fast. She resisted the urge to say, "Damn my foot. Why don't you just let *me* be the judge of what hurts too much?"

Instead she withdrew, convinced that Hans came from one of those curious societies where women were not supposed to take the lead in sexual matters. She waited. And waited. Finally, during the next sleep period, she asked what was wrong. Wasn't he interested? Didn't he find her attractive?

"Of course I do." He kept his voice low and glanced across toward the two aliens. As far as Darya could tell they were both sound asleep, in an untidy sprawl of intermeshed limbs. "But what about *them?*"

"What *about* 'em? I hope you're not suggesting they should join in."

"Don't be disgusting. But if they wake up, they'll see us."

So that was it. A privacy taboo, just like the one on Moldave. And apparently a strong one. Hans would not be able to do anything as long as they were cooped up in the ship with J'merlia and Kallik, even though the aliens could have nothing beyond a possible academic interest in human mating procedures.

But their indifference did not change the situation for Hans Rebka. Darya had given up.

"Too many eyes for you," she repeated. "I know. Don't worry about it, Hans. So how much longer before we reach Gargantua?"

"About forty hours." He was relieved to change the subject. "I can't stop wondering—what do you think we are going to find there?"

He looked at Darya expectantly. She had no answer, though she admitted the justice of his question. After all, she was the one who had actually *seen* the dark sphere gobble up Louis Nenda's ship and head off to Gargantua. Hans had been too busy trying to stop Nenda from shooting them out of the sky. But did she really expect to find the Builders there, now that she'd had plenty of time to think about it?

For Darya, that was the ultimate question. The Builders had disappeared from the spiral arm more than five million years earlier, but she had been pursuing them in one way or another for all of her adult life. It had begun with a single Builder artifact, the Sentinel, visible from her birthworld of Sentinel Gate. Darya had first seen it as an infant. She had grown up with that shining and striated sphere glowing in her night sky. Inaccessible to humans and to all human constructs, the unreachable interior of Sentinel had come to symbolize for her the whole mystery of the lost Builders. Her conviction that Summertide was somehow connected with Builder artifacts had brought her to Dobelle, and the events at Summertide had provided a new insight: the alignment of planetary and stellar positions that caused Summertide was *itself* an artifact, the whole stellar system a construct of the long-vanished master engineers.

But Hans Rebka's question still demanded an answer. Had she become so obsessed with the Builders, and everything to do with them, that she saw Builder influence everywhere? It was not uncommon for a scientist to live with a theory for so long that it took control. Data and observations were forced to fit the theory, rather than being used to test it and if necessary reject it. How did she know she was not guilty of that same failing?

"I know what I saw, Hans. But beyond the evidence of my eyes—however you weight that—all I can offer are my own deductions, however you weight *them.* Can you pick up an image of Gargantua with the external sensors?"

"Should be able to." He craned his head around. "And we ought to be able to look at it right here—we're line-of-sight for the projectors. Don't move. I'll be back in a minute."

It did not take that long. Twenty seconds at the display controls of the *Summer Dreamboat* gave Hans Rebka a three-dimensional image in the space above the twin berths. He carried the remote control unit over to Darya, letting her use it to pinpoint the target and zoom as she chose.

The planet sat in the center of the globe of view. And what a change since the last time that Darya had seen it. Then the light of Gargantua had been screened by the protective filters of the *Dreamboat*'s viewing port. The planet had been gigantic, sure enough, bulking across half the field of view, but it had also been faint, faded to a spectral shade by the brilliant torrents of light sleeting in from Mandel and Amaranth. Now Gargantua was a sphere not much bigger than Darya's thumbnail, but it glowed like a jewel, rich oranges and ochers of high-quality zircon and hessonite against a black background scattered with faint stars. There was just a hint of banding to mark the axis of the planet's rotation, and the four bright points of light in suspiciously accurate alignment with the equator had to be Gargantua's major satellites. Darya knew that a thousand other sizable fragments of debris orbited closer to the planet, but from this distance they were invisible. Their paths must have become a monstrous jumble after the perturbations of periastron passage close to Mandel and Amaranth.

Not the harmony of the spheres, but a rough charivari of tangled orbits. Navigation through them would be a problem.

She studied the image, then used the remote marker to indicate a point a quarter of a radius away from the planetary terminator.

"When the ray of light first appeared, it came from just about there." She closed her eyes for a moment, recalling what she had seen. "But it wasn't ordinary light, or it would have been invisible in empty space. I could see it all the way, and I could follow its line right back to that point."

"But couldn't it have come from a lot farther away—way out past Gargantua?"

"No. Because by the time the silver sphere turned into a hole in space, swallowed up Louis Nenda's ship, and zoomed off along the light-line, the ray's point of origin had *moved*. It was right next to Gargantua by the time I lost sight of it. The only way you can explain that is if it came from something *in orbit* around Gargantua."

Darya closed her eyes again. She had a bit of a headache, and recalling the last desperate minutes close to Summertide had somehow made her dizzy and disoriented. Her eyes did not want to focus. She must have been staring for too long at the image on the display. She squinted up at Gargantua. The giant planet was receding fast from Mandel, on a complex orbit controlled both by Mandel and its dwarf stellar companion. But the *Dreamboat* was moving faster yet. It was catching up.

"A few more hours, Hans." She suddenly felt slow and lazy. "Just a few more hours. We'll start to see all the little satellites. Begin to have an idea where we're going. Won't we?" She was puzzled by her own words, and by the odd sound of her own voice. "Where are we going? I don't know where we're going."

He did not answer. She made a big effort and turned to him, to find that he was not looking at her at all. He was staring at J'merlia and Kallik.

"Still asleep," he said.

"Yeah. Still asleep." Darya smiled. " 'S all right, Hans, I'm not going to attack you."

But he was sitting up and swinging his legs over the side of the bunk. His face was redder than usual, and the line of the scar that ran from his left temple to the point of his jaw showed clearly.

"Something's wrong. Kallik never sleeps for more than half·an hour at a time. Stay there."

She watched as he hurried over to the central control panel of the *Dreamboat,* studied it, and swore aloud. He reached forward. There was a whir of atmospheric conditioners, and Darya felt a cold and sudden draft in her face. She muttered a protest. He ignored her. He was bending over the inert forms of J'merlia and Kallik; then, suddenly, he appeared at her side again.

"How are you feeling? Come on, sit up."

Darya found herself being levered to an upright sitting position. The chilly air brought her to fuller wakefulness, and she shivered. "I'm all right. What's wrong?"

"Atmosphere. The ship took a real beating when we lifted off from Quake. Something was knocked out of whack in the air plant. I've put in a temporary override, and we'll do manual control till we know what happened."

For the first time, his urgency reached through to her.

"Are we all right? And Kallik and J'merlia?"

"Now we are, all of us. We're quite safe. But we weren't. Maybe J'merlia and Kallik could have breathed what we were getting a few minutes ago—they have a high tolerance for bad air—but you and I couldn't. Too much monoxide. Another half hour like that, we'd have been dead."

Dead! Darya felt a cold wave across her body, nothing to do with the chilly cabin breeze. When they had faced death at Summertide, the dangers had been obvious to all of them. But Death could arrive in other ways, never making an appointment or announcing his presence, creeping in to take a person when she was least expecting him . . .

She could not relax. Hans Rebka had stretched out on the bunk again by Darya's side. She moved close to him, needing human contact. He was breathing hard, and a moment later they were touching along most of their bodies. She could feel him trembling. But then she realized that the tremors were in his hands, touching her face and reaching beneath her shirt to her breasts. In the next few seconds it became obvious that he was highly excited.

They clung to each other without speaking. Finally Darya craned her head up, to stare past Hans at the sleeping forms of J'merlia and Kallik.

What about them—suppose they wake up? She was on the point of saying it. She caught herself. Shut up, dummy. What are you trying to do?

She made one concession to modesty, reaching up past him

to turn the light off above the bunks. He did not seem to care; after a few more seconds, neither did Darya. Neither, she was sure, did J'merlia and Kallik.

An hour later the two aliens were still asleep. So was Hans. Darya lay with her eyes closed, reflecting that one aspect of male human behavior varied little from Fourth Alliance to Phemus Circle.

And I'm beginning to understand him better, she thought. He's a sweet man, but he's a strange one. A close call from death doesn't frighten him. It makes him *excited*—excited enough to ignore his own taboos. I don't think he gave Kallik and J'merlia one thought . . . nor did I, for that matter. I suppose it's not the approach of death that's the stimulus, it's the knowledge that you *survived* . . . Maybe that's the way with all the men of the Perimeter worlds, and the women, too. It certainly worked well for Hans.

She smiled to herself. Pity it didn't work for me. Death doesn't excite me, it scares me. I enjoyed myself, but I didn't even come close. Never mind. There'll be other chances.

At last she opened her eyes. They had not bothered to turn off the projection unit. Gargantua hung above her head, perceptibly bigger. She could see the markings on the swollen face, and the planet had turned a quarter of a revolution since the last time she had looked at it. The huge and permanent atmospheric vortex known as the Eye of Gargantua sat in the center of the disk. It was staring straight at her: orange-red, hypnotic, baleful.

Darya found herself unable to breathe.

So there'll be other chances, will there? the Eye's expression said. *Don't count on it. I know something about death, too.*

CHAPTER 4

E. CRIMSON TALLY: Permanent record for transfer upon return to Persephone.

Today I reached my initial destination, the planet Opal of the Dobelle system. Today I also drew a major and disturbing conclusion concerning my mission.

It is this: The decision made by Senior Technician Sue Xantippe Harbeson Ando was an appropriate one, although not for the reasons she gave me. For it turns out that the slow, inefficient method of information transfer via human channels yields information that I would never have received by direct access to the data banks. This is true for a simple reason: *some important information is not in the data banks.*

The central data banks of the Fourth Alliance are incomplete! Who could have foreseen that? Worse still, I now have reason to believe that they are sometimes *in error,* so much so that I can no longer rely on them.

I would now like to present the evidence that supports these conclusions.

Item one: My journey to Opal required that I pass through four transition points of the Bose Network. This I knew before departure. The data banks had also indicated that each Bose Transition Point serves as a nexus for the transportation of different species; thus members of the Cecropia Federation and the Zardalu Communion might be encountered there, as well as humans of the Fourth Alliance and the Phemus Circle.

This information proved accurate. At the third transition point, 290 light-years from Sol, in a region already verging on the Phemus Circle zone and adjoining both Fourth Alliance and Cecropia Federation territories, I saw and recognized Cecropians, Lo'tfians, Varnians, Hymenopts, and Ditrons.

The data banks make the relationship between these species very clear. Lo'tfians and Ditrons serve as slave species to Cecropians. Hymenopts and Varnians are sometimes free beings, but are usually slave to humans living in the territories of the Zardalu Communion. (Slave to the land-cephalopod Zardalu also, should any still exist; but none has been encountered since the Great Rising, in pre-Expansion times.)

The data banks also make it clear that, despite the independence of the Cecropian and Zardalu clades, all these species recognize the superiority of humans of the Fourth Alliance. They defer to them, acknowledging the higher nature of human intellect and achievements, and regarding Earth and surrounding Alliance territories as the cultural and scientific center of the spiral arm.

That is not the case! I, a Fourth Alliance human in outward appearance, received no preferential treatment whatsoever. In fact, quite the opposite. In the great terminus of Bose Access Node 145, I emerged to find an overcrowded transit point. To reach my required departure zone it was necessary for me to pass close to a group of other travelers, Cecropians, Zardalu humans, and Hymenopts prominent among them. My request for prompt passage was ignored. More than that, a Cecropian pushed me out of the way as though I did not exist!

When I remonstrated to another human traveler, he said, "Your first trip, is it? You're going to run into a lot of things that aren't in the travel guides. Or they're going to run into you, like that Cecropian." He laughed. "As far as she's concerned, you don't exist, you see. Humans are missing the right pheromones for Cecropians to detect, so they consider we're hardly there. And anyway, since they're an older civilization than humans, they kind of look down on us. Don't ever hope for politeness from a Cecropian. She knows you're an upstart little monkey. And get out of the way if she pushes; she's a lot bigger than you."

I do not believe that I could have received such information, except directly from a human source. It is totally inconsistent with the perspective offered by the central data base.

Item two: The Fourth Alliance central data bank indicates that Alliance science is superior to that of the other clades, and that Alliance technology is even more so.

I am forced to dispute that notion.

The first three Bose Transition Points that I passed through after leaving Sol-space were constructed and operated by Fourth Alliance humans. The fourth one, as I learned upon my arrival, was built and is maintained by the Cecropia Federation. With time to spare before my shuttle ship to Dobelle, I studied this transition point in some detail. It is obvious that the facility is technologically at least the equal of the Fourth Alliance nodes; operationally it is far better designed. Moreover, it is cleaner, safer, and less noisy.

The data bank is again misleading, for a reason I cannot conjecture. Alliance technology is not universally superior, and in at least some instances it is inferior. But direct observation was necessary to draw that conclusion.

Item three: The data base indicates that humanity reached the stars employing carefully constructed and logical theories of the nature of the physical world. The laws of physics, mathematics, and logic underpin all human activities, says the data base, no matter how diverse the application.

I believe those facts may be accurate, as they relate to human *history*. But they seem irrelevant to current human actions on Opal. Indeed, from recent conversations I deduce that they apply little anywhere in the Phemus Circle. Either humans here are deranged, or they operate with a subtlety of logic beyond anything to be found in the files of the central data base.

These disturbing conclusions are drawn from my own direct observations, supplemented by discussion with natives concerning the recent traumatic events known as Summertide, as follows:

The dangers of Summertide were enormous. Death and destruction were planetwide and appalling. A logical race would have concluded that Opal is not a world suitable for human occupation and would have begun birth-limitation procedures in preparation for relocation to some new planetary environment. Such action would be consistent with the profiles of a logical humanity, as described in the central data banks.

And what did the people of Opal do, once Summertide was over? They embarked on a reproductive orgy, one guaranteed to raise the population in a few years' time and thereby make it far more difficult to evacuate the planet. They justify this by professing—and perhaps, in truth, feeling—a powerful affection for the very place that recently killed so many of their friends and families.

And to "celebrate" their own survival, they have been inhaling and ingesting large quantities of addictive drugs and powerful carcinogens, thereby substantially shortening their already diminished life expectancies. Suspecting that for some reason the natives might be misleading me, as a newcomer, about the effects of these substances, I ingested a small amount myself on an experimental basis. My metabolism was seriously impaired for several hours.

Those ill effects were not, I should add, a consequence of my different background and origins. Indeed, I find that a similar impairment is common among the natives. And far from being puzzled by their own contralogical activities, they actually proclaim them to one another—unashamedly, and often in boastful terms.

Item four: The central language banks claim to be complete, with a full and idiomatic representation of every form of written and spoken communication in the spiral arm.

That cannot be true, for this reason: Upon my arrival on Opal, I met with a human male who identified himself as Commissioner Birdie Kelly. He informed me that of the names given to me as potential contacts, all but one were either presumed dead, or away exploring other parts of the Mandel system. The single exception is Councilor Julius Graves, and I will be meeting with him in a few hours' time. That was good to know, and I said so.

I had no trouble understanding every word of my conversation with Commissioner Kelly. Certainly there was no reason to assume that recent language changes on Opal might be causing miscommunication between us.

However, after a meeting of a little less than twenty minutes, the commissioner told me that he had another appointment. I left. And once I was outside the room he spoke, presumably to himself. He must have believed me to be out of earshot, but I was grown from first-rate genetic stock and my hearing is more sensitive than that of most humans.

"Well, Mister E. C. Tally," he said. " 'May I speak,' indeed. May I babble, more like. You're a funny duck, and no mistake. I wonder why you flew in."

A duck is an animal indigenous to Earth, imported to Opal where it thrives. Clearly, a human being is not a duck, nor does a human closely resemble one. And since I resemble a human, I cannot therefore be mistaken for a duck. It is not easy to see how Commissioner Birdie Kelly could make such an error, unless the language banks themselves contain errors.

These matters call for introspection.

CHAPTER 5

THE UNIVERSE IS all extremes. Monstrous gravity fields, or next-to-nothing ones; extreme cold, or heat so intense that solids and liquids cannot exist; multimillion atmosphere pressures, or near-vacuum.

Ice or fire. Niflheim or Muspelheim: the ancient alternatives, imagined by humans long before the Expansion.

It's *planets* that are the oddities, the strange neutral zone between suns and space, the thin interface where moderate temperatures and pressures and gravity fields can exist. And if planets are anomalies, then planets *able to support life* are rarer yet—a zero-measure subset in that set of strangeness.

And within that alien totality, where do humans fit?

"Willing to share your thoughts?" Hans Rebka's voice interrupted Darya's bleak musings.

She smiled but did not speak. She had been gazing out of the port of the *Summer Dreamboat,* her head filled with the unsatisfying present and the far-off dreams of Sentinel Gate. She was 800 light-years from home. Instead of the Sentinel, Gargantua filled the sky, as big as at Summertide and far more dominant. The Eye was a smoky whirlpool of gases, wide enough to swallow a dozen human worlds.

"You want me to help you?" she asked.

"You couldn't if you wanted to." Hans Rebka jerked his head toward the control panel. "They won't let me get near it. I think Kallik's having fun."

It was nice to know that someone was. The arrival in orbit around Gargantua had depressed Darya enormously—to come so far, with such vague goals, and then find nothing toward which she could point and say, "There! That's it. That's just what I hoped we'd find here."

Instead they had found what she should have expected. A planet, big enough to be at the fusion threshold, unapproachable by humans because of its dense, poisonous atmosphere and giant gravity field. Dancing attendance on Gargantua were its four major satellites, with their own atmospheres and oceans; but the air was mostly nitrogen, plus an acrid photochemical smog of ethane and hydrogen cyanide, and the oceans were liquid ethane and methane. The surfaces, recently heated by close approach to Mandel and Amaranth, were dropping back to a couple of hundred degrees below freezing.

If they were to find anything, the best bet was on one of the hundreds of smaller, airless satellites. Kallik and J'merlia were patiently identifying those, tagging each with its own set of orbital elements for future identification; the intertwining orbits were impossible to follow by eye, and a tough job even for the *Dreamboat*'s computer. Finally the team would examine "anything interesting," which was the vague criterion that Darya had provided.

"How many have they done?" Darya was not too sure she wanted to hear the answer. Because when they had worked their way through all the larger fragments she had no suggestion as to what they should do next, beyond the bitter option of an empty-handed return to Dobelle.

Hans Rebka shrugged, but J'merlia had heard the question. The lemon eyes turned on their short eyestalks. "Forty-eight."

He went on to answer the unasked question. "At this time, we have found nothing. Not even a prospect of high-value mineral deposits."

Of course not. Don't be so dumb, J'merlia. This is part of the Phemus Circle, remember? Metal-poor and mineral-poor and everything-poor. The whole Mandel system had been scoured for metals and minerals back when it was first colonized. If anything had been out here it would have been mined and picked clean centuries ago.

Darya managed not to say all that. She realized that she was angry with everything. She began to feel guilty. The two aliens were doing all the work, while she sat back, watched, and complained. "How many still to go, J'merlia?"

"Hundreds, at least. Every time we look more closely we find more small bodies. And each one is a time-consuming task. The problem is the orbital elements—we need many minutes of observation before we can assign them accurately. And we need accuracy, because the fragments move. We have to be sure we are not missing one, or doing some of them twice. The old catalogs help, but the recent perturbations make them unreliable."

"Then we'll probably be sitting here for a long time—at least a few days. What do you think, Hans? Maybe it's time to pick one of the planetoids, somewhere we can spread ourselves a bit until the search is over. We've got suits with us; at least we can stretch our legs and get out of each other's hair for an hour or two."

"We already have a . . . ck-candidate for such a place." Kallik had also been listening and watching. Her command of human speech was approaching perfection, but it could still betray her occasionally in moments of excitement. "We noted it when we first . . . ss-saw it. J'merlia?"

The Lo'tfian nodded. "It was already in the old catalog. It carries an identification as Dreyfus-27, and at one time a survey expedition used it as a base of operations. There should be tunneling, perhaps an airtight chamber. It can be reached from our present orbit with a minimal energy expenditure. Would you like to see its stored description?"

Darya had accepted J'merlia's suggestion with indecent haste. She knew that, but she didn't regret it. Motion, bustle, activity, that was what she needed at the moment—even if it *was* only motion and bustle, something as useless as fixing up a barren lump of rock so that humans and aliens might call it home for a few days.

Close approach to Dreyfus-27 had confirmed the data suggested by the *Summer Dreamboat*'s remote sensors. The planetoid was a dark, cratered body only ten kilometers in diameter, swinging in low orbit around Gargantua. A thousand years before, traces of nickel and iron in the outer layers of Dreyfus-27 had encouraged prospectors to drill the interior. The rubble and tailings that still formed a meters-deep coat to the planetoid's rugged surface showed that no deposits worth refining had been found, but the automated drilling equipment of the miners had not given up easily. Dreyfus-27 had been tunneled and retunneled, carved and bored and fractured and drilled until dozens of crisscrossing shafts and corridors and chambers riddled the inside.

Without air and appreciable gravity, those tunnels had not changed since the day they had been abandoned. The new arrivals could read the final frustration of the miners in the jumbled heaps of debris and half-completed living quarters. The prospectors had started out with high hopes, enough for them to plan a permanent base appropriate to extended mining operations. Those hopes had slowly evaporated. One day they had just downed tools and left. But although they had stopped halfway in making Dreyfus-27 fully habitable, their efforts were more than enough for the short-term needs of the crew of the *Dreamboat*.

"Seal it at the top, and this will do," Darya said. She and J'merlia had found an almost empty cylindrical chamber with a narrow entrance, five hundred meters below the surface, and had tested the walls to make sure that they could hold the pressure of an atmosphere. "The thermal insulation is as good as the day it was installed. Let's go back up. Once we pump some air in here we can open our suits. That will be wonderful."

She looked around her. The chamber was clear of major rock fragments, but powdery grit covered the passivine wall lining and flew up at every contact and vibration.

Wonderful? she thought. My God, I'm slipping down the ladder, rung by rung. A couple of months ago I'd have been appalled at the idea of spending ten minutes in a place like this. Now I can hardly wait to settle in.

J'merlia was already at home. The Lo'tfians were a burrow race, and the land surface of their home planet formed one vast, interconnected warren. He had been scuttling excitedly from one chamber and corridor to the next. Now he nodded his head and led the way back up the weak gravity gradient.

Darya, less nimble in free-fall, was left far behind. When she came close to the surface she was surprised to find the tunnel illuminated from outside. Dreyfus-27 was tumbling slowly around its long axis, with a period of a little more than one hour. When they had gone down into the interior of the planetoid, Gargantua had filled the sky above their entry tunnel; now the shaft was lit at its upper end by the fading and wintry sunlight of Mandel.

The ship hovered where they had left it, moored a hundred meters above the surface. Darya took the connecting cable and pulled herself easily along it. J'merlia was still in the tiny airlock when she got there, and she had to wait outside until the lock cycle was completed. She looked down. From this height she could see most of one irregular hemisphere of Dreyfus-27. The wan light made the surface more than ever into a jumbled wasteland of broken rocks. Harsh contours of light and dark were hardly softened by the microscopic dust particles and ice crystals thrown up by the arrival of the *Summer Dreamboat*. There were hundreds of other sizable fragments in orbit around Gargantua, all of them presumably much like this one. Was she crazy, to imagine that the secrets of the vanished Builders might be hidden in such a desert?

Hans Rebka was standing by the lock when she emerged from it. Darya switched her suit to full open and waited a couple of seconds for two-way transparency to be established.

"J'merlia says you found something good," Rebka began. "He's really excited."

"I thought it was a mess—just a whole labyrinth of tunnels. But he loved it down there. I guess it's like home for him. Look at them now."

J'merlia had moved across to the ship's control panel, where Kallik was sitting in a sprawl of extended legs, exactly as she had been when Darya left. For the past two days the Hymenopt had been painstakingly locating, tracking, and monitoring the minor satellites of Gargantua, never moving from her position at the controls. Now the Lo'tfian and the Hymenopt were chattering excitedly together, in the clicks and whistles of the latter's own language that neither Darya nor Hans had mastered. The whistling and chittering grew louder and more intense, until Darya said, "Hey, stop that, you'll deafen us," and added to Rebka, "I sure didn't see anything all *that* exciting in the interior."

He nodded. "What's with them? J'merlia! Kallik! Calm down."

J'merlia gave one final, earsplitting whistle before he turned to the humans. "Apologies, our sincere apologies. But Kallik has wonderful news. She picked up a signal, two minutes ago—from the *Have-It-All*!"

"Louis Nenda's ship? I don't believe it." Rebka moved across the cabin to stand by the control panel. "Darya said they were accelerated away from Quake at hundreds of gees. Any signal equipment inside that ship would have been crushed flat."

The Hymenopt's smooth black head turned to face the humans. "Not ss-so. I found a definite ss-signal, although a very weak one."

"You mean the *Have-It-All* is there, but in trouble?"

"Not necessarily in trouble. It is not a distress beacon, it is intended only to aid location."

"Then why didn't we pick it up earlier, when you did a scan of the entire region?"

"Because it becomes activated by an input ss-signal. Our

first s-scan was passive, using reflected stellar radiation. But now I am using active microwave, to scan the surface of rock fragments for composition and detailed images."

The Hymenopt's mandibles gaped with excitement and joy. "With apologies and respect, we cannot hide our pleasure. The sh-ship was not destroyed! It survives, it has power, it must be in good ck-ck-condition. Just as J'merlia and I hoped, our masters may not have died at Summertide. Louis Nenda and Atvar H'sial may be alive—and just a few hours' flight away!"

ENTRY 37: LO'TFIAN.

Distribution: The center of Lo'tfian civilization, and the only habitat of the species' females, remains the minor planet *Lo'tfi*. Since these females are exclusively burrow dwellers, the planetary surface reveals no sign of their presence; the subterranean regions of the planet, however, are believed to have been extensively modified as breeding and metamorphosis warrens. There is no direct proof of this, since no non-Lo'tfian has ever entered the burrows.

Male Lo'tfians are to be found in large numbers roaming the surface of Lo'tfi, and in small numbers on every world of the Cecropia Federation and Fourth Alliance where Cecropians interact with other intelligences of the spiral arm.

Physical Characteristics: The physical form of Lo'tfian females is not known by direct examination, though they are certainly blind and exceed the males in size and probably in intelligence. Their general physiology is believed to resemble that of the Lo'tfian males.

The males are thin-bodied, eight-legged arthropods, with excellent hearing and vision. They have an ability to communicate pheromonally, which makes them the preferred interpreters for Cecropians. Their two lidless compound eyes can be individually or jointly focused, enabling either stereo sight or simultaneous monocular viewing of two fields of vision. The eyes have spectral sensitivity from 0.29 to 0.91 micrometers, permitting them to see something of both ultraviolet and infrared radiation. (The Lo'tfian "rainbow" distinguishes eleven colors, compared with the conventional ROYGBIV seven of humans.)

The blind Lo'tfian females are known to be highly intelligent. The intellectual level of the Lo'tfian males, however, is a much-debated subject. On the one hand, until the arrival of Cecropians on Lo'tfi, no Lo'tfian exhibited curiosity toward anything beyond the planet. This is understandable for the burrowing females, but not for the males who roamed the surface and saw stars and planets every night. In addition, Lo'tfian male interpreters for Cecropians function as pure translation devices, never commenting on or adding to the statements of their masters.

On the other hand, Lo'tfian males are superb linguists, and when deprived of their Cecropian dominatrixes they are certainly capable of independent thought and action. Male Lo'tfians who are taken off-planet are illiterate, but they pick up reading and writing so easily and rapidly that these abilities are surely part of their genetic stock.

The prevailing theory to resolve this paradox comes from limited studies of Lo'tfian physiology. The male brain, it is believed, is highly organized and possesses powerful intelligence. However, it contains an unknown physical inhibitor, chemical in nature, that forbids the employment of that intelligence when in the presence of a Lo'tfian female. Confronted by such a female, the reasoning ability of the male Lo'tfian simply switches off. (A much weaker form of this phenomenon has been attributed to other species. See *Human* entry of this catalog.) The same mechanism is believed to be at work to a lesser extent when the Lo'tfian male encounters Cecropians and other intelligences. If the theory is true, no one is ever exposed to full Lo'tfian intelligence in face-to-face meetings with them.

History: From other evidence on the planet Lo'tfi, the planet's dominant organisms are members of an old race, existing in their present physical form and enjoying their present life patterns for at least ten million years. If there are written records, they are maintained in the burrows by the dominant females and are unavailable to outside inspection.

Culture: Lo'tfian males living on the surface of their home planet or absent from it display no interest in mating. They are in a mature form they refer to as "Second Stage" or "Postlarval." Since the adult form of the species possesses two well-defined sexes, and since it is highly unlikely that the burrow-dwelling larval stage prior to metamorphosis is capable of reproduction, mating presumably takes place when the males return to the burrows carrying food. At that time, male intelligence is inhibited and sex drives will dominate. Since Lo'tfian females are continuously intelligent, they define and control all Lo'tfian culture.

It is interesting to speculate on the social organization that might be set up by a group of Lo'tfian males, far removed from their females or other intelligent beings. These speculations remain academic, since such circumstances have not so far arisen and are unlikely to do so. Male Lo'tfians become agitated and exhibit irrational behavior when access to intelligent companions, of their own or other species, is denied them.

—From the *Universal Species Catalog*
(Subclass: Sapients).

CHAPTER 6

A JOURNEY OUT to Gargantua sounded difficult and dangerous. Birdie Kelly had been dreading the prospect. As he got to know Julius and Steven Graves better he liked the idea even less; and when E. C. Tally's presence on the trip was thrown in for good measure, Birdie's level of apprehension was raised to new heights.

Yet that final addition proved to be the saver. In some way that Birdie could not explain, Steven Graves and E. C. Tally canceled each other out. Maybe it was because they never stopped arguing. The annoyance level of their arguments was enough to reduce most other irritations to background level, and it allowed Birdie to take his mind off the unpleasant reality of the journey.

That reality had started even before they lifted off from Opal. All three had gone to the edge of one of the Slings, to inspect the ship that Birdie had been offered for the journey. Tally had lagged behind the other two, showing an unnatural interest in a species of domestic waterfowl swimming just offshore.

"You're saying he's a bloody robot!" Birdie complained, when he was sure he could not be overheard. "Well, why didn't somebody tell me that when he first arrived? No wonder he comes across like such an idiot."

"He's not a robot." Julius Graves was eyeing the interplanetary transit vessel with disfavor. The ship was certainly big—ten times the size they needed—but the outer hull was scarred and rusted. On Miranda it would have seen the scrap heap a century earlier. "I really shouldn't have said anything at all, except that sometime it might be important for you to know. E. Crimson Tally is an embodied computer. His available data base should be huge, even though he lacks human experience and local knowledge."

"Same difference. Computer, robot. And data base about what? He doesn't seem to know anything useful."

"He's not a computer, or a robot. He has a human body."

Birdie shuddered. "That's awful. Whose was it before he got it?"

"Nobody's. It was grown for him from a library template." Graves had climbed up to stare through a hatch into the ship's vast and desolate interior. He sniffed. "Phew. What did you say this was used for last time?"

"Ore freighter." Birdie peered in. "At least, that's what they told me. Can't imagine what sort of ore looked like that. Or smelled like it." He pulled his head out fast. Even he was impressed by the filth inside. "But I still don't know what Tally's doing here."

"Blame me for that. If I had returned to Miranda as planned, E. C. Tally would have gone with me. He tells me that he was sent to Opal with three goals. First, to determine firsthand the significance of recent events here; second, to accompany me wherever I go; and third, to bring me back with him to Alliance headquarters." Graves rubbed his hand over the hatch cover and stared at the results with distaste. "Look, this won't do. The whole inside hull will have to be cleaned out completely before it's fit for use."

"No problem."

No problem, because Birdie knew that the chances of getting anyone to clean it out were zero; but there was no point in telling that to Graves. It occurred to Birdie that he would willingly settle for the last of those three stated mission objectives for E. C. Tally—all his own problems would go away if only Graves and Tally would just *leave*. And didn't it display the most monstrous and the most typical gall, for the Alliance Council to sit hundreds of light-years away and try to call the shots through a half-witted robot?

Tally's next act had not helped his popularity with Birdie. He had finished his puzzled inspection of the ducks, then wandered over to examine the inside and outside of the ship.

"May I speak?" he said at last.

Birdie swore. "Will you for God's sake stop *saying* that? Even when I say no, you speak anyway."

"My apologies, Commissioner Kelly. Since my request for some reason causes you discomfort, I will try to desist . . . even though politeness was a basic element of my prime indoctrination. However, I am sure you will be interested in what I have to say now. I have been engaged in computation and analysis. Based on this ship's history and current condition, I calculate a sixty-six percent chance of catastrophic failure on any extended journey, such as that planned to the planet Gargantua."

Julius Graves gave a loud grunt of disapproval. Birdie shuddered and felt inclined to echo it. Had he survived Summertide, then, only to be wiped out in space? Not if he could help it. But surely he didn't need to do anything. This was the moment where Graves would exercise his override authority as a council member and veto the whole journey, no matter what E. C. Tally wanted to do. It was unacceptably dangerous.

"I am sorry, Tally," Graves said—there, he was going to use his authority, just the way Birdie had hoped. "But we are forced to take exception to your statement. Steven calculates that there is a *sixty* percent chance of catastrophic failure—no more!"

"I beg to differ." Tally looked down his well-designed nose at Graves. "I think that if you itemize the parameter inputs appropriate to the case, as follows, you will find these additional sources of danger . . ."

And away they went.

The Steven Graves vs. E. Crimson Tally stakes; that was the way Birdie was coming to think of it. As the *Incomparable*—Birdie was inclined to agree with that name for the rotting hulk—creaked and groaned its smelly and rust-covered way to the outer system, Steven Graves and E. C. Tally went on with their endless arguments.

Who was the winner? Birdie was not sure. The trip out to Gargantua was long and—thank God!—uneventful, and there were few people around to argue the point with. From sheer perversity Birdie went to an unlikely source—and consulted Julius Graves about the Steven-Tally dispute.

The councilor took the question perfectly seriously, wrinkling his bald, scarred forehead before he replied.

"I believe that I can be impartial. And I think it is a standoff. E. C. Tally has the advantage over Steven when it comes to anything involving computational speed—which is no surprise, given that his basic circuitry is many trillions of times as fast. The real surprise is that Steven can do as well as he does. So far as I can tell—Steven and I have discussed this several times—Tally employs direct formula computation whenever possible. Steven, on the other hand, makes extensive use of precomputed and memorized lookup tables and interpolation. Normally Tally will reach a conclusion faster on anything calling for straight computation—but not always.

"Steven's advantage comes in other areas. Like any human, he enjoys a degree of parallelism that no computer, embodied or not, has ever achieved. To take one simple example, Steven and you and I are capable of remarkable feats of pattern recognition. We can distinguish and name an object familiar to us in a fraction of second, no matter how far off or at what angle we see it. You know who I am at once when we meet, regardless of lighting conditions or distance. Given the slow speed of organic memory, that cannot require more than about one hundred full cycles of our brains, which means tremendous parallel processing. To do the same job of recognition, the inorganic brain of E. C. Tally needs hundreds of billions of serial calculation cycles. Naturally, he will eventually reach the same result. But in this case, Steven will often be faster."

"Two heads are better than one, you mean." Birdie was unsmiling. "Either one of them may win. Sounds like we ought to hear from both Steven and E. C. Tally before we make any decision."

"There is a certain logic to that idea. The other surprise is in information storage. Steven has far slower access, but he has better information packing density. He knows many more *facts* than E. C. Tally, but he takes longer to retrieve them." Graves thought for a few moments longer. "And, of course, the final weakness of E. C. Tally is unrelated to computation speed or to memory capacity. It is his inability to allow for the effects of *emotion* when considering human issues. He will always do his best to make the right decision—his makeup gives him no choice—but his judgment on both human and alien issues will always be impaired. And the farther he is away from the environment in which his principal experience was drawn, the more suspect his decision processes will be." Graves peered around, making sure that Tally was not lurking somewhere near. "It occurs to me that you and I had better keep a close eye on him. Especially you. He will seek to hide his motives from me, because he knows that I am part of the Council. You must inform me at once if his actions ever appear dangerously simplistic, or insensitive to the subtleties of organic intelligence."

Birdie nodded. At the first opportunity he went for a quiet chat with E. C. Tally.

"Your observations have merit," Tally said carefully, after a few milliseconds' pause for substantial introspection. "The minds of Julius and Steven Graves possess certain attributes that may supplement mine. There is virtue in massively parallel processing, although on the whole it does not compensate for the painfully sluggish speed of an Organic's neural circuits." Tally looked carefully around him. "However, Julius and Steven Graves possess one weakness that could be fatal.

In an emergency they—especially Julius—will tend to make judgments that are clouded by emotion. I was warned of this by the Council. Perhaps you can assist me here. Graves will seek to hide the effects of his emotions from me, because he knows that I will be reporting to the Council. You must tell me at once if his actions ever appear dangerously emotional, or unduly colored by the hormonal influences of organic intelligence."

"Sure. You can count on me."

"Hmm. Indeed?" There was a moment's pause. "Aha! You employ the verb *idiomatically,* not literally." E. C. Tally nodded with heavy satisfaction. "Yes, indeed you do. Logic, and the slowness of your arithmetic circuits, require that must be the case. It is rewarding to know that the ways of organic intelligence are becoming apparent to me."

He wandered off through the interior, with its lingering aroma of rancid fat.

Birdie felt a moment's satisfaction, which was quickly replaced by a disturbing thought: Graves is as crazy as a Varnian, and E. C. Tally is no better. What's wrong with me, when *both* sets of weirdos take me into their confidence?

ENTRY 18: VARNIAN.

Distribution: The Varnian cladeworld, Evarnor, orbits an F-type star near the center of the ellipsoidal gas cloud known in the Fourth Alliance as the Swan of Hercules. The cloud lies approximately 170 light-years from Sol, in a direction bisecting the angle between the galactic normal and the vector to the galactic center.

Varnians spread from their original home via sublight-speed ships to thirteen other planets prior to their discovery by human explorers. All fourteen of these Varnian worlds lie within or on the boundaries of the Swan of Hercules.

Subsequent to that first discovery (in E. 1983, by the members of the Dmitriev Ark), small groups of Varnians have been spread by human contact throughout the Fourth Alliance and the Cecropia Federation. Spiral-arm regulations prohibit the formation of any colony of Varnians in excess of four thousand members, except on Evarnor itself or on one of the original thirteen Varnian colony worlds. Despite Varnian petition, this edict is judged unlikely to change in the foreseeable future (see *Culture*, below).

The population of Varnians throughout the spiral arm is estimated at 220 million. Although in no danger of extinction, they represent one of the rarer intelligences of the region.

Physical Characteristics: The Varnians are versatile metamorphs, capable of extensive physical transformation. Since Evarnor is a low-temperature planet, close to the limit for oxygen breathers, the Varnians who live there adopt in repose a spherical configuration that maximizes heat conservation. They extrude variable-width pseudopods as required, but they rarely deviate far from the overall spheroid.

Varnians in warmer environments are less constrained in appearance. In the presence of members of another species they will often mimic their main features, from the basic elements of endoskeleton, limb structure, and epidermal appearance, to such refinements as eye color, hair follicles, and behavioral patterns. There are no known limits to such mimicry ("Don't judge a Varnian by the warmth of her smile").

History: The Varnian story appears as a constant battle with racial insanity. If any species points up the distinction between intelligence and rational behavior, this is it. Archeological records, obtained by human and Cecropian workers, show that Varnian civilization went through at least five sudden and total extinctions, with subsequent slow returns from barbarism. Each collapse occurred without warning, following a long stable period of peaceful development. The estimated cycle time has been as short as forty thousand years (Second Eclipse) and as long as seven hundred thousand (Fourth Eclipse).

The loss of all but scanty records of those five disasters makes reconstruction of past events difficult; however, the spread of Varnian civilization across fourteen planets of twelve suns during three different eras proves that an advanced technology was achieved in at least those cycles.

The continuous written history of the Varnians can be traced back for twenty-two thousand years, to the time of the beginning of the Sixth Emergence.

Culture: Today's Varnian civilization is tranquil, unambitious, and apparently stable. It has been so for thirty thousand years, with no sign of an impending sixth species-wide disaster. However, the Per'nathon-Magreeu symbiote (PM) suggested in E. 2731 that this is no cause for complacency. It was PM's analysis of Varnian culture that finally led to the restriction on colony size to four thousand members anywhere beyond the original fourteen Varnian worlds.

PM, in a systematic analysis of Varnian languages, noted that although there are over 140 semantic groups, languages, and local dialects in use among Varnians, none of those possesses a word meaning cynicism, self-criticism, or skepticism. They also pointed out that the basic collapse of Varnian civilization took place only on Evarnor, with the failure of other colonies arising from their material dependence on the cladeworld. In addition, the several different collapses do not all appear to have arisen for the same reason. Finally, PM remarked that the autopsies of Varnian brains reveal no meme-inhibitor complex.

PM concluded that the Varnian collapses were a resonance phenomenon, the consequence of positive feedback among large Varnian groups. Lacking the necessary faculty of reasoned skepticism, the Varnians are uniquely vulnerable to negative memetic influences. Destructive memes, spreading unchecked through the whole population, feed on themselves, to the point where individual Varnians become incapable of rational thought. The memetic plagues are terminated only by a civilization's collapse, with the associated loss of rapid communication among large groups.

PM set the absolute lower limit of interacting Varnians for such a phenomenon at twenty thousand participants. The onset of instability will not normally be seen until the number of individuals involved is in the millions. The present maximum value of four thousand for general colony size is extremely conservative.

—From the *Universal Species Catalog* (Subclass: Sapients).

CHAPTER 7

WITHOUT THE AID of the beacon they would never have found Louis Nenda's ship. Darya became convinced of that as the *Summer Dreamboat* crept closer to it. For the past hundred kilometers they had been flying through a cloud of debris—lumps of rock, water-ice, and ammonia-ice ranging from boulders the size of a house down to pea-sized hail. Even the smaller pieces could be dangerous. The clutter scattered radio signals, too, and determining the precise location of the *Have-It-All* became a trial-and-error process. No wonder the beacon had been so faint.

"I don't understand this at all," Hans Rebka complained. "Why are there so many fragments, all so close to their ship? We're having to avoid more and more of them." He was at the controls with Kallik at his side. Darya had retired to the bunks, and J'merlia had been left behind on Dreyfus-27, along with a complete record of everything seen so far and instructions to explore and maybe refurbish the old mine shafts and tunnels.

"It cannot be the result of chance." Kallik was still tracking and monitoring, using range and range-rate data to determine trajectories. She whistled and clucked to herself as she added to the data base she had already formed. "If these fragments were in normal orbits about Gargantua, they would have dispersed, long ago, to form an extended toroidal ck-c-cloud with Gargantua at its center. Since they have not, and since physical laws have not been suspended here . . ." She leaned forward, her forward-facing black eyes intent on the display screen. "Ck-ck. I believe I have the explanation. Tell me if you s-s-see it also. Is not something there, another object, close to the location of the *Have-It-All*?"

Darya stood up from the bunk and moved forward to examine the display. Amid the diffuse reflections she saw the hint of a brighter ring of light, at roughly the computed position of Nenda's ship.

"I see something. Hans, it's another planetoid, right in the middle of the mess. In fact it explains why there *is* a mess. The whole cloud of fragments is orbiting around it, while it orbits Gargantua."

"I ck-concur. It is the reason that they have not dispersed."

"But it makes things more mysterious, not less." Hans Rebka changed the contrast of the display, so that the bright circle stood out more clearly from the background. "Look at that thing. It's tiny—a couple of kilometers across, no more. We'd never have seen it with the ordinary sort of search methods."

"You mean it shouldn't have enough mass to hold anything in orbit around it."

"Right. But it does. And we're being accelerated toward it. I'm forced to make adjustments to our own motion."

The *Summer Dreamboat* was sliding through a denser froth of orbiting fragments as the body ahead of them became larger and sharper on the display.

"And look at that outline," Darya said softly. "If that's not a perfect sphere, it's close enough to have fooled me."

Kallik was busy superimposing the latest fix for the position of Nenda's ship on the largest display screen. It became clear that the other vessel sat on or very close to the round body. The Hymenopt studied the combined image in silence for a few moments. "The *Have-It-All* is not moving relative to the planetoid. There must be enough ss-ss-surface gravity to hold it firmly in one position."

Rebka turned the *Dreamboat* and increased the thrust.

"Kallik, do a calculation for me. Assume that thing is a couple of kilometers in diameter, and suppose it's made of solid rock. What should the surface gravity be? I'd like a reasonable maximum figure."

"Ah." The Hymenopt touched four limbs to the keyboard in front of her. "A small fraction of a centimeter per second," she said in a few moments, "Maybe one three-thousandth of a standard gravity, no more."

"I thought so. But we're experiencing that already, while we're still fifty kilometers out! If I extrapolate all the way down, the gravity on the surface of that thing must be getting close to one gee. That's flat-out impossible, for any material we've ever heard of."

As Rebka was speaking the *Dreamboat* made a sudden jerking move to one side. Darya was thrown back onto the bunk. The other two saved themselves by clutching at the control panel.

"What was *that*?" Darya remained flat on her back as the ship took a second leap in a different direction.

"Meteorite-avoidance system." Rebka hauled himself back into position. "I put it on automatic, because there's so much stuff around here I wasn't sure we'd see it all. Good thing I did. Hold on, here comes another. And another. God, they're piling in from everywhere."

The new jerking thrusts came before he had finished speaking, throwing him forward onto the controls. He grabbed desperately for handholds.

"Where are they coming from?" Every time Darya tried to sit up, the ship made a leap in some other unpredictable direction. There was a solid thump on the outside hull, loud enough to be frightening, and the few objects that were not secured in the galley came sailing through into the cabin and rattled around there. "Can you see them?"

Even as she asked that question, her mind was posing a more abstract one. How could orbiting lumps of rock be vectoring in at them, all at once and from all directions? Random processes did not work that way.

Kallik, with hands to spare, was doing better than Hans Rebka. Without saying a word she was at work on the control panel. The ship spun on its axis, and Darya felt a powerful, steady thrust added to the jerks and surges of the collision-avoidance system.

From her position in the bunk she could still see the main display screen. It showed a circle of light surrounded by bright glittering motes. As she watched it came swooping closer at alarming speed. When they seemed ready to plunge right into its center, the ship pivoted on its axis and decelerated at maximum power. Darya was again pressed flat to the bunk's mattress. She heard a startled grunt from Hans Rebka and a thump as he fell to the floor.

Darya felt a few seconds of maximum force on her body; then all acceleration ceased. The drive turned off. Darya found herself lying in something close to normal gravity. She lifted her head.

Hans Rebka was picking himself up painfully from the floor. Kallik was still seated, clutching with four hands at the control panel. The Hymenopt stared at them with the semicircle of rear-facing eyes and bobbed her head.

"My apologies. It was wrong to take such action without seeking permission. However, I judged it necessary if this ship and its occupants were to ss-ss-survive."

Rebka was rubbing his right shoulder and hip. "Damn it, Kallik, there was no need to panic. The collision-avoidance system is designed to handle multiple approaches—though I must say, I've never known a bombardment like that."

"Nor will you again, in normal ss-ss-circumstances."

"But what made you think we'd be any safer here, on the surface of the planetoid?" Darya had looked out of the port and confirmed her first impression. The *Summer Dreamboat* was sitting on a solid surface, in a substantial gravity field.

Kallik gestured out of the same port. The upper part of another ship was visible around the tight curve of the planetoid. "For two reasons. First, it was clear from the fact that the *Have-It-All* could sit on the surface with a working beacon, and therefore with working antennas, that there could be no continuous rain of materials here at the surface of the planetoid. I already thought that meant safety, even before I saw what was triggering the collision-avoidance system."

"Rocks and ice?"

"No." The black cranium turned slowly back and forth. "When I caught sight of the objects raining in on us, I had a second reason for descending rapidly. The attackers were free-space forms. I knew they would avoid any substantial gravity field, and we would be safe here." The Hymenopt turned to face Darya. "Those were not rocks or ice, Professor Lang. We were attacked by *Phages.*"

Hans Rebka looked startled. But Darya jerked upright in the bunk and clapped her hands together with excitement. "Phages! That's terrific."

"Terrific?" Rebka stared at her in disbelief. "I don't know how much exposure you've had to Phages, Darya, but I can tell you this: they may be slow, but they're *nasty.*"

"And these Phages are not so slow," Kallik said calmly. "They are faster than any of which I have seen reports."

"Which makes them worse." Rebka stared at the excited Darya. "Do you *want* to be killed?"

"Of course I don't. We made it through Summertide together, and yet you still ask me a question like that?" Darya had trouble keeping a smile off her face. "I want to live as much as you do. But put yourself in my position. I drag us all the way out here to the middle of nowhere, telling you we'll discover clues to the Builders. And then all we find are dreary bits of rock and old mine-workings. Until a few minutes ago I thought that might be all that we *would* find. But you know as well as I do, Phages are found around Builder artifacts, and only there. They may even *be* Builder ar-

tifacts—a number of specialists have suggested that theory."
She stood up and went to stare out of the ship's port at the
gleaming and suspiciously regular surface of the planetoid. "I
was right, Hans. I felt it back on Quake, and I feel it more
than ever now. We're getting there! The Builders have been
gone for a long time—but we're close to finding out where
they went."

Kallik wanted to scramble into a suit and head off at once
across the surface of the planetoid. Louis Nenda's ship was
in plain sight, a few hundred meters away, and she was itching to hurry over to it. The need to know if her master was
alive or dead made her abandon any thought of caution.

It took a direct order from Hans Rebka to stop her. "Absolutely not," he said. "I can think of ten ways you might get
killed, and there must be twenty more I don't know about.
When you go, one of us goes with you. And you don't go yet."
At his insistence Kallik settled down on her stubby abdomen
and joined the other two in making a first survey of their
surroundings.

Even from a distance, the body on which the *Dreamboat*
rested had appeared anomalously massive and anomalously
spherical. An hour of observation and measurement added
other peculiarities. When Kallik and Hans Rebka finally put
on their suits and made a first descent onto the planetoid's
surface, Darya stayed behind, monitored their progress, and
entered the physical data into the *Dreamboat*'s log. A copy
was going to J'merlia on Dreyfus-27, together with a note of
their safe landing and their location. Darya prepared another
copy for tight-beam transmission to Opal, with a request that
it be forwarded via the Bose Network to Sentinel Gate.

She smiled to herself as she reviewed the message before
sending it out. Just dull statistics, most people would say. She
was giving little but the facts. But there would be high excitement over these particular dull statistics when they reached
her colleagues on Sentinel Gate and were passed on in turn
to Builder specialists in the spiral arm. Every last one of them
would want to be here.

She kept an eye on Kallik and Hans, who were moving

cautiously away from the *Summer Dreamboat*, and played back the message before sending it to Opal.

Surface Temperature: 281 K; THE SURFACE OF THE BODY IS *WARM,* ABOVE THE FREEZING POINT OF WATER. GIVEN ITS ENVIRONMENT, REMOTE FROM MANDEL, IT SHOULD BE HUNDREDS OF DEGREES COLDER.

Figure: THE BODY IS A PERFECT SPHERE TO WITHIN THE LIMITS OF OBSERVATION; RADIUS, 1.16 KILOMETERS.

Surface Gravity: 0.65 GEE; GIVEN ITS SIZE, IT SHOULD BE LESS THAN A THOUSANDTH OF THIS VALUE.

Mass: 128 TRILLION TONS.

Density: ASSUMING HOMOGENEOUS COMPOSITION, 19,600 TONS PER CUBIC METER. NOTE THAT ALTHOUGH THIS IS LESS THAN SOME CECROPIAN COMMERCIAL MATERIALS, IT IS ABOUT 1,000 TIMES AS DENSE AS ANY NATURALLY OCCURRING SUBSTANCE.

Atmosphere: 16 PERCENT OXYGEN, 1 PERCENT CARBON DIOXIDE, 83 PERCENT XENON. THIS IS UNLIKE THE ATMOSPHERE OF ANY PLANET IN THE SPIRAL ARM; THE XENON CONTENT IS AN UNHEARD-OF CONCENTRATION; AND A BODY OF THIS SIZE SHOULD POSSESS NO ATMOSPHERE AT ALL. NOTE THAT THIS ATMOSPHERE WILL SUSTAIN LIFE FOR ALL OXYGEN-BREATHING FORMS OF THE SPIRAL ARM.

Material Composition: THE OUTER SURFACE HAS THE APPEARANCE OF SMOOTH, FUSED SILICA. THE INTERNAL COMPOSITION IS UNKNOWN, BUT IT IS OPAQUE TO ELECTROMAGNETIC RADIATION OF ANY WAVELENGTH.

Darya halted the data readout and looked out of the port. Kallik and Rebka had been crouching down, close to the surface. She had asked them to do additional materials testing outside, hoping to add something to this piece of the planetoid's description.

"Any results yet, Hans?"

Rebka straightened up. "We didn't get what you wanted, but we've probably got all we're going to. We couldn't take samples. The surface is too hard to cut, and it's impervious to heat. But we've been hitting it with precise impulses and monitoring the seismic return wavefronts. The phase delays are very peculiar. We think it's as you suggested—the whole thing is hollow, maybe with a honeycomb structure."

Kallik stood up also. "Which makes the high ss-ss-surface gravity even odder, since this is a hollow body."

"Right. I'll add that to the physical description. You can give me more detailed data when you get back. No other problems?"

"None so far. In a little while we're going to head for Nenda's ship. Keep monitoring."

"I will." With considerable satisfaction, Darya added a section to the readout:

General Description: THE BODY APPEARS TO BE HOLLOW, PROBABLY WITH INTERNAL CHAMBERS. GIVEN ITS ANOMALOUS PHYSICAL PARAMETERS, IT MUST BE OF ARTIFICIAL ORIGIN. THE PLANETOID'S AGE HAS NOT YET BEEN ESTABLISHED. THERE IS A GOOD POSSIBILITY THAT IT IS A BUILDER ARTIFACT. THAT HYPOTHESIS IS GIVEN SUPPORT BY THE FACT THAT PHAGES ARE TO BE FOUND CLOSE BY IN LARGE NUMBERS, LESS THAN A HUNDRED KILOMETERS AWAY FROM THE BODY'S SURFACE.

Darya paused. Better leave it at that, and not stick her neck out too far. But personally she was sure it was an artifact. And if that was the case it should be given its own name and ID number, like every other Builder artifact.

She added a final note to the message. "The artificial planetoid has been assigned the provisional Universal Artifact Catalog number 1237, and the provisional name"—she recalled the bright motes on the sphere's image, now vanished—"the provisional name of *Glister.*"

"Darya?" Hans Rebka's voice came as she was making the final entry. "Darya, we're over at the *Have-It-All* now. It seems to be in working order, but you ought to see it for yourself. Can you put your suit on and walk over?"

"I'll be there in five minutes." Darya initiated the message transmission, put the *Summer Dreamboat* into self-protect mode, and moved across to the lock. In less than a minute she was outside.

She looked up. Gargantua loomed in the distance beyond the other ship. High above her head the Phages were invisible, too small to be seen from fifty or a hundred kilometers away, but she had no doubt that they were still there. Phages were always there when they were not wanted.

And what Phages! Phages smart enough to track a falling ship. Phages fast enough to head for that ship. Phages fast enough to come close to catching it.

Darya began to move slowly across the curved and polished surface. The horizon was only a couple of hundred meters away. As Louis Nenda's ship came more and more into view she could not help glancing up every few seconds, to make sure that some marauding Phage was not diving down on her.

Phages didn't enter powerful gravity fields; in fact, they shunned them. Sure. That was the conventional wisdom. Until today she had believed it herself. But why assume that conventional wisdom applied to these Phages, and this situation, when everything else about them was so bizarre?

It occurred to Darya that Kallik had taken a bigger risk than they realized when she had brought them down here. The alien surface of Glister might be no safer than Phage-infested space. But Kallik's own need to know what had happened to Louis Nenda had made her blind to risk.

Darya arrived at the lock of the *Have-It-All.* One thing was for sure: given the behavior of these new Phages, she would have to do a major rewrite of that section of the *Lang Universal Artifact Catalog.* Good timing. She was supposed to begin work on the fifth edition when she got back home.

When she got back home . . .

She stared out across the smooth, glassy surface of Glister before she entered the lock. The little ship they had arrived on was the only familiar object. The *Summer Dreamboat* had started its life as a teenager's toy; now it was far from home, looking oddly lonely and defenseless.

Would it ever see its birthworld again? And would she see hers?

Darya closed the hatch. When she got home. Better make that *if* she got home.

ARTIFACT: PHAGE.

Exploration History: The first Phages were reported by humans during the exploration of Flambeau, in E. 1233. Subsequently, it was learned that Phages had been observed and avoided by Cecropian explorers for at least five thousand years. The first human entry of a Phage maw was made in E. 1234 during the Maelstrom conflict (no survivors).

Phage-avoidance systems came into widespread use in E. 2103, and are now standard equipment in Builder exploration.

Physical Description: The Phages are all externally identical, and probably internally similar though functionally variable. No sensor (or explorer) has ever returned from a Phage interior.

Each Phage has the form of a gray, regular dodecahedron, of side forty-eight meters. The surface is roughly textured, with mass sensors at the edge of each face. Maws can be opened at the center of any face and can ingest objects of up to thirty meters' radius and of apparently indefinite length. (In E. 2238, Sawyer and S'kropa fed a solid silicaceous fragment of cylindrical cross-section and twenty-five meters' radius to a Phage of the Dendrite Artifact. With an ingestion rate of one kilometer per day, 425 kilometers of material, corresponding to the full length of the fragment, were absorbed. No mass change was detected in the Phage, nor a change in any other of its physical parameters.)

Phages are capable of slow independent locomotion, with a mean rate of one or two meters per standard day. No Phage has ever been seen to move at a velocity in excess of one meter per hour with respect to the local frame.

Intended Purpose: Unknown. Were it not for the fact that Phages have been found in association with over 300 of the 1,200 known artifacts, and only in such association, any relationship to the Builders would be questioned. They differ greatly in scale and number from all other Builder constructs.

It has been speculated that the Phages served as general scavengers for the Builders, since they are apparently able to ingest and break down any materials made by the clades and anything made by the Builders with the single exception of the structural hulls and the paraforms (e.g., the external shell of Paradox, the surface of Sentinel, and the concentric hollow tubes of Maelstrom).

—From the *Lang Universal Artifact Catalog,*
Fourth Edition.

CHAPTER 8

LOUIS NENDA'S SHIP was undamaged. Inside and out, every piece of equipment was in working order. The main drive showed signs of overload, but it still tested at close to full power.

"I'm sure that overload happened while they were in orbit around Quake," Darya said. "I told you, I saw them putting in every bit of thrust they had to try and get away from that silver sphere."

"Yeah. But you also said they were accelerated away by the sphere at hundreds of gees, enough to flatten everything." Hans Rebka waved an arm at the orderly interior. "Nothing flat here that I can see."

"Which is not difficult to explain." Kallik was crouched down on the floor by the *Have-It-All*'s hatch, sniffing and clicking to herself. "If the ship were to be accelerated by gravity or any other form of body force, neither it nor its occupants would be harmed. They would feel as though they moved in free-fall, no matter how high the acceleration appeared to an outside observer."

"Which should mean that if the ship is undamaged, so are Louis Nenda and Atvar H'sial." Rebka was inspecting the main control panel. "And the engines haven't been powered down. They're on standby, ready to fly this minute. Which leaves us with one question." He stared at Darya and shrugged. "Where the devil are they?"

They had searched the *Have-It-All* from side to side and top to bottom. There was ample evidence that Atvar H'sial and Louis Nenda had been there. But there was no sign of them, and no suits were missing from the lockers.

"Master Nenda was certainly here," Kallik said, "more than three days ago, and less than one week."

"How do you know?"

"I can smell him. In his quarters, at the controls, and here near the hatch. J'merlia, if he were here, could place the time more accurately. He has a finer sense of smell."

"I don't see how that would help us. Not even if J'merlia could smell it to the millisecond." Rebka was walking moodily around the big cabin, examining the decorated wall panels and running his fingers across the luxurious fittings. "Darya, I know you said that the sphere that carried this ship away was silver at first, then it turned to black—"

"Turned to nothing, I said. It was like a hole in space."

"All right, turned to nothing. But couldn't it have changed again? One odd thing thing about this place—wha'd'ya call it, Glister?—is that it's a perfect sphere. Spherical planetoids don't occur in nature. Hasn't it occurred to you that it may be the *same* sphere, the one that you saw?"

"Of course I've had that thought. I had it before we even landed. But it only leaves a bigger mystery. *Something* sent a beam from near Gargantua, at Summertide, and the sphere that I saw ascended it. If this sphere was *my* sphere, what sent the signal?"

"All right, so maybe this isn't *your* sphere." Rebka seemed amused by her proprietary tone. "I'll drop that, and ask you again: Where are they?"

"Give me a minute. I may have a logical answer; whether

or not you like it is another matter." Darya sat down on one of Nenda's comfortable couches to organize her thoughts. As she did so she surveyed her surroundings, comparing them with the familiar, stripped-down, and spartan fixtures of the *Dreamboat.*

The contrast was great. The whole inside of Nenda's starship was filled with alien devices and manufacturing techniques. The technology used here had been perfected long before by the Zardalu, before their thousand-world empire had collapsed, and been picked up piecemeal after that collapse to become the common property of the mix of species that now made up the Zardalu Communion.

But even more than it spoke of alien technology, the *Have-It-All* proclaimed another message: that of *wealth.*

Darya had never seen such opulence—and she was from a rich world. If Louis Nenda was a criminal, as everyone seemed to think, then crime certainly paid.

In one other area, her first view of the interior of Nenda's ship was forcing a change in Darya's thinking. She had first met Kallik on Opal and on Quake, and had seen her then as a callously treated under-being, little better than a shackled and servile pet of the Karelian human, Louis Nenda. But Kallik's quarters on the *Have-It-All* were as good as Nenda's own, and far better than *anyone* enjoyed in the worlds of the Phemus Circle. Kallik had her own study, equipped with powerful computers and scientific instruments. She had her own sleeping area, decorated with choice and expensive examples of Hymenopt art.

Even villains deserved justice. Darya filed that thought away for future reference. Nenda might act the monster—might *be* a monster—but his generous private treatment of Kallik was at variance with his public image. Nenda had certainly been crude, lecherous, coarse, and boorish with Darya. But was that the *real* Louis Nenda, or was it a pose?

"Well?" Hans Rebka was staring at her impatiently. Darya came back to the present with a jerk and realized that her thoughts had strayed off in a quite unexpected and inappropriate direction.

"I'm sorry," she said. "Point one: Nenda and Atvar H'sial

were alive when the ship got here. Kallik is sure of that. Point two: There are no suits missing. Point three: The air on the surface of this planetoid is breathable. Point four—not proved, but a good working assumption: This planetoid is hollow. Point five—another working hypothesis: The inside of Glister contains the same sort of air as there is on the surface. Put them together: if Louis Nenda and Atvar H'sial are still alive—or even if they're dead—we know where they can be found." She pointed at the floor.

"Inside Glister." Rebka was frowning. "That's what I decided, too, while you were sitting there daydreaming. I don't much like that idea."

"I never said you would."

"It gives us another problem."

"I know. To see if we're right, we have to get inside. And we haven't seen any sign of an opening or a hatch."

"On the descent, we certainly didn't." Rebka sat down in the control chair. "But that's not surprising—we had other things on our minds. There could be ways in just a hundred meters away, or there could be openings around the other side that we've never seen."

"And we won't find them sitting here." Darya stood up. She was full of an irrational energy. "You know what? I want to find Nenda and Atvar H'sial, and spit in their eye for trying to kill us on Quake. But even if they didn't exist, I'd want to find a way to the interior. And so would you. You pretend you're not interested in Builder artifacts, but you're the man who was all ready to risk a descent into Paradox, before you were sent to Dobelle. And this *is* an artifact. I've studied all twelve hundred and thirty-six of them, and I'm sure of it. Come on, let's take a look outside." Darya placed her hand on the control that would move her suit from full open to closed mode, then paused. "The air out there is supposed to be breathable. I might as well test it a little. Keep your eye on me."

She headed for the lock, expecting to hear Rebka's voice ordering her to stop. Instead he said in an amused tone, "I swear, if it isn't one of you wanting to run off and do something crazy, it's the other. Wait for me."

"And me," Kallik said.

"And don't worry about the air," Rebka added. "After the analysis was finished and came out positive I put my suit on partial transparency. Glister's atmosphere is fine."

"And you call *me* crazy." Darya stepped through into the lock.

In the time they had been inside Nenda's ship, Glister had made a quarter-turn on its axis. Gargantua was visible as a half disk, while Mandel and Amaranth were hidden behind the planetoid. Darya emerged to an overhead dazzle of orbiting fragments and a cold, orange twilight. The air was odorless, tasteless, and chilly in her nose and lungs. Her breath showed as a puff of white fog when she exhaled.

What now?

Darya stared around at the featureless horizon. She began to walk forward, moving across Glister in the direction away from the *Dreamboat.* As she went she scanned the surface ahead. It had not occurred to her before, but without light from Mandel, visibility was going to be much reduced. Even using the image intensifiers in her suit she could not see details more than fifty meters away.

Darya slowed her pace. Kallik was a lightning calculator, but the Hymenopt was fifty meters behind and Darya would have to work it out for herself. A little more than a kilometer in radius. So the surface area of Glister was a bit less than seventeen square kilometers. And she could see things clearly for at most fifty meters in each direction. Assume that they split up and found an efficient way of covering the whole area. Then each of them would have to walk over fifty kilometers to be sure of finding whatever might be there.

Not good enough. And she should have thought it through before she left the ship. Darya waited for Rebka and Kallik to catch up with her.

"I've changed my mind." She outlined the problem. "It will take us too long. I think that we ought to go back inside and use Nenda's ship; he doesn't need it at the moment. And we should do a low-orbit traverse of Glister, a few hundred meters up, and use every sensor on board to explore the surface. Anything odd that we find—cracks, openings, hatches, markings, whatever—we'll have the ship's computer make a note of it, and then later we take a closer look ourselves. On foot. Can you fly the *Have-It-All,* Hans? If not, we can go back and use the *Dreamboat.* Though I'm sure the equipment there isn't as good."

"It isn't. As you saw, Nenda travels first-class. I can fly his ship. And I bet that Kallik can fly it at least as well as me."

"I have flown it often, on both planetary and stellar missions," the Hymenopt concurred.

"So let's go back inside." Darya was turning toward the ship when she noticed an odd effect on the horizon behind Hans Rebka. It was as though she were suffering slight vertical double vision, with a thin brighter layer added above the sphere's original curved boundary. As she watched, the region thickened and solidified; faint sparkles appeared within it as random points of light. Part of Glister looked the way it had when she first saw it, from far out in space. Darya halted for a closer inspection.

Increased intensity added color. The cloud became a gauzy orange patch, lying close to Glister's uniform horizon, and extended over more than a quarter of the circle. As Darya watched the nimbus grew in size. The twinkle of interior lights became brighter.

"Hans!" She pointed. "Look there. Did you see anything like that before, when you were out on the surface?"

He stared, and at once took her arm to begin pulling her toward the *Have-It-All.*

"We sure didn't. Come on. And hurry."

"What is it?"

"Damned if I know. I've never seen anything like it in my life. I think maybe me and Kallik weren't too smart when we banged on the surface to learn more about the interior structure. Bit like knocking on the door to say, hey, we've arrived." He was still holding her arm. "Come on, both of you, get moving. I prefer to watch that thing, whatever it is, from inside the ship—with the shields up. Close your suit completely, just in case. And *don't look back.*"

Darya at once felt an irresistible urge to look behind her. The orange shimmer was bigger, spreading more than a third of the way across the horizon and perceptibly closer. Kallik had not moved, but that did not mean she would be left behind. When she decided to travel, the Hymenopt's eight wiry legs could carry her a hundred meters in a couple of seconds.

"It has a discrete structure." Kallik's calm voice came through Darya's suit phone. "The points of lights are reflections of incident radiation from Gargantua on individual small components, each no more than a few centimeters across. Their angles change constantly, which is why they sparkle like that. To appear as bright as they are, those components must be almost perfect reflectors. I can see no sort of connection between the parts."

The leading edge of the cloud was within twenty meters of the Hymenopt when Kallik finally turned. The thin black legs became a blur, and a second later she was by Darya's side. "I concur with Captain Rebka. This is a phenomenon outside my experience."

"Outside anyone's." The *Have-It-All* was only forty meters away. Darya could not resist looking back again. The cloud was not gaining. They could crowd inside the airlock and have it closed before the twinkling fog arrived. With the ship on standby, there was a good chance they could even take off from Glister before the leading edge touched the hull.

"Ahead!" Kallik spoke at the same moment as Hans Rebka began to swear.

Darya turned. A gauzy light was in front of them, rising like a sparkling vapor up through Glister's impervious surface. It thickened and spread as she watched, forming a tenuous barrier between them and the starship.

Rebka jerked to a halt, and they stared around them. The cloud behind was still moving forward. It had become opaque, and its edges were spreading wider. In a few more seconds its borders would meet with those of the fog ahead, to encircle the three completely.

Kallik was already moving forward. Rebka shouted at her. "Kallik! Come back. That is an order."

"Ck-ck." The Hymenopt kept moving. "With apologies, Captain Rebka, it is an order I cannot obey. I must not risk the life of a human when perhaps that can be avoided. I will report my experiences for as long as I am able."

Kallik was entering the cloud. It swirled up around her thin legs and tubby body. She was quickly reduced to a sparkling outline of light.

"I am now able to see the structure of individual components." The voice was as calm as ever. "They appear to be unconnected, and each one is different and has independent mobility. They have a definite crystalline nature. In their appearance I am reminded of water-snowflakes—there is the same diversity of form and fractal structure. I feel them pressing against my suit, but there is no sensation beyond simple external pressure. And now . . . they are *within* my suit— despite the fact that it is set for full opacity! Apparently they penetrate our protective materials as easily as they move through the planetoid's surface. I question whether a ship's shields can offer any obstacle or protection.

"The flakes are now in contact with my thorax and abdomen. They are touching me, sensing me, as though in examination of my structure. They are *inside* me, I feel them. Their temperature is difficult to estimate, but it cannot be extreme. I feel no discomfort."

Kallik had vanished from sight. Her voice briefly faded, then came back to full strength. "Can you hear me, Captain Rebka? Please reply if you can."

"Loud and clear, Kallik. Keep talking."

"I will do so. I have now taken seven paces into the cloud, and it is tenuous but quite opaque. I can no longer see the sky or the surface of the planetoid. I also register a power drain from my suit, but so far I am able to compensate. *Eleven paces.* There is minor resistance to my forward progress, although not enough to impede my movements. The surface beneath my feet feels unchanged. I am having no trouble breathing, thinking, or moving my limbs.

"*Eighteen paces.* The resistance to my motion has lessened. Visibility is improving, and already I can see the outline of Master Nenda's ship ahead of me. *Twenty-two paces.* I can see the stars again. Most of the cloud is behind me. I am standing on the surface of the planetoid, and I appear to be physically unaffected by my passage through it. *Twenty-seven paces.* I am totally clear.

"Captain Rebka, I humbly suggest that both of you proceed through the cloud at once and join me here. I will prepare the *Have-It-All*'s lock for multiple entries and the controls for takeoff. Can you still hear me?"

"I hear you. We're on our way, we'll see you in a couple of minutes." Hans Rebka was pulling at Darya's arm again, but she needed no urging. Together they stepped into the sparkling orange glow. Darya began to count steps.

At seven paces the view around her faded. The stars overhead clouded and dissolved. She saw delicate crystals, hundreds of them, a handbreadth from her face. She heard Rebka's voice: "Seven paces, Kallik. We're almost a third of the way."

Eleven steps. Small points of pressure were being applied directly to her body, *within* her body. Like Kallik, Darya could not say if their touch was hot or cold. She felt that the crystals were touching her innermost self, measuring her, *evaluating* her. She found herself holding her breath, reluctant to inhale the cloud of crystals. She plowed on. There was a definite resistance to her forward motion, almost like walking underwater.

"Fourteen paces," said a gargling and distorted voice. That was Rebka, and he *sounded* as if he were underwater.

Eighteen steps. According to Kallik, she should start to see something more than the sparkling mist. Darya peered ahead of her. She could see only foggy points of light. Resistance to her progress was increasing.

It was not supposed to happen this way!

She struggled to force herself ahead, but the surface beneath her feet afforded less traction. She felt it becoming spongy, giving beneath her weight.

She wanted to sink to her knees, lean forward, and explore that insubstantial ground with her hands. But instead of releasing her, the sparkling points of light were holding her more and more tightly. She could barely move her arms and legs.

"Darya?" She heard Hans Rebka's voice faintly in her suit

phone. It was the thinnest thread of sound, miles and miles away, the signal full of static.

She made a final effort to push herself forward. Her limbs would not move. She was fully conscious but fixed in position, as firmly as a fly in amber.

Keep your head! she told herself. Don't let yourself get panicky.

"Hans!" She tried to call to him, struggling to keep the fear from her voice. That concern was unnecessary, for no sound came from her throat. And now no sound was reaching her ears, not even the faint static that was always present with suit phones. The touch of the crystals on her body was fading, but still she could not move. The sparkling mist had given way to an absolute blackness.

"Hans!" It was a soundless scream. Fear had taken over. *"Hans!"*

She listened, and she waited.

Nothing. No sound, no sight, no touch. No sensations of any kind. Not even pain.

Was this the way that life was to end, in universal darkness? Had the death that she had escaped so closely on Quake followed her to claim her here?

Darya waited. And waited.

She had a sudden vision of a personal hell that lay beyond death itself: to be held fully conscious, for eternity, unable to move, see, speak, hear, or feel.

Kallik had walked unscathed through the crystal fog. She had no reason to think that Darya Lang and Hans Rebka would fare any differently.

She heard his voice say, "Seven paces, Kallik. We're almost a third of the way." That was satisfactory. She listened for the next progress report, at twelve or fourteen steps.

It did not come when she expected; but before there was time to be alarmed, the barrier of sparkling mist in front of her changed, to form a series of swirling vortices that were sucked back into the hard surface. She waited, eagerly watching for the other two to appear out of the wreaths of fog.

The mist thinned. No familiar human outlines emerged. In

another few seconds the fog had vanished completely. The surface ahead of Kallik was bare.

She ran forward, at a speed that only those who threatened a Hymenopt with deadly violence would ever see. Two seconds and a hundred and fifty meters later she stopped. Given the snail's pace of human movement, there was no way that Hans Rebka and Darya Lang could have traveled so far in the time available.

Kallik reared up to her full height and employed every eye in her head.

She saw Gargantua, looming on the horizon. She saw Louis Nenda's ship, and beyond it the *Summer Dreamboat,* almost hidden by the tight curvature of the planetoid.

And that was all.

Kallik stood alone on the barren surface of Glister.

CHAPTER 9

THE HIERARCHY WAS clear in J'merlia's mind: humans were inferior to Cecropians, but they were well above Lo'tfians and Hymenopts, who were in turn vastly superior to Varnians, Ditrons, Bercia, and the dozens of other ragtag and marginally intelligent species of the spiral arm.

That hierarchy also defined a command chain. In the absence of Atvar H'sial or another Cecropian, J'merlia would obey the orders of a human without question. He did not have to *like* it, but he certainly had to do as he was told.

So J'merlia had not complained when he was ordered to remain on Dreyfus-27 while the other three went off to look for Louis Nenda and Atvar H'sial on the *Have-It-All*. All the same, he was desperately envious of Kallik. The Hymenopt was on her way to seek her master, perhaps to help him, while J'merlia stayed here making Dreyfus-27 a more habitable habitat. Suppose that Atvar H'sial needed help? Who would provide it, if J'merlia was not there? Who could even *commu-*

nicate with a Cecropian, via pheromonal transfer? Not Darya Lang, or Hans Rebka, or Kallik.

The cleanup operation had been given no particular starting time, so J'merlia did not feel obliged to begin at once to improve the living quarters of Dreyfus-27. Instead he remained in his suit on the rocky surface, close to the communications unit that Hans Rebka had removed from the *Dreamboat.*

His experiences would have to be vicarious ones, gleaned from the verbal and occasional visual messages sent back to him. That was still better than nothing, and J'merlia possessed strong interspecies empathy. He had exulted when Kallik reported the first image of the *Have-It-All* on the *Dreamboat*'s sensors. He had waited in agony when all signals suddenly became garbled during the dive to the surface of Glister. He had rejoiced when the report came of their safe landing, and when he learned of the apparently undamaged condition of Louis Nenda's ship. He had puzzled over the anomalous physical parameters of the planetoid itself, and the presence of a swarm of energetic Phages surrounding it. And he had nodded agreement at Darya Lang's suggestion that Glister must itself be an artifact.

The *Dreamboat*'s final message for the record indicated that Darya Lang was placing the ship on remote-controlled status, while she went out onto the surface of Glister to join Hans Rebka and Kallik in their direct inspection of Louis Nenda's starship.

J'merlia shivered with excitement and anticipation. The next communication would be the crucial one. The *Have-It-All* seemed undamaged, and that was wonderful. But were Louis Nenda and Atvar H'sial alive or dead? J'merlia waited six hours for an answer, crouched unmoving by the com unit.

The long-awaited transmission came as a voice signal— from Kallik! "Report #11031," she began. "09:88:3101. Unit ID R-86945."

Louis Nenda's ID. So the *Have-It-All* was certainly in working order. But even before the real message began, J'merlia knew from the slow and strained speech that something had gone terribly wrong.

"This is Kallik. The whereabouts of Captain Rebka and Professor Lang are unknown to me. I am alone on the surface of Glister . . ."

The Hymenopt gave a concise and unhappy summary of events since Darya Lang's last message. She ended: "It is unclear whether Masters Nenda and Atvar H'sial are living or dead. The same is true of Professor Lang and Captain Rebka. Logic suggests that regardless of their condition they will be found, if anywhere near here, in the interior of Glister. I know of no way to achieve entry to the sphere. I propose to fly the *Have-It-All* on a low-altitude survey, seeking possible entry points. Such a discovery is a low-probability event, but I will try it before exploring more risky alternatives."

J'merlia looked at the message-source locator. Kallik was on a planetoid in a higher orbit than Dreyfus-27, so she was steadily falling behind. In another half hour Glister would be hidden behind the curved bulk of Gargantua. Messages would become impossible for a while. Already the signal was distorted by electronic noise, faded and broken.

J'merlia switched to his own transmission mode. "Kallik. What are we going to do? The masters are gone." His voice rose to a wail. "There is no one left to direct us!"

He waited impatiently through the three-second round-trip delay. Kallik was the smart one; she would have answers.

"I understand," a faint voice said, "and I have the same problem. All we can do is try to imagine what the masters would want, and function accordingly. For the moment, your position is clear. You were instructed to remain on Dreyfus-27. You should do so. My own position is more . . . difficult."

There was a long pause. J'merlia could guess at Kallik's suffering, and he sympathized strongly with it. The Hymenopt had disobeyed an order from Rebka when she walked forward into the fog, but that was not the problem. J'merlia would have done the same thing, to keep humans from risk. But Kallik had then been convinced by her own safe passage that Rebka and Lang could proceed unharmed through the shining mist. She had told them so—and she had been wrong. Her action may have led to their deaths. Kallik could not sit and wait, as J'merlia was waiting. She had to find a way to atone for her mistake.

"If my survey does not reveal an entry point," Kallik went on at last, "and I have little confidence that it will, then one other avenue is open to me. Our first attempts to penetrate the surface of Glister were unsuccessful. We could not cut into it or burn any mark in it. But the cloud that we saw came from *within* Glister. It emerged from an apparently solid surface. And yet when the cloud touched me, I feel sure that it possessed solid components. We tend to ascribe supernatural powers to the Builders, and therefore we ignore simple explanations. But it occurs to me that a gaseous or liquid form of surface, held to rigidity by an intense electromagnetic field, would be easy to achieve even with our technology. If that is the case, local cancellation of the field will permit entry to or exit from Glister. The instruments to explore that possibility are here, on the *Have-It-All* . . ." Her voice disappeared, then came back more weakly. ". . . prefer a more conventional mode of access, but . . . as last resort."

The signal was going, but Kallik sounded determined again, free of J'merlia's own sense of desolation and foreboding. Perhaps it was because she had the ships available to her, he thought. She could *do* something. If everyone on Glister was dead, Kallik could even fly home to seek a new master. J'merlia could not go anywhere, could not imagine any other master than Atvar H'sial. Maybe Kallik was less accustomed to slave status, with its freedom from difficult choices.

"Kallik, please call me. As soon as you can. I do not like to be alone."

After a too-long delay: "Certainly. I will contact you . . . line-of-sight communication . . . but . . . fading again . . . six hours . . ."

The signal was almost gone. "If you do not hear . . . whatever you must . . . patient." The final word was a whisper against the hiss of interference.

J'merlia huddled over the communication set. Be patient. What else *could* he do?

First Atvar H'sial and Louis Nenda. Then Darya Lang and

Hans Rebka. Everything and everyone, little by little, taken away from J'merlia.

Kallik was all he had left, the only remaining contact within hundreds of millions of kilometers. And now?

He listened and listened. She was gone.

By the standards of any normal inhabitant of Lo'tfi, J'merlia was already insane.

He had to be. Lo'tfians were communal animals. Only a crazy being could stand to be plucked out of the home environment to serve a Cecropian dominatrix as her interpreter. As far as the Cecropians were concerned, Lo'tfian slaves were selected for their ability to learn the Cecropian pheromonal form of speech; but from the Lo'tfian perspective, selection took care of itself through quite a different mechanism.

Any Lo'tfian could learn the Cecropian form of communication; with their talent for languages, that was easy. But only a few rare males, mentally off-balance to the point of madness, could bear to be yanked away from the society of the warrens.

Separation was worse than it could ever be for a human. When Lo'tfi was first discovered by the Cecropians, the dominant species roaming the surface of that planet possessed intelligence without technology. For millions of years, male Lo'tfians had lived most of their pleasant and peaceful lives out under the clear, cold skies of Lo'tfi. They had minimal intellectual curiosity. Any difficult decisions were made for them by the blind females, snuggled away in the burrows. The food-seeking males had seen the stars, but incuriously, as an element of the world that told them only when certain plants would be available to collect.

The arrival of the Cecropians, bearing the news that around those bright points of light circled other worlds populated by other beings, had been received with tolerant disinterest by the burrow females. They had little interest in the surface, and even less in what lay beyond. Communication had been established at a leisurely pace. The Cecropians, it transpired, had no interest in conquering the planet, or in living there. They hated those cold, clear skies. And they did not want to exploit Lo'tfi. The Cecropian terms for peaceful coexistence were simple. All they sought were beings with the sense organs to understand human sonic and Cecropian pheromonal speech, and the intelligence to learn both forms of language.

The loss of a small number of surplus Lo'tfian males, as the only price for being left alone, was acceptable to the negotiators—and anyway, argued the burrow females making the deal, wasn't anyone crazy enough to go of bad breeding stock, even if he stayed?

J'merlia had left Lo'tfi, to become servant and interpreter to Atvar H'sial. In Lo'tfian terms he was therefore demented already. Now he was contemplating an action that would put his previous insanities into the shade.

Six hours. Twelve hours. Twenty. And never a signal from Kallik, or anyone else. Never a reply to his own, increasingly frantic, messages.

The orbits of Dreyfus-27 and Glister had passed and repassed. At first J'merlia had been able to force himself to set the unit into recording mode while he did a little work on the interior of Dreyfus-27. As the hours passed, the urge to remain near the communicator became stronger and stronger.

At thirty hours he had waited as long as he could stand. Hans Rebka had told him to remain on Dreyfus-27. Kallik had told him the same thing. But they and Darya Lang were in *danger*.

The *Summer Dreamboat* was already in remote-controlled status. He used the communicator to bring it on a maximum-velocity trajectory to Dreyfus-27.

The ship ran the gauntlet of the Phage belt and arrived with another dent in the hull from a glancing blow. J'merlia gave it one moment's inspection to make sure that the damage was superficial, then boarded the *Dreamboat* and set a least-time return course.

No messages came in during the flight back to Glister. In his preoccupation with the problem at hand, J'merlia did not think to send any record of his decision to abandon Dreyfus-27 in favor of a trip to the planetoid.

At two thousand kilometers Glister became visible. So did

the matrix of pinpoint lights whirling in orbit around the little sphere. J'merlia gripped the controls himself, ready to override the collision avoidance system if he had to. The computer was ready for the free-fall trajectories of natural bodies, not the directed attack of energetic Phages; Kallik might have been able to devise alternative programs in the time available, but J'merlia certainly could not.

Two hundred kilometers. There was a jerk of violent acceleration. A close approach—near enough to stare down a Phage's dark pentagonal maw as it whizzed past only forty meters away. Eighty kilometers. Another, closer, miss, and a second violent thrust to the left. Fifty. The *Dreamboat* began decelerating so hard that J'merlia's front claws could not move on the controls. He sat rigid, staring out of the port as the ship corkscrewed its way through a sea of Phages. He counted scores of near misses.

When he was convinced that the ship was doomed, they were suddenly clear and in the final moments of descent. The whine of overstressed engines died to a high-pitched whisper. J'merlia, already in his suit, activated the display screens for an all-around look at the surface.

Nothing. No orange shimmer, no moving humans, no sign of the *Have-It-All.*

But from his position close to the surface he could see less than one percent of the surface of the planetoid, and during the flight down there had been no time for a visual search. Maybe Kallik and the other ship were just a few hundred meters away, hidden behind the curve of Glister. And Kallik had been wrong. That surface was not totally featureless. He could see something, a slate-grey mass peeping above the horizon.

According to Kallik and Hans Rebka, the atmosphere outside was breathable. But according to them, the whole place was safe. J'merlia put his suit to full opacity and stepped outside. He started to walk across the smooth surface toward the drab surface lumpiness.

Halfway there he paused. Was that thing what it seemed to be? He stared for a long time, then turned his lemon-colored compound eyes upward. Was it imagination, or were they moving still lower and faster than Darya Lang's report had suggested?

He turned and went back to the *Dreamboat,* placing the ship into full self-protect mode.

On the surface once more, he again began to walk around the curve of Glister. That crumpled mass might have been there when the others arrived on the planetoid, hidden beyond the horizon. It might have been there for a million years. J'merlia certainly hoped so.

But it might be a very recent and ominous addition. Every few steps, he found himself pausing to scan the sky.

Was it? It certainly looked that way, although every Builder specialist swore one would never be found in a substantial gravity field.

The closer he came, the more the object he was approaching looked like the gray remnant of a shattered Phage.

CHAPTER 10

WHERE WAS SHE?

Darya's first thought when the shimmering mist faded was huge relief. Nothing had changed. She was standing exactly where she had been when the cloud swept over them. Ahead of her was the same convex, gray, faintly luminous plain, barren of features, stretching away from her feet to a near horizon. The light that shone down upon it was the same cold, orange gloom.

But there was no sign of the *Have-It-All*, or of Kallik. And the strange light did not cast shadows.

Darya raised her eyes. Gargantua had vanished. The pinpoint brilliance of stars and orbiting fragments was gone. In their place was a smooth overhead illumination, as featureless as the floor beneath her feet.

She felt a touch on her arm.

"All right? No aftereffects?" Hans Rebka sounded as unruffled as she had ever heard him.

What was the old saying? If you're calm *now* it means you just don't understand the problem. "What happened to us? Where are we? How long were we unconscious?"

"I'll pass on the first two. But I don't think we were unconscious at all. We were held for less than five minutes."

She grabbed his arm, needing the sheer *feel* of a human being. "It seemed like forever. How do you know how long it was?"

"I counted." He was staring hard at the curved horizon, measuring it with his eye. "It's something you learn on Teufel if you're trapped outside during the *Remouleur*—that's the dawn wind—and you have to go to earth. Count your heartbeats. It does two things: lets you estimate time intervals, and proves you're still alive. I just counted to two hundred and thirty. If you'll stand right there for a minute, I think I'll be able to answer your second question. I know where we are."

, He walked away fifty paces, turned, then called to Darya, "I'm going to hold my hand out and gradually lower it. Let me know when it goes below the horizon."

When she called to him "Now!" he nodded in satisfaction and came hurrying back to her. "I thought so from my first look; now I'm sure. The surface we are on is still a sphere, or very close to it—but the radius is *less* than before. You can see it in the way the surface curves away on each side."

"So we're on another sphere, *inside* Glister."

"That's my best guess." He pointed up. "Kallik and the *Have-It-All* are right up there, through the ceiling. But there's no way to reach them, unless we can persuade that cloud to come back and carry us through."

"Don't say that!" Darya had been staring around her.

"Why not? Uh oh. Damnation. Is it listening to me? Here we go again."

As though responding to his words, an orange shimmer was flowing up and around them from the smooth gray surface. Darya resisted the urge to run. She was sure it would do no good. Instead she reached for Hans Rebka's hand and held it tightly. This time when the twinkling points cut off all light, sound, and mobility, the result was far less disturbing.

She waited, sensing the faint throb of her own pulse and counting steadily.

One hundred and forty-one . . . two . . . three. The fog was dispersing. One hundred and fifty-eight . . . nine. It was gone. She was free, still gripping his hand hard enough to hurt.

At her side, Rebka grunted in surprise. "Well, it may be no better, but at least it's *different.*"

They had sunk through to another level. The curvature of the surface was no longer noticeable, because there was no visible horizon against which to check it. They stood in a connected series of chambers. All around them structures ran in an eye-baffling zigzag of webs, pipes, nets, and partitions, from slate-gray floor to glowing ceiling. The "windows" between the chambers were set at random heights, and there were few openings at floor level. Whatever inhabited these chambers did not move like humans.

Nor did they walk through walls. Darya noticed that the retreating fog of orange lights did not penetrate the new structures. Instead it crawled around and over them, to wriggle its way through the small openings in nets and webs.

She glanced down to her feet. The outer layers of Glister had been unnaturally clean and totally dust-free, but here there were fragments of broken pipe and long lengths of cable. Everything had the neglected and disused look of a room that had not seen a cleanup in a million years. And yet the walls themselves seemed perfectly solid.

Rebka had been making his own inspection. He walked to one of the partitions, and as soon as the twinkling lights had left it he slapped his palm hard against the flat surface. He did the same thing to one of the fine-meshed webs and shook his head.

"Perfectly solid, and strong. We won't push those aside. If we want to go anywhere, we'll have to follow the holes in the walls—if we can climb up to them."

Since their arrival on Glister, Darya had felt increasingly useless. She just didn't know what to *do.* Whereas Hans was so used to trouble, he took it all in stride. She could contribute nothing. Unless it was information . . .

"Hans! What would you say the gravity field is here?"

He stopped his careful inspection of the walls and webs. "A standard gravity, give or take twenty percent. Why? Is it giving you trouble?"

"No. But it's *more* than it was, back on the surface. If Glister had a uniform density, or most of the mass was near the outside, then the field would *decrease* as you went closer to the center. So there has to be a big field source down near the middle. And it can't be a normal mass; nothing natural is that dense."

"So it's something new. Let's go and take a look below." Rebka began to walk slowly down one of the corridors, a hallway wide enough for the local vertical to change appreciably across its width.

Darya followed, pausing often to examine the wall materials and the complicated interlocking nets that covered most of the "windows." Her nervousness disappeared as she realized that this was truly a new Builder artifact—the first one discovered in more than four hundred years. And she was the first scientist ever to examine it. Even if she could escape, she should first give the place the most thorough examination of which she was capable. Otherwise she would never forgive herself—and neither would a thousand other Builder specialists.

So it was panic button off, observation hat on. What else could be said about their surroundings?

Many of the partitions slanted up all the way from floor to glowing ceiling. With their help she could judge the height of the chamber. It was *high*—maybe sixty meters. Nothing human needed that much space; but it was consistent with the enormous chambers found on other Builder artifacts.

She stepped to one wall and examined the material. Close up, it displayed a fine, grainy structure like baked brick. From the appearance it seemed brittle, as though one sharp blow would shatter it, but she knew from experience with Builder materials that that was an illusion. The structure would possess a material strength beyond anything else in the spiral arm. Left to stand for a million years in a corrosive atmosphere of oxygen, chlorine, or fluorine, it would not crumble. Bathed in boiling acids for centuries, it would not dissolve.

Darya had no idea how long this chamber had been unoccupied, but the surfaces should have been as dust-free as if they were polished daily. And they were not. There was dust *everywhere.*

Maintenance on Glister was sloppily done, if it was done at all.

Darya took the knife from her suit belt and jabbed at the gray wall. The tip was a single crystal of dislocation-free carbon-iridium, the hardest and sharpest material that human technology could create. And yet the blade did not make even a nick. She moved to one of the tight-drawn nets and tried to cut through a thin strand. She could see no mark when she was done. Even the thinnest web would be an impossible barrier to anything that could not, like the cloud, dissolve to small individual components. It was hard to believe that the dust all around them had come from gradual flaking away from the walls. There had to be some other source. Somewhere on Glister there had to be other materials, not built to Builder standards of near-infinite permanence.

Hans Rebka had been waiting impatiently as she chipped at the wall and sawed at the net. "It'll take you a long time to cut your way out like that," he said. "Come on. We have to keep moving."

He did not say what Darya had already thought. The air here might be breathable—though why, and how? There was nothing to create or maintain an atmosphere acceptable to humans—but beyond air, they needed other things to stay alive. Twelve hours had passed since their last meal, and although she was too nervous to feel hungry, Darya's throat was painfully dry.

They walked on, side by side, taking any floor-level connection between chambers and slowly descending through a long succession of sloping corridors. At last they came to a room containing the first sign of working equipment inside Glister—a massive cylinder that began to hum as they approached. It took in air and blew it out through a series of small vents. Rebka placed his hand and then his face close to one of the apertures.

"It's an air unit," he said. "And I think we just started it going. Somehow it reacted to our presence. Here's something for you to think about: If units like this maintain a breathable atmosphere *inside* Glister, what does it *outside?*"

"Probably nothing. There's nothing up there to do anything, no machinery at all. The surface must be permeable, at least sometimes and somewhere. That's how we were carried in here. Right through the floor."

"So all we have to do is work out a way to make the ceilings permeable again, and out we go. Of course, we need a way to jump straight up about a hundred meters." He stared upward. "The hell with it. I'd still like to know how the unit knew the atmosphere is good enough for both humans and Hymenopts."

"Right. Or what kind of atmosphere Glister had, before the *Have-It-All* arrived. Why would it need one, until we got here? Maybe it didn't have one at all."

Rebka gave her a startled glance. "Now that's what I call *real* custom service. Air designed to order. Now you're making *me* nervous."

They walked on past the air unit and half a dozen other constructs whose purpose Darya could only guess at. She itched to stay and examine them, but Hans was urging her forward.

The eighth device was a waist-high cylinder with a surface like a honeycomb, riddled with hexagonal openings each big enough to accommodate a human fist. The outside of the panel was cold and beaded with drops of moisture. Rebka touched one, sniffed his finger, and touched it to his lips.

"Water. Drinkable, I think, but it tastes flat."

Darya followed his example. "Distilled. It's a hundred percent pure, with no salts and minerals. You're just not used to clean water. You can drink it."

"Just now I'll drink anything. But we won't get much from panel condensation." He peered into one of the openings. "I'm going to try something. Don't stand too close."

"Hans!"

But already he was reaching his arm deep into the aperture.

He drew out a cupped handful of water and took a cautious sip. "It's all right. Come and take some. At least we won't die of thirst.

"And following up on your earlier line of thought," he added as they reached in to fill the bottles attached to their suits, "I wonder what liquid *that* was producing a week ago. Ethanol? Hydrochloric acid?"

"Or liquid methane. What do you think the *temperature* was on the surface of Glister, when Gargantua was a long way from Mandel?"

They moved on, to reach a point where the uniform curvature of the convex floor was broken by a descending ramp. Rebka stood on the brink and stared down.

"That's pretty steep. Looks slick, too. More like a chute than a corridor, and I can't see the bottom. Once we go down there, I'm not sure we'll be able to climb back up."

"We need food. We can't get back to the surface, and we can't stay here forever."

"Agreed." He sat down on the edge. "I'm going to slide. Wait until I call back and tell you it's all right."

"No!" Darya was surprised at the strength of her own reaction. She came forward and sat next to him. "You're not leaving me up here by myself. If you go, I go."

"Then hold tight." They eased side by side over the edge.

The chute was less steep than it looked. After a sheer start it curved into a gentle spiral. They skidded down and soon reached terminal velocity of no more than a fast walking pace. As they descended, the light changed. The cold orange that mimicked Gargantua's reflected glow was replaced by a bright yellow-white that came from ahead of them and reflected from the smooth walls of the chute. Finally the gradient became so shallow that they could no longer slide forward.

Rebka stood up. "The free ride's over. I wonder what this was intended for originally. Unless you think *it* wasn't here, either, until we came along and needed it."

They had emerged to stand at the edge of a domed chamber, a giant's serving dish fifty meters across. The floor ahead formed a shallow bowl, gently sloping all the way into the center, and above them stood an arched ceiling in the form of a perfect hemisphere. Hans and Darya stared around the chamber, adjusting to the white dazzle. To eyes accustomed for the last few hours to cold hues and dusty slate-gray, the new environment was sheer brilliance. The circular floor of the room was marked off like an archery target, in bright concentric rings of different colors. From the boundaries of those gaudy rings rose hemispheres, faintly visible, forming a nested set. Corridor entrances, or perhaps the delivery points of chutes like the one that they had just descended, stood at intervals around the outer perimeter of the chamber. A single dazzling globe at the room's apex provided illumination.

And in the middle of the chamber, at the central depression directly below the light . . .

Darya gasped. "Look, Hans. It's *them!*"

The smallest translucent dome stood around the bright blue bull's-eye of the innermost ring. At its center was a raised dais, a meter and a half tall; upon that, facing outward, stood a dozen transparent structures like great glass seats.

Side by side in two of those seats, held by some invisible support, sat Louis Nenda and Atvar H'sial.

Darya began to move forward, but she was restrained by Hans Rebka's hand on her arm.

"This is the time to be most careful. I think they're both unconscious. Look at them closely."

Darya stood and stared. Between them and the central dais rose the half-dozen translucent nested hemispheres. They interfered with her view of Nenda and Atvar H'sial, but Darya could still see enough detail to prompt new questions.

Louis Nenda's overall appearance was at first sight no different from the last time she had seen him. The arms of the short, swarthy body rippled with muscle, and the shirt was wide open at the neck to show a powerful and thickly haired chest.

Or *was* that hair? It looked wrong, discolored and uneven. She turned to Rebka.

"His chest—"

"I see it." Hans Rebka was blinking and squinting, having

the same problem with perspective as Darya. The hemispheres introduced a subtle distortion to the scene. "It's all covered with moles and pockmarks. Did you ever see his bare chest before?"

"No. He always kept it covered."

"Then I don't think it's a recent change. I bet he was like that when he arrived on Opal."

"But what is it?"

"A Zardalu-technology augment. The first records on Nenda when he requested access to Opal said he was augmented, but they didn't say how. Now we know. Those nodules and pits are pheromone generators and receptors. It's a rare and expensive operation—and it's painful, like all the Zardalu augments. But that's how he could work directly with Atvar H'sial. They can *talk* to each other, without needing J'merlia." Rebka studied the other man for a few seconds longer. "My guess is that he's physically unchanged, and just unconscious. It's a lot harder to tell about Atvar H'sial. What do you think?"

Darya moved her attention to the Cecropian. She had spent more time with Atvar H'sial, so her estimate of condition ought to be better. Except that the Cecropians were so alien, in every respect . . .

Even seated, with her six jointed legs tucked away underneath her, Atvar H'sial towered over the Karelian human Louis Nenda. A dark-red, segmented underside was surmounted by a short neck with scarlet-and-white ruffles, and above that stood a white, eyeless head. The thin proboscis that grew from the middle of the face could reach out and serve as a delicate sense organ, but at the moment it was curled down to tuck neatly away in a pouch on the bottom of the pleated chin.

Neither the Cecropian nor the Karelian human had the empty look of death. But was Atvar H'sial conscious?

"Atvar H'sial!" Darya called as loudly as she could.

If the alien was at all aware of her surroundings, that should produce a response. Originating in the clouded planet of a red dwarf star, the Cecropians had never developed sight. Instead they "saw" by echolocation, sending high-frequency sonic pulses from the pleated resonator in the chin. They received and interpreted incoming signals through yellow open horns set in the middle of the broad head. As one result Cecropians had incredibly sensitive hearing, all through and far beyond the human frequency range.

"H'sial! Atvar H'sial!" Darya shouted again.

There was no reaction. The yellow horns did not turn in her direction, and the pair of fernlike antennas above them, disproportionately long even for that great body, remained furled. With hearing usurped for vision, Cecropians "spoke" to each other chemically, with a full and rich language, through the emission and receipt of pheromones. The unfurled antennas could detect and identify single molecules of many thousands of different airborne odors. If Atvar H'sial were conscious, those delicate two-meter-long fans would surely have stretched out, sniffing the air, seeking pheromones from the source of the sound.

"She's unconscious, too. I feel sure of it." Darya was moving forward to the place where the outermost ring of color began on the floor. Before she reached the edge of that first annulus of vivid yellow, Hans Rebka again restrained her.

"We don't know *why* they are unconscious. It looks safe enough in there, but it may not be. You stay here, and I'll go in."

"No." Darya moved more quickly down the slope of the shallow bowl. "Why *you* again? It's time we started sharing the risks."

"I have more experience."

"Fine. That means you'll know how to get me out of trouble if I need you. I'll go in just a little way." Darya was already stepping gingerly through the haze of the first hemisphere. She put her feet down carefully, feeling the ground ahead.

"All right, I'm through that one." She turned to look at Hans. He did not seem any different. She did not feel it. "No problem so far. Didn't notice anything, no resistance to motion. I'm going to cross the yellow zone."

She stared ahead. Yellow to green to purple. Five paces for each—it should be easy. Halfway between the second and third hemispheres she paused, confused for a moment about what she was doing.

"Are you all right?" She heard his call from behind her. She turned. "Sure. I'm going to . . . the center."

And then she paused, oddly uncertain of her goal. She found it necessary to look all around her before she knew what was happening.

There, in the middle, where Atvar H'sial and Louis Nenda are sitting, she reminded herself. In the chairs.

"I'm halfway there," she called. "Nearly done the green. Next stop, purple."

She was moving again. Bright lights, bright colors. Yellow to green to purple to red to blue. Five zones. Not following the usual order, though, red to orange to yellow to green to . . . the order in—what's that thing called? Hard to remember. The rainbow. Yeah, that's it.

These colors are not like the colors in the . . . whatever. Damn it, I've lost the word again. Keep moving. Only two more to go, and I'll reach what's-their-names. Yellow to green to purple to red . . . to—what was the name of that color—to yellow to . . . green . . .

Darya's eyes were wide open. She was lying on a hard, flat surface, staring up at a domed blue ceiling. Hans Rebka was bending over her, his face sweaty and pale.

She sat up slowly. In front of her was the great chamber, with its circular rings of color. At the center stood the dais with its two silent forms.

"What am I doing lying here? And why are you letting me sleep? We won't be able to help those two if we spend time loafing around."

"Are you all right?" At her impatient nod Hans said, "Take your time. Tell me the very last thing that you remember."

"Why, I was saying that I wanted to go into the rings, to bring Louis Nenda and Atvar H'sial out, and you were trying to talk me out of it. And then I was all ready to put my foot—" She was suddenly puzzled. "I was at the edge of the yellow ring, and now we're ten steps outside it. What happened, did I pass out?"

"More than that." His face was anxious. "Don't you remember crossing the yellow ring, and then the green one, and starting in on the purple one?"

"I didn't. I couldn't have. I only started out a minute ago. I just put my foot onto the yellow zone, and then—" She stared at him. "Are you telling me . . ."

"You said it a minute ago. You passed out. But not here." He pointed. "Way over there. You were halfway to the dais when your voice went all confused and dreamy, then you sat down on the floor. And then you lay down and stopped talking. That was three hours ago, not one minute. You were unconscious in there for nearly all that time."

"And you came in after me? That was crazy. You could have passed out, too."

"I didn't go all the way in. I didn't dare. I've seen something like this before—and you've written about it in your artifact catalog. It was your suggestion that this is a Builder artifact that told me what the problem had to be."

"Unconsciousness? That's not a Builder effect."

"Not unconsciousness. Memory loss. It's the same thing that happens to people who try to explore Paradox, except that what it does there is far worse. You only lost a few hours. They come out with their memories wiped clean. I've seen victims who tried to enter and came out more helpless than newborn babies."

Excitement replaced alarm. Darya had studied the artifacts since childhood, but until Summertide she had seen only Sentinel firsthand. "You're saying that there's a Lotus field inside those hemispheres. That's absolutely *fascinating.*"

She could see from Rebka's look that the word was not one he would have chosen. She hurried on. "But if it *is* a Lotus field, however were you able to get me out? If it affected me like that, it would do the same to you."

"It would have. It did, a little bit. You were all right in the yellow ring, you still knew what you were doing, so I was willing to risk that much. I went that far. But the field would have caught me, too, if I'd gone all the way in to get you. Then we'd have lain there helpless until we starved to death, or somebody else came along to kill us or get us out."

"But you got me out."

"I did. But I didn't go in for you. I stood in the yellow zone and I hauled you out from there, like a hooked fish. Why do you think you were in so long? I had to find something to use as a grapple. It wasn't easy. It took me hours to find something I could use, then another hour to fish for you."

Darya turned to face the center of the chamber. "Atvar H'sial and Louis Nenda are right in the middle of it. Do you think their memories are wiped clean?"

"I can't say, but if this is anything like Paradox the field may affect the approach route and not the middle. They could be fine—or they could be wiped. We won't know until we get them out."

"Can you do for them what you did for me—haul them clear?"

"Not with this." Rebka indicated the length of noosed cable that lay on the floor at Darya's side. "It's too short, and they look like they're tied somehow to those seats."

"So how do we get them out?"

"We don't. Not for the moment." Rebka helped her to her feet. "We have to find some other way to do it. Come on. At least I know a bit more about the layout of this place—I ran up and down half the corridors off this room, scavenging for something I could use as a rope. This is a wild place—some parts are spotless; others have a ten-million-year dust layer. But don't ask me what any of it is *for*—that's a total mystery."

Darya allowed him to lead her to a doorway, three entrances farther around the room's perimeter. "It's hard to see why Glister is here at all," she said. "But it's not the prize mystery."

"Plenty of choices for that." Rebka sounded weary, but Darya knew from experience that he would ignore fatigue until he actually collapsed. "I can list a bundle," he went on. "The fast Phages. The atmosphere on the surface. The way we got inside. The equipment that provides air and water.

The Lotus field in the chamber we just left. They're all candidates. Take your pick."

"You haven't listed the one most on my mind." The path was spiraling down, heading in a gentle, curving ramp toward the middle of Glister. Darya was thirsty—and suddenly so hungry that it was hard to think of anything else.

How long since she had eaten? It felt like forever. Her mind might have been switched off for three hours, but her stomach had not been. It kept careful track of missed meals.

"The tough one is this," she said at last. "Why did the orange cloud on the surface let Kallik pass through untouched, but grab *us,* and Louis Nenda and Atvar H'sial, and bring us down here? There's something on Glister that *knows the difference* between humans, Cecropians, and Hymenopts. *That's* the biggest mystery of all."

ENTRY 19: HYMENOPT.

Distribution: The Hymenopt cladeworld is not definitely known, but it is believed to be one of the eighty worlds subjected to large-scale surface reshaping by the Zardalu, roughly twenty thousand years ago.

Hymenopt societies flourish today on eighteen of those worlds, having been transported there by the Zardalu and abandoned at the time of the Great Rising. Eight of these colonies subsequently became technologically advanced enough to achieve interplanetary travel. One Hymenopt world was an independent discoverer of the Bose Drive, but for cultural reasons it limited its use.

After the Great Rising the Hymenopt worlds were lost from spiral-arm communication, until finally they were rediscovered by the Decantil Survey and Census of territories of the Zardalu Communion.

Since then, slave Hymenopts have been taken to all worlds of the Communion, and also to dozens of planets of the Cecropia Federation. The total Hymenopt population is unknown, but certainly it is in the tens of billions.

Physical Characteristics: The Hymenopts in their own colonies contain six separate functional groups, designated as Regents, Recorders, Defenders, Feeders, Breeders, and Workers. There is a progression among these forms, in that Breeders following metamorphosis become Feeders, and finally Regents, while Defenders in the later stages of their lives become Recorders. Workers maintain the same form all their lives.

It should be noted that the only Hymenopts employed as slaves are the Workers. The others do not leave their colonies. Thus when another species of the spiral arm refers to "a Hymenopt," that is by implication a Hymenopt *Worker.* The following physical description applies to them alone.

Hymenopt Workers are sterile female eight-legged arthropods. The paws on all limbs are prehensile and capable of the manipulation of small objects; however, only the four forelimbs are normally used for delicate work. Despite the fancied resemblance of the Hymenopt Workers to the Earth

Hymenoptera, which led to their naming by Decantil Survey biologists, the physiological similarity is at best superficial. The Hymenopts do, however, possess a tough exoskeleton and a powerful sting at the end of the rounded abdomen. (This, combined with their speed of movement, suggests that the slavery of a Hymenopt Worker is a matter of choice and habit, rather than force.)

Hymenopts see with a ring of simple (i.e., not compound) eyes, circling a smooth head. The need for all-around vision encourages them to remain upright on most occasions, although for rapid movement they revert to a horizontal position. The Hymenopts' eyes are sensitive to a range of wavelengths from 0.3 to 1.0 micrometers, which more than spans the range of human optics. Their sensitivity to low light levels is superior to that of humans; this has led some exobiologists to offer an unconvincing identification of the Hymenopt cladeworld based on fainter sunlight and stellar spectral properties.

History: The earliest history of the Hymenopts has been lost, together with knowledge of their cladeworld. Today, the planet of Ker is generally considered to be the center of Hymenopt civilization, and it is certainly the principal storage point for Hymenopt records.

It was on Ker that the Bose Drive was discovered, seven thousand years ago. That invention led to a dominance of Ker among other Hymenopts which has never been challenged. According to the Ker archives, some form of Hymenopt oral history and race memory extends back sixty thousand generations. Since a breeding cycle lasts for seventy standard years, Hymenopts have therefore been intelligent, with a well-developed language, for over half a million years. By contrast, written records on Ker go back less than ten thousand.

Ker is the moving force, main market center, and principal beneficiary of the sale of Hymenopt slaves. Its inhabitants are eager to maintain that role, and they follow general Hymenopt practice by discouraging interaction and commerce with any other species, except for the purpose of Hymenopt slave trading.

Culture: In the Hymenopt worlds, societal control equals *breeding* control. Since the other five groups are sterile, the Breeders in principle possess unique power; however, each Breeder knows that she will one day undergo metamorphosis to Feeder (responsible for feeding the young) and then to Regent (responsible for all colony development decisions). These three groups therefore cooperate to constitute the "Superior Triad" of Hymenopt culture, with the Workers, Recorders, and Defenders forming the "Inferior Triad." It would be unthinkable for one member of the Superior Triad to sell another member for use as a slave.

Crossbreeding outside the colony is recognized as genetically beneficial, but travel is tightly controlled. It is approved in advance, and applies only to mating. No Hymenopt colony desires, or permits, uncontrolled transfers of individuals. This factor, more than any other, limits Hymenopt interest in interstellar, or even interplanetary, commerce. The slave trade of Ker is the single significant exception.

—From the *Universal Species Catalog*
(Subclass: Sapients).

CHAPTER 11

THE FOLLOWING FACTS were deemed too an-
ecdotal for the formality of the *Universal Species Catalog*
(Subclass: Sapients). Few beings of the spiral arm, however,
would dispute them:

AN ADULT HYMENOPT HAS REFLEXES TEN TIMES AS FAST AS ANY
HUMAN'S.

A HYMENOPT CAN RUN A HUNDRED METERS IN LESS THAN TWO
SECONDS.

USED IN CONCERT, A HYMENOPT'S EIGHT TRIPLE-JOINTED LEGS
WILL PROPEL HER TEN METERS INTO THE AIR UNDER TWO STAN-
DARD GRAVITIES.

THE RETRACTED YELLOW STING IN THE END OF A HYMENOPT'S
STUBBY ABDOMEN CAN BE READIED IN A FRACTION OF A SECOND
TO DELIVER STIMULANTS, ANESTHETICS, HALLUCINOGENS, OR LE-
THAL NEUROTOXINS. THEY ARE EFFECTIVE ON ALL KNOWN INTELLI-
GENT ORGANISMS.

WITH VOLUNTARILY REDUCED METABOLISM, A HYMENOPT CAN SURVIVE FOR FIVE MONTHS WITHOUT FOOD OR WATER; ENCYSTED, SHE WILL ENDURE FOR FOUR TIMES AS LONG.

A HYMENOPT IS AS INTELLIGENT AS A CECROPIAN OR A HUMAN, WITH MORE MENTAL STAMINA THAN EITHER.

Kallik, of course, knew all these things. And yet it never occurred to her that her own slave status was in any way unnatural. In fact, she thought it inevitable. Her race memory extended back well over ten thousand years, to the time when every Hymenopt had been a slave.

Hymenopt race memory lacked the precision of nerve-cell memory. The few billion bits available for its total storage reduced recollection to a mere caricature of the original direct experience. Yet the brain, insistent on offering race memories in the same format as other experiences, clothed the skeleton of recollection in a synthetic flesh of its own creation.

Thus, Kallik "remembered" the long enslavement of her species as a series of visual flashes; but no amount of effort would make those images detailed. If she made the attempt, the result was the product of her own imagination.

She could make a picture in her mind of the Zardalu, the land-cephalopod masters who had ruled the thousand worlds of the Zardalu Communion until the Great Rising. If she thought hard, she could make specific images: of stony beaks, big and strong enough to crush a Hymenopt's body . . . but she could not see how they fitted to the Zardalu body. Of huge, round eyes . . . but they were floating free and disembodied, high above her head. Of hulking bodies, girded with supporting straps and slick with fatty secretions that allowed the Masters to survive on land . . . but the legs that carried those bodies were vague shadow legs, undefined in size, color, or number.

She had only the most confused memory of the disappearance of the Zardalu: her mind fed back a whirl of flying bodies, a green fire, a world turned black, a sun exploding. And then, great calm; an absence of all Zardalu images.

For Kallik's social class, the Great Rising and the vanishing of the tyrant Zardalu brought little change. She had been born a Worker; had she remained on the Homeworld she would have remained one. Her role would always have been Worker, rather than Regent, Recorder, Defender, Feeder, or Breeder. She had been bred for slavery, born for slavery, raised for slavery, and sold for slavery. Nothing made her so uncomfortable as a total absence of masters. She *needed* them—humans, Cecropians, or Hymenopts.

The disappearance of Lang and Rebka stimulated her to frantic activity. She moved at once to make a low-altitude survey of the surface of Glister, traversing the slowly rotating planetoid on a path that would allow a close inspection of every square meter.

The survey took over an hour. It was wasted time. Kallik remained convinced that Glister was hollow, but the sphere showed no trace of external structure. Nothing suggested a way to reach the hidden interior. In fact, if Kallik had not *seen,* with her own multiple pairs of black eyes, that sparkling cloud absorbed into the surface, she would have judged Glister's exterior totally impermeable.

When the futile ground survey was over Kallik raised her eyes again to scan the heavens far above the ship. She was no nearer finding Rebka and Lang, and—ominously—the Phages were no longer remaining at a safe distance. The presence of the *Have-It-All,* moving in its survey orbit around the planetoid, seemed to madden them. Three times Kallik had seen a Phage dropping in on a trajectory that carried it to within a couple of kilometers above the ship. Each approach came a little closer. Now she could see two more Phages, dropping in low.

She returned the *Have-It-All* to the surface of Glister, roughly where they had first found it, and went to her own quarters. The time for tentative measures was past. She selected equipment and carried it down from the ship to the surface. It would measure the E-M field associated with Glister and compute an external field to cancel it in magnitude and phase.

She sent a terse message to Opal, explaining what she was about to do. She could not signal to J'merlia, since Dreyfus-27 was still shielded by the mass of Gargantua.

Kallik dragged the field generator and inhibitor forty meters away from the *Have-It-All.* She had one more problem to solve. If she focused the field on the surface with a five- or ten-meter effective range, the device itself would sink through into Glister if the surface became fluid or gaseous. The only way to prevent that was to run a pair of lines attached to the generator right around the body of the sphere, one following a geodesic around the "equator" and the other a geodesic over the "poles." Downward forces would then be held by tension in the cables, and supported by the surface strength of the whole of Glister.

Kallik paused for thought.

The lines would be supported, unless of course the *local* field cancellation somehow caused a *global* cancellation. Then Glister would become a ball of gas or liquid, and Kallik, the *Have-It-All,* and the *Summer Dreamboat* would plunge together into the unknown interior.

A Hymenopt had no shoulders to shrug. Instead, Kallik clucked and chirped softly to herself while she made the final connections of the thin, dislocation-free cables to the field generator. She was a fatalist. So Glister might become liquid. Well, no one ever promised that life would be risk-free. She hurried back to the *Have-It-All* and left a message for J'merlia on the recorder of the ship, the equivalent of "So long, it's been nice knowing you." If she returned safely, she could erase it.

She turned on the power, stood back, and watched.

The result was at first disappointing. The generator was a compact device, operating with microwave energy beamed from the *Have-It-All.* There was nothing to show that it was in operation, and the equipment stood exactly as she had left it, with no sound or movement.

Then she heard it; a faint creaking of the thin, tight-strung cables, protesting as they took up the strain of the generator's weight. The unit itself stood on three solid legs, but now the bottom few centimeters of those legs were invisible. They had sunk through into the surface of Glister.

Kallik moved cautiously toward the field generator. Its position was stable, moving neither downward nor upward. She touched one of the taut support lines, estimating the tension. From the feel of it, the generator would have dropped right on through without them. The surface looked subtly different for a radius of about five meters from the field's center, where the support lines bent downward and disappeared.

Kallik reached down. Her forelimb penetrated the gray surface, but she felt nothing.

She had brought with her from the ship half-a-dozen spent power canisters. She lobbed one to land by the field generator. The surface did not change in appearance, but the metal canister vanished at once and without a trace. The absence of ripples around the point of disappearance argued for a gaseous rather than a liquid region around the generator.

Kallik retreated a couple of steps. So it would swallow a power canister easily, and perhaps a Hymenopt with no more difficulty. But was the canceled field zone deep enough to provide true access to the interior? Or did it come to a solid bottom, a few meters down?

Kallik knew that she would not find answers by standing and thinking about it.

She went back to the ship and procured another length of cable, securing it first to a brace on the *Have-It-All*'s main hull and then cinching it around her own midriff. If someone came along and decided to fly the *Have-It-All* off on an interplanetary mission while Kallik was down inside Glister, she would be in deep trouble.

But she was in deep trouble anyway.

She moved to the edge of the zone of change. For a few seconds she paused there, hesitating. There was no guarantee that what she was doing would help Darya Lang and Hans Rebka—still less that it was the *best* way to help them. If there was a better solution, it was her duty to find it.

As she stood thinking there was a *whoosh!* of disturbed air not far overhead. It was a Phage, hurtling by no more than fifty meters from the surface. The dark maw was closed, but it could open in a few seconds.

Kallik whistled an invocation to Ressess-tress, the leading nondeity of the Hymenopts' official atheism. She blinked all her eyes, stepped forward, and dropped through into the impalpable surface of Glister.

CHAPTER 12

THE *INCOMPARABLE* — INCOMPARABLY
rattly, rusty, cumbersome, and smelly—was approaching
Gargantua. Birdie Kelly and Julius Graves focused their attention on the satellites and waited for a detailed view of
Glister itself, while E. C. Tally stared steadily at a display of
the giant planet. He had been sitting silently for fifteen hours,
since the moment when the *Incomparable*'s sensors had provided their first good look at Gargantua.

That was fine with Birdie Kelly. Tally's designers had recognized that the embodied computer's body would need rest,
but apparently his inorganic brain functioned continuously.
Over the past three days, Birdie had been wakened from
sound sleep a dozen times with a touch and a polite "May I
speak?"

Eventually Birdie had lost it. "Damn it, Tally. *No more
questions.* Why don't you go and ask Graves something for

a change? Julius and Steven between 'em know ten times as much as I do."

"No, Commissioner Kelly, that is not true." E. C. Tally shook his head, practicing the accepted human gesture for dissent and the conventional human pause before offering a reply. "They know much more than ten times as much as you do. Perhaps one hundred times? Let me think about that."

The first sight of Gargantua had kept him quiet for a while. But now he was perking up and coming out of his reverie over by the display screens. To Birdie's relief, though, he was turning to Julius Graves.

"If I may speak: with respect to the communications that we have received from Darya Lang and from Kallik. Professor Lang suggests that Glister is a Builder artifact, and Kallik agrees. Does any other evidence suggest the presence of Builder activity in the vicinity of Gargantua?"

"No. The nearest artifact to Gargantua is the Umbilical, connecting Quake and Opal." The voice was Steven Graves's. "And it is the only one reported in the Mandel stellar system."

"Thank you. That is what my own data banks show, but I wondered if there might be inadequacies, as there have been in other areas." Tally reached out and tapped the screen, where Gargantua filled the display. "Would you please examine this and offer your opinion?"

His index finger was squarely on an orange-and-umber spot below Gargantua's equator.

"The bright oval?" Graves asked. He looked for only a moment, then turned his attention to the other screen, where the sensors were set for analysis of a volume of space surrounding Glister. "I'm sorry. I have no information about that."

But to his own great amazement, Birdie did. He finally knew something that Graves did not! "It's called the Eye of Gargantua," he burst out. "It's a great big whirlpool of gases, a permanent hurricane about forty thousand kilometers across." He pointed to the screen. "You can even see the vortices on the image, trailing away from it on both sides."

"I can see them. Do you know for how long the Eye of Gargantua has existed?"

"Not really. But it's been around for as long as the Dobelle system has been colonized. Thousands of years. When people came out here exploring for minerals, ages ago, the survey teams all took pictures of it. Every kids' book talks about it and has a drawing of it. It's a famous bit of the stellar system, one of the 'natural wonders' you learn about in school."

"You are speaking metaphorically. I learned nothing in school, for I did not attend it." E. C. Tally frowned. He had been experimenting with that expression as a way of indicating a paradox or dichotomy of choice, and he felt that the look had reached a satisfactory level of performance. "But knowledge is not the issue. The Eye of Gargantua should not be described to children as one of the natural wonders of the stellar system. For a good reason: it is not one."

"Not one *what?*" Birdie cursed to himself. He should have known better than to have jumped into a conversation with Tally.

"The Eye of Gargantua is not a natural wonder of the stellar system. Because it is not *natural.*"

"Then what the blazes is it?"

"I do not know." Tally attempted another human gesture, a shrug of the shoulders. "But I know what it is not. I have been calculating continuously for the past fifteen hours, with all plausible boundary conditions. The system that we see is not a stable solution of the time-dependent, three-dimensional Navier-Stokes equation for gaseous motion. It should have dissipated itself, in weeks or months. In order for the Eye of Gargantua to exist, some large additional source of atmospheric circulation must be present right there." He touched the screen. "At the center of the eye, where you can see the vortex—"

"Phages!" Julius Graves broke in excitedly. "They're there all right. We're getting an image of fragments around Glister, but it's not like the one that Rebka and Lang sent back from their first sighting. The cloud around it extends all the way down to the surface. If those are all Phages . . ."

"Can we fly down through them, as did Captain Rebka and Professor Lang?" Tally addressed Birdie Kelly, as the most experienced pilot. "They reached the surface safely."

"Fly down there—in this scumbucket?" Birdie glared around at the controls and fittings of the ore freighter. "We sure as hell can't. Take a look at us. The drive don't work at more than half power, there's no weapons to pop Phages with, and we're about as mobile as a Dowser. If those are all Phages down there, and they're half as nippy as Captain Rebka says, we've got problems. Maybe if they get a good *sniff* of this ship before they start chewing, we'll have a chance. I know Phages are supposed to eat anything, but there have to be limits."

"A sniff—"

"I was *joking,* E.C. What I mean is, we'd better stay well out of the way."

"But we don't have to rely on the *Incomparable* to get us there," Julius Graves said. "We can use the *Summer Dreamboat.* It took the others safely past the Phages, and Professor Lang said in her last message that she left it on remote control. We can call it up to us, and fly it down."

"But what about Rebka and Lang and Kallik?" Birdie did not like the assumption that they were all going down to Glister, danger or no danger. "They'll need a ship if they want to get out of there in a hurry."

"They'll have one—the *Have-It-All.* It's still there if they need it. And we can surely borrow the *Dreamboat* for a few hours. We'll have it back to them before they even know it's gone. But it will take a while for the *Dreamboat* to get here. We ought to give the command at once. So if you will please proceed, Commissioner . . ."

It *was* a Phage on the surface of Glister.

Or maybe it was best to say that it was the devastated remains of one. J'merlia had approached as closely as he cared to and confirmed that the heap of slate-gray debris contained regular pentagonal elements. But he could see nothing of organs or an internal structure, and other factors made him question that this was a Phage as they were known in the rest of the spiral arm. For one thing, Phages were supposed to be just about indestructible. This one looked as though it had hurtled vertically and at high velocity into the surface of Glister. It should have smashed a giant hole. But the impact had left no mark, or else the mark had since vanished.

What could Glister be made of, to remain unscathed after such a blow?

J'merlia lifted lemon-yellow eyes on their short eyestalks to the heavens and looked for more Phages. They were there, whipping past overhead. Lower on every pass, if he was any judge.

He trotted on, scanning the surface of Glister for anything familiar. It was less than five minutes before he came across a taut cable running from horizon to horizon. He followed it and soon saw the *Have-It-All.* He hurried to the ship hoping to find Kallik or the missing humans, but a quick look inside showed that the cabins were deserted; the message from Kallik confirmed that. Forty meters away stood a piece of equipment, partially sunk into Glister's smooth gray surface. Four tight-stretched lines at ninety degrees to each other appeared to support the machine.

J'merlia decided that the lines probably ran all the way around the planetoid. There was no point in following them. He went closer to the machine and recognized it as a field monitor and inhibitor. If it was operating as Kallik had suggested, the surface around it might offer no resistance to weight. J'merlia went forward cautiously to the place where one of the lines vanished into Glister's interior. When he placed a forelimb on the surface at that point, it went down without resistance. The smooth gray appeared totally insubstantial.

He straightened up. Another cable ran from a stout stanchion on the *Have-It-All*'s hull all the way to the point where it plunged into the unblemished surface by the field inhibitor. Anyone might try to climb down that rope, into the unknown gray region—or, more likely, use it as a way to return to the outside of Glister.

J'merlia went back to the ship and gave it a more thorough

inspection. As when Rebka and Lang had found it, everything was in working order. Given an hour or two to familiarize himself with the controls, he could make a fair shot at flying it anywhere in the spiral arm via the Bose Network Transition Points.

Which more and more felt like a good idea. Every few minutes now he heard the whistle of Phages overhead. Something was maddening them, and that something was probably the presence of newcomers on the surface of Glister. The place was not safe anymore; even as he watched, a Phage came sailing by with open maw, no more than a hundred meters above the *Have-It-All.*

It was only a matter of time before some furiously energized Phage, by accident or design, made a direct hit on him or on the ship. He had to get away from the planetoid, or he would soon be of no use to anyone.

J'merlia was feeling increasingly uncomfortable with his own actions. He had come to Glister with a poorly defined idea of saving Rebka, Lang, and Kallik, and perhaps Atvar H'sial and Louis Nenda. But having arrived here he had no idea what to do next. He lacked Kallik's initiative and decisiveness. It certainly seemed a poor idea to follow her to the interior of Glister. On the other hand it was no better to stay on the surface, because that option appeared more dangerous with every minute.

J'merlia sat in the cabin of the *Have-It-All* and dithered.

He had had enough of this free-thinking misery; what he longed for was a master to give him directions.

His own orders had been to stay on Dreyfus-27. It was the one thing he had been told to do, and he had disobeyed. He did not want to go back to Dreyfus-27—it was too far from Glister—but maybe he should take a good intermediate step. He could fly the *Summer Dreamboat* far enough from Glister to be safe from the Phages, yet close enough to monitor everything that happened on the planetoid's surface. Then if Kallik or one of the others appeared, J'merlia could have the ship down to pick them up in a few minutes.

It was not a good solution, but it was a reasonable compromise. He hesitated for a few minutes more, until a Phage came whistling past almost close enough to grab him.

The *Summer Dreamboat* was no more than two minutes' travel at a rapid trot. J'merlia closed the cabin of the *Have-It-All* and set off for the other ship.

He was less than a hundred meters away when it rose smoothly from the surface of Glister. As J'merlia gaped up, it hurtled away at maximum acceleration into the glimmering void above his head.

CHAPTER 13

SEEN FROM A distance with the great bulk of Gargantua as backdrop, Glister was an insignificant mote. Without the telltale signal from the *Have-It-All*'s beacon, the planetoid would have been too small to notice, lost amid a thousand larger fragments.

But viewed from the *inside* . . .

The floors, bulging walls, and arched ceilings of the lower levels were formed of broad interlocking hoops, each one pleated and rigid and glowing with its own faint phosphorescence. It was like walking through the curling alimentary canal of a giant alien beast. Some sections were filled with nets and cables, like those found on the higher levels, while others were totally empty; occasional areas were littered with pieces of equipment placed apparently at random.

Darya was muttering to herself as Hans Rebka led the way deeper and deeper, on through endless corridors.

"What's that?" he asked over his shoulder as she swore more loudly than usual.

"Calculations. Depressing ones. The radius of Glister is one-point-one-six kilometers. Even if each interior level is fifty meters high, that's a hundred and twenty square kilometers of floor. How long is it going to take us to look at it all?"

"Don't worry about it. You'll starve to death first."

Hans Rebka had to be hungry, too, but he was defiantly cheerful. Starvation, or even the mention of it, did not make Darya cheerful. It made her grouchy. Back on Sentinel Gate she had not missed a meal in twenty years. That thought was no help at all. "We don't seem to be finding anything useful. Where do you think you're taking us?"

Hans did not answer. In spite of her grumbles, it was Darya who had insisted on stopping every few minutes to take a close look at some novel structure or machine. Every object in the interior of Glister was a product of the Builders' technology and therefore a source of fascination to the professor in her. She could recognize many of them, devices that occurred in some of the other 1236 known Builder artifacts scattered around the spiral arm, but a number were totally unfamiliar, and she wanted to inspect them closely and estimate their function. Rebka was the one who had to drag her away, every time, insisting that they must find the control center of Glister before they did anything else. Since the planetoid was artificial and habitable, *something* had to be keeping it in working order.

Rebka had not mentioned his own secret fear. Gravity was increasing steadily as they wound their way down toward the center of Glister. Now it was close to two gees. Beneath their feet must be some powerful field source. They could still walk easily enough—but what would they do if it rose higher yet? No one knew what gravity field the Builders had found natural. A central control room for Glister might occupy a high-gee environment that neither he nor Darya could tolerate.

From the curvature of the floor he estimated that they were still about six hundred meters from the center of Glister. Given a choice of paths, he had always descended. It was only an instinct, the belief that the most important regions of the planetoid ought to be near the center rather than on some upper level. If he was wrong, he would have doomed both of them.

In spite of all that, Rebka was quite enjoying himself. This was what life was all about. Exploring things that no human had ever seen before, with an interesting companion—what more could a man ask, unless it was for a little food?

"I think we're coming to something," he said. "The light ahead is different. It's getting fainter."

The answering growl behind Rebka sounded skeptical. He wondered if it was just Darya's stomach. As the illumination from walls and ceiling faded, he stepped forward more cautiously. Soon he could see nothing ahead, not even the floor, but his instincts told him they were approaching something new.

"Stay there." He kept his voice down to the softest whisper. "I don't know what's ahead, but I want to feel my way for a bit before we shine a light." Even those breathed words sounded strange, hollow and echoing.

He went down on hands and knees and felt his way forward. Five meters farther on, his left hand found itself groping into empty space. He reached out as far as he could on both sides. Nothing. The tunnel ended in a blind drop. There was no light below, or in any direction. He crawled back to join Darya and placed his mouth next to her ear.

"We'll have to use your flashlight," he whispered. "Take a look ahead. Be careful how you shine it—straight down on the floor first, then raise it up slowly." He moved aside to allow her to come level with him, then paced her carefully forward.

"No farther now!" He stopped her. "There's nothing ahead."

Darya nodded, unseen in the darkness. The light beam shone on the floor at her feet, then moved out over the lip in front of them. As it came higher its narrow beam reflected faintly off a distant wall. Darya inched forward, shining the light downward. One more step, and she would be over the edge.

The ledge she stood on was halfway up the wall of a great

open room, with a sheer drop below that plunged twenty meters before it curved around to form the bowl-shaped empty floor of the chamber.

Darya stepped back a pace. In this gravity field, any fall could be fatal. She shone the beam higher. Above them was a vaulted ceiling, confirming the spherical shape of the chamber. The domed vault was featureless, without lights or support struts. The whole room had to be at least sixty meters across.

"Something's there." Hans kept his voice to a whisper, but the echoes came rolling in from across the room, reluctant to die. *There . . . there . . . there . . . there.*

"Right in the middle. Shine the light in the center."

Darya pointed the flashlight straight ahead. Hovering in the middle of the room without any visible support was a silvery sphere about ten meters across. She thought at once of the sphere that had risen from the broken surface of Quake at Summertide, but this one was hundreds of times smaller.

And it was more active. The ball had been hanging in a fixed position, but as the beam touched it the surface became a play of motion. The flashlight reflected an undulatory pattern, like slow waves on a ball of rippling mercury. The waves grew and steadied. The sphere began to deform and elongate.

There . . . there . . . there . . . there . . . A rusty, creaking voice filled the chamber, as deep and ancient as the sea. *There . . . there . . . there . . . there. Center . . . center . . . center . . . center.*

Darya was so excited that she could hardly hold the flashlight steady. The sphere had become a distorted ellipsoid. A frond of silver began to grow upward from the top, slowly evolving to a five-sided flower that turned to face Darya and Hans. Open pentagonal disks extruded from the front of the ball, pointing toward the flashlight beam. A long, thin tail grew down, extending to the floor of the chamber. In three minutes the featureless sphere became a horned and tailed devil-beast, with a flowerlike head that sought the source of the intrusion.

A flickering green light shone from an aperture in the body of the demon and illuminated Hans and Darya. The inside of the great chamber shimmered with its reflection. Darya turned off the flashlight.

Human form . . . human . . . human. Too soon . . . soon . . . soon . . . The weary voice came echoing across to them. *Who . . . who . . . who . . . who . . .*

Hans and Darya turned to look at each other.

He shrugged. "What do we have to lose?" He faced into the chamber and spoke at normal volume. "Can you understand me? We are humans. We were brought against our will into this planetoid. We do not know how to leave it."

The flower head was nodding toward them. The light from the being's body modulated in color and intensity as it bobbed up and down in the middle of the chamber.

"It's no good," Darya said. "You can't expect it to understand a word." But while she was speaking the voice began again.

Brought inside . . . inside. Yes, we understand human . . . human . . . human . . . You were brought inside to be . . . others, in case others were needed . . . you may not be needed. You were to stay there . . . near the outside . . . not come here . . .

Darya stepped closer to the edge. "Who are you? Where did you come from? What is this place?"

"One question at a time," Rebka said softly, "or it won't have any idea what you're asking."

But the demon figure in front of them was already speaking again, and more fluently. *I am The-One-Who-Waits . . . The one who waited in the heart of the double world, in the Connection Zone . . . I came from the heart of that world, when it opened to the signal . . .*

"From inside Quake," Darya said. "At Summertide! It must have come in the big silver sphere, the one that grabbed the *Have-It-All.*"

. . . for which I had waited long. In human time, one fortieth of a galactic revolution. I waited—

"That's six million years! Are you a Builder?"

"Don't keep interrupting, Darya. Let it talk!"

—waited long for the Event. I am not a Builder, only a

servant of the Builders. I am The-One-Who-Waits. Who seeks the Builders?

"I do!" Darya moved dangerously close to the edge. "All my life, ever since I was a child, I've studied the Builders, wanted to know more about them. The Builders have been my life's work."

The Builders are not here. The ones who fly outside are not true Builders. This is the Connection Zone . . . the testing place, where we wait for the question to be answered. Wait.

The green light was extinguished and the chamber plunged again into darkness. Darya was teetering on the edge of the drop until Hans Rebka seized her arm and pulled her back to safety.

She shook herself loose; she did not feel even a twinge of nervousness. "Did you hear that, Hans? The *Connection* Zone! The Builders aren't here, but there's access to them from inside Glister. I knew it! They can be reached from here!"

"*Maybe* they can. Darya, calm down." Rebka grabbed her again, pulled her close, and spoke with his mouth next to her ear. "Did you hear me? Cool off, and think before you jump to conclusions. You've been in communication for about two minutes with something that says it's at least six million years old, and you're willing to take everything it says at face value. What makes you think you understand what it means, or it understands you? Lots of what it said makes no sense—'the ones who fly outside are not true Builders.' That's not information, it's gibberish. More than that, where did it learn to speak our language? How did it even recognize the human *shape*, if it's been locked away inside Quake for six million years? There were no humans *anywhere* that long ago."

But the green light was pulsing again, illuminating them and the whole of the domed chamber.

The testing proceeds. The rusty voice spoke again. *It comes close to completion . . . close enough to be sure that the modified one is a true human, and acceptable. It is not necessary for you to be here . . .*

"Then take us back to the surface," Rebka said.

"No!" Darya moved in front of him. "Hans, if we go back now we may as well never have come here at all. There are so many things we might be able to find out here about the Builders. We may never have as good an opportunity."

You seek the Builders, the creaking voice went on, as though neither human had spoken. *I am not a Builder, and I cannot guarantee the result. But if it is your desire to encounter the Builders—*

"It is!"

Then, GO.

"No. Darya, will you for God's sake wait a minute! We don't know—"

Rebka's shout was too late. They were standing on the brink of the tunnel as the edge turned suddenly to vapor.

Free-fall!

Rebka looked down to his feet. They were accelerating at a couple of gees along a featureless vertical shaft that ended half a kilometer below them in a darkness so total that the eye rejected its existence.

"What is it?" Rebka heard Darya's despairing cry beside him.

"It's Glister's gravity field—whatever creates it—maybe a . . ." He did not finish the phrase. If they were falling toward the event horizon of a black hole they would know about it soon enough—know it for maybe a millisecond, before tidal differential forces reduced their bodies to component elementary particles.

"Hans!" Darya screamed.

Two hundred meters to go, still accelerating, faster than ever. Maybe a second left. And now the darkness possessed a structure, like a roiling whirlpool of black oil, curling and tumbling onto itself. They were heading into the churning heart of that dark vortex.

Rebka's empty stomach was churning, too.

A fraction of a second to go.

Childhood on Teufel had taught him one thing above all others: there was always a way out of every fix—if you were smart enough.

You just had to *think*.

Think.

Apparently he was not smart enough. He was still thinking, unproductively, as he dropped into the depths of that writhing blackness.

CHAPTER 14

THE UNMANNED *SUMMER* *Dreamboat* had arrived in one piece and in working order.

That was the good news. The bad news was that it had been touch and go.

Five grazing encounters with Phages had delivered hammer blows to the *Dreamboat*'s hull, one strong enough to dent and puncture the top of the cabin. The repair was not difficult, and Birdie Kelly was already half finished. But the significance of those five near misses was not the damage that they had done. It was what they revealed about the state of the Phages. Steven Graves and E. C. Tally had monitored the ascent of the *Dreamboat* and were agreed for once: the little ship's survival, even with all collision-avoidance systems active, had been mainly a matter of luck. The Phages were more active than ever, all the way down to the surface of Glister. A descent with accelerations that humans could stand had less than a one percent chance of success.

The *Summer Dreamboat* had been moved for repairs into the capacious ore hold of the *Incomparable*. Graves and Tally were floating free in the air-filled interior, talking and talking.

And watching me work, Birdie thought. Same as usual. The other two were long on talk, but when anything calling for physical effort came along they managed to leave all the *doing* to him. And they lacked a decent sense of danger. Birdie hated to work with heroes. He had listened to Steven and E. C. Tally casually talk odds of a hundred to one against, and shuddered. Fortunately, Julius Graves seemed to have more rational views.

"Those odds are totally unacceptable," he was saying. "When you and Steven are in agreement, I am forced to listen. We cannot afford to take such a risk."

"May I speak?"

"Which means we have a real problem," Graves continued, ignoring Tally's request. "J'merlia is on Dreyfus-27. Probably deep inside it, since he does not answer our calls. So he can't help. And everyone else is on Glister. And we have no safe way of getting to them." He paused. "Did you say something, E.C.?"

"Steven and I agreed on the probability of survival if the *Summer Dreamboat* simply makes a direct descent to Glister. Or rather, we disagreed in the third significant digit of the calculated result. But there are other options. It depends on the probability level which one uses to define 'safe.' For example, there is a technique that would raise the probability of a successful landing of the *Summer Dreamboat* onto the surface of Glister to a value in excess of zero-point-eight-four."

"A five-out-of-six chance of getting there in one piece?" Julius Graves glared at Tally. "Why didn't you mention it earlier?"

"For three reasons. First, it came to me only after a review of analogous situations, of other places and times. That review was completed only thirty seconds ago. Second, the technique should provide a safe landing, but the odds of a safe subsequent ascent are incalculable without additional data concerning the surface of Glister. And third, the procedure would probably lead to the loss of a valuable asset: the *Incomparable.* "

"Commissioner Kelly." Graves turned to Birdie. "The *Incomparable* is the property of the government of Dobelle. As the representative of that government, how would you view its possible loss?"

Birdie had finished the patch on the *Dreamboat*'s hull and burned his thumb doing it. He pushed himself off and glared around the *Incomparable*'s hold as he floated up to grab a support beam at Tally's side.

"It's a filthy barrel of rust and rot, it stinks like a dead ponker, and it should have been thrown on the scrap heap fifty years ago. If I never see it again, that's too soon."

Tally was frowning at him. "Am I to take it, then, that you would sanction the potential loss of the *Incomparable?*"

"In one word, matey, yes."

"Then if I may speak, I will outline the technique. It is something that can be found in the older parts of the data banks. In old times, when human individuals wished to accomplish an objective that certain other guarding entities sought to prevent, they often employed a method known as *creating a diversion . . .* "

Agreement in principle did not guarantee agreement in practice. E. C. Tally and Steven Graves had argued endlessly about the best method. Should the *Incomparable* be sent in well ahead of the *Dreamboat,* passing through the periphery of the cloud of orbiting Phages and seeking to draw them away from Glister? Or was it better to fly the old ore freighter on a trajectory that would impact Glister, and take the *Dreamboat* in not far behind, relying on its being ignored in the presence of the freighter's larger and more tempting target?

Tally and Steven Graves had finally agreed on one thing—that they had insufficient data.

"Since there is not enough information to make a reasoned choice," Tally said apologetically to Birdie Kelly, "the only thing I can suggest is that we resort to aleatoric procedure."

"What's 'aleatoric' mean, when it's at home?" Birdie was reaching into his jacket pocket.

"An aleatoric procedure is one that contains chance and random elements."

"Why, that's just the way I was thinking myself." Birdie produced a deck of cards and shuffled it expertly. He held it out to Tally. "Pick a card, E. C., any card. Red, and the ships fly a long way apart from each other. Black, and we tuck ourselves up the old *Incomparable*'s tailpipe."

Tally selected a card from the spread and turned it over. "It is black." He had stared in great curiosity when Birdie shuffled the deck. "What you did just then—it was difficult to see, but is it designed to randomize the sequence?"

"You might say that." Birdie gave E. C. Tally a thoughtful glance. "Didn't you ever play cards?"

"Never."

"If we get out of this alive, why don't I teach you?"

"Thank you. That would be informative."

"And don't you worry," Birdie patted Tally on the shoulder. "We won't be playing for high stakes. At first."

"That could have been us." Julius Graves was staring straight up. "Not a comforting thought."

They had finally decided that since the *Dreamboat* needed time and maneuvering space to land on Glister, it would be a mistake to have the *Incomparable* fly in all the way to the surface. Instead, the bigger ship had been programmed to zoom down to ten kilometers and then veer away from the planetoid, with luck luring the cloud of attacking Phages with it.

As the *Dreamboat* increased the power level of its drive for the last hundred-meter deceleration to the surface, the *Incomparable* could be seen skirting the northern horizon of Glister. The old ship was at the center of a dense cluster of marauding Phages. Already it had sustained a dozen direct hits. The drive was still flaring, but Phage maws had gouged great chunks from the body of the freighter. About twenty

Phages clung to the flanks of the *Incomparable,* like dogs worrying an old bull.

"They'll be back," Julius Graves went on. "The way they're going, they'll have swallowed the freighter completely in another half hour. And Phages don't get indigestion, or lose their appetite, no matter what they ingest."

Birdie Kelly had chosen an approach trajectory to bring them no more than fifty meters from the *Have-It-All,* on the side of the ship away from Kallik's field inhibitor. There had been no time to examine that installation during their descent, and would not have been even if the *Dreamboat's* evasive movements from a handful of isolated Phages had been smooth enough to permit it. Now they had to hurry over to the inhibitor and decide what to do before any Phages returned to harass them.

The two men and the embodied computer had their suits set to full opacity. Kallik, Darya Lang, and Hans Rebka had certainly been able to breathe the atmosphere; and just as certainly, they had disappeared from the surface of Glister. Their vanishing and failure to reappear was unlikely to be the result of Glister's air—but it could be. As E. C. Tally pointed out, quoting from the most ancient part of the data banks, "Taking a *calculated risk,* sir, does not oblige one to act *rashly.*"

While Graves and Tally went on to the site of the field inhibitor, Birdie took a quick look inside the *Have-It-All.* He headed first for the control room. The ship was untouched, ready to fly within a few seconds of giving the command. That gave Birdie his first warm feeling for quite a while. He patted the control console and hurried back outside.

He had half expected to see the surface of Glister littered with crashed Phages, but there were only two crumpled remains in sight. Did they lose interest if no organic life-forms were present? That was a new thought—though not an encouraging one, to an organic life-form.

Birdie followed the stretched cable from the *Have-It-All's* stanchion to the place where Graves and E. C. Tally were standing. Tally had his hand on the line, close to the point where it disappeared into the gray surface, and he was tugging on it vigorously. As Birdie came up to them Tally released the cable, reached down, and pushed his hand easily *into* the slate-colored plane.

"Observe," he said. "The field inhibitor is still operating, with near-perfect field cancellation. The surface offers negligible resistance to the penetration of my hand, and at this point it must, I think, be a weakly secured gaseous form. But the cable itself offers considerable resistance to its own withdrawal. We conclude that it must be secured at its lower end, within the interior of Glister."

"In other words," Graves said, "it's tied to something."

Now that he was close enough, Birdie could see that the surface for a radius of a few meters around the field inhibitor appeared slightly indistinct. And the legs of the inhibitor equipment stood not *on* Glister, but buried a few centimeters in that hazy gray.

"So who shall be first?" Graves asked.

"First for what?" But Birdie knew the answer to that question before he asked it. The one thing that made no sense was to come all the way here, run the gauntlet through that belt of aggressive Phages, and then sit and wait for the same Phages to come back and dive-bomb them. The only way to go was *down,* into that gray horridness.

Tally had taken hold of the cable without waiting for discussion. "It is possible that I will be unable to return messages to you through the suit communications system," he said calmly. "However, when I reach a point where it is appropriate for another to descend, I will strike the cable—thus." He hit it with the palm of his suited hand. "Feel for the vibration."

He pushed his feet over the edge and swung hand-over-hand down the cable. His body disappeared easily into a gray opacity. When only his head showed above the smoky surface he paused.

"It occurs to me that my words leave the required action for some possible future situations inadequately defined. A contingency may arise in which I become unable to strike the cable in the manner that I described. If I do not signal in a reasonable time, say, one thousand seconds, you should assume that contingency."

"Don't worry your head about that," Birdie said. "We'll assume it."

"That is satisfactory." E. C. Tally disappeared completely. A second later his head popped up again from the gray haze. "May I ask, if I do not signal in one thousand seconds, what action you propose to take?"

Birdie stared off to the horizon. The hulk of the *Incomparable* had vanished—devoured, or flown far away, he could not tell. There was a cloud of glittering motes visible in the same direction. The same Phages, probably, sensing motion on the surface of Glister and coming back for another go at it.

Except that these Phages were not interested in the surface of Glister. They wanted to have a go at humans. At *him*.

"I don't know what action we'll take, E. C.," Birdie said. "But don't be surprised if it happens before you count out your thousand seconds."

The cable went down ten meters through gray obscurity, then emerged into a spherical region with another gray floor and a ceiling above it that glowed with cold orange light.

Birdie clung to the line, high up near the ceiling, and peered downward.

It was a long drop—a horrid long drop, for somebody from a planet where the buildings were never more than a couple of stories high; and there was no sign of E. C. Tally down there. But the cable went on, straight downward, into the floor.

Birdie slightly relaxed the grip of his hands and knees and continued his controlled descent. When he came to the part of the second floor where the line ran through, that surface proved just as insubstantial as the first one. The field inhibitor had been focused downward, and for all Birdie knew, its effect went right through Glister and out the other side. He allowed himself to drop on through. Somewhere above him, Julius Graves was waiting for his signal, as he had waited for E. C. Tally's. But this was no time to give it, suspended in midair.

The gray fog filled his nose and mouth, passing through his supposedly sealed suit as though it did not exist. The gas was thin, tasteless, and odorless, and it did not interfere with Birdie's breathing. In another ten meters he was through that and dropping again toward a spherical surface.

This level was more promising. There were structures and partitions and webs, dividing the space into giant, oddly shaped rooms. Birdie was coming down into one of the bigger open areas. He released the line with his crossed legs, let go with his hands, and dropped the last few feet. The gravity was more than he had realized. He landed heavily and flopped backward to a sitting position. Before he stood up he took a quick look around.

Dull gray walls. A jumble of nets and unconnected support lines on the floor, right by his side. He was sitting on a length of flexible netting, springy enough to be a bed. The cable he had come down ran off to the right, to a descending ramp that became part of a brightly lit tunnel.

Off on that right side—he stopped, stared, and stared again. On that right side, close to the entry to the downward ramp, was E. C. Tally.

And crouched next to him, eight legs splayed, was J'merlia.

Birdie scrambled to his feet. The Lo'tfian was supposed to be hundreds of thousands of kilometers away, on Dreyfus-27. What was he doing here?

Birdie jerked at the line he was holding, to send a signal back to Graves that it was safe to descend, and hurried across to the other two.

"You were right about messages, E.C.," he said. "I assume you tried to send something through your suit communicator, but we didn't hear a thing."

"Nor I from you. The surface is presumably impervious to electromagnetic signals, though it permits material objects to pass through with no difficulty." E. C. Tally gestured to J'merlia. "It is not necessary for you to introduce the two of us, Commissioner Kelly. We have already done that. Although J'merlia and I never met before, I recognized the Lo'tfian form from stored records."

"That's as may be. But what's *he* doing *here*? Why aren't

you over on Dreyfus, J'merlia, the way Captain Rebka's messages said you would be?"

"I beg forgiveness for that act. I came to Glister to seek the masters, Atvar H'sial and Louis Nenda, and also the Hymenopt Kallik. But when I was on the surface, I was forced to seek refuge in the interior from the attack of Phages. The ship that I had arrived in, the *Summer Dreamboat,* took off from the surface and left me helpless."

"Sorry, J'merlia, that was our doing—we needed it to come down in. But you were a bit ambitious, wouldn't you say, looking for Nenda and H'sial and Kallik? Seeing as how we've all no idea where any one of them is. You'd have been better off staying on Dreyfus, out of harm's way. Phages are bad news."

"With apologies, Commissioner Kelly. The Phages are, as you say, amazingly aggressive. It was unwise of me to come here. But there is good news also. I know where the masters are! And the Hymenopt Kallik. They are all three together, in a chamber closer to the center of Glister."

"I can't believe it." Birdie turned to E. C. Tally. "Is J'merlia telling the truth?"

"I have no direct evidence that supports his statement. But if you will accept indirect evidence, according to the central data banks the species that lead the spiral arm in deliberate falsehood are humans and Cecropians. Everyone else, including J'merlia and all Lo'tfians, is far behind."

"With respect, Commissioner Kelly, you may verify that I speak the truth. All you need to do is act as I did—follow the cable. It led me all the way from the surface, to where the masters and Kallik can be found."

"Which would certainly be direct evidence." E. C. Tally gestured to Birdie. "Go ahead, Commissioner, with J'merlia. When Councilor Graves joins me we will come after you. The cable provides an unambiguous trail for us to pursue."

Birdie found himself following the thin figure of J'merlia down an angled and jointed tunnel, whose sudden changes of direction made his head spin. The tunnel branched occasionally, and parts were so dimly lit that the walls could not be seen, but J'merlia followed the thin line wherever it led. Birdie trailed along behind, his hand touching the Lo'tfian's back. Their emergence into a giant domed chamber came as a shock.

The downward-curving floor formed a shallow circular bowl, marked off in concentric rings of pure color. Under the brilliant overhead light their reflection hurt the eyes. From the meeting place of each pair of rings rose insubstantial hemispheres, arching up over the middle of the chamber. The line that J'merlia had been following led toward that center, straight as a spoke on a wheel. Halfway in it stopped. Kallik was lying on the floor there, a compact dark bundle on the boundary between a purple and a red ring. In two front paws she held the spool for the line, and the other end had been wrapped securely around her body.

And *beyond* Kallik's unconscious form . . .

The innermost ring was blue, purest blue, a monochromatic 0.47-micrometer blue. At its center stood a raised dais of the same color, with a dozen glassy seats upon it. In two of those seats lolled the unmistakable forms of Louis Nenda and Atvar H'sial.

Birdie started forward. He was restrained by J'merlia's grip on his sleeve.

"With respect, Commissioner, it may be unwise to proceed farther."

"Why? They don't look dead, just unconscious. But they could be in bad shape. We have to get 'em out and take care of them, soon as we can."

"Assuredly. My first reaction was the same as yours, that I must proceed at once and rescue the masters. But then I thought to myself, the Hymenopt Kallik surely operated with the same imperative. She saw the masters, she went forward toward them—and she did not reach them. When I realized that, I also realized that the worst way for me to serve the masters would be to become unconscious, as they are. I returned for safety to the second outer chamber. I had formulated no safe plan of action when the human, E. Crimson Tally, appeared."

"He's not a human. Tally's an embodied computer." Birdie did not go into details. He was too busy thinking about the other things that J'merlia had said.

"Why didn't you just grab hold of the line and pull Kallik out?" he went on. "She doesn't weigh much."

"I was unable to do so, Commissioner. Try it, if you wish."

Birdie seized the end of the line and heaved, as hard as he could. Kallik did not move a millimeter, and the line inside the pattern of rings did not even leave the floor. It was held there, fused to the surface or secured by some form of field. Birdie was still tugging and swearing when E. C. Tally and Julius Graves arrived.

There were five minutes of questions, suggestions, and counter-suggestions. At the end of it no one had bettered J'merlia's first proposal: that it was safe to do now what he had been reluctant to do before. He would enter the hemispheres and attempt to retrieve Kallik. If he failed, for any reason, the others would be on hand to help him. He would wear a line around him, so that if he became unconscious he could be pulled out.

"Which we know doesn't work for Kallik," Birdie said.

But he had no better ideas. They all watched in silence as J'merlia walked forward steadily, passing through the yellow and green rings and half of the purple one. At that point he hesitated. The thin head began to turn, and the pale-yellow eyes on their short eyestalks moved dreamily from side to side.

"J'merlia!" Julius Graves shouted at him—loudly. The Lo'tfian stared around in a vague and puzzled way. He folded his thin hind legs and began to sit down.

"That's enough!" Graves was already pulling on the line. "Get him out, quick—while he can still stand."

J'merlia came reeling back from inside the pattern of rings. At the edge of the green annulus he jerked up to his full height and peered around him, but he allowed the others to haul him all the way out. On the edge of the yellow ring he sank down to his belly.

"What happened?" Tally asked. "You were progressing well, and then you halted."

"I don't remember." J'merlia crouched down on all his limbs and turned his eyestalks to stare back into the circle. "I was going in. Steadily, without difficulty. And then all at once I was going *out,* facing the other direction and being pulled clear."

"A Lotus field." Graves was nodding his head soberly. "Once Darya Lang pointed out that Glister is a Builder creation, we might have expected it. There are Lotus fields on many artifacts. The most famous one surrounds and protects Paradox. But J'merlia is lucky—he was exposed to only peripheral-field strength. Only the most recent of his memories were erased."

"Which may not be true of Kallik," E. C. Tally said. "And still less of Louis Nenda and Atvar H'sial. The Lotus field of Paradox erases all memories."

"From men," J'merlia said, "and from Lo'tfians and Hymenopts. But from machines? Or from computers?"

The others turned to look at E. C. Tally. He nodded. "According to the records, all memories are lost in Paradox, from Organics or Inorganics. However." He bent down to release the line from J'merlia and place it around his own body. "However, this is not Paradox. The Lotus field here may not be the same. An experiment is in order."

They watched in silence as he cautiously stepped into the yellow ring, then passed across the five-meter band that led to the green. In the middle of the green annulus he paused and looked back.

"I feel some slight disturbance of circuits." His voice was calm. "It is not enough to inhibit performance, nor to prevent my further progress. I will proceed."

He walked on, descending across the shallow bowl of the floor. Five paces short of the place where J'merlia had faltered, he paused again.

"I must return." His voice had become halting and slow. "I cannot retain information. It is being destroyed in both current and backup files . . . I record a loss of fourteen thousand sectors in the past three seconds." He turned and took one hesitant step away from the center. Then he seemed to freeze.

"Twenty-three thousand more sectors are gone," he said dreamily. "The rate is increasing."

"That's enough." Graves heaved on the line, and Tally came bobbing and weaving back to the periphery of the chamber. At the edge he halted and shook off Birdie Kelly's supporting hands.

"Do not worry, Commissioner Kelly. I have lost some data—all recent—but I am still fully functional. Most of my stored memory has not been affected."

"But we've answered the main question," Graves said. "The field is just as effective on organic or inorganic memories. So we can't get them out—any of them."

"We must." J'merlia stood up and made a movement as though he was ready to run back toward the middle of the chamber. "The masters are in there! Kallik is there! We cannot abandon them."

"I am sorry, J'merlia." Graves walked across to place himself between the Lo'tfian and the silent forms at the center of the room. "If we could do something to help Kallik and the others, we would—even though Atvar H'sial and Louis Nenda tried to kill us, back on Quake. But we can't do a thing to get them out."

"That statement is plausible, but not proven." E. C. Tally had been standing motionless. Now he raised his hands to touch the sides of his head. "I would like to question it. When I was receiving my original indoctrination, before I set out for Dobelle, there were calibration problems. To make the required adjustments, it was necessary to remove my brain."

Tally ignored Birdie Kelly's gasp of horror. He was feeling carefully around his temples. "I pointed out to the technicians at the time that my embodied design was intended for continuous sensory input. They employed a neural bundle connecting my brain to my spine. I lost sensory feeds and body control for a few seconds as the attachment was being made, but I was otherwise unaffected. Now, my observations suggest that J'merlia is the strongest and most agile of us. If he were to ascend the cable all the way to the surface, enter the *Have-It-All,* and return with a long high-capacity neural cable . . ."

* * *

Birdie Kelly had never seen anything so disgusting in his whole life. And that was saying something.

E. C. Tally lay on his side on the gently curving floor, eyes closed. A coil of high-capacity cable lay by him. His head was supported on a folded blanket taken from the *Have-It-All,* and he was giving calm directions to Julius Graves and J'merlia.

"The skull is of course real bone, and the skin was grown naturally. But for convenience of access the blood vessels were terminated in the rear section, on a line one centimeter above my ears. The blood supply to the upper skull has been rerouted to veins and arteries in my forehead. The upper cranium is hinged at the front and secured with a line of pins at the back. You will see the access line when the hair is lifted. If you raise the skin at the back you should see the pressure points, marked in blue on the bone."

Graves inserted a thin spatula into the horizontal gap a few inches above E. C. Tally's rear hairline. As he levered upward there was a gleam of white bone. Three blue dots were revealed on the smooth rear of the skull.

"I see them. Three of them?"

"That is correct. Very good. When those pressure points are simultaneously depressed, the rear pins release. You will find that the whole upper cranium lifts forward about the hinged line in the forehead. The skin, veins, and arteries there should stretch, but they will remain intact above the hinged region." When Graves hesitated, Tally added, "Do not concern yourself about my sensations. Naturally, the warning signals that you know as pain have been modified in my case. I will feel nothing that you recognize as discomfort."

Graves nodded, and while J'merlia held the spatula in position he reached in and pressed the three marked places on the white bone. There was a sharp click. The rear part of the skull jerked upward a couple of millimeters, revealing a narrow dark slit.

"That looks like poor design," Graves said. "Isn't there a danger that the release could be triggered accidentally?"

"Not while I am functional. I must cooperate, or be incapable of internal state transitions, before the release can take place. Now—grasp the rear hair and lift the upper cranium, rotating it about the forward hinge."

The whole cap of the skull eased upward under Graves's gentle pressure. Birdie saw the inside of the hemisphere, with its intricate network of red blood vessels. Below it was a bulging gray ovoid, sitting in the skull case as snugly as an egg in an eggcup.

"Very good." Tally remained completely still. "You will now see what appear to be the meninges—the outer protective membranes of the human brain. In my case they are of course artificial. I was embodied with my own independent power supply, so there is no need for anything other than a neural body/brain interface. You will find the neural interface when you lift me out of the skull cavity. Lift me only a few centimeters, and proceed with caution. It would be undesirable to disable the interface prematurely. A strong pull would unseat the connection."

Graves was reaching into Tally's head and cautiously lifting out a roughly spherical object, small enough to hold comfortably in his two cupped hands. As the wrinkled ball was raised, a short coiled spiral was revealed. It ran between the bottom of the embodied computer and the lower hindbrain of E. C. Tally's body, above the end of the spinal column. Clear liquid dripped from the coil onto Graves's hands as the computer brain was lifted free of its body.

"Now," Tally continued. "The next phase should be simple, but I will not be able to guide you through it. Commissioner Kelly, you and J'merlia must make sure that my body does not move—there may be some reflex muscle activity. Councilor Graves, you must break the connection between me and the body, and then connect it again through the high-capacity cable. Do it as quickly as you can, consistent with care, but do not worry if it takes a minute or two. This body's own hindbrain will permit it to function normally for at least that long, while I am absent. Also, do not be afraid to touch the inside of the skull cavity. This body is well protected against infection. Carry on, please, as soon as you feel ready."

Graves nodded. There was another click as he reached in and delicately separated the body and the sphere of the embodied computer. E. C. Tally's limbs jerked against Birdie and J'merlia's restraining grasp; then the body slumped and steadied.

The ends of the neural cable had been placed close to hand. Julius Graves picked up the male connector. After a few seconds of effort he inserted it snugly into position at the upper end of the body's hindbrain.

"Half the job done." He was breathing loudly through his mouth. "But the other one doesn't want to go in. Hold him still." Graves's fingers were slippery with cerebrospinal fluid. He could not force home the connector attaching the computer brain to the neural cable.

"Hold on a minute." Birdie Kelly wiped his hands down his pants, then reached across to take both the brain and the connector from Graves. He pressed the plug home hard onto the multiple prongs of the computer's receptor.

"Gently!" Graves said. But the body of E. C. Tally was already sitting up and lifting free of J'merlia's grip.

"Hmm—kkh—khmmm." The torso shivered, and the eyes snapped open.

Graves bent close. "E. C. Tally! Can you hear me?"

"Very well." The topless head turned. "Excuse me, Councilor, but there is no need to shout like that. This body is equipped with excellent sensory apparatus."

The skull was still gaping wide, the empty cranium inverted and hanging upside down in front of Tally's bright blue eyes. Birdie Kelly stared at that empty skull, split open like a coconut, and at the neural cable that ran from the base of the brain to the little sphere in his right hand. *His* torso wanted to shiver, too. Life on Opal was tough, but it had not prepared him for this sort of thing.

As Birdie watched, Tally reached up, took the open skull case in both hands, and casually rotated it back into position. "It won't quite close, I'm afraid," he said, "because the neural connector inhibits the seal. If possible we should tie it in place. It would be inconvenient to have the upper cranium detached and lost."

He turned to glance at the sphere that Birdie was holding. "Handle me with care if you please, Commissioner Kelly. What you have in your hands represents a substantial investment of Fourth Alliance property. I'm afraid that the body has already suffered minor damage, since it was not anticipated that we would need to perform brain removal in an unprepared facility." A thin trickle of blood was running down the left side of Tally's forehead. He wiped it away casually, stared around the chamber, and continued. "Also, my motor and sensory performance is somewhat impaired. The signal-carrying capacity of the neural cable is less than that of the original connection. I am able to see with rather less definition, colors are muted, and I sense that my muscular control is diminished. However, it should certainly be adequate for our purposes."

He rose to his feet, staggering a little before he caught his balance. At his direction J'merlia and Graves tied a makeshift bandage around his head, adding an extra wrapping to hold both the upper cranium and the external neural cable in position. Birdie Kelly was still holding the brain in nervous hands, doing his best to avoid jiggling it or putting any pressure on it.

"Are you sure you are ready?" Graves asked. "Don't you want to practice moving?"

But Tally was already stepping forward. "That would be pointless," he said. "My coordination would not improve. But as one precaution, let me do this." He picked up the strong line that he had used on his previous foray toward the center of the room and tied it around his waist. "You can always haul me back here. So now, if J'merlia will pay out the neural cable, Commissioner Kelly, as necessary . . ."

Tally took two staggering steps forward and began to weave his way down the gentle slope that led to the center of the chamber. He was soon into the first of the concentric rings. At the far edge of the yellow annulus he paused for a moment, while the others froze. Then he was off again, heading for the silent figure of Kallik. Birdie Kelly watched him, afraid even to blink, as J'merlia paid out cable from the reel that he was holding, at a pace just enough to prevent the line from tightening or drooping to touch the floor. There was something wholly unnatural about that human form, head bloody and bandaged, moving into the shallow and brightly lit cauldron of gaudy colors. He staggered as he walked, and the two cables trailing behind him swayed and jerked with a life and rhythm of their own.

"Come out at once if you feel you are losing memories," Graves called.

Tally waved an arm without slowing his progress. "Certainly. Though I do not expect that to happen. How can it, when *I* am with you in the hands of Commissioner Kelly?"

He was already past the green ring and moving on to the purple one. Two seconds more, and he was sinking slowly to sit on the floor beside Kallik, careful to keep his head upright. His fingers touched the Hymenopt's furry thorax. "She is alive. Unconscious, but not apparently injured. I cannot lift the line around her from the floor, but if I release her from it I see no difficulty in carrying her out."

Tally stood up and peered toward the center of the chamber. "But first, I think it is better if I proceed all the way in, and examine the situation there. I can retrieve Kallik as I return."

Not what I'd do, Birdie thought. A bird in the hand . . . He glanced at the sphere of the now-disembodied computer. It was strange that the only way to pass messages to the real E. C. Tally was to call them to the brainless body moving slowly toward the middle of the room, and have the sensory input fed back through the cable to the brain that Birdie was holding.

Tally was moving more slowly. The low central platform was only fifteen meters away, but he took twenty cautious seconds to reach it. Two steps from the silent figure of Louis Nenda, he paused.

"There is something peculiar about the dais itself. As I have approached it, an interior structure has gradually become visible. It is a set of dodecahedra, invisible from fifteen meters. At ten I saw a hazy outline, like gray smoke. Now the pattern is apparently solid. Tendrils run from two of the dodecahedral faces and surround the heads of Louis

Nenda and Atvar H'sial. That must be why the bodies can remain seated upright, although both are unconscious.''

Birdie glanced at Graves, then peered toward the platform. From where he stood it looked empty except for the outward-facing seats, the Cecropian, and the human.

"I propose to try to remove Nenda from the platform first," Tally said. "I have no idea if there will be resistance, active or passive."

He took the final two steps, reached up, and grasped Louis Nenda by the shoulders. He began to lift. To the watchers it appeared that the two bodies moved to an unstable position, leaning back far from the vertical.

"There is definite resistance," Tally said. "But also there is progress. We are a few centimeters farther from the platform, and the connecting tendril has thinned. It is starting to turn in on itself, like a ring of blown smoke—" He lurched backward suddenly, and fell to the floor with Nenda on top of him. "—and now the tendril has gone completely. Be ready to reel in the line and the neural cable. We are coming out."

With Nenda's body set over his right shoulder in a fireman's lift, Tally began to walk slowly back from the center of the chamber. Another minute, and he was by the side of Julius Graves. Together they lowered Louis Nenda to the floor.

Birdie Kelly stared at the pitted and noduled chest, gray and disfigured. "Look at that. What did they do to him?"

Graves bent low, studying the roughened skin. "Nothing was done here, according to Steven. This is a Zardalu augment, designed to permit a human to speak to a Cecropian via pheromonal transfer. We thought this was a lost technology, and a banned one. There must be places in the Communion where the old slave races had mastered and retained parts of the Zardalu sciences."

Tally had already turned and was heading back toward the middle of the vaulted chamber. Cable was pulling through J'merlia's too-tight grip. He began to pay it out again just as Louis Nenda grunted and his lips twitched.

"Where the hell am I?" The eyes opened and glared around. The squat figure began trying to sit up.

"That's a good sign," Graves said. "He can speak, so at least he hasn't been wiped totally clean." He turned to Nenda. "You're inside a planetoid near Gargantua. Do you remember coming here?"

Nenda shook his dark head and struggled to his feet. "Not a glimmer." His speech was labored and swollen-tongued.

"So what's the last thing you do remember?"

Nenda ignored the question. He was too busy staring at the others. "How about that. Fancy you showing up. Julius Graves. And Birdie Kelly. And J'merlia. And all alive."

"All alive, and no thanks to you." Graves leaned close. "Come on, Nenda, this is important. What's the last thing you recall, before you went unconscious?"

Nenda rubbed his hand over his unshaven jaw. "Last thing I remember?" He gave Graves a cautious look. "Mmm. Last thing I remember, Atvar H'sial an' me were lifting off Quake in the *Have-It-All.* Summertide was nearly there. I guess it came, and I guess it went."

"You don't remember firing on another ship?"

"Firing? Me?" Nenda cleared his throat. "No way. I didn't fire on anything."

"Remember it or not, you'll have to answer for that when we get back to Opal. You've already been formally charged with lethal assault."

"Won't be the first time someone's accused an innocent man." Nenda was recovering fast, the black eyes blinking furiously. "What happened to At? She was with me on the ship."

"Atvar H'sial?" Graves turned toward the middle of the great chamber. He nodded. "In there. Good. I see they're on the way out now."

J'merlia was squeaking with excitement. While Graves and Nenda were talking, E. C. Tally had returned to the dais, pulled Atvar H'sial clear, and was staggering back toward them. He was doubled over with the weight of the great Cecropian body. Nenda followed Graves's gesture, taking in the bandaged, tottering form, the cable leading from its head to where they stood, the recumbent figure of Kallik four paces behind, and the backdrop of the great, vaulted chamber.

"Hey, what's going on here? What'd you do to At?"

"We did nothing, and we're not sure what's going on. All we know is that you and Atvar H'sial were unconscious in the middle of this chamber, and we have been trying to rescue you."

"And Kallik? What did you do to my Hymenopt?"

"She became unconscious, trying to get you out."

J'merlia was jumping up and down with excitement as Tally emerged from the outermost ring. As the Lo'tfian helped to lower Atvar H'sial to the floor, Tally staggered a couple of paces farther and sat down suddenly. The blue eyes closed, and his hands went up to touch his bandaged head.

"This body is regrettably close to its physical limit." He spoke in a whisper. "I must rest for a few moments. However, we can be pleased with our progress. I am confident that the difficult part is all over. Kallik weighs little. I will take a brief pause to recuperate, and then I will carry her out of the chamber. She is ready to be moved."

"Hell, I can get her." Nenda was pushing forward. "You sit down, take it easy. She's mine, and she's my responsibility."

"No." Graves caught his arm. "Go in there and you'll be in the same condition as she is in—as *you* were in. The chamber contains a Lotus field. That is why it was necessary to disembody E. C. Tally before he entered." He pointed at the rough-surfaced sphere that Kelly was handing to J'merlia. "His brain remained here."

Nenda took another and more thoughtful look at the crouched body and the cable running from its bandaged head. "Good enough," he said after a few moments. "I'd better look after At, though—she'll be coming round in a minute, from the look of her, and she might get violent. Don't worry, I know how to handle her."

The Cecropian's black wing cases had opened to reveal four delicate vestigial wings marked by red and white elongated eyespots. The end of the proboscis was moving out from its home in the pleated chin, and the yellow trumpetlike horns on the head were lifting.

At the same time, the brain-empty body of E. C. Tally was

struggling to its feet. His eyes opened slowly. "I must go now and recover Kallik."

"It's too soon." Graves moved to Tally's side.

"No. It must be soon. The interface is beginning to be affected by seepage of cerebrospinal fluid. The performance of the neural connect is diminishing, and I am receiving worsening sensory inputs. I will go to Kallik while I am still able to see her. Otherwise, we must begin all over again."

Tally did not wait for approval. The body gave a stuttering step forward, then leaned to one side. It began a crablike shuffle down the slope, heading for the unconscious Hymenopt. Tally's body had taken ten steps and had almost reached Kallik when Atvar H'sial gave a shrill, earsplitting scream, rose fully upright, and leapt toward Julius Graves.

In the next half second Birdie Kelly saw everything and could do nothing.

The Cecropian ran into Graves first and sent him sprawling. Then the councilor and the Cecropian together collided with Birdie. One of her legs knocked him flying and sent the reel of cable spinning away to the periphery of the room. At the same time the brain of E. C. Tally, too securely held by the Lo'tfian, jerked free of the cable and rolled away with J'merlia inside the yellow ring and toward the chamber's center. As the neural connect was broken, Tally's body, moving toward Kallik, crumpled and fell to the floor. Another of Atvar H'sial's legs came sweeping across Birdie and knocked him flat on his back.

He lay staring up at the ceiling. He could not move. All that he could see was a part of the chamber's domed ceiling, Julius Graves's equally domed bald head, and part of one of Atvar H'sial's wing cases. A big weight was sitting on his chest. He was half-stunned from the bruising impact of the back of his head on the floor, his nose was bleeding, and half his teeth felt as though they had been jarred loose.

If E. C. Tally had not assured them that the difficult part was all over, Birdie would never have guessed it.

ENTRY 22: CECROPIAN.

Distribution: The Cecropia Federation occupies a flattened crescent region of the spiral arm, 300 light-years across and 750 long. Its axis stretches from an overlapping boundary with the Fourth Alliance, toward the general direction of the galactic center. The cladeworld of the Federation lies slightly to the north of the central galactic plane.

Cecropians are found on inner-system clouded planets of red dwarf stars through this whole region, for a total of more than 900 inhabited planets and an estimated population of 160 billion. Trader groups of Cecropians, of unknown total numbers, are also found scattered through the region of the Zardalu Communion.

Physical Characteristics: Cecropians are six-legged arthropods, the adult female form massing about two hundred kilos and standing three meters in full extension. The dark-red segmented body is topped by a short neck surrounded by ruffles of scarlet and white. Above it sits a large, white, eyeless head. The middle of the head is dominated by a long proboscis that combines the functions of feeling organ and eating aperture. The Cecropian's normal diet is wholly liquid.

The twin yellow horns that sit in the middle of the head are sensitive hearing organs. They receive return signals from the sonic resonator located in the pleated chin. Having evolved on a cloudy globe circling a faint red dwarf star, the eyeless Cecropians see by echolocation using high-frequency sonic pulses.

With normal hearing usurped for vision, speech between Cecropians is accomplished via chemical messengers. This pheromonal transfer permits a full and rich language, one with unique powers to convey not only thoughts, but emotions and nuances of feeling. The long antennas (two meters when fully unfurled) on the top of the head can detect and identify single molecules of many thousands of different airborne odors. However, any species that does not generate the pheromones appropriate to Cecropian speech is generally considered negligible by the Cecropians themselves, almost to the point of being deemed nonexistent.

The Cecropians evolved from much smaller winged ancestors. They long since lost the power of flight, but retain their black wing cases and four dark vestigial wings with red and white elongated eyespots. Those wings are now used only for thermal absorption and temperature control.

Note: The size and appearance described above applies only to Cecropian females, who wholly dominate their society. The males are smaller, apparently speechless, and interested only in feeding, fighting, and mating. They are not permitted interaction with other intelligences of the spiral arm. Any other possible roles that they play in Cecropian society are unclear.

History: The evolution of the sightless Cecropians from atmosphere-bound species to star-spanning superculture is the spiral arm's most convincing proof of the power of intelligence.

The Cecropians developed on a dark and cloud-covered world. Seeing by echolocation is useless across a vacuum. It requires air or some other material substance to carry the signals. Thus the Cecropians could never receive direct information of anything beyond their own atmosphere. They were aware of the presence of their own sun, only because its weak radiation was a source of warmth. However, the very existence of light, or any electromagnetic radiation, required a deductive, theoretical process, followed by the development of suitable technology.

Following those first steps, the Cecropians thirty thousand years ago turned their observing instruments to the sky. They deduced by observation and analysis the existence of a universe beyond their homeworld and beyond their own sun. They recognized the importance of the stars, measured their distances and their sizes, and at last built ships to travel to and explore them. The Cecropians discovered the Bose Network five thousand years before humans. The failure of humans and Cecropians to encounter each other during the early days of spiral-arm exploration derived from the total lack of Cecropian interest in G-2 yellow dwarf stellar systems. Interspecies interaction began only with the human discovery and use of the Bose Network, also employed by the Cecropians.

Culture: Although some other species (notably the Lo'tfians) are able to employ pheromonal messengers for the purposes of speech, the Cecropians are the only known intelligent species to be *restricted* to that method of communication. As a result, Cecropians have remained intellectually isolated from the rest of the intelligences of the spiral arm, even though they indulge in commerce and employ a number of other forms as slave species.

The key to Cecropian culture, with its unique view of other life-forms, is perhaps best illustrated by the most famous of their legends, as follows:

The Great Creator formed the Universe, and then, because she was lonely, she gave the gift of intelligence to a Cecropian. The first intelligent Cecropian went to the Great Creator, complaining that the supposed "gift" was no blessing. It brought only self-knowledge, responsibility, and sorrow. The Great Creator agreed and promised that if the Cecropian agreed to keep intelligence, as compensation it would receive the whole rest of the Universe. Every star, every planet, and every other species, intelligent or nonintelligent, would be for Cecropian use, to do with exactly as they wished. They would, in fact, exist only for the convenience of Cecropians.

The Cecropian agreed. This view of all other beings persists in Cecropians to this day.

> —From the *Universal Species Catalog*
> (Subclass: Sapients).

CHAPTER 15

AT THE LAST moment the swirling void below turned blood-red. Darya felt herself stretched from head to toe, while forces of compression rippled their way along her body. Just as they became intolerable she flashed into the heart of the red glare. Before she could record any new sensation she was through, falling in open space.

Hans was at her side, still holding her arm. Straight ahead, rushing toward them, was the bloated sphere of Gargantua.

It filled half the sky. There was no way that they could avoid collision with the planet. In one heartbeat it doubled in apparent size, and from the way that the gas-giant's appearance was changing Darya could determine their exact impact point. They were accelerating into the unwinking Eye of Gargantua. The Eye had become a huge spiraling swirl of orange and umber, with a point at its center as black and lifeless as intergalactic space.

What was that dark pupil? Darya could not guess, but she

knew that she would never find out. They would not get that far. They would burn up in one flash of light, human meteors consumed by the outer atmosphere of the planet. As they came closer Darya saw that they were heading right into the empty pupil of the Eye, following the center line of another dark vortex that narrowed all the way in.

As Hans vanished from her side, Darya entered the tunnel of the vortex. Within it she could feel nothing—no air, no light, no forces. On all sides were the cloudy orange swirls of the Eye, but she heard and felt no touch of atmosphere.

The vortex was closing, a tightening spiral that shrank until it became no wider than her body. Darya was plunging along the centermost line, deep into the maelstrom of the Eye. Forces again racked her body, but now they were *twisting,* from head to neck to chest to hips to legs to feet. As they became unbearable there was a final agonizing shear, and she found herself again in open space.

She felt no acceleration, but she could see that she was moving.

Faster and faster. As she watched, Mandel was in front of her . . . was off to the left . . . was shining from behind . . . was no bigger than a pinpoint of light when she turned her head.

After half a minute of total confusion, the analytical part of her brain asserted itself. She was seeing the universe as a series of still images, but there was no force of acceleration and there was no sign of an external gravity field. She must be pausing at each location for a fraction of a second before undergoing an instantaneous translation to another position. It was the universe in stop-motion, experienced as a series of freeze-frames. Although she was not traveling faster than light through ordinary space-time, she was certainly reaching each new location in less time than light would take. And since there was no sign of Doppler shift in the starscape around her, she must be sitting *at rest* between transitions, until the next one transported her to a new place.

It was a series of Bose Transitions, but without the Bose Network stations needed for all human interstellar travel. Each jump must have been at least a few million kilometers—

and increasing. Mandel was no brighter now than any other star in the sky.

How fast was she moving in inertial space? She would have to estimate her rate of change of position. Darya looked around for a reference frame. She could see a blue supergiant, off to her right. It was surely no closer than a hundred light-years. Yet it was changing its apparent position at maybe a degree a second. Which meant she was moving at close to two light-years a second.

And still accelerating, if that word could be applied to her series of instantaneous translations. As she watched, the constellations ahead were beginning to change, to melt, to reconfigure themselves into unfamiliar patterns.

The blue supergiant was already drifting away behind her. Darya stared all around, looking for some new reference point. She could find only one. The gauzy fabric of the Milky Way was a band of light, far away to her left. It had become the single constant of her new environment.

Darya fixed her eyes on that familiar sight—and realized, with a shiver, that it was beginning to move. She was plunging downward, out of the galactic plane. The globular clusters of the Magellanic Clouds were in front of her. They had emerged from the clutter of the spiral arm to form glittering spheres of stars.

How fast? How far?

She could not say. But in order for her motion relative to the whole Galaxy to be noticed, she had to be skipping hundreds of light-years in each transition. Another minute, and much of the Galaxy's matter lay below her. She was far below the spiral arm and catching a hint of a monstrous flattened disk. Below her feet she could see the sweeping curve of the spiral itself. Individual stars were disappearing, moment by moment, into a sea of spangles that glittered around dark dust clouds and lit the filaments of gaseous nebulas with multicolored gemstones.

As she watched the stars faded again, merging to become the hazy light of distant millions. Far off to her left the disk had swelled up and thickened. She was far enough from the main plane to be clear of obscuring gas and dust clouds. She gazed in wonder at the glowing bulge of the galactic center. Hers were surely the first human eyes to see past the spiral arm to the densely packed galactic nucleus and to the massive black hole that formed the hub of the Galaxy.

How far? How fast?

She seemed to be moving straight away from the galactic disk, and now the blaze of the central hub was off at an angle of forty-five degrees to her direction of motion. With her lungs frozen and her heart stopped in her chest, Darya made her estimate. The Phemus Circle territories were about thirty thousand light-years from the center of the Galaxy, so she must be about that far from the galactic plane. And the angle of the hub was changing, at maybe ten degrees a minute. That gave her a speed of a hundred and seventy-five light-years a second.

Ten thousand light-years a minute. A million light-years in an hour and a half. The Andromeda Galaxy in twice that time.

Even as that thought came, the mad drive ended. The universe stopped its giddy rush and clicked into a fixed position.

Ahead of Darya in the open void sat a great space structure, agleam with internal lights, sprawling across half the sky, of a size impossible to estimate. Darya had the sense that it was huge, that those trailing pseudopods of antennas and twisting tubes of bright matter, spinning away into space from the central dodecahedron, were millions of kilometers long.

Before she could confirm that impression, there came a final transition. Stars, galaxies, and stellar clusters vanished. Darya found herself standing on a level plain. Overhead was nothing. At her feet, defining the level surface itself, were a billion twinkling orange lights.

And next to her, his suit open so that he could scratch his chin, stood Hans Rebka.

"Well," he said. "We-ell, that's one for the record books. Try and describe *that* in your trip report."

He was silent for a few moments, breathing deep and staring around him. "Maybe we ought to trade ideas," he said finally. "If either of us has any. For a start, where in the hell are we?"

"You opened your suit!"

"No." He shook his head. "I never had time to *close* it when we dropped—nor did you."

To Darya's astonishment she saw that he was right. Her own suit was fully transparent. "But we were out in open space—airless vacuum."

"I thought so, too. I don't remember needing to breathe, though."

"How long were we there? Did you count heartbeats?"

He smiled ruefully. "Sorry. I don't know if I even *had* heartbeats. I was too busy trying to figure out what was happening—where you had gone, where I was going."

"I think I know. Not what was happening, but where we went and where we are now."

"Then you're six steps ahead of me." He gestured out at the endless plain in front of them. "Limbo, didn't it used to be called? A nowhere place where lost souls went."

"We're not lost. We were brought here, deliberately. And it was my fault. I told The-One-Who-Waits how keen I was to meet the Builders. It took what I said at face value."

"Didn't work, though, did it? I don't see any sign of them."

"Give them time. We only just got here. Do you remember flying down into the Eye of Gargantua?"

"Until the day I die. Which I'd like to think is a fair way off, but I'm beginning to wonder."

"The Eye is the entry point to a Builder transportation system. It must have been there as long as humans have been in the Mandel system, maybe long before that; but it's no surprise that no one ever discovered it. A ship's crew would have to be crazy to fly down into it."

"Explorer ships' crews *are* crazy. People did plenty of mad things when this system was first being colonized. I know that ships went down deep into Gargantua's atmosphere and came back out—some of them. But I don't think that would be enough to do what we did. We had to be given that first boost from Glister, to rifle us exactly down the middle of the vortex.

When I was in there it seemed to just fit my shoulders. There wasn't room for another person, let alone a ship."

"I had the same feeling. I wondered where you'd gone, but I knew there wasn't room for both of us. All right. So we had a first boost from the gravity generator on Glister, then a second boost from a shearing field in the Eye of Gargantua. That put us square into the main transportation system, and then right out of the spiral arm. Thirty thousand light-years, I estimate."

"I wondered about that. I looked around, and I could see the whole damned galaxy, spread out like a dinner plate— though the way I'm feeling, I hate to even *mention* the word 'dinner.'"

"And then one final transition, to bring us in here." Darya gazed around, up to the segmented dark ceiling, and then across the glittering plain of the floor.

"Where we can stand and stare until we starve. Any more ideas, Professor?"

"Some." Now that the mind-numbing journey was over she was beginning to think again. "I don't believe we were brought all this way to starve. The-One-Who-Waits sent us, so something must know we're here. And although this is part of the Builders' own living place, I'll bet it has been *prepared* for us, or beings like us." Darya swung her hand around a ninety-degree arc of the level floor. "See the flat surface? That's not natural for a Builder structure."

"We don't know how Builders think. Nobody ever met one."

"True. But we know how they *build*. When you've studied Builder artifacts as long as I have, you begin to form ideas about the Builders themselves. You can't *prove* things, but you learn to trust your instincts. We don't know where the Builders evolved, or when, but I'm sure it was in an aerial or free-space environment. At the very least, it was a place where gravity doesn't mean the same thing as it does to us. The Builders work naturally in all three dimensions, every direction equal. Their artifacts don't provide any feel for 'up' or 'down.' A level plain like this is something that *humans* like. You don't encounter it in the artifacts. You don't expect a gravity field close to one gee in a structure like this, either—complete with a breathable atmosphere. And look at that." She pointed to the ceiling, apparently kilometers above them. "You can see it's built of pentagonal segments. That's common to many Builder structures. So I think we're inside a dodecahedron, a shape you find over and over in Builder artifacts, and I think they just added a flat floor and air and gravity for the benefit of beings like us. I'm not sure this plain is anything like as big as it looks, either. You know the Builders can play tricks with space that confuse our sense of distance."

"They can. But I think this place is really big, no matter what tricks are being performed."

Hans Rebka had not raised his voice, but Darya's stomach tightened at the sudden tension in it. Hans was not supposed to get nervous. That was her privilege.

"It's certainly big," he went on, "if *that* is anything to judge by."

He was pointing off to their left. Darya at first saw nothing. Then she realized that above the twinkling sea of orange spangles shone the steadier light of a bright sphere. It was tiny at first, no more than a shiny marble of silver, but as she watched it grew steadily. It was advancing across the level plain, apparently at a constant speed. There was no way to judge its distance, or to tell if it was rolling or traveling by some other method.

"Welcoming committee," Rebka said, almost under his breath. "Everybody smile."

It was not rolling. Darya was somehow sure of that, even though she could see no signs of surface marking. She had the feeling that it was flying or floating, its bottom only a fraction of a millimeter above the orange cloud of sequins.

And it was not small at all. It was sizable. It was growing. It was *huge,* three times the size of The-One-Who-Waits. It towered over them, and still it was not close.

Twenty paces away it halted. A steady series of ripples moved across the spherical surface, like waves on a ball of mercury. As they grew in amplitude the globular form bulged up to form a stem. On top of it a familiar pentagonal flowerlike head drooped to face them. Five-sided disks were extruded from the front of the sphere, while a silver tail stretched down to moor the object to the floor. A flickering green light shone from a newly formed aperture in the central belly.

There was a long silence.

"All right, sweetie," Rebka said in a gruff whisper. "What now?"

"If this is like The-One-Who-Waits, it needs to hear us speak a few words before it can key in to our language." Darya raised her voice. "My name is Darya Lang, originally from the planet Sentinel Gate. This is Hans Rebka, from the planet Teufel. We are human, and we arrived from the star Mandel and the planet Gargantua. Are you like The-One-Who-Waits?"

There was a ten-second silence.

"One—Who—Waits," a groaning voice said. Its tone was deeper than that of the sphere on Glister, and it sounded even more tired. "The One Who . . . Waits. Human . . . human . . . hu-u-man . . . hmmm."

"Needs a pep pill," Rebka said softly. "Are you a Builder?" he called to the horned and tailed nightmare floating in front of them.

The being drifted a few paces closer. "Human, human, human, human . . . At last. You are here. But two are the same. Where is . . . the other?"

"The other," Rebka said. "What's it mean?"

Darya shook her head. "There is no other," she said loudly. "We do not understand. We are the only ones here. We ask again, are you like The-One-Who-Waits?"

The silver body was humming, with a low tone almost too deep for human ears. "There must be . . . another . . . or the arrival is not complete. We have two forms only . . . but the message said that the third one was on the way and would soon arrive . . ." There was another long silence. "I am not like The-One-Who-Waits, although we were created in the same way."

"Not a Builder," Darya said in a quick whisper. "I knew

it. We're seeing things that the Builders *made,* just like The-One-Who-Waits. Maybe some kind of computers, incredibly old. And I don't think that they're—well, that they're *working* quite right."

That was a new thought for Darya, and one hard to accept. Usually Builder artifacts seemed to perform as well after five million years as the day they were made. But The-One-Who-Waits, and now this new being, gave Darya an odd feeling of disorganization and randomness. Perhaps not even the Builders could make machines last forever.

"I am not . . . a computer." The being's hearing must have been more sensitive than a human's, or it was directly reading their minds. "I am Inorganic, but a grown Inorganic. The-One-Who-Waits stayed always close to Old-Home, but I was grown here. I am . . . I am . . . a *Speaker-Between.* An Interlocutor. The one who must . . . interface with you and the others. The task of The-One-Who-Waits is done. But the task of Speaker-Between cannot start until the third one is here." The weary voice was slowing, fading. "The third one. Then . . . the task of Speaker-Between can begin. Until then . . ."

The surface of the great silver body began to ripple. The five-sided flower on top was shortening.

"Hey! Speaker-Between! You can't stop there." Rebka ran forward across the surface, his shoes kicking up sprays of glittering orange. "And you can't leave us here. We're humans. Humans need food, and water, and air."

"That is known." The body was swelling at the base and descending toward the flat surface, while the silver tail withdrew into it. "Do not worry. The place has been prepared for your kind. Since the third is already on the way, you will have no need for stasis. Enter . . . and eat, drink, rest."

The silver globe of Speaker-Between had deformed to a bulging hemisphere with a wide arched aperture at the center. "Enter," the fading voice said again. The opening moved around to face the two humans. "Enter . . . now."

Rebka swore and backed away. "Don't go near it."

"No." Darya was moving forward. "I don't know what's

inside, but so far nothing here has tried to hurt us. If they wanted to kill us, they could have done it easily. Come on. What do we have to lose?"

"Other than our lives?" But he was following her.

The opening that they entered was filled with the green glow of hidden lights. From the outside it could have been of any depth. One step inside, and Darya realized that she was actually in a small entrance lock, three meters deep. When she went across to the inner door and pushed it aside, an open chamber with slate-gray, somber walls and a high ceiling was revealed.

Too high. She walked through and stared upward. Forty meters, to that arched, pentagonal center? It had to be at least that—which meant that she was in a room taller than the *outside* dimensions of Speaker-Between. And that was physically impossible. Before she could move there came a sighing, slithering noise. Sections of the chamber's level floor in front of her began to buckle and lift. Partitions and furniture grew upward, thrusting like strange plants through a soft, springy surface.

"A place prepared for *us?* I'm not so sure of that." Hans Rebka advanced cautiously past her, toward a cylindrical structure that was still emerging from the floor. It had a bulbous, rounded upper end, and it was supported on a cluster of splayed legs. "Now this is really interesting. It's a food-storage unit and food synthesizer. I've seen one like it, but not in use. It was in a *museum.*"

"It's not typical Builder technology."

"I'm sure it's not." An oddly perplexed expression crept into Rebka's eyes. "If I didn't know better, I'd start wondering . . ."

The top of the cylinder was surrounded by a thin fog, and a layer of ice crystals covered its surface. Rebka touched it cautiously with one fingertip, then jerked away.

"Freezing cold." He turned up the opacity level of his suit to provide thermal insulation and reached out with a protected hand to pull a curved lever set into the upper part of the cylinder. It moved reluctantly to a new position. Part of the cylinder body turned, revealing the interior. Three shelves stood inside, loaded with sealed white packages.

"You're the biologist, Darya. Do you recognize any of these?" Rebka reached in and quickly lifted out a handful of flat packages and smooth ovoids, placing them on the saucer-like beveled top of the cylinder. "Don't touch them with your bare hand or you may get frostbite. They're really cold. We can't eat yet, but you can tell your stomach we may be getting close."

Darya set her suit gauntlet to full opacity and peeled open a rounded packet. It was a fruit, mottled green and yellow, with a thin rind and a fleshy stalk at one end. She turned it over, examining texture and density and scraping a thin sliver from the surface, then allowed the gauntlet to heat it. When it grew warm in her hand she sniffed it, tasted it, and shook her head.

"Fruit aren't my line, but I've never seen anything like this before. And I don't think I've ever read anything about it, either. It could be from an Alliance world, but it's not a popular fruit, because they tend to be grown everywhere. Do you really think it's edible?"

"If it's not, why would they have stored it here? I'm using your logic, Darya—if they want to kill us, they can find easier ways. I think we can eat this, and the other food. Speaker-Between didn't seem too happy to see the two of us, because it was expecting something else. But we're part of the show, too. We have to be fed and watered. And you don't bring somebody thirty thousand light-years and then let them accidentally poison themselves. My worry is a bit different." He rapped the bulging side of the cylinder. "I know construction methods in the Phemus Circle and the Fourth Alliance, and I've been exposed to the way they do things in the Cecropia Federation. But this isn't like any of them. It's—"

He was interrupted by the creaking sound of long-neglected hinges. Thirty meters away, the whole side of the room was sinking ponderously into the floor. Beyond it stood another chamber, even larger, with a long bank of objects like outsized coffins at its center.

Darya counted fourteen units, each one a pentagonal cylinder seven meters long, four wide, and four high.

"Now those *are* Builder technology," she said. "Very definitely. Remember Flambeau, near the boundary between the Alliance and the Cecropia Federation? That artifact is filled with units just like this, a lot of them even bigger. They're all empty, but they're in working order."

"What do they do? I've never seen anything like these before." Rebka was walking cautiously forward toward the nearest of the fourteen. Each of the monster coffins had a transparent port mounted in its pentagonal end. He put his face close to it, rubbed at the dusty surface with his gauntleted hand, and peered in.

"No one is sure what they were intended for *originally.*" Darya rapped the side of the unit, and it produced a hollow booming sound. "But we know they can be used to preserve things pretty much indefinitely—objects, or organisms—and we assume that was their main purpose. There's a stasis field inside each unit, externally controlled. You can see the settings on the end there. Clock rates in the interior have been measured for the Flambeau units, and they run an average of sixty million times slower than outside. Spend a century in one of those stasis tanks, and if you remained conscious you'd feel as though one minute had passed."

Rebka did not seem to be listening. He was still poised with his face against the port.

She tapped his shoulder. "Hey, Hans. Come up for air. What's so fascinating in there? Let me take a peek."

She moved to his side. The stasis tank did not seem to be empty, but its inside was almost dark. Darya could see vague outlines, but for details she would have to wait a couple of minutes until her eyes had adjusted to the interior light level.

She took his arm and squeezed it. "Can you see what's in there? Come on, if it's interesting don't keep me in suspense."

Still he did not speak, but at Darya's words and touch he finally turned to face her.

She looked at his twitching face, and her grip on his arm slackened. Her hand dropped to her side.

Nothing shocked Hans Rebka. Nothing ever touched his iron self-control.

Except that now the control had gone. And behind his eyes lurked an unreasoning terror that Darya had never expected to see.

CHAPTER 16

AFTER ATVAR H'SIAL had knocked Julius Graves headlong into Birdie Kelly, broken the connection between E. C. Tally's brain and body, and sent J'merlia rolling and spinning into the pattern of concentric rings, Louis Nenda did not hesitate.

As the Cecropian went scuttling out of the chamber, wing cases wide open, Nenda followed at once.

Let the mess back there sort itself out!

He was cursing—silently. It was no use shouting. Atvar H'sial had astonishing hearing, but she did not understand human speech. And his own pheromonal augment was worthless when she was in full flight, because the necessary molecules had no chance to diffuse into her receptors.

The near-darkness of Glister's interior made no difference to Atvar H'sial. Her echolocation vision worked as well in pitch blackness as in bright sunlight; but it made things hellishly difficult for Louis Nenda. A Cecropian did not care where she moved, into chambers light or dark, just so long as there was air to carry sound waves. But *he* sure cared. He was bouncing off dark walls, tangling in nets, tripping over loose cables, diving down steep slopes without any idea what he would meet at the bottom. And all the time he had not the slightest idea where she was heading. He doubted that she knew it herself.

Enough of this, he thought.

He slowed down after a particularly bruising collision with an invisible partition. It would be too easy to knock himself out, and he could not afford that.

The good news was that he could track her, infallibly. The Zardalu augment had been designed for pheromonal speech, with all its subtleties, so simply following another's scent through Glister's sterile interior was ridiculously easy. Even if she crossed and recrossed her own path, the strength of the trail would show him exactly where she had gone.

The corridors of Glister turned and twisted, apparently at random. He patiently followed the unmistakable airborne molecules of Cecropian physiology, turn by turn, wherever they led. The only thing he could be sure of was that they were descending, following a gravity gradient to regions of steadily increasing field. But the stronger field increased the danger of injury from a fall. He slowed his pace still further, confident that Atvar H'sial could not get away from him. As he walked he began to make plans.

One word with Graves had been enough to convince him that telling the truth to the councilor would be a terrible idea. He had fought back his own initial urge on awakening— violent flight—because Atvar H'sial was still trapped in the Lotus field. At that point it had made sense to blame the field itself and "forget" anything that had happened back on Quake.

Of course, he remembered it all perfectly: the wild ascent from the planet's surface, the capture of the *Have-It-All* by the dark sphere, the giddy plunge through space, their arrival at Gargantua and the little planetoid that orbited it—and, finally, the release of the ship onto the surface, while the sphere that had captured and held them moved inside. He had been aware of events right up to the moment on the planetoid's surface when the orange cloud surged up around them. He even had a vague memory after that, of being carried down, down, down through multiple levels of the interior. Then came a blank, until he had wakened to find Julius Graves crouched over him.

Graves's mention of the Lotus field allowed him to piece together most of the rest. He and Atvar H'sial had been locked in the field—but *why,* when it would have made more sense just to kill them—until the others had come along. And finally that crazy robot with the human body and pop-top skull case had dredged them out.

Pity that Atvar H'sial had run wild before E. C. Tally had been able to get Kallik, too. Nenda missed his Hymenopt servant. No matter. There was plenty of time for Tally to pull Kallik free now—if ever they could stick Tally's popout brain back in his dumb head and connect it so it worked.

Louis Nenda paused. He was standing in an unlit passageway, but the pheromonal scent was increasing in strength. He concentrated and generated his own message, sending it diffusing out from his chest nodules. "Atvar H'sial? Where are you? I can't see you—you gotta steer me in."

As usual, he found it easiest to speak his message at the same time as it was generated chemically. It was not necessary to identify himself. If the Cecropian received any message at all, Nenda's individual molecular signature would be built into it.

"I am here. Wait." The messenger molecules drifted in through the darkness. A few seconds later, Atvar H'sial's hard claw took Nenda's hand. "Follow. Tell me if the thermal source ahead is also for you a source of seeing radiation."

"Why'd you take off like that?" Nenda allowed himself to be led through the darkness, until he saw a glimmer of light ahead. "Why didn't you wait until they got Kallik out? She's my Hymenopt—she shouldn't be doin' work for them."

"Just as J'merlia is mine, and he should not be serving humans. But he is." The Cecropian led them into a long rectangular room, warmed and dimly lit by a uniform ruddy glow from the walls. "The failure to recover J'merlia and

Kallik is, I agree, regrettable, but I judged it necessary. As soon as I became conscious I smelled danger to you and me. Councilor Graves was dominant in that group. He had a clear intention to restrict our freedom at once. I was not sure we could prevent that. With an imperfect understanding of events, it is always better to remain unimpeded in one's actions. Therefore, we had to escape."

"How'd you know I'd follow you?"

There was no explicit message of reply, but the chemical messengers of grim humor wafted to Nenda's chest receptors.

"All right, At. So I don't like the idea of being locked up, any more than you do. What now? We're not safe. Graves and the rest of them can come after us anytime. J'merlia can track you, easy as I could. We're still in deep stuff."

"I do not disagree." The Cecropian crouched in front of Nenda, lowering herself so that the blind white head was on a level with his. The open yellow trumpet horns quivered on either side of the eyeless face. "We must pool information, Louis Nenda, before we make a decision. I lack data items that you perhaps gained from Julius Graves. For example, where are we now? Why were we brought here? How much time did we spend unconscious? And where is our ship, the *Have-It-All*, and is it in working condition for our escape?"

"I can take a shot at answering some of those."

Nenda rubbed at his cheek and chin as he provided Atvar H'sial with a summary of his own experiences since waking from the Lotus field. There was a three- or four-day stubble there, but that did not tell him much; he had no idea how fast hair grew inside the field. Some of what he told Atvar H'sial had to be guesswork.

"So if you believe Graves," he concluded, "we're still inside a hollow planetoid, goin' round Gargantua. Same one as we were brought to after Summertide, for a bet. Graves says he's got no more idea than we have as to *why* we were dragged here, or why we were stuck in the middle of that room like two drugged flies. You can be damn sure it wasn't done for our benefit, though. I don't know how long we were held there. Enough for Graves and the rest of 'em to get their hands on a ship after Summertide and fly it out to Gargantua.

Don't ask me where that computer with the strung-out brain-box came from. I never saw him before, or anything like him. Mebbe they brought him from Opal. I think they went back there before they started for here, because Birdie Kelly is with 'em, too."

"I registered Kelly's presence. Do not worry about him. Graves is the principal danger; also perhaps the embodied computer, but not Birdie Kelly."

"Yeah. And Graves told me he wants to take us back home and charge us with lethal assault. He'll do his best to keep us in one piece till then, otherwise he'd never have stopped me going back into the Lotus field for Kallik. Graves seems pretty sure he *can* take us back for trial, so there has to be at least one ship available—the one they came in, or the *Have-It-All,* or maybe both of 'em. We should be able to escape, if we can just find our way back to the surface."

The great blind head was nodding, a foot from Nenda's face. "Very good, Louis. So I have one more question: *When* should we choose to escape?"

"As soon as we can. It won't be more than a couple of hours before Graves is on our trail again. Why hang around?"

"For one excellent reason." Atvar H'sial swept a jointed forelimb in a long arc, covering the room they stood in. "Examine. I have not had time for a complete survey, but as I moved through the chambers of this planetoid I saw evidence of Builder technology unlike anything known to the spiral arm. This is a treasure house, a cornucopia of new equipment with a value too great to estimate. It can be ours, Louis."

Nenda reached out and patted the Cecropian's wrinkled proboscis. "Good old At. You never give up, do you? Ever. And people tell me I'm the greedy one. Got any ideas how we prevent interference from Graves?"

"Some. But first things first." Atvar H'sial unfolded her legs and rose to her full height. "If profit is to be maximized, this must be treated as a multistage endeavor. We will need great capital to exploit this planetoid, and we must plan to return here when we have suitable financing. To obtain that, before we leave we must select a few items of machinery and equipment, small and light enough to take with us for trade to the richest worlds of the spiral arm. I could do that, but you are more experienced. And as soon as we have decided what to take, we must evade Julius Graves and his group, and leave."

"Then we'd better get a move on, before they come looking." Nenda reached out to grasp one of the Cecropian's forelimbs, hoisting himself to his feet. "You're right, I do like to price goodies. 'Specially when I know I won't be paying for 'em. Let's go to it, At, and pick 'em out."

After the first few minutes Louis Nenda was willing to admit Cecropian superiority for the exploration of Glister. He could see dead ends easily enough, when the light level permitted. But Atvar H'sial, with her sensitive sonar and echolocation, could "see" around bends in corridors, and know ahead of time when she was approaching a large open area. And she did so just as well in total darkness.

Nenda did not bother after a while to peer ahead. He focused on what he was best at, walking behind Atvar H'sial and making a mental catalog of novel equipment and artifacts as they came to them. There was plenty of choice. In less than half an hour he reached forward and tapped her carapace.

"I think we're done. I've tagged a dozen portable items, an' I don't think we can handle more than that."

Atvar H'sial halted and the white head turned. "You are the expert on salable commodities; but I would like to hear your list."

"All right. I'll give 'em in order, top choice first. That little water-maker in the second room we looked at. Remember it? No sign of a power source, no sign of a supply. But five hundred cubic meters a minute of clean water production. You could name your own price for a few of them on Xerarchos or Siccity, or any of the dust worlds."

"I agree. It was also a leading item on my own list. Do you know its mass?"

"I can lift it, that's all I care about. Then for number-two choice, I liked that cubical box on gimbals three chambers back, the one with the open top and a blue haze over it."

"Indeed? I observed that object. But I found nothing remarkable about it."

"That's because you don't see using light. When I looked down into the open top I could see stars. But when I turned the box on the gimbals, I was looking at Gargantua, right through the planetoid. It's an all-direction see-through—let's you look at distant objects and not be bothered by near ones. It'd be marvelous for ship navigation in dust clouds.

"My number-three choice is harder to justify. The sphere, the one that was floating, not attached to anything, in the room we just left."

"To my viewing it appeared entirely featureless."

"To me, too. But it was a lot cooler than everything around it."

"Which should be physically impossible."

"That's why we want it. Impossible gadgets are always the most valuable. I've no idea how it works, an' I don't care. But I can tell you a dozen places that would pay a lot for it, looking to maybe find a closed infinite heat sink. Number four—"

"Enough. I am persuaded. I accept your list. But there is one more thing that I would like to do, before we collect the items of choice and seek egress from the planetoid." Atvar H'sial motioned in front of her with one forelimb. The yellow horns faced ahead, open as wide as they would go and scanning slowly from side to side. "There is another chamber ahead; a huge, open one, possessing anomalous acoustical properties. At certain frequencies, it appears completely empty. At others, I detect a spherical object at its center."

"You think we might find something specially valuable? No point taking risks, just to be nosy."

"I cannot estimate the value. I will only say that an object transparent at certain acoustic frequencies is as potentially valuable to Cecropian society as glass, transparent to certain frequencies of light, is to humans. I know exactly where we could sell such a discovery. To me, it might be the most precious thing on this world."

Atvar H'sial was advancing slowly as she spoke, to a place where the tunnel ended in a blind drop. Nenda moved to her side and took a look down. After one startled glance he swore and stepped back. She had an indifference to heights that came from her remote flying ancestors, but he did not share it. They were on the brink of a twenty-meter drop, slowly curving away below to a bowl-shaped floor.

Atvar H'sial was pointing to the middle of the chamber. "There. Do you sense anything with your eyes?"

"Yeah. It's a silver sphere." Nenda took another step back. "I don't like this, At. We oughta get out of here."

"In one moment. To my senses, that sphere is *changing*. Do you observe it, also?"

Nenda, set to retreat, stood and stared in spite of himself.

Atvar H'sial was right. The sphere was changing while he watched. And in a way that tricked the eye. The whole surface began to ripple, like oscillations on a ball of mercury. Those vibrations became a pattern of standing waves, growing in amplitude until they changed the whole shape. A five-sided flowerlike head was sprouting above, while a slender barbed tail extended down toward the floor of the chamber.

Ahh. A sighing voice echoed through the whole chamber. *Ahhh. At last.*

A green light flickered from an aperture in the deformed sphere's center. It shone on Atvar H'sial, lighting up the crouched, insectile form and great blind head. Louis hid away behind her.

At last, the voice said again. It sounded as old as time itself. A strange, pungent aroma came drifting across the room. *At last . . . we can begin. You are here. The testing is complete. The duties of The-One-Who-Waits are ending, and the selection process can begin. Are you ready?*

The creature poised in the center of the chamber was unlike anything that Louis Nenda had met in thirty years of travel around the spiral arm. But what was Atvar H'sial seeing? The Cecropian seemed frozen, her long antennas unfurled and bristling. The being in the middle of the chamber had been partially invisible to her sonar. Did she see it at all now, and recognize the danger?

"At!" Nenda sent the pheromonal signal with maximum urgency. "I don't know if you're getting the same message as

I am from that thing, but believe me, we're in trouble. It wants us. Don't reply to me, just back up."

You are the form, the voice was saying, and the green light had focused on the Cecropian. *The third awaited form. Do not move*—Atvar H'sial had finally taken a step backward, bumping into Louis Nenda—*the transition is ready to begin.*

Louis Nenda reached forward, grabbing one of the Cecropian's forelimbs. "At! No messing about. Let's get out of here!" He turned and took one step.

Too late.

Before his second step the floor vanished. He was falling freely, plummeting down a vertical shaft. He looked down. Nothing, only darkness that baffled the eye. He looked up. Above him was Atvar H'sial, wing cases fully extended, vestigial wings wide open, all six legs tensed. She was poised for a hard landing—on top of Louis Nenda.

He looked down again, seeking the bottom of the shaft. He could not see a thing, but given the small size of the planetoid, the end of the fall had to be no more than a second or two away.

And then what? Nothing pleasant, that was for sure.

Nenda fell and swore. Hindsight was wonderful. They had been a little bit too greedy. He and Atvar H'sial should have left when they could, as soon as they had picked out all they needed.

He stared down into a rolling, viscous blackness and had time for a final thought: They would have been better off staying with Julius Graves. At the moment, a formal trial for lethal assault seemed positively inviting.

CHAPTER 17

WHEN LOUIS NENDA and Atvar H'sial went scurrying into the darkness, Birdie Kelly was not at all sorry to see the back of them. Graves might want to arrest the pair, but the Karelian human Nenda had always struck Birdie as crude and violent, and the silent, winged Cecropian gave him the creeps.

Good riddance to both. Birdie pushed Julius Graves off him, struggled to his feet, and looked around.

Things were a mess. He was not sure where to begin.

Graves was winded and gasping for breath, but otherwise he seemed all right. Birdie ignored him. Kallik was unconscious, lying on the floor halfway to the center of the room, and Birdie could do nothing for her.

The body of E. C. Tally, a little closer, was in the worst shape. It lay motionless, with the cable trailing from the bleeding head and ending in a bare plug a few feet from where

Birdie stood. There was nothing to be done for Tally, either, because his body was deep in the Lotus field.

Birdie looked for J'merlia. The Lo'tfian was lying on the curved floor, just inside the pattern of concentric rings, and he was still holding E. C. Tally's disconnected brain firmly in two of his forelimbs. If he had been knocked out, too, or affected by the Lotus field . . .

But as Birdie watched, J'merlia began to move, crawling out toward the perimeter of the outer circle. Birdie took the loose end of the neural connect cable and went around to meet him.

"Where is Atvar H'sial?" J'merlia asked as soon as he crossed the boundary of the yellow ring.

"Ran for it. With Louis Nenda. We'll worry about them later. Here." Birdie held out the connector. "Turn Tally's brain around this way, and let's see if we can plug him in again."

The connection was supposed to be handled delicately, but it had been yanked free with great force. Now the neural bundles refused to mesh easily into position. The plug slipped out of the socket when it was released. Birdie knew nothing about the care and maintenance of embodied computers, but he said a prayer, placed the connector into position again, and pushed—this time a lot harder.

Down on the curved bowl of the floor, the body of E. C. Tally jerked and spasmed. There was a grunt and a *whoosh*, of lungs violently expelling air.

"Tally!" J'merlia called. "Can you hear me?"

The battered figure with its bloody head was on hands and knees, struggling to stand up. It failed on half a dozen tries, supporting itself on its bruised forearms each time it fell forward. At last the body stayed upright.

"I hee-ar . . . poo-erly." The speech was garbled. "It is diffigult . . . to speag. Some of my gonnegtor interfaces were des-troyed when they were pulled out. Others are . . . de-graded. I am seeging to gompensate. Do not worry, I was designed with high-cirguit redundancy. I am . . . improving. I will be all right. I will be *fine.*"

Birdie was not so sure. As Tally said those last words, he had fallen flat on his face again.

"Take it *slowly,* E.C. We have plenty of time."

"Brr-err," E. C. Tally replied. "Grarr-erff." But he was making progress. He was standing again, shaky but upright. As Birdie and J'merlia watched, he took two tentative steps— in exactly the wrong direction.

"No. E.C.!" Birdie shouted. "Wrong way. Come toward the outside. You're heading for the middle of the room."

"I am well . . . aware of that." The head turned slowly, to look back at them. The voice was reproving. "Since it will be necessary at some point to retrieve the Hymenopt Gallig, surely it is more efficient to do so now, and thereby egonomize on both time and motion."

E. C. Tally was improving all right, Birdie thought—if a return to his usual wrongheadedness could be considered an improvement. But he carefully paid out neural cable while Tally limped forward until he reached Kallik. Blood streamed from the open skull as Tally bent down and laboriously cradled the little Hymenopt in his arms.

"We are goming out now. Prepare to restore me . . . to the granial gavity, as soon as I reach you. Sensory inputs via the gonnegt gable are degenerating. Please geep talging, so that I gan sense your diregtion. I gan no longer see."

"This way—this way—this way—" J'merlia called, but he did not wait. When Tally was still inside the yellow ring the Lo'tfian rushed forward, took part of Kallik's weight, and led the way back to Birdie Kelly. As Kallik was released, E. C. Tally groaned and sank to the floor beside her.

"Quickly." Julius Graves had finally recovered his wind enough to be helpful. He was removing the bandage from Tally's skull. "Steven says that there will be permanent damage if an impaired neural connector is used for more than a minute or two. We are close to that limit already."

As the bandage came off Birdie turned the cranium on its hinged flap. "All right, E.C., here we go. We'll have you back on-line in a few seconds.

"Now!" he said to J'merlia, who stood ready. The connector came free of the disembodied brain, at the same moment as Birdie pulled the cable out of the hindbrain socket. Tally's body slumped against Birdie. The blue eyes closed.

Julius Graves took the short connecting spiral of the computer's hindbrain connection and set it carefully into its usual position. There was a brief spasm of Tally's limbs, but before anyone had time to worry the eyes had flickered open.

"Very good," E. C. Tally said. "We suffered a loss of interface for only two-point-four seconds. All sensory and motor functions appear to be normal. Now, the closing of the cranial cavity is something that I prefer to do for myself. So if you do not mind—"

He reached up, pushed away Graves's supporting hands, and grasped the open top of the skull. He turned it backward on its hinge. Birdie, standing behind him, had another quick view of a red network of blood vessels in the skull's lining; then the cranium tilted to fit snugly over the protective membranes of Tally's spherical brain. Tally exerted vertical pressure. There was a faint click. The skull was again a battered but seamless whole.

As E. C. Tally calmly reached up a forearm to wipe blood from his eyes, the other three could begin to attend to other worries. Birdie realized that Kallik was conscious and silently watching.

"Are you feeling all right?"

The Hymenopt shook her head. "Physically, I am functioning normally. But mentally, I am very confused. Confused as to how I came to be here, but even more as to how *you* come to be here. The last thing I remember was going down there." She pointed toward the center of the chamber. "My master was at the center. Now he has vanished, and so has Atvar H'sial. Where are they?"

"Good question." Birdie was automatically coiling up the neural cable. Old habits of neatness died hard. "J'merlia, can you bring Kallik up to date, while the rest of us decide where we go from here?"

He turned to Julius Graves. "I'm not in charge, never have been. But I want to find Professor Lang and Captain Rebka as much as you do, and help them if they need help. And I know you want to get your hands on Nenda and that Cecropian, and give 'em what's due. But don't you think it's time we forgot all that and started acting rational? I mean, like getting out of here and going someplace where we know what's happening to us."

Listening to himself, Birdie was amazed at his own nerve. Here he was, a real nobody, telling a representative of the central council what he ought to do. But Graves did not seem annoyed. The bald head was nodding slowly, and the radiation-scarred face wore a serious expression.

"Commissioner Kelly, I cannot argue with you. You, as well as J'merlia, Kallik, and E. C. Tally, have been drawn into a situation of great danger, for no better reason than my desire to bring Louis Nenda and Atvar H'sial to justice, and to satisfy my own curiosity. That is unfair, and it is also unreasonable. I intend to continue to explore Glister. I hope to find Nenda and H'sial, and also Hans Rebka and Darya Lang. But that is not your responsibility. As of this moment you are officially relieved. You, E. C. Tally, J'merlia, and Kallik are all free to return to the surface. Take the *Summer Dreamboat,* go back to Opal, and report. Leave the other ship for my use, and for the others if I can find and rescue them."

It was a better answer than Birdie dreamed of getting. He stood to attention. "Yes, *sir!* Kallik, J'merlia. E.C.? All ready to go?"

But the embodied computer was shaking his head. "Go, Birdie Kelly, as soon as you are prepared. However, I cannot accompany you. I was sent to the Dobelle system with a mission: find out what happened at Summertide, and learn why Captain Rebka and the others elected to remain there afterward. Full answers have not been provided, and my query registers remain unfulfilled. I must go with Councilor Graves."

Which left the two aliens. Even as Birdie turned to them, he suspected that he was going to be disappointed. Kallik was hopping up and down, emitting the chirps and whistles that told of high excitement.

"The masters are alive! The masters are alive! J'merlia says that they are conscious, and somewhere within Glister. Honored humans, please grant us permission to seek them and offer again our services."

"You still want to go after those two crooks?" Birdie did not have much hope after that speech, but he tried. "Kallik, they deserted you and J'merlia and left you to die on Quake. They ran away from you here, when you were still stuck in the Lotus field with no idea when or how you'd get out. They don't care what happens to you. You don't owe them anything."

"But they are the *masters!* Our true and wonderful and only masters." Kallik turned to Graves. "Revered Councilor, please grant us permission to accompany you. We will obey any orders that you choose to give us. Let Commissioner Kelly go home—but please do not send us with him to Opal. Let us remain with you and seek the masters."

Hearing her, and looking at J'merlia and E. C. Tally, Birdie had his own moment of truth. They were all suggesting that he should try to fly—*alone*—through that blizzard of murderous Phages. Without Kallik to help as navigator, his survival chances were close to zero. And then if by some fluke he did make it, he would have to fly all the way to Opal facing the bitter fact of his own lack of courage.

What a choice: a fool, or a coward. And the coward had a near-certain chance of being killed as he tried to fly away from Glister. Birdie might be safer here.

He sighed. "I was just joking. I'd rather find out what happened to the others. Lead on, Councilor. We're all in this together."

"Wonderful. I am glad you will stay. You are a great asset." Graves gave him an admiring smile.

Birdie cringed. If there was one thing worse than being a coward, it was being mistaken for a hero.

Kallik's lonely wandering through the interior of Glister before the others arrived was paying off. As she moved the Hymenopt had mapped out in her head a rough plan of many of the chambers and corridors. She already knew that the lower levels were high-gee environments, unsuitable for human or Cecropian habitation. And she was also fairly sure that there was no way they could reach the surface, other than the one she had created with the field inhibitor. To reach that, Nenda and Atvar H'sial would have to pass again through the chamber with the Lotus field. Since they had not done so, they must still be somewhere in the lower levels of Glister's interior.

Julius Graves led the way, followed by the two aliens. Tally was next, still holding the reel of neural cable that Birdie had rewound. There might be no more Lotus fields in the interior—Kallik knew of none—but it was best to take precautions.

Birdie came last. The rear was no safer than anywhere else, but he wanted to be alone to think. He was still brooding over his decision to stay on Glister. He had blown it. It had occurred to him, too late, that he ought at least to have gone back to the surface and taken a *look* at what was going on there. For all he knew, the Phages had wandered away to seek other targets. He might have had a clear ride home. And even if they had not gone, he could have come back here and been no worse off than he was now.

They had been descending steadily, through a succession of corridors, sliding ramps, and chambers of all shapes and sizes. At this point Birdie was not sure he could find his own way back, but that did not matter too much because E. C. Tally would have every turn and twist recorded in his inorganic data banks.

Birdie bumped suddenly into the back of the embodied computer. Graves, in front of the others, had paused, and Birdie had not been paying attention.

The councilor turned. "Something is ahead." His deep, hollow voice was reduced to a hoarse whisper. "There are peculiar sounds. You wait here. J'merlia and I will proceed. We will return in five minutes or less. If we do not, Commissioner Kelly will be in charge of all subsequent actions."

He was gone before Birdie could object. *All subsequent actions.* He was being promoted from peon to president, with no idea what he ought to do. "How do I know when five minutes is up?" he asked E. C. Tally.

"I will keep you informed. My internal clock is accurate to

the femtosecond." Tally held up one grimy finger. "Since Councilor Graves's final words to you it is exactly . . . forty-six seconds. Forty-seven. Forty-eight. Forty-nine. Fifty."

"Stop that, E.C. I can't think when you keep on counting."

"Indeed? How strange. I have no such trouble. I offer condolences for your restriction to serial processing."

"Talking like that is just as bad. Keep quiet. Just tell me when it's every minute."

"Very well, Commissioner. But one minute has already passed."

"So tell me when it's two." Birdie turned to Kallik. "You have better ears than we do. Did you hear any sounds from in front of us?"

Kallik paused to reflect. "Sounds, yes," she said at last. "But nothing remotely human. Wheezing, and groaning. Like a venting Dowser."

"Now come on, Kallik. There can't possibly be a Dowser here—it would fill up the whole planetoid. Were there any *words?*"

"Possibly. Not in a language that I am able to comprehend. But J'merlia is a far better linguist than I am, perhaps you should ask him."

"He's not here—he's with Graves."

"When he returns."

"But if he returns, I won't need—"

"Two minutes," Tally said loudly. "May I speak?"

"My God, E.C., what now? I told you to keep quiet. Oh, go on then, spit it out."

"I am concerned by our immediate environment. As you may know, the functioning of my brain requires shielding from electromagnetic fields. As a result, the protective membranes contain sensitive field monitors. The corridor in which we are standing contains evidence of field inhibitors, and that evidence becomes stronger the farther that we go."

"So what? Don't you think we have more important things to worry about?"

"No. Assuming that the field inhibitors are functional, and that the interior structure of Glister relies upon the same methods as the surface for its stability, we would experience a significant change in environment were the field inhibitors to be turned on. As they could be, at any time."

"Change of environment. What do you mean, a change of environment?"

"In simple terms, we would fall through the floor. After that, I cannot say. I have no information as to what lies below. But let me observe that the outer parts of Glister average fifty meters between successive interior layers. A fifty-meter drop in this high a gravity field would render everyone of our party inoperative, with the possible exception of Kallik."

"Gawdy!" Birdie stepped sharply backward and stared down at his feet. "A fifty-meter fall? We'd all be mushed."

Before he could say more there was a patter of multiple feet in the tunnel ahead of them. J'merlia came scuttling back.

"It is all right," he said excitedly. "Councilor Graves says that it is safe to move forward to join him. He is in conversation with a being who dwells within Glister. It can converse in human speech—and it knows the present whereabouts of Atvar H'sial and Louis Nenda! It means us no harm, and we are in no danger. Please follow me."

"Now hold on a minute. And you, too, Kallik." Birdie grabbed the short fur on the back of the Hymenopt, restraining her—though if she had decided to go, nothing he or any human could have done would have stopped her. "You can tell us we're safe, J'merlia, but that's not what E.C. says—according to him, the tunnel floor could dissolve underneath us, any time. We'd all fall through and be killed. The farther we go, the worse it gets. Can't whoever it is wait just a bit, while we check if we're safe?"

"I do not know." J'merlia stood thinking for a moment, his narrow head cocked to one side.

"I suppose it can," he said at last. "After all, it's been waiting for six million years. Maybe a few minutes more won't matter too much."

From the internal files of the embodied computer E. Crimson Tally: A note for the permanent and public record, concerning new anomalies of human behavior.

A recent experience leads me to suspect that the information banks employed in the briefing of embodied computers are so flawed in their representation of human reactions that their data are not merely useless but positively pernicious.

My observation is prompted by this recent experience:

After the removal and reinsertion of my brain, it was not clear to me that I would be able to perform at my previous level. Although my brain itself of course functioned as well as ever, the body's condition was obviously physically degraded. Moreover, I believed that my interface was impaired, although I knew that I was not the best judge of that.

Tests would easily have confirmed or denied the hypothesis of reduced function. However, without any procedures for performance evaluation, the humans of the group have treated me with noticeably *increased* respect following the event of brain removal and subsequent violent interruption of the interface.

Logic suggests only one explanation. Namely, the presence of a bloodied bandage around my head, which to any rational being warns of reduced function, has been taken instead as an *elevator* of status. Physical damage in humans demands increased respect. The more battered my skull, the greater the deference with which I am treated!

One wonders to what extremes this might be carried. If the top of my head were missing permanently, would all my actions be increasingly venerated?

Probably.

And if I were to be destroyed completely?

This matter demands introspection.

CHAPTER 18

BIRDIE HAD WORKED twenty-six and a half years—which felt like forever—for the government of Opal. Based on that, he had often said that humans were the most ornery, crackpot, cuss-headed critters in the universe.

But he would not say it anymore. There were others, he had just decided, who had humans beat for madness, from here to Doomsday.

They had been standing at the end of the tunnel, over a horrible sheer drop into nothing. And there was Julius Graves, with that big bald head of his, leaning out over the edge looking at a thing like a big silver teapot, with a flower for a spout, floating on nothing. And Julius, or maybe it was Steven, was *talking* to it, as if it were his long-lost brother.

"I do not follow your meaning, The-One-Who-Waits," he said. "This is our first visit. We have never been here before."

And the teapot had talked back!

Not at first, though. First it made a noise that sounded to

Birdie like a set of bagpipes that needed pumping up. Then it wheezed. Then it screeched like a steam blower. Then it said, imitating Graves's accent, "Not you, the individuals. That was not my meaning. You, the *species.*"

Which seemed to make no more sense to Graves than it did to Birdie, because the councilor had wrinkled up his bulging bald head and said, "Our *species* has been here before?"

There was another groan, like the sound made by a dying Dowser—Kallik had been right about that. Then: "The necessary members of your species came here. We had more than were needed. One would have been sufficient. But three humans came, including the one with the special additions."

At that Kallik gave a screech right in Birdie's ear, louder than anything the teapot-creature had produced. "Additions!" she said. "Augmentation. That must mean the master Nenda. He was here, and he is still alive."

The-One-Who-Waits must have understood her, because it went on. "One with augmentation, yes, alive, and there was also a necessary one of the *other* form, the great blind one with the secret speech. She, too, was passed along."

And that set J'merlia off, as bad as Kallik. "Oh, Atvar H'sial," he said, grabbing Birdie's arm and moaning the Cecropian name like a hymn. "Oh, Atvar H'sial. Alive. Commissioner Kelly, is that not wonderful news?"

Birdie chose not to answer. It seemed to him that the survival of any bug was no big deal, and especially one that had used J'merlia as a slave. But he was learning fast. Lo'tfians and Hymenopts had their own weird rules of what was important.

J'merlia's wails had not put The-One-Who-Waits off its stride for a minute. The teapot spout opened a bit more at the end, and the body quivered a little bit. Then it said, "So sufficient was already passed along. The three species are here. Your further presence is unnecessary. We will set in motion a safe passage for all of you to your homeworlds."

It seemed a bit early to start doing handstands and breaking out the liquor, but those words were still the best thing that Birdie had heard since they left Opal. Safe passage to their homeworlds—they were all going home! If The-One-

Who-Waits had not been hanging five steps away in the middle of nothing, Birdie would have been tempted to hang around its neck and kiss it.

But then came the worst bit, the thing that Birdie could not believe. J'merlia and Kallik stepped forward and set up a wailing and a chittering and a whistling enough to deafen. "No, no, that cannot be. We must follow the masters. You must pass us along also. We cannot return without the masters."

That had finally seemed to put The-One-Who-Waits off a bit. It made a horrible throat-, stomach-, and bowel-clearing noise. "Is it your wish to be passed along also? Is that the meaning of your words?"

Birdie decided that sitting around waiting for six million years must leave one none too bright. But Kallik and J'merlia did not seem to agree. "It is, it is," they piped up. "Pass us along, it is our fondest desire. Pass us along."

"Such an action is possible," The-One-Who-Waits admitted. "It presents no difficulties, although the transit time cannot of course be exactly predicted. But for the others, the three humans, a safe passage to your homeworlds . . ."

This was it! "Yes!" Birdie said. "To our home—"

"No," Julius Graves said before Birdie could get out another word. "Not me. That would be totally inappropriate. My task is not complete. I must determine what happened to Professor Lang and Captain Rebka. And I must seek to arrest Louis Nenda and Atvar H'sial and return them to the Alliance for justice. Pass me along also, if you would be so kind."

It had to be one of the most stupid statements that Birdie had ever heard in his whole life. Atvar H'sial and Louis Nenda had been shipped off to nowhere, with any luck all the way to hell, and instead of saying bye-bye, good riddance, and let's all go home, Julius Graves wanted to chase after them!

"Then—" The-One-Who-Waits said. But it had waited a second too long. E. C. Tally jumped in.

"May I speak? I cannot possibly return to Sol with my own task so incomplete. I was charged to learn what happened at Summertide, and why. I am no nearer to an answer now than the day I left the tank on Persephone. Logic suggests that the

answer must involve the actions of Atvar H'sial and Louis
Nenda. It is appropriate that I also be 'given passage,' whatever that expression may signify, to join the others."

That confirmed Birdie's view that E. C. Tally was a robotic
idiot. If the embodied computer was half as smart as he ought
to be, he would have headed for home and made up some
yarn about Summertide when he got there. Any six-year-old
on Opal could have managed that. But Tally must have had
bad training, so he only knew how to tell the truth.

When J'merlia and Kallik moved forward, Birdie had been
left at the back of the group. Now he stepped to the front, too
close to the edge for comfort. He knew just what he wanted—
to be sent to Opal, home, and beauty, nice and safe, the way
The-One-Who-Waits was promising.

"I'd like—" he began.

But still he had no chance to say it, because the teapot
started vibrating like a struck gong. Birdie was convinced that
it was getting ready to do something drastic, and he jumped
smartly backward. While he was doing it, Graves hopped in
and started talking again. From the tone of voice it was
Steven.

"Before we are all passed along to join the others," he said,
"I have questions. About this planetoid, and the Builders, and
why they *need* humans and Cecropians. And where we will
be going. And who you are, and what your own role is in all
this. And what are the *three* species you mentioned. Those
are questions that I feel sure you can answer, as perhaps no
one else can. So if you would be so kind . . ."

Birdie was sure that Steven would be told to shut up. But
instead The-One-Who-Waits gave another of those rude
noises that would discourage Birdie from ever inviting it to
parties. It stopped vibrating all over and hung in the air for
a while. Finally it came drifting closer.

"Questions," it said. To Birdie it sounded exhausted, as
though it had been planning to go off somewhere quiet and
take another six-million-year nap, and Graves was interfering
with the scheme. "That is perhaps . . . predictable. And not
unreasonable."

The-One-Who-Waits kept moving forward until it was actually crowding them back on the ledge. No one touched it, but Birdie could tell that the silver surface was cold, cold enough to put a chill into the air all around it. Close up, he still could not see what the other was made of, but there were teeny little ripples running over the surface, no more than a millimeter or two high. The-One-Who-Waits had to be at least partly liquid. As it settled down on its tail, Birdie could see its shape sag, bulging out at the bottom.

"Very well," it said at last. "I will talk to you. It is best if I begin with my own history . . ."

Birdie groaned to himself. Wouldn't you just know it! Six million years old, and more alien than anything in the whole spiral arm—but no different in some ways from the rest of them.

Given a choice of subjects, The-One-Who-Waits was going to talk about *himself.*

CHAPTER 19

A FLAG BURIED deep in Rebka's brain told him what he was looking at in the tank. He had never seen anything like it before, but the skin of his arms tingled and hair stood up on the back of his neck.

"Hans?" Darya said again. "Move over. It's my turn."

She tugged at the sleeve of his suit. Then something in his rigid posture told her that this was nothing trivial, and he was not going to move. She crowded closer to him and again peered in through the tank's transparent port.

It took a while for her eyes to adapt to the reduced light level. But while she was still making that visual adjustment, her brain objected loud and clear: *Alert! This is a stasis tank!* There should be *no* light inside, none at all. Not while the tank was preserving the stasis condition. What was going on?

But by then she could see, and all rational thinking had stopped. No more than three feet from her face was a great, lidded eye, as big across as her stretched hand. That cerulean orb was almost closed. It sat in a broad, bulbous head of midnight blue, over a meter wide. Between the broad-spaced eyes was a cruel hooked beak, curving upward, easily big enough to seize and crack a human skull.

The rest of the body sprawled its length seven meters along the tank; but Darya needed to see no more.

"Zardalu." The word came from her lips as a whisper, forced out against her will.

Hans Rebka stirred beside her. The soft-spoken word had broken his own trance.

"Yeah. Tell me I'm dreaming. There's no such thing. Not anymore."

"And it's *alive*—look, Hans, it's moving."

And with that remark, Darya's own sense of scientific curiosity came flooding back. The Zardalu had been exterminated in the spiral arm many thousands of years earlier. Although they were still the galactic bogeymen, everything about them was theory, myth, or legend. No one knew any details—not of their physiology, their evolution, or their habits. No one even knew how the cephalopods, originally a marine form, had been able to survive and breathe on land.

But Darya suddenly realized that she could answer that last question. She saw a sluggish ripple of peristalsis running along the length of the great body. The Zardalu must be breathing using a modification of the technique employed by ordinary marine cephalopods for propulsion—except that instead of drawing in and expelling *water* like a squid, the Zardalu employed that same muscular action to take in and expel *air*.

And for locomotion?

She stared at the body. The upper part was a round-topped cylinder, with bands of smooth muscle running down it. The eyes and beak were placed about one meter down. Below the beak sat a long vertical slit, surrounded by flexible muscular tissue. There was no difference in width between head and torso, but below that long gash of the mouth was a necklace of round-mouthed pouches, about six inches wide and circling the whole body. Darya could see pale blue ovals of different sizes nestled within the pouches. Stretched out along and beyond the main body was a loose tangle of thick tentacles, also pale blue. They were amply strong enough to walk on, though a set of broad straps wrapped around their thickest parts. Two of the tentacles ended in finely dividing ropy tips.

If those thin filaments were capable of independent control, Darya thought, a Zardalu would have manipulative powers beyond any human—beyond any other being in the spiral arm.

She felt an uncomfortable awe. The Zardalu might fill her with dread, but at the same time she knew that they were beautiful. It was a beauty that came from the perfect matching of form and function. The combination of muscular power with delicate touch could not be missed. The only anomaly was the webbing that girded the upper part of the tentacles.

"What are the straps for, Hans?" she whispered. "They can't be for physical support. Do you think they're for *carrying*—offspring, or supplies and weapons?"

But Rebka was still staring at the slow ripple of movement along the body. "Darya, this shouldn't be happening. It's impossible. Remember, this is a *stasis* unit. Everything's frozen, just like time has stopped. But that thing in there is *breathing*—slow, but enough to see. And look at that eye."

There was a flicker of movement in the heavy lid. While they watched, the tip of one thick tentacle twitched and curled a few centimeters.

Rebka stepped sharply away from the tank. "Darya, that Zardalu isn't in stasis. It may have been, a few hours ago. But now it's starting to wake up. I've no idea how long reanimation will take, but Speaker-Between must have started the process as soon as we arrived. He said that there were 'two forms only' here, and I assumed that he meant the two of us. But now it looks as though he meant two *species,* Human and Zardalu. We have to try to find him and warn him. He probably has no idea what the Zardalu were like."

He was already moving from one stasis tank to the next, peering in for only a moment at each.

"They're all the same. All starting to wake."

He hurried back to the food-supply unit, grabbing handfuls of still-frozen packets and stuffing them into his pockets. Darya marveled that at a time like this he could still think of food. She remembered how hungry she had been feeling, but at the moment she could not have eaten a thing.

He turned impatiently to her. "Come on."

She obeyed—reluctantly. It was against all her instincts, to leave something so novel, about which so many students and experts on the cultures of the spiral arm had expended so much speculative effort. Hans might be right when he said that Speaker-Between might have no idea what the Zardalu were like; but that was just as true of *human* knowledge of the Zardalu. There was speculation and theory, but no one *knew* anything. And here she was, with a perfect opportunity to determine a few facts.

Only one thing made her follow right after Rebka: the fear that had crept up her spine unbidden, like a capillary flow of ice water, when she first saw that dark-blue skin and bulky body. She did not *want* to be alone with a Zardalu, even an unconscious one.

According to all expert knowledge, humans had never encountered Zardalu. The Great Rising had happened before humanity moved into space. But there could be deeper wisdom than anything in the data banks. The submerged depths of Darya's brain told her that there *had* been encounters, back before human recorded history.

And they had been bloody and merciless meetings. Sometime, long before, the Zardalu scouts had taken a close look at Earth. They had been stopped before they could colonize. Not by any action of early humans, but by the Great Rising. Dozens of intelligent races and scores of planets had been annihilated in that rebellion. And Earth had benefited, unknowing, from their sacrifice. The Zardalu had been exterminated.

Or almost exterminated.

Darya found herself shaking all over as she went after Hans. He was right. They had to find Speaker-Between and warn him, even if they were not sure what they were warning him *about*.

Reaching the Interlocutor should in principle be trivially easy. They had entered the sphere of his body and never left it. Therefore they must still be inside Speaker-Between.

But Darya did not believe it. She did not trust the evidence of her senses anymore. The chambers containing the stasis tanks and the Zardalu were just too big to fit inside Speaker-Between. The Builders had a control of the geometry of space-time beyond anything dreamed of by the current inhabitants of the spiral arm. For all she knew, Speaker-Between could be very far away—thousands of light-years, as humans measured things.

She glanced behind her as she followed Hans Rebka to the two doors of the chamber—the same doors through which they had entered, less than an hour before. The great coffins still sat silent. But now that she knew their contents, that silence had become ominous, a calm that heralded coming activity. She was strangely uncomfortable about leaving that chamber, and even more uneasy about staying there.

As they passed through the first sliding door and then the second one, Darya knew at once that her instincts had been correct. The outside *had* changed. They were emerging not into the level and infinite plain where they had encountered Speaker-Between, but to a somber gray-walled room. And instead of high-ceilinged emptiness, or the webs, cables, nets, and partitions of Glister, Hans and Darya were standing before hundreds of ivory-white cubes, ranging in size from boxes small enough to tuck easily under one arm, to towering objects taller than a human. The cubes were scattered across the floor of the rectangular room, like dice cast by a giant.

Nothing moved. There was no sign of Speaker-Between.

To Darya's surprise, after Rebka's careful inspection of their surroundings he walked forward to look at a couple of boxes. They stood side by side and came about up to his knees. He sat down on one of them, reached into his pocket, and pulled out a packet. As she stared he opened it and started to peel the thin-skinned fruit that it contained.

"It's still a bit cold on the inside," he said after a few moments. "But we can't afford to be too picky."

"Hans! The Zardalu. We have to find Speaker-Between."

"You mean we'd like to." He bit off a small piece of the fruit, chewed it, and frowned. "Not too great, but it's better than nothing. Look, Darya, I want to find Speaker-Between and talk to him as much as you do. But how? I hoped we'd find that we were still inside him, so coming out would bring us back to talk to him. It didn't work. This place is stranger than anything I've ever seen in my life, and I doubt if you're any more at home than I am. You saw the size of this artifact when we were approaching it. We could spend the rest of our lives looking for somebody, but if he doesn't *want* to be found, we'd never get near him."

Darya visualized the monstrous space construct that they had seen on the final transition of their approach, its delicate filaments stretching out millions of kilometers. Rebka was right. Its size was too big to contemplate, let alone search. But the idea of *not* searching . . .

"You mean you're just going to sit there and do nothing?"

"No. I could make a case for that—when you don't know what to do, do nothing. I'm going to sit and *eat*. And you should do the same." He patted the box beside him. "Right here. You're the logical one, Darya. Think it through. We have no idea where Speaker-Between is, or how to go about looking for him. And we don't know our way around here—I mean, we don't even know this place's *topology*. But if you were to ask the most *likely* place for Speaker-Between to show up, I'd say it's right here where he left us. And if you were to ask me the best way for us to spend our time, I'd say we should do two things. We should eat and rest, and we should stay where we can easily keep an eye on what's happening back in that other room, with the Zardalu. We really ought to eat in there, too, but staring at those tanks I know I couldn't manage a bite."

Signs of human frailty in Hans Rebka? Darya did not know if she approved of that or not. She sat down on a white box with a fine snowflake pattern on its sides. The top was slightly warm to the touch. It gave a fraction of an inch under her weight, just enough to make it comfortable.

Maybe it was not weakness in Rebka at all. *When you don't know what to do, do nothing.* One might think that would be her philosophy, the research worker who had lived in her study for twenty years. But instead she felt a huge urge to *do something*—anything. It was Rebka, the born trouble-shooter who had lived through a hundred close scrapes, who could sit and relax.

Darya accepted a lump of cool yellow fruit. *Eat.* She ate. She found it slightly astringent, with a granular texture that encouraged hard chewing. No aftereffects. Rebka was right about that, too. They surely would not have been brought all this way only to be poisoned or left to starve. Except—what right did they have to make any assumptions about alien thought processes, when everything that had happened since they arrived at Gargantua had been a total mystery?

She accepted three more pieces of unfamiliar food. Still her stomach was making no objections, but she wished that what they were eating could be warmed. She felt chilled. Shivering, she set her suit at a higher level of opacity. She was ready to ask for more fruit when she noticed that Rebka was sitting up straighter on his seat and staring around him. She followed his look and saw nothing.

"What is it?"

He shook his head. "I don't know. Only . . ." He was focusing his attention on the far side of the room. "Feel it? It's not my imagination. A draft—and getting stronger."

A *cold* draft. Darya realized that she had been feeling it for a while, without knowing what it was. There were chilly breezes blowing past them, ruffling his hair and tugging gently at her suit.

"What's causing it?" But Darya knew the answer, even as Hans was shaking his head in bewilderment. She could see a swirling pattern forming on the far side of the room. A rotating cylinder of air had darkened there, streaked horizontally like muddy water on glass. It formed a vortex column that ran from floor to ceiling. She stood up and grabbed Rebka's arm.

"Hans. We have to get out of here and back to the other chamber—it's getting stronger."

The circulation pattern created by the vortex was becoming powerful enough to generate a minor gale, driving around the whole inside of the room. Who could say how fierce it would get? If it continued to strengthen, she and Hans would be swept off their feet.

He was nodding, not trying to speak over the scream of wind. Holding on to each other, they fought their way back to the shelter of the doorway. Rebka turned in the entrance.

"Wait for a second before we go through." He had to shout in her ear to be heard. "It's still getting stronger. But it's *closing*—look."

The spinning cylinder of air was drawing in on itself. From a width of five meters, it tightened as they watched to become no wider than a man's outstretched arms. Its heart became an oily, soft-edged black, so dark and dense that the wall of the chamber could not be seen through it. The scream of wind in the room grew to a new intensity, hurting Darya's ears.

She backed farther into the doorway. The force of the wind was terrifying. The vortex loomed darker, more and more dangerous. She reached out to pull Rebka back—he was leaning into the room, even while gusts tore at his hair and buffeted his body. Her fingers grabbed the back of his suit. The wail of rushing air rose higher and higher.

She tugged. Rebka fell off balance backward. She bumped into the closed door.

In that same instant, everything stopped. The wind dropped, the sounds faded.

There was a moment of total silence in the chamber; and then, in that uncanny stillness, there came a soft pop no louder than a cork being removed from a bottle. The vortex changed in color to a blood-red, and began to fade.

Another moment, and the silence was broken more substantially. Out of the thinning heart of the spinning column staggered a form. A *human* form.

It was Louis Nenda. He was greenish yellow in complexion, stripped to the waist, and cursing loudly and horribly.

The little black satchel that he always carried with him flapped against his bare chest. Two steps behind him, creeping along miserably with all six limbs to the ground, came the giant blind figure of Atvar H'sial.

* * *

Back on Quake they had been enemies. Nenda and Atvar H'sial had tried to kill Darya Lang and Hans Rebka, and Rebka, at least, would have been happy to return the compliment.

Thirty thousand light-years made quite a difference. They greeted each other like long-lost brothers and sisters.

"But where in hell *are* we?" Nenda asked when his nausea had eased enough to allow any form of speech beyond swearing.

"A long way from home," Rebka said.

"Ratballs, I know *that*. But where?"

As they exchanged information—what little of it they had—Darya learned that her own journey here had been a pleasure trip compared with what had happened to the two new arrivals.

"Stop an' go," Nenda said. "Go an' stop, all the way." He belched loudly. "Jerkin' around, turned ass-over-teacup, right way up one minute and wrong way up the next. Went on forever. I'd've puked fifty times, if I'd had anything in my guts." He was silent for a few moments. "At says it was just as bad for her. And yet you come so easy. There must be more than one way to get here. We traveled steerage class and got the rough one."

"But the fast one, too," Rebka said. "By the look of it, you and Atvar H'sial left Glister days after us. We thought we were only on the way for a few minutes, but it could have been a lot more—we don't know how long we were stuck in nowhere, between transitions."

"Well, I thought we were on the way for *weeks*." Nenda belched again. "Gar. That's better. Thirty thousand light-years, you said? Long way from home. Let that be a lesson to you, At. Greed don't pay."

"Can she understand you?" Darya had been staring at the pitted and nodulated area of Nenda's bare chest, watching it quiver and pulse as Nenda spoke.

"Sure. At least, whenever I use the augment she can. I speak the words at the same time, usually, because that way it's easier to know what I want to say. But At picks it all up. Watch. You hear me, At?"

The blind white head nodded.

"See. You ought to have an augment put in, too, so you can chat with At an' the other Cecropians." He stared at Darya's chest. "Mind you, I'd hate to see them nice boobs messed up."

Any sympathy that Darya might have had for the Karelian human evaporated. "If I were you, Louis Nenda, I'd save my breath to plead with the judge. You have formal charges waiting for you, as soon as we get back to the spiral arm. Councilor Graves already filed them."

"Charges for what? I didn't do a thing."

"Your ship fired at us," Rebka said. "You tried to destroy the *Summer Dreamboat* after Summertide."

"I did?" Nenda's face was blandly innocent. "You sure it was me, Captain, and not three other guys? I never even heard of no *Summer Dreamboat.* I don't remember firing at anything. Doesn't sound like the sort of thing I'd do at all. Do you think we fired at a ship, At?" He paused. The Cecropian did not move. "No way. See, she agrees with me."

"She's as guilty as you are!"

"You mean as innocent."

Rebka's face had lost its usual pallor. "Damn you, I don't think I'll even wait until we get back home. I can file charges on you right here, just as well as Graves can." He took a step closer to Nenda.

The other man did not move. "So you're feeling mad. Big deal. Go on, try to arrest me—and tell me where you'll lock me up. Maybe you'll shut me away with your girlfriend here. I'd like that. So would she." He grinned admiringly at Darya. "How about it, sweetie? You'll have more fun with me than you've ever had with him."

"If you're trying to change the subject, it won't work." Rebka moved until he and Nenda were eyeball to eyeball. "Do you really want to see if I can arrest you? Try a few more cracks like that."

Nenda turned to Darya and gave her a wink. "See how mad he gets, when anybody else tries for a piece?"

He had been watching Rebka out of the corner of his eye, and he batted away the hand that grabbed for his wrist. Then the two men were standing with arms braced, glaring at each other.

Darya could not believe it. She had never seen Rebka lose his temper before—and Louis Nenda had never been anything but cool and cynical. What was doing it to them? Tension? Fatigue?

No. She could see their expressions. They were trying each other out, testing to see which rooster was top of the dunghill.

So that was how people behaved on the primitive outworlds. Everyone would think she was making this up if she told them all about it back on Sentinel Gate.

The two men were still standing with arms locked. Darya reached over and tugged at Rebka's right hand. "Stop it!" she shouted at them. "Both of you. You're acting like wild beasts."

They ignored her, but Atvar H'sial reached out with two jointed forelimbs, grabbed each man around the waist in one clawed paw, and lifted them high in the air. She pulled them effortlessly away from each other. After a second or two she allowed their feet to touch the ground, but she still held them far apart.

The blind head turned toward Darya, while the proboscis unfurled and produced a soft hissing sound.

"I know," Darya said. "They *are* like animals, aren't they? Hold them for a minute or two longer." She spread her arms wide, as though pushing the men farther apart. Atvar H'sial might not understand her words, but she surely could take her meaning.

Darya went to stand between them. "Listen to me, you two. I don't know which of you is more stupid, but you can have your idiocy contest later. I want to say just one word to you." She paused, waiting until they turned their attention fully to her. "Zardalu! D'you hear me? *Zardalu.*"

"Huh?" Louis Nenda's hands had still been reaching out toward Rebka. They dropped to his sides. "What are you talking about?"

Darya gestured at the doorway behind her. "In there. Fourteen Zardalu."

"Crap! There's not been a Zardalu in the spiral arm for thousands of years. They're extinct."

"You're not in the spiral arm anymore, boy. You're thirty thousand light-years out of the plane of the galaxy. And back in that room there's fourteen stasis tanks, with a Zardalu in each one. *Alive.*"

"I don't believe it. Nobody's ever seen a Zardalu, not even a stuffed or a mummified one." Nenda turned to Hans Rebka. "You hear her? She trying to make a joke?"

"No joke." Rebka straightened his suit, where Nenda had pulled it half off his shoulders. "She's telling the truth. They're in stasis tanks, but I don't know how long that will last. The stasis was beginning to end when we saw them."

"You mean you stood there and picked a fight with me, when there's *Zardalu* waking up in there? And you call *me* dumb! You have to be crazy."

"What do you mean, *I* picked a fight!"

Darya stepped between them again. "You're *both* crazy, and you're both to blame. Are you going to start over? Because if you are, I hope Atvar H'sial understands enough to crack your heads together and knock some sense into you."

"She does. She will." Nenda stared at the closed door. Suddenly he was his old calm self. "Zardalu. I don't know what you're smoking, but maybe we better get in there. I'll tell At what's been happening. She's like me, though—she won't really believe it until she takes a peek for herself."

He turned to Atvar H'sial. "You're not gonna like this, At." The gray pheromone nodules on his chest pulsed in unison with his human speech. "These two jokers say there's *Zardalu* in there. You heard me. Fourteen of 'em, in stasis but alive and gettin' ready to trot. I know, I know."

The Cecropian had squatted back onto her hindmost limbs, furled the antennas above her head, and tucked her proboscis into its pleated holder.

"She don't like to hear that," Nenda said. "She says a Cecropian ain't afraid of anything in the universe, but Zardalu images are part of her race memory. A bad part. Nobody knows why."

Hans Rebka was sliding open the first of the two doors. "Let's hope she doesn't find out. I'd suggest that you and Atvar H'sial hang back a bit—just in case."

He opened the second door. Darya held her breath, then released it with a sigh of relief. The great pentagonal cylinders lay exactly as they had left them, silent and closed.

"All right." Hans Rebka moved forward. "You wanted proof, here it is. Take a look in there."

Nenda walked cautiously to the transparent port in the end of the stasis tank and peered in through it. After a few seconds he gave a long sigh.

"I know," Rebka said softly. "Impressive, eh? And scary, too. We have to find a way to turn that stasis field back on, before they wake up and try to get out."

But Louis Nenda was shaking his head. "I don't know what game you're playing, *Captain* Rebka and *Professor* Lang. I just know it's a stupid one."

He stepped away from the long casket.

"There's thirteen more to look at, but I'll bet money they're all like this one." He turned to face Darya. "It's *empty,* sweetheart. Empty as a Ditron's brainbox. What do you have to say about *that?*"

ENTRY 42: DITRON.

Distribution: Never having achieved an independent spaceflight capability, Ditrons are found in large numbers only on their native world (*Ditrona,* officially Luris III, Cecropia Federation, Sector Five). Transported Ditron colonies can also be found on the neighboring worlds of Prinal (Luris II) and Ivergne (Luris V). In the early days of the Cecropian expansion, Ditrons were taken to the other stellar systems, but generally they did not thrive there. Diet deficiencies were blamed at the time, but more recent analyses make it clear that psychological dependencies were as much a factor. Ditrons, at the third stage of their life cycle, fail to survive if the group size dwindles below twenty.

Physical Characteristics: It is necessary to consider separately the three stages of the Ditron life cycle, conventionally designated as S-1, S-2, and S-3. The Ditrons are unique among known intelligent species in that their highest mental levels are achieved not in their most mature form, but rather in their premature and premating (S-2) stage.

The larval form (S-1) is born live, in a litter of no less than five and no more than thirteen offspring. The newborn Ditron masses less than one kilogram, but it has full mobility and is able to eat at once. It is near-blind, possesses sevenfold radial symmetry, is asexual, herbivorous, and lacks measureable intelligence.

S-1 lasts for one Ditron summer season (three-fourths of a standard year) at the end of which time a body mass of twenty-five kilos has been achieved and metamorphosis begins. S-1 moves below ground, as a flat, pale-yellow disk about one meter in diameter. It emerges in the spring as S-2, a slender, dark-orange, many-legged carnivore with bilateral symmetry and a fierce appetite. An S-2 Ditron will prey on anything except its own S-1 and S-3 forms. It possesses no known language, but from its behavior patterns it is judged to be of undeniable intelligence. Consideration of the S-2 Ditron first led to that species' assignment as an intelligent form.

In this life stage the Ditron is solitary, energetic, and antisocial. Attempts to export S-2 Ditrons to other worlds have all failed, not because the organism dies but because it never ceases to feed voraciously, to attack its captors at every opportunity, and to try to escape. A confined S-2 will solve within minutes a maze that will hold most humans or Cecropians for an hour or more.

S-2 lasts for fourteen years, during all of which time the Ditron grows constantly. At the end of this period it masses twelve tons and is fifteen meters long. No more formidable predator exists in the spiral arm (archaeological workers on Luris III have discovered an ancestral form of the Ditron S-2 that was almost twice the S-2's present size, and apparently just as voracious; it probably, however, lacked intelligence).

The transition to S-3 arrives suddenly, and apparently without warning to the S-2 itself. It is conjectured that the first sign of a change to S-3 state is a substantial fall in Ditron S-2 intelligence, and a sudden urge for clustering. The formerly antisocial creature seeks out and protects the cocoon clusters of other changing S-2s. Up to a hundred Ditrons tunnel deep into sites by soft riverbanks, where each spins its own protective cocoon. New arrivals protect the site from predators, before themselves beginning to tunnel. Metamorphosis takes place over a two-year period. Emerging S-3s have dwindled to a body mass of less than one ton. The material of the residual cocoon is a valuable prize, for anyone able to thwart the guardianship offered by the protective S-2s.

The form of the S-3 is a large-headed upright biped, brownish-red in color, two-eyed, and with bilateral symmetry. Its alert appearance and large brainbox persuaded early explorers of Luris III that the S-3 must be a more intelligent and certainly more friendly form than its S-2 progenitor.

Unfortunately, the head of the S-3 is employed mainly as a resonance cavity. It enables the creature to produce mating calls that can be heard over large distances, but the skull contains mostly air. The brain itself is little more than the couple of hundred grams of material required to allow an S-3 to find a mate, to copulate, and to bring forth the S-1 larval form.

The attempt to use Ditrons as a slave species has been made many times, because the S-3 is undeniably docile and tractable and enjoys company; but the main result has been frustration to the Ditron owners. Only the Cecropians continue to cultivate S-3 slaves, either as pets or for purposes that remain obscure.

History: Ditrons possess no written or oral history. Paleontological research shows that these beings have changed little in form, though considerably in size, over the past three million years.

Culture: None. S-1 and S-3 Ditrons are mindless. S-2 Ditrons, undeniably intelligent, build no structures, use no tools, wear no clothing, and keep no records. All attempts at communication with S-2s have been ignored.

—From the *Universal Species Catalog*
(Subclass: Sapients).

CHAPTER 20

THE PERIOD BEFORE the coming of intelligence had been quiet, peaceful, and eons long. The final emergence was a miracle in itself; and like all miracles, nothing before it presaged its arrival.

The nutrients in the middle atmosphere of the gas-giant were rich and abundant; the climate was unvarying; a total absence of competition removed any stimulus to evolution.

The dominant life-form drifted idly in its buoyant sea of high-pressure hydrogen and helium, loose aggregations of cells that combined, dissociated, and recombined with endless variety. The results were sometimes simple, sometimes complex, and always without self-awareness. They had persisted unchanged for eight hundred million years.

When it came, the pressure was provided from without, and from far away. A supernova, nine light-years from the Mandel system, sent a sleet of hard radiation and superfast particles driving into the upper atmosphere of Gargantua.

The dominant life-form, tens of thousands of kilometers down, was well protected; it drowsed on. But small and primitive multicelled creatures, eking out their own existence almost at the edge of space, felt the full force of the incident flux. They had been harmless, unable to compete with the loosely organized but more efficient assemblies of life below; now they mutated in the killing storm of radiation. The survivors grew voracious and desperate, and expanded their biosphere—downward. Like vermin, they began to infest the deep habitats and to modify the food chains there.

The Sleepers below had to quicken—or die. At first their numbers dwindled. They mindlessly sought refuge in the depths, down in the unfathomable abyss near the rocky solid core, where living conditions were harsh and food less plentiful.

It was not enough. The vermin followed them, gnawing at their evanescent structures, interfering with their placid drift at the whim of currents and temperature gradients.

The Sleepers had a simple choice: adapt or die. Since permanence of form was essential to survival, they became unified structures. They formed tough skins to protect those structures, integuments hard enough to resist the vermin's attack. They developed mobility for escape. They learned to recognize and avoid the swarms of starving nibblers. They themselves became rapid and aggressive eaters.

And they developed *cunning*. Not long afterward came self-awareness. In a few million years, technology followed. The Sleepers pursued the vermin back to the upper edge of the atmosphere, for the first time claiming that domain as their own.

Now they found themselves familiar with and at home in environments ranging from million-atmosphere pressures at the interface with Gargantua's rocky central core, to the near-vacuum of the planet's ionosphere. They developed materials that could endure those extremes of pressure, and as great extremes of radiation and temperature. Finally they decided to move to a place where the still-annoying vermin could not follow: space itself.

The technology went with them. The Sleepers became the

Builders. They spread with no haste from star to star in the spiral arm. Never again would they occupy a planet. Their homeworld became Homeworld, and finally Old-Home, abandoned but not forgotten. It remained the central nexus of the Builders' transportation system.

They were Sleepers no more; and yet in one essential way they were as they had always been. The active and aggressive behavior patterns forced upon them by the vermin were only a few million years deep. They were overlaid like a thin veneer on a deeper behavior, one derived from that idyllic and near-infinite era of idle drifting.

The Builders made their great spaceborne artifacts, with a communication network that stretched across and beyond the spiral arm; but they did so almost absentmindedly, with no more than a small part of their collective consciousness. They were Builders, certainly; but more than that they were *Thinkers*. For them, contemplation was the highest and the preferred activity. Action was a sometimes necessary but always unwelcome digression.

The new stability persisted for almost two hundred million years, while the Builders busied themselves in a leisurely analysis of the nature of the universe itself. Then came a new *Great Problem*, more troublesome even than the vermin. And further change was forced upon them . . .

The-One-Who-Waits fell silent. At some hidden command the lights in the great chamber dimmed further. The alien lifted a few centimeters above the surface of the tunnel, where in front of it sat Julius Graves, with J'merlia and Kallik on each side. E. C. Tally and Birdie Kelly were just behind, cross-legged on the hard tunnel floor and stiff-jointed from two hours of silent attention. When it had finally become fluent in human speech, the voice of The-One-Who-Waits had proved to be slow and hypnotic, forcing the listeners to ignore their surroundings and their own physical needs.

Birdie stirred and inspected each of the others in turn. E. C. Tally was in the worst shape of anyone. The embodied computer was leaning forward and supporting himself wearily on his hands and elbows. Apparently the need for rest and recuperation had not been sufficiently explained to him; before long, by the look of it, Tally would collapse from simple exhaustion.

At the front, Graves sat with his face invisible to Birdie. The two aliens by his side had expressions unreadable at the best of times. The only thing they seemed to care about was finding Louis Nenda and Atvar H'sial, so that they could grovel again to their old masters. They were sprawled on the floor, all jointed legs, staring up at the shining body a few feet away from them.

"And what was the new *Great Problem*?" Graves asked.

"That information was not considered useful to me." The weary voice sounded more tired than ever, as though it would welcome a rapid end to the conversation. "I, of course, was *created* by the Builders, long ago, so although my data sources here are large, they are limited to information judged necessary for my effective functioning. You will obtain more answers than I can give you when you reach Serenity—the main artifact, far from the main galactic plane."

"And we will find the Builders there?" Graves had become the official spokesman of the group.

"That information also is not available here." The-One-Who-Waits paused. "The present whereabouts of the Builders are unknown to me. But this I know, that you must work with Speaker-Between, the Interlocutor, one who wears my shape. When the Builders chose to move to Serenity, they also postponed certain other decisions until particular events occurred. Those events are now imminent, and involve Speaker-Between."

"When did the Builders leave the spiral arm?"

"I am not exactly sure." The-One-Who-Waits made a now-familiar soft bubbling noise, like water boiling over, and went on. "I myself waited for six million of your years, in the interior of that planet you call Quake. But of course, I was already old before that . . . I am not sure how old. Mmmm. Ten million of your years? Twelve?"

There was another substantial silence, during which Birdie wondered if Builder constructs could suffer from senility.

"I would be waiting still," The-One-Who-Waits went on,

"but a few weeks ago the signals were at last received. They indicated that every Builder structure in the spiral arm had finally been visited by a member of one of the chosen intelligent species.

"The plan could at last proceed. The tidal energies available at Quake during Summertide were harnessed to open the planet. They permitted me to be sent to the vicinity of Old-Home. I came to the gate of the transportation system, where we are now.

"Very soon you will enter that gate, at your own request. Unless you have a final question?"

"If we may not meet the Builders, even on Serenity, can't you at least describe to us what they look like?" Graves said.

"It is not necessary for me to do so. You are already familiar with ones who wear the external appearance of the Builders: the Phages."

"There's a popular theory that says the Phages are artifacts," Steven Graves said. "Are you saying that the Phages were *constructed* by the Builders in their own image, to look like them?"

"No. The Phages *are* Builders—devolved forms, debased and degenerate. Their intelligence has been lost. They are able to propagate themselves, and to perform the most elementary acts of matter and energy absorption, and that is all. For all the time that I have known, they have been a nuisance to every free-space structure in the spiral arm. Planetary interiors, like the inside of Quake, are safe, and intense gravity fields discourage their presence."

"What happened, to turn Builders into Phages?" Graves asked.

"I cannot say." The-One-Who-Waits was stirring, lifting higher off the floor. "I know only that it was another consequence of the *Great Problem,* the one that led the Builders to leave the spiral arm and seek a long stasis in the Artifact.

"Now, no more questions. It is time for you to enter the gate."

Birdie looked all around him. All this talk about a gate. There was nothing in sight that resembled a gate, even vaguely.

"I don't know where your gate is," he began. "But about that safe passage that you promised us, back to our home planets—"

He was in midsentence when the floor evaporated beneath his feet. He heard a rushing sound all around him. Birdie took one look down. He was falling, dropping into nothingness.

He closed his eyes.

Looking back on what happened next, Birdie decided he must have kept his eyes squeezed tight shut until he felt firm ground again beneath his feet. Or then again, maybe he had just fainted. He was not willing to argue that point. He knew only two things for sure: First, when the others described the journey, he had no idea what they were talking about. He did not remember one thing about it.

Second, when he did finally open his eyes . . .

He was standing on a flat, endless plain, beneath a dull and featureless ceiling of glowing grayness.

And he was not alone. Surrounding him, looming over him, reaching out toward him with pale-blue tentacles, even before his eyes had finished opening, were—

—the stuff of nightmares.

He saw a dozen hulking bodies of midnight blue. They were closing in, sharp beaks gaping.

At that point Birdie felt more than ready to close his eyes and faint again.

ENTRY 16: ZARDALU.

Distribution: Like all information concerning the Zardalu, species-distribution data are based on fragmentary historical records and on incomplete race memory of other species. The great empire known as the *Zardalu Communion* is believed to have formed a roughly hemispherical region, over a thousand light-years across and centered on 1400 ly, 22 hours, 27° north (coordinates in galactic-plane angular measure, radial distances with respect to Sol; coordinate shifts to Cecropia reference frame are given in Appendix B). The face of the hemisphere comprising the Zardalu Communion is roughly tangent to the edge of Crawlspace (see HUMAN entry), and the lower part of the hemisphere itself overlaps the Cecropia Federation (see CECROPIA entry).

At its height, just before the Great Rising of approximately eleven thousand years ago, the Zardalu Communion ruled in excess of one thousand worlds. There is evidence that preliminary missions to worlds of the Fourth Alliance and of the Cecropia Federation took place just before the Rising, and that the Zardalu intended to expand into those regions.

Despite rumors today of hidden worlds inhabited by Zardalu—rumors that possess the force and persistence of multispecies legend—it should be noted that *no Zardalu has been encountered since the Great Rising.* It can be confidently stated that the Zardalu are extinct, and have been extinct for eleven thousand years.

Physical Characteristics: No physical remains or pictures have been discovered. The Zardalu records were systematically destroyed, along with all evidence of Zardalu existence, at the time of the Great Rising. The following data represent a consensus derived from race memories, largely of the Hymenopts. They are undoubtedly subject to the distortion natural for a slave species remembering their former masters:

The Zardalu were land-cephalopods, possessing between six and twelve tentacles. Their size is not known with any precision, but it is certain that they were considerably larger

204

than a Hymenopt (which seldom stands above one and a half meters, even with legs fully extended). A suggested plausible height for a standing Zardalu would be three meters, although Hymenopt impressions record it as at least twice that.

Evidence suggests that the Zardalu possessed smooth, grease-coated skin ranging in color from pale powder-blue (tentacles) to deep blue-black (main torso). The head possessed large, lidded eyes, a formidable beak, and one main ingestion mouth.

Details of interior anatomy are not available. The existence of an endoskeleton, or the lack of one, is purely conjectural. Based upon their large size, and upon their ability to move and function well on land, it seems likely that the Zardalu possessed at least a rudimentary skeleton, or substantial interior sheaths and bands of semirigid cartilaginous material.

No information is available concerning Zardalu intelligence or culture level, and nothing is known about the Zardalu mating or family habits. They retain to this day the reputation of having been prodigious breeders, but that reputation is not based on scientific evidence.

History : Almost nothing can be said here with any authority, beyond this: Based on their wide distribution and integrated empire, the Zardalu must have developed space travel at least twenty thousand years before Cecropians or Humans, and possibly much longer ago than that.

The original homeworld of the Zardalu clade remains unknown, although its name, Genizee, is well established in legend. Quite likely it was one of the dozens of worlds cindered and sterilized in the bitter struggle of the Great Rising. Certainly any of the subject races able to find and annihilate the home of the Zardalu would have done so, without hesitation.

Culture: Five words summarize all recollections of Zardalu culture: imperialistic, powerful, determined, expansionist, and ruthless. It is a perverse testament to the Zardalu that they still evoke such strong images in the minds of intelligent beings everywhere, even though they have been gone for over ten millennia.

—From the *Universal Species Catalog*
(Subclass: Sapients).

CHAPTER 21

DARYA ARRIVED BACK in the silent chamber a little bit early, before the other three. In the past four hours she had become convinced that the search was going nowhere. She was also tired, and becoming hungry again.

Even so, she could not sit down until she had taken a look inside each of the big tanks. Logically she knew that the coffins would be empty. It made no sense for the Zardalu to have gone back into stasis, even assuming that they knew how the tanks worked.

But logic had nothing to do with it. She had to see for herself and make *sure*.

Atvar H'sial crept quietly into the room a few minutes later, right on time. She and Darya nodded to each other. That was about as far as they could go without Louis Nenda as interpreter, but Darya was sure that the Cecropian had also found nothing useful. She could read that much from body language, just as Atvar H'sial must be able to read her.

Rebka and Nenda came in together. They looked angry and worried.

"Nothing?" Darya asked.

They shook their heads simultaneously.

"Washout," Nenda said. "No Builders, no Speaker-Between, no Zardalu. Bugger 'em all. From the look of it, we'd take ten thousand years searching this place properly. Screw it." Just as Darya had done, he and Rebka went compulsively across to the tanks and peered inside to make sure that they were empty.

"It's worse than I thought," Nenda said when he came back. "At says she didn't catch one whiff of them, nowhere. And she can smell a gnat's armpit at a hundred kilometers. Stinkers like them ought to be a cinch. They've vanished, every one of them. What do we do *now,* boys and girls?"

It was smell that had persuaded Nenda, not any argument offered by Darya or Hans Rebka. When Atvar H'sial had risen high, poked her big white head inside one of the big tanks, pulled forth on one claw a trace of fatty smear, and assured them all that nothing smelled remotely like that anywhere in the spiral arm, Nenda had become an instant believer. The Cecropian knew scents better than any human knew sights. Darya had put her own head into one of the tanks and caught the faintest whiff of ammonia and rancid grease.

Rebka was sitting on top of one of the coffins, his chin cupped in his hands. "What do we do?" he repeated. "Well, I guess that we keep looking. Speaker-Between said the action would start when all three species were present. We didn't know what he was talking about then, but now we do."

"We're all here," Nenda said. "Humans, Cecropians, and Zardalu. Great—except we can't find the Zardalu."

"*We* can't. But I'll bet that Speaker-Between can. This is his home ground."

"Yeah—and *we* can't find Speaker-Between." Nenda walked forward to stand in front of the tank and stare up insultingly at Rebka. "Great work, Captain. If you're so convinced Speaker-Between will find us, I don't know why we bothered looking."

Rebka did not move. "Because I'd like to tell him about the Zardalu before *they* tell him," he said quietly. "Just in case he doesn't know their reputation. Got any ideas, smart guy? I'm ready to be amazed."

"That shouldn't take much."

"All right." Darya stepped between them. "That will do. Or I'll set Atvar H'sial on both of you. I thought we agreed, we can't afford to bicker and fight until we're out of this mess."

"I said I'd *cooperate*. I never said I'd bow down in front of him, or that I'd agree with him when he said something really dumb—"

Nenda was interrupted by Atvar H'sial, who came gliding through the air to land by his side. She grabbed him by the arm with one clawed forepaw and pulled him backward so that his head was in contact with the front of her carapace.

"Hey, At," he said. "Whose side are you on? Now just stop that!"

He had been drawn close to the Cecropian and turned bodily to face the chamber entrances. *"What!"* His chest nodules were pulsing. "Are you sure?"

He twisted and called back to Darya. "Behind the tanks. Get a move on! You, too, Captain."

"What's happening?" Rebka eased off the top of the stasis tank, but he came forward instead of moving into hiding.

"At says she's getting a whiff of Zardalu. From out there." Nenda nodded toward the entrance. "She's hearing sounds, too, faint ones. Somethin's coming this way."

"Tell Atvar H'sial to get behind the tanks with Darya. You, too. I'll stay here."

"We playing heroes, Captain?" Nenda rubbed at his bare and pitted chest. "That's fine with me." He turned his body. "Come on, At, let go of me."

The Cecropian did not move. She was crouched forward, her long antennas unfurled and extended as far as they would go. She pulled Nenda closer to her lower carapace.

"Go on," Rebka said. "What are you both waiting for?"

But Nenda had stopped pushing at Atvar H'sial's encircling forelimbs and was peering at the entrance. "I changed my mind. I got to stay here."

"Why, man?" Rebka advanced to stand at his side. "We shouldn't all wait here if there's Zardalu on the way."

"Agreed. So you get back in there with the professor." Nenda turned his head and gave Rebka a curiously distant glance. "At says she smells Hymenopt. Not just any old Hymenopt, either—she smells *Kallik*. I stay."

The next minute was filled with tense inactivity. Nothing emerged from the chamber entrance. Atvar H'sial offered no further information or comment via Louis Nenda. No one else could hear, see, or smell anything unusual. Darya, feeling both foolish and cowardly, came from behind the tanks and moved forward to join the other three. Hans Rebka gave her a sharp look, but he did not suggest that she go back.

The smell came first, a faint and alien whiff that drifted in on the currents of air circulation. Darya did not recognize it. The sudden lump in her chest had to be pure nerves. But she craned forward, straining to see into the gloom beyond the tunnel's mouth, looking for something that loomed three times the height of a human.

"Almost here, according to At." Nenda's gruff voice was reduced to a whisper. "Coupla' seconds more. Hold your hats on."

A shape was moving out of the darkness, slowly, with an odd sideways motion. One moment it could hardly be seen, the next it was fully visible.

Darya heard a bark of laughter from Louis Nenda, standing to her left. She felt like echoing it. The menace had arrived. It was no seven-meter land-cephalopod, supporting itself on a massive sprawl of tentacled limbs. Instead she was looking at a human male, slightly below average height. He wore a bloody bandage around his head, and from his awkward movement he had something badly wrong with his legs or his central nervous system.

He shuffled forward to within a couple of paces of the group. "Some of you do not know me," he said. His voice was quite matter-of-fact. "But I know all of you. You are Darya Lang, Hans Rebka, Louis Nenda, and the Cecropian, Atvar

H'sial. My name is E. C. Tally. I am here to deliver a message, and to ask a question. But first, tell me who is the leader of this group."

Hans Rebka and Louis Nenda glared at each other until Nenda shrugged. "Go ahead. Be my guest."

Rebka turned to E. C. Tally. "I am. What's your question?"

"First, I must make a statement. I am here only as a messenger. The rest of the group that came here with me consists of the humans Julius Graves and Birdie Kelly, the Lo'tfian, J'merlia, and the Hymenopt, Kallik. They are now prisoners of that species known in the spiral arm as *Zardalu*. The others will be executed at once should you seek to free them by violence. I should add that my cooperation was forced by their threat to execute Councilor Graves on the spot if I did not function as requested. And now, the question. Are there members here of other intelligences of the spiral arm, or are you the only ones? Please give the answer loudly and clearly."

"I can't give a definite answer. All I can say is that we are the only ones here *that we know of.*"

"Logic demands that no fuller answer can be justified. I am sure that will be satisfactory. In fact—"

Rebka and the others in the group were no longer listening. Moving out behind the embodied computer and overshadowing him completely came three huge forms. The one in the middle was carrying Kallik, holding her upside down with two tentacles wrapped firmly around the abdomen, so that the gleaming yellow sting could not be employed. That alone was enough to leave Rebka gasping. No organism in the spiral arm should have been able to restrain an adult Hymenopt, one-on-one. But Kallik was not struggling. Her eyes were open, and one of her hind limbs was twisted at a peculiar angle. The cruel blue beak hovered close to the back of Kallik's neck, ready to bite.

The other two Zardalu were carrying nothing but improvised clubs fashioned from the twisted exteriors of food containers. They were almost identical in appearance, except for the necklaces of round-mouthed pouches running around the body below the slitted mouths. In the Zardalu standing on the right, the pale-blue ovals within those pouches were far more prominent, bulging out far from the tight flesh.

The beak of the Zardalu in the center moved, to produce a high-pitched chittering sound. Kallik replied. There was another brief exchange of clicks and whistles.

"Hey, Kallik," Nenda called.

The Hymenopt did not look at him. "E. C. Tally's function as messenger is now over," she said woodenly. "He cannot communicate with the Zardalu, and he is regarded as expendable. He was sent here first as a decoy, in case a killing trap had been set up around this chamber. I *can* communicate with you, and also with the Zardalu. I will therefore be the interpreter for all subsequent messages. The leader of the Zardalu is the one who is holding me. She is to be identified for message purposes as Holder."

"Son of a bitch," Nenda whispered, just loud enough for Rebka to hear. "What have they done to her? That's not my Kallik, the real Kallik."

"They came here prepared for a fight," Rebka said, just as softly. "Ten thousand years in stasis, and still they wake up ready to take on the universe. Watch what you do and say. We can't afford to make one wrong move."

"Tell me about it."

The Zardalu on the left stretched out two of the pale-blue midbody tentacles and pulled E. C. Tally effortlessly back toward it. At the same moment, Kallik was turned in midair by the Zardalu that held her and placed on the ground in front of Louis Nenda. She stood favoring her twisted hind limb. The ring of bright black eyes in the Hymenopt's round head stared up at him unblinking. Nenda nodded slowly. He did not speak.

"Holder knows that you are my former master," Kallik said. "She orders me to tell you that I now serve Holder, and Holder alone."

Louis Nenda swallowed. Darya could see his jaw muscles clenching and unclenching. "I hear you," he said at last. "Tell Holder that I received the message, and I understand it."

"And ask Holder," Rebka added, "what they want from

us. Tell her that we are recent arrivals. We do not know our way around here. We do not know how to reach Speaker-Between, or any other inhabitant of this artifact."

"Holder is aware of many of these things," Kallik said, after another brief exchange with the Zardalu who stood behind her. The Hymenopt's eyes flickered shut, one by one, in a curious pattern, before she continued. "She does not know Speaker-Between's wishes, and she does not care. She and her companions have a single objective. If you help them to achieve it, you and the hostage group will be allowed to live. If you do not cooperate, or if you attempt opposition or treachery, you and all your offspring will die."

"Nice terms. All right, we understand. What's their objective?"

"It is to be released from this place and given a ship for their use. They must be allowed to leave here, without pursuit, and go wherever they choose. For that to happen, Holder and the others know that they will need the cooperation of the beings, whoever they may be, who rule this place. She knows that you are not the rulers."

"That's all got nothing to do with us. What are we supposed to do?"

"Something very simple. Holder also knows that the rulers of this place wish to perform their own experiments using Zardalu, Humans, and Cecropians. Holder is willing to leave one Zardalu here for that purpose. She has already made the selection of that individual. When the ruler beings of this world come to meet with you again, you are to state that you will cooperate with them only after one condition has been fulfilled: namely, all the Zardalu, save one, must have been permitted to leave here in a fully equipped interstellar ship, to go to a destination of their choosing. After that event you Humans and Cecropians will be free to act as you choose, to cooperate with the rulers here or to resist them."

"Tell Holder, wait for one minute." Rebka turned to the other two humans. "You heard all that. I don't think we can do anything except agree, or say we do. But we ought to tell Atvar H'sial what's going on."

"She knows already," Nenda said. "Look at her." The

Cecropian's blind white head was nodding. "I've been giving her pheromonal translations as we went. She agrees, we have no choice but to cooperate."

"Darya?"

"What else can we do, if we don't want Birdie Kelly or Councilor Graves killed?"

"Not a thing." Rebka turned again to Kallik. "You probably followed that, but here is our official response. Tell Holder that we agree to her terms. Tell her we have no idea when we will be contacted by Speaker-Between, or by any other of the beings who control this artifact. But when they do get in touch with us, we will tell them that the price for our cooperation is the release of all the Zardalu, except one. And we will refuse to cooperate until that has been done."

Kallik nodded and again began a clicking and whistling conversation with the Zardalu. A tentacle reached out, seized Kallik around the midsection, and drew her back.

"Holder orders me to tell you that you have made a wise decision," the Hymenopt said. "Naturally, the hostages will continue to be held. However, one of them is close to a terminal condition and is not worth keeping. Holder will use that being, and one other small thing, as examples. She wishes to prove to you the seriousness of Zardalu intention, and to point out to all of you the folly of possible treachery. Holder says, do not try to follow. She will return, at a time of her choosing."

As Kallik finished speaking, the Zardalu leader reached out with another tentacle and grabbed the Hymenopt's injured hind limb. Kallik gave a whistling scream of pain as her leg was twisted off at the upper joint, pulled free of the body, and thrown to land at Louis Nenda's feet.

At the same moment, the Zardalu who had been holding E. C. Tally pushed him forward. The rough, sharp-edged club that it was holding swung sideways with frightful force, to contact Tally's head just above ear level. The whole top of the skull sheared off and flew away across the chamber.

The Zardalu retreated into the tunnel with Kallik. The body of E. C. Tally sprawled motionless in front of Darya Lang. Blood dribbled from the topless head.

* * *

The three humans did not move at once to pick up E. C. Tally. It was left to Atvar H'sial, less knowledgeable about human physiology and human survival needs, to move across to him and lift the ruined body to an upright position. She carried it to where the battered top of the skull was lying on the floor.

"What's she doing?" Darya Lang asked. Her voice was shaking. "He's dead."

Louis Nenda had been sitting slumped on the ground, muttering to himself. At Darya's words he looked up and hurried to his feet.

"She's doing what I should have been doing, if I had any sense. Tally *looks* like a human, but he isn't one. Graves says he's an embodied computer. Back on the planetoid he had his brain popped right out of his head, and it didn't worry him a bit. Come on. Maybe there's some way to get him functioning again."

At first sight it seemed a forlorn hope. The body was limp and lifeless, and the top of the skull had been ripped away to reveal the stark white of broken bone.

"First thing," Nenda said. "Gotta stop the bleeding."

"No." Hans Rebka was reaching into the brain cavity. "That looks bad, but it's not the worst problem. We've got to get his brain back in charge of his body, quickly, or he's done for. Tell Atvar H'sial to hold him. *Tightly.*" The arms and legs were beginning to jerk as Rebka felt under the brain. "See, here's the problem. That blow jarred the neural connection loose. I'm trying to reseat it. Anything happening?"

"Ye-e-s. Yes, indeed." It was E. C. Tally who answered, in a slurred and gurgling voice. "Thank—you. It was apparent to me . . . at once, that the blow had severed the brain-body interface, but without . . . sensory inputs I had no idea what happened next. Nor could I . . . communicate the problem." The bright-blue eyes opened and blinked away blood. Tally glanced around him. "I am now functional. Relatively speaking. I am operating with backup-mode interfaces, but for the time being they appear to be adequate. Where are the Zardalu?"

"Gone. For the moment." Darya had taken the loose top of the skull from Atvar H'sial and was gazing at it hopelessly. It was a mass of bloody, matted hair and sharp-edged bone. "They took Kallik with them."

"They will surely be back. Allow me." Tally reached out and removed the cap of skin, hair, and bone from Darya's hands. He studied it, his blue eyes intent. "The front hinges are gone, completely sheared away. But the rear pins appear intact. They may hold it in position, provided that I do not make sudden movements or allow my head to move far away from the vertical."

He became silent again.

"Are you all right?" Rebka asked.

Tally waved a hand at him. "I have been running diagnostic programs. I had hoped that the only major problem would be the inevitable necrosis of the skull, deprived of its blood supply. But now I know that there are other more serious difficulties. This body is close to end-point failure. It cannot function for more than another few hours; twenty at the outside, in continuous operation. Perhaps twice that long if it is given adequate rest. After that I will become unable to move; then I will lose all sensory inputs. It is important that I transfer potentially useful information to you at once, before any of this happens."

As Tally spoke he was trying to maneuver the loose skull into position. It would not seat cleanly. After a few seconds he gave up the effort. "There is also more structural damage than I thought. We may as well bandage it as best we can and forget it. This is as good a result as I am able to achieve." He sat on the floor with his hands to his head, while Hans Rebka carefully wound the bandage again around the bloodied hair and skin.

"Now," Tally went on. "May I speak? Prepare yourselves to receive information from me. It would be a tragedy if facts that I have already collected could not be passed to you because of my own motor systems malfunctions."

"You can start anytime. I'm listening." The episode with the Zardalu had left Louis Nenda pale, but not from fear. He was scowling, and his nostrils were dilated. "Any information you can give about those blue bastards, I want."

"There is one factor that Julius Graves says is of overwhelming importance. He instructed me to tell it to you, if any possible opportunity arose. Did you see the ring of pouches on each of the Zardalu?"

"Like a bead necklace, all the way around their bodies? Sure. Hard to miss 'em."

"But you probably do not know what they are. They are *reproductive* pouches. Young are developing within each of the swollen beads. The Zardalu appear to be hermaphroditic, and any one of them will produce multiple live offspring. We saw young ones, actually appearing. And they eat ravenously, as soon as they are born."

"There's plenty of food available around here."

"Adequate for us, and for the adult Zardalu forms. But the immature Zardalu are mainly *meat-eaters.* According to what Kallik heard, the Zardalu consider that inferior young will develop if feeding is restricted to what is available from the food suppliers here."

"What do you mean, *inferior?*" Nenda asked. "We're all eating it. Inferior how?"

"I do not know. But Julius Graves is convinced that unless the Zardalu are allowed to leave soon and go where they wish, you and the hostages will be seen as a necessary food supply for their young. Compliance with their demands is most urgent."

Darya was nauseated. But Rebka just shrugged, and Nenda said, "So we're all gonna be kiddie munchies. Great. I don't see how knowin' that does much for us. What else do you have?"

"I can take you at once to the chamber where the Zardalu are located, if that is your wish."

Rebka glanced at the others. "Not quite the top item on our agenda, is it? We don't know what we'd do with it if we had it. Maybe we'd like that later. What else?"

"Something whose value cannot be determined, though Steven Graves argues that it is significant. Kallik is the only one who can communicate with them. The Hymenopts were the slaves of the Zardalu in the distant past, and the Hymenopt language has not changed. Kallik said—"

"Hold on a minute, Tally," Hans Rebka interrupted. "You keep on telling us Kallik said this, Kallik said that. I don't think we can trust a single thing that Kallik tells us. The Zardalu have taken her over completely."

"Uh-uh." Nenda shook his head. "It looked that way, but it ain't so. Kallik and me, we've got codes we use when we can't speak. You couldn't read that flickering pattern of her eyes, when she was down groveling in front of the middle Zardalu. But I could. She was saying to me, over and over, *'Wait. Not yet.'* She knew I was ready to bust out, an' she was telling me it wasn't the time."

"Did she say anything else to you?" Rebka asked. "Any details of their weapons, or maybe their weak spots?"

"Hey, be reasonable. Those eye codes aren't a real *language.* But I'll tell you one thing Kallik told me, indirectly. The Zardalu are *strong.* Nothing should be able to hold an adult Hymenopt. We couldn't do it, if we all tried at once. That Zardalu did it easy. We'll need something special if we're gonna fight 'em."

"But Kallik was weakened," Darya said. "Even before they tore her leg off, she was injured. She might be dead by now."

"Naw." Nenda was turning back to Tally. "You lot just don't know your Hymenopts. Takes a lot more than that to worry Kallik—she's regrowing that leg right now, won't think twice about it. But it makes the point even stronger, and it's not such a nice one. See, if a Zardalu could hold *her,* and do that to her, it'd turn any of us into mincemeat. And talking of mincemeat, let's hear the rest from Tally before the baby Zardalu start squeakin' for dinner. What else did Kallik say?"

The embodied computer had sunk down to a sitting position and was holding the sides of his head. "She was listening to them when we were first captured, before they realized that she could understand Zardalu speech. By the way, Kallik does not hold a high opinion of their intelligence. They did not worry themselves with what they had *already* said in

front of her, even *after* they learned that she could understand them. She heard much of their conversation. Apparently they were captured by The-One-Who-Waits, or
something like him, during the very last days of the Great
Rising. They were transported here already in stasis. At that
time, planet after planet ruled by the Zardalu Communion
had joined the revolution. Zardalu were being systematically
exterminated, and their last few outposts overrun and wiped
out. These fourteen individuals had fled to space to escape.
They were the last ones left. Kallik says *they think that they
are the only surviving members of their species.*"

"I hope they're right," Rebka said. "Be thankful if they
are."

"But that's why they are so absolutely determined to escape from here, and to lie low while they recuperate. Their
strength has always been their breeding powers. Given a quiet
planet and a century or two, there will be hundreds of millions of Zardalu. They will again be organized, and ready to
start over."

The tall form of Atvar H'sial had crouched silent through
all the talk. Now she stirred and turned the open yellow
trumpets on each side of her head toward Louis Nenda.

"I agree with that," he said. He turned back to the others.
"I've been filling At in as we went along on what Tally's been
saying. She makes a good point. If the Zardalu were captured
and put in stasis back near one of their home planets, and they
only just came out of it, it's possible they don't have any idea
where they are now. Me and At never spoke to Speaker-
Between, but I get the idea he's a bit obscure. And the Zardalu must be confused as hell, just coming out of stasis.
Maybe they think they can jump into a ship and take off, and
find a place to hide within a few light-years. That ain't so, but
let's make sure that *we're* not the ones who tell 'em. At says
the smart thing to do is let 'em have a ship, help 'em take off
out of here—and *then* let the blue bastards find they're thirty
thousand light-years from anywhere, and screw 'em six ways
from Tuesday."

"That's fine," Rebka said. "Assuming that Speaker-

Between goes along with it. But I don't see why he would. If he hasn't told them already where they are, he'll probably tell them next time he meets them."

"We can't stop that. But we can make sure it doesn't come from *us*. And maybe steer the conversation in other directions if we get the chance. Might not be hard, if these Zardalu aren't the brightest specimens." Louis Nenda stared at E. C. Tally, whose head was drooping forward onto his chest. "Go on. What else?"

Tally did not speak.

"Leave him alone," Darya said. "He's on his last legs."

"How do you know?"

"Just look at him. He's swaying."

"He may be worse later." Nenda bent down and peered at Tally's drooping eyelids. "The body's resting, but he's not asleep. And this could be our last chance. Give him a jab, Professor, get him going."

"No." This time it was Hans Rebka who spoke. "You're not an expert on embodied computers, Nenda. Neither am I. Tally knows the condition of that body better than any human ever could. If he thinks he has to have rest, he rests. We don't argue."

"So what are the rest of us supposed to do? Sit around here, and wait till the Zardalu ring the dinner bell?"

"More or less." Rebka moved forward and dragged E. C. Tally along the smooth floor, until he could prop him up against a wall. "We've been on the go for days. Every one of us looks ready to drop. We need rest. I'm going to follow Tally's example and take a short nap. If you have any sense you'll do the same. We can take turns to keep watch. And if you all want to be ready for action when the Zardalu come back, better make sure you're not exhausted."

He sat down by Tally's side. "Otherwise . . . Well, otherwise when that bell rings, you may find you're the first course on the menu."

CHAPTER 22

TWO HOURS LATER Darya Lang was alone and prowling the space behind the stasis tanks. Hans Rebka and Louis Nenda had eaten; then Rebka had said with no sign of emotion, "Nice and quiet now. Better get some sleep."

He and Nenda lay down next to Atvar H'sial. All three dropped off at once, apparently without a care in the world.

Sleep. Darya could no more sleep than she could have breathed fluorine.

She glared at the snoring Hans Rebka. She had been having an affair with a robot, a being who lacked all normal fears and feelings. And Nenda was just as bad, if not worse, lying there flat on his back with his mouth open.

E. C. Tally had remained in an upright position, but the embodied computer was also silent. Darya did not dare to try to talk to him. His brain might be engaged in computation, but his body was resting as best it could. Tally was too far gone for rest to extend to restoration.

The bad thing was that Rebka was quite right, and she knew it. It *was* important to rest and keep up one's strength. She had managed to force down a little food, so that was a success. But whenever she closed her eyes the memory of those towering blue-black forms came rushing back, along with a jumble of frightening thoughts. Where were the Zardalu, right now? What was happening to Graves, Birdie Kelly, Kallik, and J'merlia? Were they all still alive?

Finally she gave up any attempt to relax. She left the chamber and went wandering into the surrounding labyrinth of corridors. Even with an imagined Zardalu behind every partition, walking around was better than sitting and watching the others sleep. Her earlier search for Speaker-Between had produced no clear sense of place, and that made her feel uncomfortable. She was a person who needed a sense of spatial context, and now she had a chance to establish one.

It took a couple of hours of systematic search to build up an architectural sense of location. The three-dimensional picture that finally formed in her brain was disconcerting. Darya found that she would reach the end of a corridor, or come out into a broad open chamber, and find viewports set into the walls. They looked out onto vast, open-space structures, long cylinders and spirals and graceful cantilevers of unguessable purpose, arching out beyond the limits of vision. As Nenda said, it would take thousands of years to explore all that complexity—and even longer to understand its function.

But as she walked, the possibility of real exploration also became less and less likely. She could certainly *see* hundreds of thousands, maybe millions, of kilometers of the Builder artifact known as Serenity. But she could not *reach* them. When she plotted out in her mind the places that she had been able to visit before she came to some kind of blind end, the accessible region shrank to modest proportions. She had been able to move only a couple of kilometers in any direction. Maybe *that* was the reason Speaker-Between was so confident that their little group could easily be contacted whenever the alien chose to do so.

The other side of that thought was more disturbing: if their movements were so constrained, escape from the Zardalu also became impossible. For if she and her companions could not move freely through the whole of Serenity, no matter where they hid they would be discovered by any determined pursuer.

Darya tried to bury that thought and keep on walking. Another point had been nagging at her subconscious, but for a while she had trouble pinning it down. It came to her only when she began to move back toward the chamber where she had left the others sleeping.

Gravity. The chamber with the stasis tanks had a field of maybe three-quarters of a standard gravity; but now that she was walking "downhill" she realized that for the past half hour she had been traveling through a region of weaker gravitational force. Carry that thought a little further, and it suggested that there had to be some source of gravitational field in the direction that she was now headed.

When Darya came back to the chamber with the stasis tanks she did not stop. Instead she went straight on through, heading toward the region of strongest gravity field.

She squashed another disquieting thought: This is the direction taken by the departing Zardalu. She wished that Tally had told them just where the Zardalu had set up their camp, but she forced herself to keep moving. In less than a kilometer, the field strengthened substantially. The tunnel she walked in branched a couple of times. Each time she followed the "downward" track. The tunnel began to spiral lower in a tightening helix.

Darya paused. The air within all the chambers remained fresh, through a gentle circulation from unknown sources. But now she could feel a stronger breeze blowing. She licked the back of each hand and held them out in front of her, palms facing and a couple of feet apart. The back of her left hand felt noticeably colder. The light wind was coming from that direction.

Darya went forward more cautiously than before. The moving air was strong enough to ruffle her exposed hair. Already she had a suspicion of what she would find. As she followed the curve of the tunnel, she caught a glimpse of movement ahead.

It was a relief to find something familiar—and yet it was still frightening. The dark, swirling vortex ahead of her, no more than thirty or so steps down the sloping path, was a close relative of the one into which she and Hans Rebka had fallen on Glister. It had the same eye-frustrating property as the circulation pattern that had, while she watched, bodied forth Louis Nenda and Atvar H'sial and then vanished.

Darya was convinced that she was staring into one end of a space transportation system. But she had no idea where she would be taken if she allowed herself to drop into it, or even if there was any way that she could survive the transition. It did *not* represent what she now realized she had been hoping to find when she began her wanderings: an escape route from the Zardalu.

The whirling vortex had a hypnotic quality, tempting her to move closer. Darya resisted and backed away. The slope became rapidly steeper, the gravity field stronger and stronger. Half a dozen more steps, and she would be sucked in, no matter how hard she tried to drag herself away.

Would it *really* take a traveler back to the spiral arm? Or did it lead on to somewhere unknown, and still farther afield? Perhaps at its end lay a true space-time singularity, a maelstrom that would reduce the doomed voyager to independent subnuclear components.

Darya was not willing to find out. But that dark vortex might be a possible last resort, a preferred final alternative to dismemberment by a Zardalu beak. She headed for the chamber where the others lay sleeping.

She went cautiously. The Zardalu were firmly in her mind, to the point where she could think of little else.

No one had said it, but Darya was quite sure that the Zardalu would not leave peacefully, even if they got what they asked for. They would want to be sure that no one could follow them—that no one knew any Zardalu still *existed*; the safest way to make sure of that was to get rid of anyone who had met them.

A sudden deep chuckle from behind her made her muscles tense and her heart leap in her chest. She spun around as something gripped her arm.

"Hey, there," a soft voice said.

It was Louis Nenda. She had heard nothing of his silent approach.

"Don't you ever do that again!"

"Nervous?" He chuckled again. "Calm down, Professor. *I* won't eat you."

"What are you doing here? Couldn't you sleep, either?"

He shrugged. "Little bit. Then I woke up. Too mad to get much rest."

"Too *mad?*"

"Mad. Angry. Pissed. As I've ever been. You saw what that Zardalu did to Kallik."

"I did. But I'm surprised *you* feel that way. She was your faithful slave, and you left her to die, down on Quake; and you fired at a ship with her in it, at Summertide."

"I told Graves and the others, I don't remember firing on no ship." He grinned. "Anyway, even if that happened, I didn't know Kallik was on board, did I?"

"But you admit that you left her to die on Quake."

"Hell, no. I'd have picked her up before things got too hot. Anyway, that's not the point. Kallik is *my* Hymenopt; she belongs to *me*. What I do with her, that's one thing. What that blue bastard did to her, that's something else. It had no right to touch her." He frowned. "What was its name?"

"Holder."

"Right. Well, let me tell you, when we have it out with 'em, nobody else touches Holder. That one's *mine*. And it's dead meat. I'm gonna have Holder's guts fried up and eat 'em for breakfast, even if they make me puke for a week after."

"You talk big when they're not here. You were as quiet as the rest of us when they were."

"I was. And so was Atvar H'sial. Me and her, and Rebka, too, we know how you play this game. You don't rush in, you don't act hasty. You watch, and you wait, and you pick your time. Don't confuse caution with cowardice, Professor."

Darya looked down at the squat, glowering figure. "You talk a good line, Nenda, but it won't help when the Zardalu come. They're three times the size of you, and ten times as strong. And they probably have weapons, and you have none."

Nenda was turning, getting ready to move on. He gave her a pitying smile. "Sweetie, you may be a smart professor, but you don't know much about the real world. You think I don't have weapons? That'll be the first time, then, since I was a little kid." He reached down to his calf, and pulled out a long, thin-bladed knife. "This is just for starters. But it'll do pretty good to make sausage skin out of Zardalu guts. And if you think that *I'm* carrying weapons, go take a look at what Atvar H'sial carries around under her wing cases. She's a real believer in self-preservation. She's smart, though. She knows you use it at the right time, and not before."

He winked at her. "Gotta go. Sleep well, now, and sweet dreams. Remember, me and At are here to look after you."

Darya glared at him as he went on, around the bend in the corridor.

"Watch where you're going," she called after him. "There's a vortex and maybe a field singularity, a few hundred meters that way. I'd be really heartbroken if you fell into it."

He did not answer. Darya continued to the chamber, oddly comforted by the encounter. Louis Nenda and Hans Rebka had at least one thing in common: so many awful things had happened to them already in their lives, nothing broke their spirit.

E. C. Tally had not moved. But Hans Rebka was awake and sitting up—and Atvar H'sial had disappeared.

"No idea," Rebka said in answer to her question. "Don't know about her, or Nenda either. Or you, until you just appeared."

"I saw Nenda." Darya gave him a quick recap of her meeting with Louis Nenda, and of her own travels. "But it's not a safe way out," she said, when she came to the vortex, and her conviction that it was the entry point to a transportation system. "It's not useful at all, until we know if it's meant to take living objects. And it can't be used even then, until we discover its termination points."

"I'm not so sure of that. Things are what people think they are. Don't rule out that vortex."

He refused to explain. And he said nothing more on the subject, except to add thoughtfully, when Darya complained that Speaker-Between had talked with them just once and then deserted them completely, "Speaker-Between and your vortex have one thing in common, and it's something we'd better not forget. They are *alien,* both of them. One of the worst mistakes we can make is to think we understand alien thought patterns—even when it's a *familiar* alien. We think it's hard to know what motivates Atvar H'sial or Kallik or one of the Zardalu; but it's a thousand times as difficult to know what a Builder or its constructs is trying to achieve."

"Do you think we and Speaker-Between are misunderstanding each other?"

"I'm sure we are. Let me give you just one example. We're all feeling angry because we've been left here alone, with no idea what comes next from Speaker-Between. We're upset because we know no way to reach him. But he has been in existence, sitting and waiting, for millions of years! From his point of view, a day—or even a year—is like the blink of an eye. He probably has no idea we're chafing over his absence."

He put his arm around her, leading the way to where Tally was sitting silent and with closed eyes.

"Darya, we have no idea when or if Speaker-Between is likely to return. If you didn't sleep at all, you ought to try again. I caught a couple of hours, and you can't imagine how much better I feel." He saw her looking around. "Don't worry, I won't leave you sleeping if the Zardalu come back. And I won't leave. I'll keep watch right here."

At his insistence, Darya lay down and closed her eyes. Given their situation, she did not expect to catch even a second of rest. She thought again of the Zardalu, of Kallik's whistle of pain as her leg was twisted from her body, of the top of Tally's skull flying across the chamber. Then she recalled Hans Rebka's calm, pale face, and Louis Nenda's anger at what had happened to Kallik, and his irrational self-confidence.

We might be as good as dead, she thought, but those two will never for a second admit it.

She opened her eyes and saw Hans Rebka watching over her. He nodded. She closed her eyes again and was asleep within thirty seconds.

Louis Nenda had not gone far after his encounter with Darya Lang. Less than three hundred meters from where she was sleeping, he was sitting cross-legged on the floor of a small, poorly lit room. Crouched across from him, her carapace close enough for him to reach out and touch, was Atvar H'sial.

"All right." Nenda's pheromonal speech pattern diffused across to the waiting Cecropian. "What did you get from the sonics?"

"Less than you hope. In fact, I think it may be wise to share this information with Captain Rebka and with Professor Lang. It has no conceivable commercial value."

"Let me hear it, though, before we decide that."

"What I saw through low-frequency sonic imaging is probably exactly what you received through your own vision. The external form of the Zardalu is impressively powerful."

"Nothing new there. One of 'em was enough to hold Kallik."

"Easily so. The more interesting information came from the whole-body ultrasonic imaging. The necklace of pouches that circle each Zardalu below the main ingestion organ contains, as E. C. Tally reported, young Zardalu in various stages of development. The broad bands of webbing around the upper part of the tentacles conceal not weapons, as I am sure you also suspected, but food and personal belongings. I do not see that as a threat. More important: the Zardalu have twin circulation centers for their body fluids. The main one, that which carries hematic oxygen, was readily accessible to ultrasonic imaging. It lies deep within the center of the main trunk, half a meter below the necklace, and half a meter below the surface."

Atvar H'sial produced simultaneously the pheromonal equivalents of a curse, a sigh, and a mocking laugh. "Regrettably, the heart is not so easily accessible to your knives as to my sonar. It lies deep. The same is true for their brain center, and for the main conduits of their central nervous system. The brain is below the heart, and the nerve column runs down from there, in the centermost line of the body. It is an efficient design for protection from harm, far better than yours or mine."

"Damnation."

"I know. I am sorry, Louis Nenda. I was able to read your emotions when Kallik's leg was torn off, and I share your ambitions. But their realization will call for more than simple violence."

"What about *your* weapons? Don't you have anything that can take 'em out of action?"

"Not permanently. It was difficult to bring effective weapons through the Bose Transition Points."

"I told Darya Lang you'd blow the Zardalu away."

"That is, unfortunately, wishful thinking. I have knives, but too short to reach the Zardalu brain or heart. I also have three flash electrostatic devices. Not intended as weapons, but they will inflict a painful surface burn. On something the size and strength of a Zardalu, however, they would be no more than irritants."

"Forget it. You might as well try and tickle 'em to death. Is that all?"

"I have one device which was not seen as a weapon in the Dose Network. It could serve me well—but at your expense, as well as that of the Zardalu."

Atvar H'sial reached back under her wing cases and produced a small black ovoid. Nenda stared at it curiously.

"Doesn't look like much. What's it do?"

"It is known as a Starburst. I have two of them. They each produce an intense flash of light in the wavelength range from oh-point-four to one-point-two micrometers. Any creature which sees by means of such radiation will be temporarily or permanently blinded, depending on ocular sensitivity and directness of exposure. I believe that Zardalu eyes operate in that wavelength region. So, unfortunately, do humans', Lo't-fians', and Hymenopts'. I, of course, will be unaffected."

"Better tell me when to shut my eyes, then. It's nice, but it don't solve any problems. How and where could you ever use it? We gotta *think*, At."

"We do; and I am obliged to point out to you that we do not have a monopoly on that process. Distasteful as it will be to you, Louis, we must work with Captain Rebka and Professor Lang. At least until such time as the Zardalu are no longer a problem. After that . . ." The great blind head swung around, as though taking in the whole of the million kilometers of Serenity that surrounded them. "After that, and only after that, can we again begin to operate in rational terms. Which is to say, *commercial* terms; for which, I suggest, there is more than tempting potential here."

"You had the same impression as I did. If we could once get the run of this place, there's things that will have the whole spiral arm drooling."

"And there is far more than we have so far been permitted to see. Somewhere in this artifact lies the technology that *built* the being that Rebka and Lang identify as Speaker-Between, and created an inter*galactic* transportation system. If those secrets can be ours—"

The Cecropian paused. The great antennas on top of the blind head suddenly unfurled like sails, two meters long and a meter wide. They turned to face back toward the chamber where she and Louis Nenda had left Tally and Rebka.

Nenda turned with her. "What's wrong, At? More Zardalu?"

"No. But I am receiving faint new aromatics, like those from The-One-Who-Waits, diffusing in from far away. Unless I am gravely mistaken, the one known as Speaker-Between is entering the stasis-tank chamber containing Rebka, Lang, and Tally. It is, I suspect, a meeting that we would be wise to attend."

CHAPTER 23

FREE MOVEMENT AROUND the interior of Serenity might be denied to humans, but there were others for whom that restriction did not apply.

Darya had new proof of that when Speaker-Between appeared. The alien construct drifted up like a silver ghost through the impervious floor of the chamber. Halfway through he stopped and began decreasing steadily in size. When Louis Nenda and Atvar H'sial came hurrying into the room and had their first sight of the Interlocutor, they were confronted by a bulging hemisphere apparently immovably embedded in the solid floor. Speaker-Between looked just like the upper half of The-One-Who-Waits.

The flower-shaped head craned forward briefly to face the new arrivals, then turned back to Rebka, Lang, and the newly awakened E. C. Tally. The embodied computer was pale and shaky, but fully alert.

"We've been waiting for you since the last meeting," Rebka

said. "There are big problems. Do you know who the Zardalu are?"

"Of course." The flower head drooped and nodded. "Since their arrival they have been my responsibility. It was I who turned off the stasis tanks to permit their reanimation. What is the purpose of your question?"

"They are awake now."

"As they should be."

"And they are dangerous. They have harmed two of our group already, and they are threatening the rest of us. I'm sure you didn't bring our group all this way just to let the Zardalu destroy us."

Speaker-Between did not reply at once. He began to intone in a low mumble: "*Human, Cecropian, Zardalu . . . Human, Cecropian, Zardalu . . .*" Then, after a few moments of silence, he said, "All are present and available. That is as it should be. The process can begin—"

"Not if it involves any of us, it can't." Rebka stepped forward, close enough to touch the shining surface of Speaker-Between. "Until you listen to us, and we get answers to a few major questions, we don't do one thing."

"That cannot be. Your involvement is . . . required."

"Well, just you try to get it, without talking to us first. We won't do it. Not a human, or a Cecropian. There's a transportation-system entry point not far from here. We'll use it if we have to."

Rebka had taken a random shot, fishing for information. But Speaker-Between's answer confirmed Darya's guess.

"That would be most unwise," the Interlocutor said. "Without suitable keys prior to use, no safe endpoint of travel is guaranteed. A transition would surely be fatal."

"We'll risk that. We won't cooperate unless we have some answers from you."

"I say to you, cooperation is *required.*" Speaker-Between was silent again for a few seconds. "But I will listen, and talk if necessary, at least briefly."

"How briefly?"

"For no more than eight of your hours."

"We don't have that long anyway. Let me tell you about the Zardalu, and what they're doing."

"I am hearing." The flower head sighed. "Speak, if you must."

Speaker-Between had listened to Hans Rebka's explanation in total silence. The others interrupted only once, with Louis Nenda's mutter of rage when Rebka came to the Zardalu treatment of Kallik.

"Very good," the Interlocutor said when Rebka came at last to the Zardalu recent threats. "That is all very good. It has begun."

"What has?"

"The process of *selection.*" Speaker-Between lifted himself through the floor, until the whole body and the horned tail were revealed to Nenda and Atvar H'sial for the first time. "The Zardalu, it seems, understand what is needed without explanation. But for the rest of you . . . listen carefully."

To the Builders, it was simply *The Problem.* Compared with that, everything from the transformation of planets to the creation of stars was trivial. And like all problems that demanded their full concentration, this one was purely abstract.

What is the long-term future of the universe?

And tagged onto that central question, as a disturbing corollary, came the other, more personal one:

What is the purpose of the Builders, and what role will they play in the evolution of the universe?

The Builders could not answer, but they were enormously long-lived and endlessly patient. They pondered those questions for two hundred million years and at last came up with a conclusion that was worse than a question: it was a *paradox.*

They concluded that chaotic elements made the long-term future of the universe *undecidable,* in the Gödelian sense of a question that could not be answered from within the framework of the universe itself; but at the same time, undecidable or not, the future of the universe *would happen.* Thus, with or without the Builders, the undecidable question would finally be answered.

Faced with paradox, the Builders made a typical Builder decision. They moved inward, burrowing deep into the nature of their own consciousness. They examined mental processes and thinking structures. They discovered individual quirks of thought and habit, but still they were unable to decide: Were those individual attributes basic to *The Problem,* or irrelevances to it?

Again, the Builders were at an impasse. Worse than that, their inability to deal with *The Problem* began to produce disastrous effects on the Builders themselves. Instead of the pattern of slow evolution and development that had marked hundreds of millions of years, a rapid process of Builder *devolution* began. Debased forms of Builder appeared: the Phages.

It was a way to escape from an intolerable mental problem. Mindless, forgetting their own individual history, ignorant of the accomplishments of their kind, the Phages were as long-lived as their intelligent brothers. Soon they became a nuisance through the whole of the spiral arm. Wherever Builders could live, so could the omnivorous Phages. With their lack of intelligence and their sluggish reflexes, they were rarely dangerous; but they became a great irritation to the equally slow-moving Builders.

Again, the Builders took refuge in their own approach to a new difficulty.

They were no closer to a solution of *The Problem,* but they did not have to hurry. They would *wait,* moving themselves into long-term stasis and leaving their servants and constructs behind, to waken them when the right time came and circumstances changed. Then they would address *The Problem* again, in a different epoch.

There was logic in that decision to wait; for although the Builders had been unable to solve *The Problem* alone, in the future they knew they might have help.

In the course of their development of the spiral arm, the Builders had seen nothing remotely like themselves; but they had noted in passing the development of other life-forms, creatures of the "little worlds," high in heavy elements, whose genesis bore little resemblance to the Builders' own gas-giant origins. The new ones were different . . .

"Different *how?*" That was Louis Nenda, posing a question asked of him by Atvar H'sial. It was the first interruption to the slow words of Speaker-Between.

"Short-lived." Speaker-Between answered without a pause. "Incredibly ephemeral, yet filled with violence, irrational lusts, illogical hopes. Far from ready to be useful, and yet . . ."

The Builders had no difficulty with *short-term* projections of the future, up to ten or twenty million years. Their analytical tools were adequate to estimate rates of species development, and to predict with high accuracy that certain life-forms were on an evolutionary path leading inevitably to self-awareness, intelligence, and technology.

It was far harder to predict where such forms would arrive *philosophically.* Would they develop their own perspective on the purpose of the universe? Would they, one day, despite their strange origins, become suitable collaborators for the Builders themselves?

No forecasting techniques of the Builders could answer that question definitively. It was again related to *The Problem,* and on that question they had already broken the edge of their intelligence.

The Builders saw clearly the emergence of three particular little-world intelligences in the spiral arm. They predicted that each might have a major impact on the future. One of those species, surely, would add the new dimension to Builder thought necessary for a reexamination of *The Problem.* One species. But which one?

That question could not be answered until the species emergence was completed and their civilizations and philosophical underpinnings were established. Only one thing seemed clear: although all three species were very different from the Builders, the one most likely to be useful in adding new insight to *The Problem* would be *the one who differed most from the Builders themselves.*

"You still keep saying we're so *different* from the Builders," Darya said. "I can see that we have far shorter lives. And we are not yet anywhere near so advanced technologically. But those don't seem like *profound* differences—time could change both of them."

"It could, and it will." The silver flower head was nodding, gleaming with internal lights. "But time cannot change certain elements common to you, the Zardalu, and the Cecropians. Common to the Lo'tfians and Hymenopts also, it appears, although those species came later and their influence on the spiral arm has been less. The element possessed by all your species is difficult to capture in a single word. I will call it *prodigality.*"

"You'd better call it something different if you want me to understand it," Louis Nenda said. "What do you mean, *prodigality?*"

"Fertility. Abundance. *Wastefulness.*" Speaker-Between hesitated, struggling with words. He had been doing a good job so far, despite a tendency to long, inscrutable pauses. Darya wondered how much was being subtly distorted by language difficulties. She itched to have her hands on one of the omnilingual translation units so common on far-off Sentinel Gate—and so rare on a poor world like Opal.

Far-off Sentinel Gate.

She realized that seen from Serenity, Opal and Sentinel Gate were next-door neighbors. Eight hundred light-years was nothing, when one was sitting thirty thousand light-years outside the Galaxy.

"Maybe it is best to offer an example," Speaker-Between went on at last. "I have functioned for many millions of years. It is likely that I will function for millions more. If I were to suffer injury, I would repair myself. If I need to do so, I can modify and improve my own operations and organization.

"I am a constructed entity, but the Builders themselves, my creators, developed naturally in the same way. They live forever, by your standards, and they are capable of *individual* self-improvement and transformation.

"Compare that with the beings of your worlds. You are short-lived, every one of you, knowing that each one of you will die, and die very soon, yet you are not obsessed by thoughts of death, or of a future without your presence. By the standards of the Builders, you are incredibly rapid breeders, and your species changes equally rapidly. Yet you are not capable of *self*-improvement, as individuals. That does not matter, for—most astonishing of all—*the survival of an individual is to you of no importance.*"

Louis Nenda gave Darya a little nudge with his elbow. "Hear that? You could sure as hell have fooled me."

"Shhh!"

"The Builders found, on many of the little worlds, wonderfully designed organisms," Speaker-Between continued. "They were highly specialized to run, or fly, or hover in the air, or hunt other creatures with great skill. But the Builders found something even more amazing. Once an individual organism fell in any way from perfect functioning, because of age or minor injury, it was *expendable.* It was allowed to die. That wonderful mechanism was thrown away, while another just as exquisite was created to take its place. That approach to life, that *prodigality,* and the idea that it could ever lead to *intelligent* life—was so alien to the Builders as to be incomprehensible. For if intelligence is any one thing, it is surely *the accumulation of experience.*

"But, the Builders argued, in that incomprehensibility lay the possibility of progress with *The Problem.* They had exhausted the familiar. Therefore, strangeness was absolutely essential to any possible advance. The Builders did not know which of the emerging intelligent life-forms was likely to prove most different from them, but they knew this: *The most alien was the one they would need.* And so they took steps to set up the necessary selection procedure.

"And it was simple. When those three species were sufficiently developed technologically to reach out from the little-worlds and explore the Builder artifacts that populate the spiral arm, they would be ready. Individuals of the three species would be taken as the opportunity occurred. They would be brought here. And here they would meet for the selection process. Stasis might be needed, to assure that representatives were available at the same time, but that was not a problem. Stasis technology has been available for 150 million years. In any case, the Builders predicted emergence close to the same time for each species.

"What was never anticipated was that the individuals of two *different* species might arrive here *together,* as happened with you two." The flower head dipped toward Nenda and Atvar H'sial. "However, that presents no problem. In fact, it simplifies matters, since I do not need to repeat an explanation. Thus, no further wait is needed."

The Interlocutor's voice began to grow deeper and softer. The silvery shape drifted slowly downward. Soon the tail disappeared into the floor, and then the bulging round of the lower body.

"For now you are here, all three species, exactly as required," Speaker-Between said dreamily. "The conditions are met. My initial task has been carried out. The selection procedure can begin.

"In fact, the actions of the Zardalu show that it has *already* begun . . ."

"Wait!" Darya cried. The flower head was all that remained above the smooth floor. "The Builders—tell us where are they located *now.*"

The slow descent halted for a second. "I know many things." The torpor of the voice had been replaced by a curious agony. "But that, *I do not know.*"

The blind head nodded. The silver pentagon drifted downward out of sight.

Hans Rebka, Louis Nenda, and Atvar H'sial had understood immediately. It was Darya Lang, the unworldly professor, and E. C. Tally, the even less worldly embodied computer, who had to have it explained to them—and still had difficulty believing the answers.

After Speaker-Between had left they asked the same questions over and over again of their companions.

"Darya, how many times do you need to be told?" Hans Rebka said at last. "Remember, we're dealing with *alien* thought processes. From *their* point of view, what they're doing is perfectly logical. They have convinced themselves that the beings who may be able to help them with their problem should have the maximum amount of what they think of as 'little world' characteristics—violence and energy and strangeness. The Builders don't want to work with more than one species at a time, so they're going to pick one out. Or rather, they'll let one species pick itself. The 'selection procedure' is designed with that in mind."

"May I speak?"

"No," Nenda said. "You may listen. I'll give it to you in words of one syllable, Tally. That's what the two of you seem to need. The Builders have set us up in a three-way knockout contest. Humans against Cecropians against Zardalu. Winner gets the big prize—survival, and a chance to work with the Builders. Losers get you-know-what."

"But that's absolutely—" Darya checked herself. She had been about to say *inhuman,* which was a ridiculous comment. Instead she changed it to "That's absolutely barbaric. *You*— Louis Nenda. You wouldn't go into a fight to the death with your friend Atvar H'sial, would you?"

"Course not." Nenda stared across at the hulking Cecropian. "Least, not till I was sure I'd *win.* Look, Professor, what I'd choose to do and not do ain't the issue. We were just told the rules. We didn't pick 'em. I think there's only one way for us to operate—and At agrees with me, she's been trackin' our talk. First, we gotta take care of the Zardalu and bust their asses. *After* that we decide how we'll squabble between humans and Cecropians."

"There are fourteen of them," Tally said quietly. "And nine of us—four of whom are already Zardalu hostages."

Nenda snorted. "What do you want to do, go and explain *arithmetic* to Speaker-Between and say it's not fair? By the time he shows up again we could all be dead."

"Nenda's right, E.C." Rebka took over again. "It doesn't matter how we got into the position we're in, or how little we like it. We have to accept it and work out how we'll survive. If we sit here and wait for the Zardalu to come back, that takes us nowhere. They'll find out we didn't reach any deal with Speaker-Between for them, and they'll blame us."

"But what can we *do?*" Darya felt she was not getting her

urgency across to Rebka. He was as cool and thoughtful as if they were having a round-table discussion of landing permits on Opal. "The Zardalu could be here any minute."

"Could, and probably will." Rebka glanced around, assessing each member of the group. "So let's find out what we've got between us, information and possessions."

"Right!" Nenda said. "Then we better do a little reconnoiter, see where they are and what they're doing. I've had experience in that, and so has At. Tally can tell us where to find 'em."

"But they're so big, and so strong . . ." Darya found it hard to say what she was really thinking, that the thought of the Zardalu gave her the shivers. And she did not like that look in Nenda's eyes, either, an odd blend of pleasure and anger.

"What can *observing* them do?" she continued. "It won't make them weaker, or us stronger."

"*Wrong.*" Nenda glared at her. "Information is strength, sweetheart. We take a peek at 'em. Then we come back here, pool all we've got and all we know. And then we *hit 'em,* quick. Zardalu, here we come! I'll bet that's the *last* thing they're expecting."

It was the last thing that Darya was expecting, too. Pool *what?* They didn't have a thing—not even information. The Zardalu held all the cards: strength, numbers, ruthlessness, hostages.

But looking at the determination on the faces of Hans Rebka and Louis Nenda, Darya did not think her views were going to count for much.

CHAPTER 24

"HAVE YOU EVER seen a human birth—a normal one, I mean, not in a tank or with an animal surrogate?" Birdie Kelly was speaking in a whisper.

Julius Graves avoided a spoken answer altogether, relying on his head shake being visible even in the low-level light.

"Well, *I* have," Birdie went on softly. "A dozen times, back on Opal. And let me tell you, it's a terrific effort for the mother, even when everything goes fine. You see it once, it makes you glad you're male. The women get pleasure out of it later, you see it on their faces when they hold their baby. But that don't make it less painful, or less hard work. But these critters . . ." He shook his head.

The two men were sitting in a corner of the room. J'merlia was a few meters away with Kallik. Occasionally they whistled and clicked gently to each other, but most of Kallik's attention was on the Zardalu.

The fourteen massive bodies lay sprawled between them

and the only entrance. Now and again a great lidded eye
would turn and blink toward Graves and Kelly; otherwise the
land-cephalopods seemed scarcely aware of human presence.
Certainly they were not worried that any of the group might
escape.

The Zardalu talked to each other in their own language,
which to Birdie sounded just like the speech that Kallik used.
Steven Graves had assured him that was an illusion. The
Zardalu vocal chords merely produced a range of frequencies
and vocal fricatives similar to a Hymenopt's; or, just as likely,
the Hymenopts had many centuries earlier been trained to
speak so that their masters would understand.

But it was not their speech that held Birdie Kelly's attention. As they spoke, or ate, or simply lay and rested, the
Zardalu were giving birth. They performed the act quickly,
easily, and casually.

Birdie and Julius Graves had watched the whole process,
while Steven Graves recorded it in his capacious memory,
against the time—the unlikely time, Birdie thought—when
he would be able to add it to the central data banks of the
Fourth Alliance. Steven had also noted his opinion that the
Zardalu had evolved in and preferred a low illumination level.
He based that on the fact that they had sought out the least
well lit chamber they could find that contained a food supply.

Steven had not tried to check his ideas against Kallik's
spotty flashes of race memory of the Zardalu. She was unreliable. The others had all seen her when the giant land-cephalopods had first appeared. What she had done then, and was
doing now, went well beyond cooperation for possible future
gain. At the first sight of the ancient masters Kallik had
dropped flat and groveled on her belly, unwilling to look up
with any of her ring of black eyes.

The Zardalu accepted her servitude as natural. The injury
to her leg had been done to confirm Holder's dominance
when Kallik was lying helpless, not because she was resisting.
Like Louis Nenda, the Zardalu must know that the loss of a
limb was not a major trauma to a Hymenopt.

As Graves and Kelly watched, another four Zardalu were

giving birth. The first sign was a rhythmic pulse in one of the swollen locations on the necklace of pouches. That was followed, in less than five minutes, by the appearance from that pouch of a rounded cone, like the tip of a shell. It was pale blue in color and quickly swelled to protrude six inches from the opening of the pouch.

At first Birdie had thought that cone-tip to be the head of the newborn. He realized his mistake when the pointed tip began to bulge farther and split open. From it emerged a smooth, rounded egg shape of pale apricot. That surprised Birdie more than he was ready to admit. He had grown to expect everything about the Zardalu, from eyes to torso to tentacle tips, to be some shade of blue.

The egg shape was the cerebral sac of a live infant, born head first. It arrived as a miniature version of the parent, except for its rudimentary tentacles. It wriggled completely free of the pouch in a couple more minutes, took a first, rippling breath, then slithered down the adult's body to a haven under the canopy of tentacles. Birdie caught a last glimpse of pale orange, then saw nothing for another few minutes. But soon the beak and mouth appeared from between the bases of two of the parent's tentacles. There was a faint whistling sound. Fragments of food selected from the containers in the center of the chamber were fed in by the parent to the complaining offspring.

From the reaction of the young Zardalu, that was not what they wanted. Within another few minutes they were pushing farther out, biting hungrily with their sharp-edged beaks at the parent's flesh.

And meanwhile, a second pouch on the necklace was steadily beginning to swell . . .

"I'm afraid they won't settle for that for very long," Graves said. "It's meat they want."

"Kallik said that they can survive on other food—if they have to." Birdie hoped he sounded more optimistic than he felt.

Graves nodded. "But they don't see any reason why they *should*. We have to change that, if we can." He began to ease his way quietly over to Kallik. The site of the Hymenopt's lost limb had already sealed, and the bud of new growth was peeping through.

"We've been waiting for over five hours now," Graves said as soon as he was close enough for her to hear his whisper. "How long before they do something new?"

As he spoke, Graves saw Birdie Kelly's reproachful look. For the past few hours there had been unspoken agreement that they would not rely on the Hymenopt for *anything*. Graves shrugged in reply. What other options did they have? They could not understand the Zardalu, even if their captors were willing to talk to them.

Kallik whistled softly to J'merlia, then said, "I do not know. They are not discussing their plans in my hearing. However, I see new signs of impatience. There are already more young ones than mature Zardalu, and they are under pressure to find a more suitable habitat. They wish to leave this place."

"Will they permit you to ask them a question, or transmit a suggestion?"

"It would not be appropriate for a slave to do so."

"But suppose that a human were to *order* you to do it?"

Kallik stared up at Julius Graves with bright, inscrutable eyes. "If the Zardalu were told that the human concerned was my former master, they *might* understand if I were to ask a question on his behalf. Or—" She paused.

"Yes?"

"Or they might be violently enraged, thinking that I offer less than total obedience to them. They might choose to kill me, as a being of divided loyalty."

Julius Graves shook his head. "Then let's forget it."

"However," Kallik went on, "I do not think that is the most probable outcome. They know that I am their only avenue of communication with you, and with the other humans. They will not want to lose that channel. What is your message?"

"I would like to propose that I be used as an emissary to Captain Rebka and the others. Tell the Zardalu that I can explain the need for rapid action by the other group, and I can point out to them why the Zardalu must leave this place as soon as possible. I would like you to emphasize that my role in human affairs has always been that of an intermediary between species. Ask them if I may serve in that role now."

Kallik held another brief, whistling conversation with J'merlia. "Wait here," she said at last. "I will try." She crawled away toward the tight cluster of Zardalu, keeping her stubby body always close to the floor and her yellow sting fully sheathed.

"And I thought *one* traitor was bad enough," Birdie Kelly said softly, as soon as Kallik was out of earshot. "You're worse than she is. At least she was *raised* to be a slave."

"You know me better than that, Commissioner. Or you ought to. I've spent my life working on interspecies problems. That's what this is, you know. I can't just sit back now and *watch.*"

"So you want to sell out to them, be another slave."

"Of course I don't. But at the moment we're just bargaining chips as far as the Zardalu are concerned. That's not good enough. We have to establish some form of direct communication with them. They need to think of us as *people*—reasoning, intelligent beings, the same as they are."

"*Them,* think of us that way. Fat chance! What makes you think they respond to reason?"

Graves nodded to where a group of midnight-blue bodies had moved to cluster around Kallik. "Improbable, perhaps. But look over there. Maybe it is working."

One of the forms had towered up onto its powerful tentacles and was moving toward them, followed by the little Hymenopt.

In front of J'merlia it stopped and bent down to stare at him with cool, pale-blue eyes, each as big as the Lo'tfian's head. Then it turned to offer the same inspection of Graves and Birdie Kelly.

A soft fluting and a series of clicks came from the cruel, sky-blue beak. Finally the Zardalu rose to its full height and stalked away across the chamber, back to its companions.

"Well?" Graves asked. "What did it say to us? Did they agree?"

Kallik was shaking her head. "With all respect, I think that perhaps it was a mistake to rouse them by asking your question. They say that I am quite adequate to provide all the communication that is needed with humans, and that if necessary J'merlia can communicate with his master, the Cecropian Atvar H'sial. Further, they say that the other group will be permitted just one more hour, to hold a meeting with the beings who control this place and arrange for the Zardalu to leave for a destination of their own choosing. If nothing is done in that time, actions will be taken."

Birdie Kelly glared at Graves. "I told you. A washout! So why did that thing even bother to come over here? What did it say to us, Kallik?"

"Not one word *to* you, I fear. But certainly words *about* you. It told me that a decision had been made. In one hour, the Zardalu will again contact the other group. If at that time no satisfactory arrangement has been made for the Zardalu to leave this place, another hostage will be sacrificed." The Hymenopt gazed at Birdie with dark, unblinking eyes. "With great regrets, Commissioner, the decision was made that you should be that sacrifice."

Birdie stared at Kallik, unable to speak. It was Julius Graves who jumped to his feet. "You go right back there, and tell them we'll *all* fight them to the death, before we let something like that happen." Graves's radiation-scarred face became pale with rage. "Commissioner Kelly is as valuable as any of us! He has as many talents as I do! We won't let them think of *any* of us as *expendable.*"

"With respect, Councilor Graves." Kallik's ring of eyes had turned away to avoid Birdie completely. "The issue was not talents, or who is expendable. You and the commissioner appear to have been judged equal in that regard."

"So what the devil was it?"

Kallik's eyes moved to Julius Graves, still avoiding Birdie. "It was something much simpler, Councilor. The Zardalu young are growing and becoming more demanding.

"You are very thin. Commissioner Kelly is undeniably *better fleshed.*"

CHAPTER 25

BIRDIE KELLY HAD never thought of himself as a hero. Quite the opposite. When other men went looking for trouble, Birdie was already looking for cover.

But this time it was different. He was the target, and there *was* no cover. He had to do *something*.

Birdie's minor shift toward bravery began as a horrified inspection of the Zardalu, particularly their hungry young. They seemed to be forever peeking out from under the protective umbrellas of tentacles, begging for food. The light-orange beaks were small, only half an inch across, but there was no doubt about their sharpness. They cut easily through any food fragment, even the hardest shells or rinds, and they made the adult Zardalu jump when the infants, dissatisfied with what was offered to them, nicked the tough flesh at the base of their parents' bodies.

After the first morbid fascination of that sight wore off, Birdie shuffled quietly over to Julius Graves. "Councilor, what are we going to do? You heard Kallik—another hour and we're done for. Me first, then all of us."

Graves was nodding, the great bald head furrowed with worry. "I know, I know. We won't let them take you, Commissioner. They'll have to fight all of us before that happens. But what can we do? They refuse to listen to me, or allow me to act as an intermediary with the others. If only they would sit down, and *talk* . . ."

Talk was not what Birdie had in mind. In his experience, people who wanted to sit down and talk were the ones who were going to lose the argument. What he would have preferred was more along the lines of a nice 88-gauge automatic cannon.

He nodded and crawled back to his place. Julius Graves was full of talk, but he was not going to do one damned thing. Certainly he would not be able to stop the Zardalu from using Birdie as baby-chow any time they felt like it.

Birdie stared again at their captors. His inspection moved from a horrified stare at the young ones to a general survey of all the land-cephalopods.

They certainly had that *look* of invulnerability. But he knew it was an illusion. Eleven thousand years earlier, species who had been trained from birth to believe in Zardalu superiority had risen to fight their tyrant masters—and won. They had exterminated the Zardalu, except for these last few remaining specimens.

There had to be some chink in the armor, some flaw that had been exploited at the time of the Great Rising . . .

It was certainly not easy to see one. Birdie had watched earlier, when two of the Zardalu picked up empty food containers and squeezed them to form rough clubs. Now he wandered over to a food container himself, and put all his weight on it. It did not budge a millimeter. Birdie sat down again with a new respect for the power of those three-meter ropy tentacles. They could pulverize him without putting one of their nonexistent hairs out of place.

So. They were as strong as they looked.

How well did they see and hear? None of the Zardalu was turned his way at the moment. Birdie drummed lightly on the side of the empty food box with his fingertips, producing a light *pa-pa-pa-pam*. No result. A few harder blows with the flat of his hand produced no reaction from the Zardalu.

Birdie stood up, slowly and quietly, went across to the side of the chamber, and began to edge his way around it. The Zardalu were close to the single exit, but on one side there was space for a human to slide along the wall without coming within tentacle range of any of them.

Birdie sidled along until he was no more than a few paces from the nearest Zardalu. He soon reached a point where he could see out of the chamber. The exit led to an open corridor. One mad dash would take him out there and on his way through the unknown interior. He rose onto the balls of his feet. At that very moment the biggest one, the one identified as Holder, fluted a few liquid sounds to where Graves, Kallik, and J'merlia were lying.

"With respect, Commissioner Kelly," Kallik called. "The Zardalu do not want you in your present location. You are commanded to return at once to join the rest of us. And when you do so, the Zardalu order you to refrain from hammering on the food containers. The noise creates unrest in the young."

Birdie nodded. The scariest thing of all was that the Zardalu did not bother to *threaten* him with consequences if he did not obey. *They* knew *he* knew. He was turning to inch his way back along the same smooth gray wall when he caught sight of movement in the outside corridor. He forced himself to keep turning, resisting the urge to stop and stare. His split-second glance had not been enough to identify the individual person, but it *was* a person, and not a Zardalu, Cecropian, or other alien. Someone human was out there, crouched low in the angle of the corridor, peeping out now and again to observe what was going on inside the chamber. And far behind, almost indistinguishable from the darker shadows, Birdie thought he had caught a glimpse of another, less familiar form.

Birdie slid steadily back along the wall and returned to sit by Julius Graves. A few minutes earlier he had been convinced that the Zardalu were hard of hearing; now he was not so sure. For all he knew they could hear the slightest whisper. And even if they could not, certainly Kallik could, and the traitorous Hymenopt would tell the Zardalu anything that she heard.

He leaned forward to put his mouth right next to Graves's ear. "Don't say anything or do anything," he breathed. "But help may be on the way."

"What?" Graves said, loud enough to be heard twenty yards off. "You'll have to speak up, Commissioner. My hearing isn't too good."

"Nothing," Birdie said hurriedly. "I didn't say a thing."

Several of the Zardalu turned to stare at them with those huge, heavy-lidded eyes of cerulean blue. Before Birdie had time to feel guilty at rousing them to attention, another land-cephalopod, closer to the door, started up onto its powerful splayed tentacles. There was a pipe-organ whistle from the ingestion organ, and the Zardalu headed out of the chamber.

Birdie had never seen anything that big move so fast and so silently. The Zardalu flashed out of the room like a silent specter of midnight blue, one moment there, the next vanished. Birdie heard the sound of rapid movement outside and a startled cry. He knew that the sound had not come from the vanished Zardalu. Those were human vocal cords, the same ones that now produced a hoarse roar of pain.

"What was that?" Graves asked. "What happened?"

Birdie did not need to answer. The vanished Zardalu was coming back into the room. It was not alone. Dangling two meters from the ground, suspended by one brawny tentacle wrapped around his neck to carry his weight and cut off his breathing, hung the kicking, purple-faced figure of Louis Nenda.

"Not to spy." Louis Nenda rubbed at his bruised throat. Released from the killing grip of the tentacle but with another sinewy extensor wrapped snugly about his chest and arms, he was reluctant to meet the gaze of either humans or aliens. He kept his eyes downcast, and he spoke in a low voice.

"Not to spy," he said again. "Or to turn against my fellow humans. I came here to—to try to—*negotiate.*"

Kallik was crouched in front of him, half her ring of eyes fixed on his expression, the others attentive to her masters. The leader of the Zardalu whistled and fluted, and its companion's grip on Nenda tightened.

"You were told in the last meeting that you were not to take the initiative," Kallik translated. "You were told to stay and arrange with the being called Speaker-Between for the Zardalu's immediate departure from this place. Are humans too stupid to understand direct commands?"

"No." Nenda was struggling for breath. The ropy arm around his chest was gradually tightening. "We held that meeting, just like we said we would. But it was no good! Speaker-Between wouldn't agree they could leave. We can't control him!"

There was a louder series of clicks from Holder as those words were passed on.

"But you suggested that you could. You must be taught a lesson," Kallik translated.

Another tentacle came forward and wrapped its ropy end section around Nenda's left leg. It began to pull. As the limb was slowly twisted and stretched downward, Nenda roared in agony.

"Let him go! Right now." Julius Graves rashly ran forward to stretch up and beat at the Zardalu's lower body. Another tentacle came up and batted him contemptuously away. At the same time, Kallik produced a rapid series of chirps and whistles.

The twisting and pulling ended, and Nenda sagged in the Zardalu's grasp.

"I have explained," Kallik said to Graves, lying winded on the floor, "that humans are quite different from Hymenopts. The removal of any limb would be far more serious in Louis Nenda's case than in mine. It would probably result in death."

Graves nodded. But as Nenda's leg was released, Holder spoke again to Kallik.

"Holder asks," the Hymenopt said to Nenda, "why should your death matter? You were once my master, and perhaps I am trying to serve you, even now. I said that is not so. But

Holder points out that the young ones are in need of proper food, and the value of your continued existence is not clear. Holder is sure that you were attempting to spy, even though you deny it. And Finder, the Zardalu who captured you, thought that it saw another stranger, far along the corridor, one that fled when you were taken. Another spy, perhaps, who escaped when you could not? But that is not the issue here. Can you suggest one reason why you should be allowed to live? If so, give it quickly."

Nenda glanced at Julius Graves and Birdie Kelly, then looked away. His face and neck were covered in sweat. "I can give Holder a reason," he said huskily. "That is why I came here. I can be very valuable to you, if you will promise that my life will be spared. And if you don't hurt me any more. I am not able to—to stand more pain."

"Holder is amused by your ignorance and presumption," Kallik replied after another brief exchange with the Zardalu leader. "A Zardalu makes no promise. But it will listen to you, rather than killing you at once. What do you possibly have that is of value?"

Nenda licked his lips. "Tell Holder this. They want to excape from here and get back to a planet in the old Zardalu Communion. Well, I can show them how to do it. Right now."

Another whistled exchange. "Holder does not believe you."

"Tell Holder that I can prove it. In her travels through this artifact, one of our party found the entry point to a Builder transportation system. She told the rest of us about it—explained exactly where it is, how to use it. It's in working order. Tell Holder I can take her there, and they can be on their way to where they want to go. They'll be gone before Speaker-Between even knows they found the entry point."

"Nenda! You can't do this." Julius Graves had dragged himself back to his feet. "God knows, I don't want you or anyone else killed. But think of what you'll be doing if you show them how to make a transition. You'll be putting Zardalu *back into the spiral arm*, letting them run free to start their—"

A muscular tentacle reached out and swatted Graves across his upper arm and shoulder. Graves cried out in pain and collapsed to the floor.

Birdie Kelly hurried across to his side. While the Zardalu held a longer conversation among themselves, he examined Graves.

"Not broken," he said softly. "A deep bruise. Maybe a cracked collarbone, though I don't think so. Hold still. Don't try to move your arm. I'll tie it against your chest." He glared across at Louis Nenda and raised his voice. "And you, you bag of slime. You're worse than Kallik. You'd better hope we don't get out of this alive. Or your name and Kallik's will be a curse everywhere in the spiral arm."

"Silence." Kallik gestured to J'merlia, who had all the time been crouched close to the floor, his pale-lemon eyes jittering nervously on their stalks from one speaker to the next. The Lo'tfian crept forward to stand next to Julius Graves.

"Help him to walk, J'merlia, if he needs it," Kallik said. "Holder has decided. We are going with Nenda—all of us. The Zardalu will inspect the transportation system. And it had better function as Nenda promises, or you will all suffer." She pointed one wiry limb at the Zardalu standing next to her, where a pale-orange oval was just visible behind the fringe of tentacles. "Holder says we should not try to escape as we travel. The young ones are hungry. They do not mind how their food is provided to them—dead, or alive."

The journey through the darker tunnels of the Builder artifact took a long time. The Zardalu were willing to investigate Louis Nenda's claim, but they were not naive enough to believe that there was no trickery or traps. They went slowly, using hostages to probe suspect areas and inspecting every corridor closely before they went into it.

Julius Graves and J'merlia were made to walk in front, as triggers for possible booby traps. They were closely followed by six Zardalu. Birdie Kelly, next in line, was amazed to see that the newly born were still emerging, even while the blue towers in front of him were gliding forward. As he watched, the bright apricot of two more miniature Zardalu emerged from their birth sacs in the necklace of pouches. As soon as they were completely born they slithered down the rubbery, oil-coated trunk to take refuge beneath the main body, sheltered by surrounding tentacles. Minutes later the little beaks appeared, begging for food. The parents fed them as they walked with scraps taken from the broad webbing satchels circling the base of their torsos.

Louis Nenda was at Kelly's side. Birdie rebuffed the other man's attempt to talk to him. After a couple of tries Nenda turned around to Kallik, who walked at the rear in the middle of the remaining eight Zardalu.

"Ask Holder somethin', will you?" he said. "Ask what happens when we get to the transportation system. Remind her how much I'm doing to help 'em. Say it's only fair that I should be set free."

There was a fluting whistle from the giant Zardalu as the message was translated.

"Holder agrees, at least in part," Kallik said. "*If* everything is as you promised, you will not be killed. If everything is *not* as you say, you should already be trembling."

Birdie turned his head. "*You* ought to be eaten, Nenda, you lousy traitor. That'd save the rest of us—because your stinking carcass would poison every Zardalu that touched it. If there's any justice, you'll be the first to go."

"Justice? Ah, but there ain't no justice, Commissioner." Nenda was staring all around him, eyes bloodshot and intense. "Not here, and not anywhere in the spiral arm. You've been around long enough to know that. There's only people like you and me, and blue bastards like the Zardalu."

Birdie glared at him. The damnable thing was that Nenda was right. There *was* no justice. There never had been, and there never would be. If there were, he would not be here at all. He would be back home on Opal, safe in bed.

Birdie made his own gloomy inspection of their surroundings as they walked on through dark corridors and big, open chambers. Even this tiny piece of the artifact was huge and eerily alien. Since arriving here and being captured by the Zardalu, he had been dragged from one place to the next, never having an opportunity to know quite where he was going or why. Now, examining the objects that they passed, Birdie realized that he could not guess the purpose of *any* of them. *Something* certainly kept the place ticking; there was fresh air in the corridors, food in the lockers, and functioning waste-disposal units for beings with needs as different as those of humans and Lo'tfians and Zardalu. But it was a wholly *hidden* something. There was no sign of *mechanisms,* no pumps or supply lines or ducting. Birdie had no idea how the artifact functioned. It was depressing to reflect that he was never likely to know.

He was pulled out of his musings when he bumped into the massive back of one of the Zardalu. Ahead of them, J'merlia and Julius Graves had suddenly stopped and turned around. They had reached the edge of a slope that spiraled gently down into darkness.

"What is wrong?" Kallik called from behind.

"It gets really steep down there," Graves said. "The tunnel is narrowing, and past this point it's no more than three or four meters wide. The gravity field is increasing, too. Once I take another ten steps I'm not sure I'll be able to pull back."

"That's all right." Nenda pushed forward through the solid rank of the Zardalu. "Stop where you are. Feel that stronger air current? It comes from the vortex itself. We're nearly there, at the ramp that leads to the transportation system."

He moved forward again, to stand at the very brink of the descending spiral. The breeze from the rotating singularity at the end of the tunnel blew his perspiration-drenched dark hair back from his face. "Kallik, tell Holder we are here. Explain that using the system is easy. All they have to do is walk down and enter the vortex itself."

He turned, trying to move back to join Birdie Kelly. But the Zardalu would not let him through. Instead, Birdie and Kallik were pushed *forward,* so that within a few seconds all the Zardalu stood to the rear of the group.

Holder fluted and whistled.

"They say we must go first," Kallik said. "All of us. Before they enter the system, we must do so. We are going with them, back to the spiral arm."

Nenda glanced over his shoulder, down the curved slope

that led to the vortex, then looked back to Kallik. "But I'm the one who brought them here! Tell 'em that, Kallik. Tell 'em they promised I'd have my freedom."

Julius Graves laughed, wincing at the pain it produced in his injured arm and shoulder. "No, Louis Nenda, they didn't promise. No Zardalu said anything like that. You heard what you wanted to hear. They never intended to allow any of us to go free. When we arrive at their destination, and they have no more use for us, you'll learn what their plans for us really are. I am not a vindictive man—a councilor cannot afford to be—but in this case I agree with Birdie Kelly. If there is justice in the universe, you will be the first to go."

"And if there is risk," Kallik said, "then Holder says you will share it. If there is danger down at the vortex, speak of it now. For perhaps with that warning your life will be spared."

Nenda turned to face the Hymenopt. He opened his mouth as though to reply, but instead he placed two fingers between his teeth and produced a high-pitched whistle followed by a loud cry: "Close your eyes! Cover them with your hands."

As he shouted, a small black ellipsoid came curving up in a smooth arc from the dark depths of the tunnel.

Nenda shot a glance at the others. He cursed. Kallik and J'merlia had at once obeyed his shouted command and tucked their heads down toward the protection of their multiple legs. But Julius Graves and Birdie Kelly were doing the worst thing possible: they were staring straight at the ovoid as it passed over their heads.

He could do nothing about Graves, but Birdie Kelly was within reach. Nenda thrust his arm out, a fraction of an inch from Birdie's face, so that the other man reflexively blinked. Nenda held his arm there and at the same moment squeezed his own eyes tight shut. He threw his other arm up to shield his face. The last thing he saw before his eyes closed was a Zardalu tentacle, reaching up toward the oval shape to smash it back where it had come.

The Zardalu was a split second too late. With his eyes closed and one forearm jammed hard across them, Louis Nenda saw the world turn bright red.

He felt his skin tingling in the flood of radiation. He stood and waited, for what felt like forever and could have been no more than half a second. The light level in the tunnel had to be just incredible if so much could bleed its way in past his arm and through his eyelids.

When everything went black he uncovered his eyes. He grabbed Birdie Kelly in both arms and pushed him over to drop to the floor of the tunnel. He landed on top of Birdie, curling into a ball as he did so.

His precautions were unnecessary. The Starburst must have triggered just a meter or two in front of the assembled Zardalu. When the brightness of a supernova flashed into being, they had all been staring at it. Now every Zardalu eye was covered by tentacles, and fluid was beginning to seep past the fine tendrils at the ends. Disorganized whistles, clicks, and moans filled the tunnel.

Nenda's own world was a maze of flickering images, with the red network of veins in his eyelids superimposed on them. But he could see—well enough to know that their problems were just beginning.

Sightless Zardalu blocked the way out of the tunnel. They were thrashing around with their tentacles, grabbing blindly at anything above waist height. The way back to the tunnel was closed by a mass of writhing, muscular snakes.

For the moment Nenda and Kelly were safe enough on the floor. So were J'merlia and Kallik. Nenda could not tell if they were able to see, but they had dropped instinctively to the ground in a splay of thin limbs.

The problem was Julius Graves. The councilor had been blinded. He was groping his way farther along the tunnel, to the place where it steepened rapidly. A couple more steps and he would fall forward, pulled by the increasing gravity field past the point of no return. In his fall, he was likely to take anyone else with him who might be in that tunnel, right down into the vortex field. Louis Nenda knew what was down there, and he could not allow that.

He dared not shout a warning to Graves. The Zardalu would home in on his call. Instead he crawled right over Birdie Kelly, who was struggling for breath with all the wind knocked out of him. Nenda came up to a half crouch and dived forward. As he hit the ground again he grabbed Graves around the knees and heaved backward.

Graves was caught with one leg in the air, ready to take another blind step. He fell sideways and to the left, crying out with pain as he landed heavily on his injured arm.

That was all the clue that the Zardalu needed. Half-a-dozen long tentacles converged at once on the place. They reached for Graves. But they found Louis Nenda.

Before he saw them he felt their touch on his leg, like oiled silk over solid rubber. He tried to escape by crawling farther down the tunnel, toward the vortex. He was too late. One sinewy arm circled his legs; another coiled around his waist. They tightened and lifted him high in the air. His head hit the tunnel roof. Then he was being dragged toward the Zardalu. Even before the pain began, he knew what was going to happen. The tentacles around his body and his legs belonged to two different aliens. One of Holder's long arms had him at the waist, but another Zardalu at the front of the group held his knees. They were both blinded, unaware of what the other was doing. And each was intent on pulling Louis Nenda within reach of its own beak.

Held high above the heads of the Zardalu, Nenda saw Darya Lang, Hans Rebka, and E. C. Tally appear in the tunnel behind them. They each held a flashburn unit. They began using them to sting and burn the Zardalu from the rear, forcing them to spin around so that they would lose their sense of direction, then driving them forward along the corridor in reflexive jerks.

But that would not help Nenda. The two holding him were in the front of the group, shielded from the humans by the Zardalu behind them.

The tentacles began to tighten on his body, pulling in opposite directions. He could not breathe. His lower back felt as if it were breaking. He was stretched, pulled apart by terrible forces. He knew what was going to happen. In another second he would be torn in two. He could do nothing to prevent it.

In his agony Nenda could not see clearly. When something black flashed past him, flying through the air toward the

Zardalu, he did not know what it was. He made a great effort and turned his head.

As he did so, the tearing forces on him slackened for a moment. He realized that the flying object he had seen was Kallik.

The Hymenopt had leapt straight out of a crouched position with all the power of her wiry legs. Her spring carried her high in the air, to the top of the head of one of the Zardalu holding Nenda. Kallik's clawed paws dug into the Zardalu's tough hide and held there. She clutched the rounded head above the blinded eyes and the wicked beak.

The Zardalu was reaching up with two of its tentacles, but Kallik did not flinch. The yellow sting appeared from its sheath at the bottom of her stubby abdomen. The furred Hymenopt body moved sideways an inch or two, seeking an exact position. The abdomen tilted. The sting sank with surgical precision into the Zardalu's head, at a point exactly between the great lidded eyes. The abdomen pulsed with a full poison discharge. The sting withdrew. A moment later Kallik dropped free and scuttled back, away from the forest of threshing arms.

The stung Zardalu made no noise, but the killing pressure around Nenda's legs slackened at once. The uplifted tentacles wilted. The great body shuddered, then froze into position. A moment later, the paralyzed Zardalu convulsed and toppled forward. It narrowly missed J'merlia and Julius Graves and lay motionless, poised on the very brink of the steep tunnel that led to the vortex.

And crawling above it, clinging upside down to the ceiling of the tunnel, came the great winged form of Atvar H'sial.

The Cecropian remained hanging on the cciling until she was past the recumbent body of the Zardalu. Then she dropped down, clear of the still-motionless tentacles, and pushed with all her strength at the hulking body. The Zardalu hung poised for a moment at the edge, then started away down the slope. Nenda heard it rolling and slithering toward the vortex at the bottom. It made no sound.

He was glad to see it go, but that did not solve his own problem. Although he was no longer being pulled apart,

Holder's tentacle still crushed his midsection and he was being drawn steadily toward the gaping sharp-edged beak.

He lacked the breath to cry out for help. Kallik, her sting sac temporarily emptied, had leapt at the second Zardalu, but she found herself gripped by a pair of tentacles. Then she and Nenda were being pulled together toward Holder's beak.

Atvar H'sial had turned from the vanished Zardalu and was watching the wild confusion in the tunnel. The yellow trumpet horns on each side of her head pointed toward Louis Nenda and Kallik as the two were pulled closer and closer to the Zardalu beak.

Atvar H'sial crouched silent, apparently inactive.

Only at the last moment, when Nenda was close enough to reach out and touch Holder's blinded eyes and opening maw, did the Cecropian act.

She took a glassy ovoid from within her wing cases. As Nenda was moved into position and the Zardalu's maw gaped at its widest, Atvar H'sial jumped.

Two hind limbs stabbed at Holder's blinded eyes. That was merely a distraction, while a forelimb thrust the oval object deep into Holder's ingestion slit. A split second after the Cecropian withdrew her arm, the maw snapped shut.

The Zardalu emitted a strange, quivering scream. The great body jerked full upright. The tentacles holding Nenda and Kallik went limp. And as he dropped to the tunnel floor, Louis Nenda saw what no sighted organism in the universe had ever seen before: a Zardalu interior, as it must appear to a Cecropian's ultrasonic imaging.

The Starburst had triggered deep inside Holder. The light it provided was so intense that the body of the Zardalu became translucent, lit from within to reveal the interior organs. A diffuse blue glow shone from the maw, from the beak, from the eyes, even from the lower part of the canopy of tentacles. Nenda could see the dark ellipsoid of the brain, nestled in the center above the long cord of the central nerve conduit. Above that he could make out the shape of the eight-chambered heart, pumping its copper-based blood through the massive body. The Starburst itself was at the back of the maw, a dazzling point of blue.

As Nenda watched, that point of light vanished. Holder became again a tall cylinder of midnight blue, supported on powerful tentacles.

Except that those tentacles would no longer support the body. They splayed wider and wider, to spread across the whole width of the corridor. The torso slumped down at their center, lower and lower, until Holder stretched full-length along the floor, head toward her companions.

Louis Nenda moved out of reach. Atvar H'sial had insisted that the Starburst was not really a weapon. It would not *explode* inside a Zardalu, and it would not kill one. But even without that, the strength of the internal illumination was enough to put the Zardalu out of action, at least in the short term.

Nenda intended to handle the longer term himself. He had promised to take care of Holder *personally,* at the moment when the Zardalu had pulled Kallik's leg off.

He drew the long knife from its holder on his calf. Maybe he could not *stab* the Zardalu's heart, because it sat too deep; but he could sure as hell *carve a way down* to it. And now he knew exactly where it lay in the body.

Nenda started forward. And then he hesitated.

Twelve Zardalu were still active. The burns that Hans Rebka, Darya Lang, and E. C. Tally had inflicted from behind were having the desired effect, spinning the Zardalu round and round, driving the pain-maddened aliens steadily forward toward the steep ramp that led down to the transportation vortex.

But that created a new problem. Nenda, Kallik, Graves, J'merlia, and Atvar H'sial were all *in front* of the Zardalu. Even though their adversaries were blinded, those tentacles and beaks had undiminished killing power. There was no way to drive them down the ramp without his whole group being forced along with them.

And the Zardalu were adapting to their blindness. Even as Nenda watched, E. C. Tally came within inches of being swept up by a thrashing, powerful arm.

The embodied robot was in awful physical shape, and he should not have been in the battle at all. He was weaving and staggering, one leg dragging useless as he moved. He stepped close to one of the Zardalu, giving it a maximum-intensity burn and forcing it to move, then tottering backward. But a sweeping arm missed him by only a split second.

Nenda swore and put away his knife.

Pleasure deferred, not pleasure denied. He would get Holder later.

It was not safe to speak, but he stood up, braving the forest of waving tentacles. He gestured to Hans Rebka. When the other finally noticed him, Nenda pointed at Graves and the others in his group, and then to the tunnel behind them.

Rebka nodded. He understood the problem. Nenda and the rest were penned in by the Zardalu. He patted the flashburn unit he was holding. Should they stop driving the Zardalu forward?

But they might begin to recover their sight at any time. Rebka and the others had to keep harassing them, to drive them over the brink before they knew of the danger.

Nenda shook his head. He made the gesture of firing a flashburn unit and shrugged. *Keep on burning them. We'll have to find the solution here for ourselves.*

Rebka nodded again. He raised a clenched fist in encouragement, stepped closer to one of the turning Zardalu, and burned its eye.

Sound thinking, Nenda thought. Make sure they stay blind. But he did not have time to watch.

He made a split-second inventory of the rest of his group. Atvar H'sial could take care of herself, better than anyone. Kallik was missing a limb, but the wound was already sealed. To a Hymenopt it was no more than a minor inconvenience. She would be all right. No time to worry about J'merlia, either—he would follow Atvar H'sial's lead.

Which left Julius Graves: blinded, battered, and bloody useless.

Nenda cursed. Typical of a councilor, to jump in and do something stupid when he did not know what was really going on. And to hand out orders into the bargain. Nenda had felt like kicking him for sticking his nose in, back in the other chamber when he was trying to lure the Zardalu to the transportation vortex and Graves had insisted on becoming involved.

He resisted the urge to roll the feebly moving Graves down the steep tunnel and be rid of him. There was always the chance that Rebka or Darya Lang might see him do it.

What was the answer?

Nenda felt the touch of a tentacle on his back. He jumped clear and looked around. In the moment he had been wondering what to do, the Zardalu had been driven a foot closer by Rebka and the others. Four feet more, and escape from those killing arms would be impossible.

He ran to J'merlia and Kallik's side, pointing up to the tunnel ceiling and waving them on. Without waiting to see the results he moved on to Atvar H'sial, placing himself right under the dark-red carapace.

"Graves." He pointed, though it was unnecessary with a pheromonal message. "The ceiling. Can you?"

Atvar H'sial nodded. "I can. If he is unconscious."

Which he was not. Not yet. Nenda moved over to Julius Graves and delivered a rabbit punch to the back of the councilor's neck, knocking him cold.

Atvar H'sial picked up the body easily in two mid-limbs and began to climb up the wall to the corridor ceiling. Nenda saw that J'merlia and Kallik were already there. They were hanging upside down, waiting for a good moment to hurry over the heads of the maddened Zardalu.

Which left only one problem. How was *he* going to get away? The Zardalu completely blocked the corridor, higher than his head. Crawling along ceilings was easy enough for bugs, impossible for him.

He could see only one answer. It was one that did not appeal at all.

Better do it now before you decide you can't face it, he told himself.

Nenda moved to the prostrate body of Holder. As the other Zardalu groped for him he forced his way headfirst into the thick tangle of Holder's limbs. The space between the base of the tentacles was scarcely as wide as his body. There was a throat-clutching smell of musk and ammonia. Nenda shivered at the greasy touch of Zardalu flesh on his face. He could not do it this way; he would choke before he was halfway. He clumsily turned around to move in feet first.

Push. A bit farther. Do it. Don't think of where you're going.

He forced himself on until he was completely hidden.

His legs were cramped against the bottom of Holder's torso. The lower body sac felt soft and unprotected. Maybe that was the point of vulnerability for the Zardalu, something that had been known in the Great Rising and then forgotten.

Nenda dismissed the thought. He could not use the information, while if Holder were to become conscious now . . .

Don't think of that, either. There was plenty else to worry about. The pain of his twisted limbs and bruised middle made him gasp when he moved—although ten seconds earlier he had been too busy to notice it.

Think *positive*. Think we're *winning*.

Maybe they were. The sounds of the fight above and about him continued. He heard the sizzle of flashburn units on Zardalu flesh, whistles and clicks of pain, the pounding of enraged tentacles against walls and floor. Powerful tentacles slapped against Holder's body.

And then he heard a new sound. It was a human being in final agony.

He risked pressing his face to the space between two tentacles and peered out.

E. C. Tally's failing body had been too slow. A Zardalu had him in four of its python arms. Hans Rebka and Darya Lang were there, running in dangerously close to burn the eyes and the maw.

To no effect. The Zardalu was filled with its own rage and blood lust. It was slowly pulling Tally apart. As Nenda watched both arms were plucked free, then the legs, one by one. Finally the bloody stump of the torso was hurled away, to smash against the corridor wall. The top of the skull case flew loose, to be cracked like an eggshell a moment later by a questing Zardalu tentacle.

Nenda pulled his head back. There was nothing to be done for Tally. At least Atvar H'sial and the others must have made it across the ceiling to the relative safety of the higher corridor level, for there was no sign of them. He had to lie low a while longer, as Lang and Rebka tried to push the disoriented Zardalu the final few meters. He looked out along the line of Holder's tentacles. Just three steps more, and they would be on the ramp to the vortex, right at the point of no return.

The stab of agony in his right thumb was so unexpected that for a moment Nenda had no idea what was happening. The half-muffled cry squeezed out of him was shock more than pain.

He lifted his hand. Clinging to it, its beak firmly set in the bleeding flesh, was a young Zardalu. As Nenda watched it swallowed a piece from the base of his thumb. In the same motion it snapped for another bite.

He smacked the creature away with his other hand and stared around him. Now that he could see better in the shade of the sheltering tentacles, he could make out four small rounded shapes, pale apricot against the blue of the unconscious parent.

The Starburst had been enough to knock out Holder, but the offspring were far from quiet. All the other infants were crawling single-mindedly toward him.

"Not today, Junior. Try a bite of this." Nenda grabbed them as they came and held them one after another to the underside of the adult Zardalu's tentacles. After a moment's hesitation they attacked the tough flesh with their sharp beaks. Holder's body began to twitch.

Nenda cursed his own stupidity. How dumb could you get? He ought to have let them keep on at him, rather than risk waking the unconscious adult.

He groped for the black satchel at his side, opened it, and pulled out random bits of food. It was his reserve supply, but if Holder woke up now Louis Nenda would never need food again.

The young Zardalu grabbed the fragments eagerly. Cannibalism was not apparently their first preference.

Holder's body rolled suddenly to the left. Nenda froze in horror. Then he realized that none of the tentacles was moving. Something was rolling the great body from *outside,* pushing it closer to the ramp. The sizzle of flashburn units was louder.

He took another look along the line of Holder's tentacles. The Zardalu were past him! He could see a confusion of stumbling bodies. While he had been preoccupied with the young ones, the adults had been herded forward. He watched them stagger one by one onto the beginning of the ramp, then overbalance and start away down the incline. Once they were on the steepest section the blind Zardalu were unable to stop. They could have no idea what was happening to them.

Going, going . . . *gone.*

The last Zardalu vanished, to cries of triumph from Rebka and the others. Nenda joined in, then realized that Holder's body was still moving toward the tunnel that led to the vortex. A couple more meters and it, too, would be rolling on its way.

"Hey!" He forced himself up from the sheltering tentacles, pushing with his legs and not worrying about arousing Holder. As his head poked free he found he was staring at the startled face of Darya Lang. She was leaning her weight against Holder's body.

"Nenda!" she said. "You're alive."

"You've got a talent for the obvious, Professor."

"You disappeared. We felt sure they'd got you—torn you to bits, or one of them took you in whole."

"Yeah. Ass first. I just took a rest in there."

"No time to chat, Nenda." That was Hans Rebka, straining on the upper part of Holder's torso. "It's starting to come round—eyes opening. Get out here and help."

Nenda forced his way free to add his weight to the others. Everyone was there except Julius Graves and E. C. Tally. Nenda put his shoulder to the Zardalu body, standing between Atvar H'sial and Birdie Kelly. Kelly nodded at him in an embarrassed way. Nenda nodded back and put his weight into the effort to move Holder.

Four strong pushes from everyone, then Rebka was shouting: "Stand back! She's going."

Nenda had one glimpse of a bleary eye, huge and heavy-

lidded, opening less than a foot from his face. Then the last
Zardalu was rolling and sliding and skidding its way faster
and faster toward the dark whirlpool of the vortex. Holder
vanished, the great body twisting around on itself as it entered
the spinning singularity.

"It is done." That was a jubilant pheromonal comment
from Atvar H'sial, straightening up. "Exactly as we planned
it. And yet you appear less than content."

Nenda bent over, rubbing his sore hand at his sore legs, his
sore back, sore midriff—sore *everything.* "We did all right.
But I promised myself Holder's guts—personally. Didn't get
the chance."

"I think perhaps you saw as much of Holder as a wise being would wish to." The Cecropian version of humor came
flooding in on Nenda. Atvar H'sial was feeling extra good.
"Upon consideration, we were very lucky. My respect for the
Zardalu as fighting machines is considerable. If we had met
them under other circumstances, when they were not disoriented by their stay in the stasis tanks and confused as to their
location . . . I confess, I am happy to see the last of them. The
tearing power of those tentacles is close to unbelievable."

"Tearing power! They got Tally! Where is he?"

Atvar H'sial gestured. What was left of the body of E. C.
Tally was slumped against a wall, twenty meters away. Darya
Lang and Hans Rebka were hurrying back along the corridor
toward it. Birdie Kelly was already there.

"He's gone," Kelly said.

But Darya Lang went down on her knees, lifting Tally's
shattered skull gently in her hands and saying, "Tally. Tally,
can you hear me?"

The limbless torso shivered. The head nodded a millimeter,
and one bruised eye slitted open to reveal a blue iris.

"I hear." The words were a whisper from purple lips. "May
I speak?"

"For God's sake, yes." Darya leaned close. "But Tally,
listen. *We did it.* The Zardalu have gone, all of them, down
the vortex. But we can't help you. I'm sorry. We don't have
medical equipment."

"I know. Don't worry. *Other* body, back on Persephone.

Waiting. Few more seconds, this body done." The slitted eye opened wide, scanned. The stump of torso tried to sit up. "Darya Lang. Hans Rebka. Birdie Kelly. Last request. *Turn me off.* Understand? One week with no sensory input . . . like trillion years for human. Understand? Please. *Turn me off.*"

"I will." Birdie Kelly knelt at his side. "How?"

"Switch. Base of brain."

"I'll find it. I promise. And when you're turned back on it will be in your new body. I'll see to it myself."

A trace of a smile appeared on Tally's guileless face. The first technicians had never gotten it right. The effect was ghastly.

"Thank you. Good-bye." The battered head lifted. "It is a strange thought to me, but I will— *miss* you. Every one of you."

The body of E. C. Tally shuddered, sighed, and died. Birdie Kelly reached down into the skull cavity, lifted the brain out, and unplugged it, then knelt with face downcast. It was illogical—this was only the temporary loss of a piece of computing equipment—but . . .

I will miss you.

The humans around Tally fell into a respectful silence.

That was broken by Julius Graves, staggering toward them from higher up the corridor where Atvar H'sial had put him down and abandoned him. For the past few minutes he had been blundering blindly into walls, futilely calling out the names of the others. They had been otherwise engaged. Now he was following the sounds of their voices. And just when he seemed to be getting close, they had all stopped talking.

Louis Nenda finally went over to him. "Come on, Councilor. The baddies are gone. It's all over. You're safe to join the party."

Graves peered at him, seeing nothing. "Louis Nenda? I think I owe you an apology. We all do. You *planned* this, didn't you?"

"Not just me. Me an' At an' Lang an' Rebka. We were all in it."

"But you had the most dangerous role—you had to lure them to the trap. That story you gave the Zardalu, about leading them to a safe escape. It was all nonsense, wasn't it?"

Mention of the Zardalu made Nenda rub again at his sore back and middle. "I don't know it was *nonsense,* exactly. Main thing is, they went into the vortex an' the hell out of here. Mebbe they had a happy landing."

"And maybe?"

"Mebbe they're all frying in hell. Hope so. Hold still." Nenda reached out and lifted Graves's eyelids. He studied the misty blue eyes for a few seconds. "Don't like the look of that. I tried to warn you about the Starburst. But I daren't give too much warning, in case the Zardalu cottoned. You must have been staring straight at it when it popped. I don't think you'll get your sight back."

Graves made an impatient gesture. "That is a detail. Back on Miranda, I'll have a new pair of eyes in less than a day. Tell me *important* things. Was anyone of our party killed?"

"E. C. Tally. We've saved his brain. Nobody else is dead. We were lucky."

"Good. That simplifies things. We won't have to waste time on medical matters." Graves gripped Nenda's arm. "We must act quickly. We have an assignment of the highest priority. Since I cannot see, the rest of you must—as soon as possible—arrange a meeting for me."

Nenda stared at him in irritation. The Zardalu were gone for two minutes, and Graves became as bossy as ever.

He felt a repeat of his earlier urge to roll the councilor down the slope and into the vortex. It would make life a lot simpler. "Meeting? With who?"

"Who else?" Graves tightened his grip and started walking Nenda forward, straight at one of the tunnel walls. "Who else, but Speaker-Between?"

CHAPTER 26

IN THE NEXT twenty-four hours Julius Graves learned what Hans Rebka and Darya Lang had long understood: Speaker-Between had his own agenda, with its own timetable. He did not choose to appear simply because a human wished to talk to him. They had to await his convenience, and the logic of that convenience could not be predicted.

With certain exceptions, the other survivors accepted that constraint. They concentrated on food, drink, and rest, and they needed all three. But Louis Nenda, muttering that being called a *hero* by everybody was worse than being called a villain, wandered off by himself; and a blind and insomniac Graves chose to follow, prowling the interior of the artifact with J'merlia as his eyes and guide. They rapidly confirmed Darya Lang's theory that the artifact of Serenity was gigantic, equal in volume and living space to the biospheres of a dozen worlds; but only a tiny fraction of that could be attained, unless the traveler learned Speaker-Between's knack of gliding through walls and floors.

Graves lacked that ability. As the hours wore on his agitation grew. He finally came back to the main chamber and joined the others, still restless.

"What's the big deal?" Birdie Kelly asked. He had become Graves's confidant, as well as the official custodian of E. C. Tally's brain, which he carried with the distracted air of a man holding an unexploded bomb. "Tally isn't suffering. Actually, he's not doing anything at all. Must be nice to be able to switch yourself off when things get nasty." Birdie became aware of Graves's sightless glare. "Anyway, with the Zardalu gone, this place is safe enough. Come on, Councilor. Lighten up."

"I'm not worrying about *Tally*. And I'm not worrying about *us*." Graves flopped moodily down by one of the big Zardalu stasis tanks. "I'm worried about *these*." He rapped the side of the tank. "And what was in them."

"The Zardalu? They're all dead."

"Are they? Can you *prove* that to me?" Graves closed his blind eyes and slumped there breathing through his mouth. As usual when he spoke to Birdie, all his questions seemed to be rhetorical.

"I know they went down the vortex," he continued, just when Kelly wondered if the councilor was falling asleep. "But who is to say that they are dead? Professor Lang is sure that the vortex is part of a *transportation system*. She says that Speaker-Between confirmed that, or at least didn't deny it. Transportation systems are not designed to kill their passengers. Suppose that the Zardalu were transported *safely*— and have finished up somewhere in the spiral arm?"

"Suppose they were?" Birdie sniffed. "Big deal! They've been gone for God knows how long, eleven thousand years or something like that, and there's only a few of them left. I'm not afraid of the Zardalu." Not when they're all dead, or thirty thousand light-years away, he added to himself. "I can't see 'em doing much damage in a couple of days."

"That's not what I'm worried about!" Graves's tone provided the "you idiot," though he did not say the words. "I'm worried about *tracing* them. If this vortex is anything like a Bose Network Transition Point, the transition trail decays exponentially with time. Today we may be able to say just where they went. Tomorrow it becomes a bit more difficult. A week from now it's a major task, and in a month it's impossible no matter what technology you have available. The Zardalu could be tucked away where no one can find them. What do you say to *that?*"

Birdie was saved from saying anything by the return of Louis Nenda. That reluctant hero nodded coldly at Graves and Kelly and went over to the food-supply cabinets. He had a second satchel slung at his side, far bigger than his usual black one. He had made it, and a crude jacket, from webbing left behind by the Zardalu. He was packing the satchel and the jacket pockets with enough food for a week.

"Wish we had a way to *heat* this," he grunted. "Cold food is lousy." He turned to Graves. "Your buddy's back, you know. Over in the next room but one."

"Buddy?"

"Old moan-'n'-groan. Speaker-Between."

Graves was on his feet at once. "What is he doing there?" But he did not wait for an answer. He was blundering out of the chamber, shouting to Lang and Rebka, who were deep in private conversation, "Professor! Captain! He is here. Now is our chance."

"Chance for what?" Hans Rebka had been busy telling age-old lies to Darya Lang, with her thorough approval. But again Graves did not wait for an answer. He allowed Nenda to lead him through the nearest chambers, while the rest of the group followed at their own pace.

Nenda's statement had been partly true. The Builder construct was *half*-visible, just the tail and lower part of the silver body. The upper part was presumably there, but it was hidden by the ceiling of the room, fifteen meters above their heads.

Graves listened to Nenda's description in total frustration. "But if he's stuck up there, how the devil am I supposed to—"

"Easy." Nenda nodded to Kallik, who had entered with Atvar H'sial and J'merlia. "Go get 'em."

The Hymenopt crouched on seven limbs—the lost eighth was regrowing fast, and nearly a foot long—and sprang straight up. She grabbed and swung on Speaker-Between's barbed tail. After a few seconds, they both began to descend.

"The Zardalu are gone." Graves started to speak even before Speaker-Between's flower-petal head was fully in view. "But it is of paramount importance that we follow them—at once!"

"If you would kindly release my tail . . ." The silver pentagon turned slowly to face Graves. "Your request cannot be fulfilled. The Zardalu indeed are gone. I therefore judge that they are losers. You were able to defeat and banish them. But the evaluation is not yet over. Is it necessary to remind you that there can be only one species judged fit to work with the Builders? I would be derelict in my own duties should I halt this evaluation before it is complete."

"You do not understand. Can you guarantee that the Zardalu were all killed when they entered the vortex?"

"One moment." Speaker-Between coalesced to a sphere, then just as rapidly rippled back to form the horned and tailed chimera. "That question is not easy to answer," he said when he was fully reconstructed. "The Zardalu suffered an unstructured transition. It is not one that is highly forbidden, and therefore it is not inevitably fatal. The Zardalu *could* have survived it. They *may* be alive. They *may* be all dead. What is the relevance of the question?"

"To you, perhaps very little. To us, and to all intelligences of the spiral arm, it is very great. If there is a chance that the Zardalu survive, it is imperative that we return to alert our fellows."

"Imperative to whom? It is not imperative to me, or to my masters." Speaker-Between floated toward Julius Graves, settling close enough for the councilor to reach out and touch him. "You do not appear to understand. There is no technical difficulty in returning you to your homes, or to any location in the spiral arm or out of it; and it may be possible to determine where the Zardalu went, though that is less sure. But those issues are academic. I say again, *the selection proce-*

dure is not complete. There remain both humans and Cecropians. Until only one remains, it is not permitted for you to leave."

"Hopeless." Graves turned to the others. "Totally hopeless. I have worked with a score of intelligences, through the whole of the spiral arm, but with this—this silver *bubble-brain* there can be no meeting of minds, no basis for negotiation."

"Mebbe. And mebbe not." Louis Nenda glanced around at the others. "D'you agree with the councilor? Nothin' to lose, nothin' to gain? 'Cause if you do, mind if I take a shot?"

"Go ahead." Hans Rebka had a little grin on his face. "Try your thing."

"All right." Nenda walked over to stand right in front of Speaker-Between. "The selection procedure isn't over, you say. I'll buy that. But the Zardalu are out of it, so it's just between two species: Cecropians, and humans. Right?"

"That is a correct conclusion."

"And it doesn't matter *how many* humans and Cecropians fight it out, does it? You were quite happy to leave us to tackle fourteen Zardalu, even though there were only a handful of humans, and a couple of aliens."

"In our experience, the number of entities is rarely the deciding factor."

"Fair enough. So the selection could be done just as well if there was only *one of each*—one human, and one Cecropian?"

"That is wholly reasonable."

"All right, then. So what's the point of keeping this whole crazy roster? Let the rest go—and *keep just two of us.* Me and Atvar H'sial. We'll fight it out between us."

"*No.*" Graves was shaking his head violently. "That is a sacrifice that I will not ask of anyone. To leave you here, while the rest of us return to safety, it would be—"

"Hey, what do you mean, *safety?* Goin' back is different for me and At than for the rest of you. Look what happens to us when we get there. We're charged with serious crimes the minute we hit civilization, and next thing you know we're jailed or brain-wiped. Not much fun in that."

"I am the person who brought those charges." Graves's skeletal face bore an expression of anguish. "I will petition to have them dropped. After what you and Atvar H'sial did, to save us from the Zardalu—"

"You can *petition*, sure you can. Maybe that'll get us off the hook. But maybe it won't. Seems to me, At and yours truly ain't much worse off *here* than we are *there*. For the rest of you, it's a different story. You get to go back home, and write your nice little reports on everything that happened. Chase the Zardalu, too, if there's time left over and they didn't fly ass-over-tentacle up their own wazoo. But *me*." He shrugged.

The flower head was nodding. "Your internal disputes are not germane to my decision. However, the proposal you make is acceptable. If one human and one Cecropian remain to complete the selection process, the rest may return to the spiral arm. It can be to your most recent departure point, or to any other place of your choosing. If you wish it, and if I can ascertain it, your destination can even be the final arrival point of the Zardalu—assuming that location is able to support life."

"No, thanks." Rebka cut off discussion, just as Graves was about to start up again. "We have to warn other people before we start chasing. We'll go back to somewhere safe."

He turned to Louis Nenda. "As for you . . . I don't usually find it hard to know what to say. But you've got me this time. All I can think of is, thanks from all of us. And pass that thank-you on to Atvar H'sial."

Nenda grinned. "I will, in a minute. First I've got to explain to At what she just volunteered for."

Graves stared at him pop-eyed. "You *are* joking, aren't you? Atvar H'sial already gave her approval for your proposal."

"Sure. Sure I'm joking." Nenda was turning casually away. "Don't worry about it. No problem."

But Kallik was stepping forward. "So it is settled, then. The rest will return. And Atvar H'sial, Louis Nenda, and their loyal servants, Kallik and J'merlia, will remain."

"Whoa, now." Nenda held up his hand. "I never said

that." He looked at Speaker-Between and Hans Rebka. "If you don't mind, At and I and J'merlia and Kallik need a few words in private. Five minutes?"

He ushered the other three out of the chamber at once, not waiting for a nod of assent.

"You see, Kallik." His voice was oddly gentle as they came to a smaller room, out of earshot of the others. "You have to understand the situation. Things are different now. Not like what they was, back in the good old days before we went to Quake. They've changed. And *you've* changed, you and J'merlia. I've been translating for Atvar H'sial as we go, and she agrees with me completely. It wouldn't be *right* for you to be slaves anymore—either of you."

"But Master Nenda, that is what we *want!* J'merlia and I, we followed you from Opal, only that we might be with you and serve you again."

"I know. Don't think we don't appreciate that, me and At." Nenda had tears in his eyes. "But it wouldn't work out, Kallik. Not now. You've been deciding your own actions ever since we left you behind on Quake. You've been thinking for yourselves, *doing* for yourselves. You've tasted independence. You've *earned* independence."

"But we do not *want* independence!" J'merlia's voice rose to a mournful wail. "Even though Atvar H'sial agrees with you, this should not be. It *must* not be."

"See? That makes my argument exactly." Nenda reached out to pat J'merlia's narrow thorax. "Listen to yourself! Atvar H'sial says what she wants you to do—an' you start *arguing* with her. Would you have done that two months ago?"

"Never!" J'merlia held up a claw to cover his compound eyes, appalled at his own temerity. "Argue with Atvar H'sial? Never. Master Nenda, with my most humble apologies and sincere regrets—"

"Stow it, J'merlia. You've proved the point. You and Kallik go on back, and start helping to run the spiral arm. You're as qualified as any species. I've known that for a long time."

"But we don't *want* to help to run the spiral arm!"

"Who does? That's what humans call the *Smart Bugs'*

Burden. You gotta go back there and carry it, even though you don't want to. Otherwise, it will be the Ditrons who'll have to organize things."

"Master Nenda, please say that you are joking! The Ditrons, why they have less brains than—than some of the—"

"Before you put your foot in it real bad, J'merlia, I'll say yeah, I was joking. But *not* about the fact that you and Kallik have to go back. For one thing, Kallik's the only intelligent being in the spiral arm who's actually *talked* to Zardalu. That might be important."

J'merlia crawled forward and placed his head close to Atvar H'sial's hind limbs. "Master Nenda, I hear you. But I do not want to leave. Atvar H'sial is my dominatrix, and has been since I was first postlarval."

"Don't gimme that—"

"Allow me, Louis, if you will." The pheromonal message from Atvar H'sial carried a glint of dry humor. "With all respect, violent action is your forte, not reasoned persuasion." The towering Cecropian crouched low to the floor and brought her smooth blind head close to J'merlia. "Let us reason together, my J'merlia. Would you agree with me when I say that any intelligent being either *is* a slave, or is *not* a slave? That those two conditions are the only two logical possibilities?"

"Of course." J'merlia, once the slave-translator for Atvar H'sial, caught every nuance of meaning in her chemical message. He shivered without knowing why, sensing already that his cause was lost.

"Now you and Kallik," Atvar H'sial continued. "You are both intelligent beings, are you not?"

"Yes."

"Therefore either you are slaves, or you are not slaves. Agreed?"

"That is true."

"And if you are *not* slaves, then it is inappropriate for you to *pretend* that you are, by stating that you must remain here to serve me and Louis Nenda. You should go back to the spiral arm with the others and begin to live the life of free beings. A nonslave should not mimic a slave. True?"

"True."

"But suppose now that you *are* slaves, both you and Kallik; then you have no choice but to *obey the orders of your masters.* And those orders are quite explicit: Louis Nenda and I order you to return to the spiral arm and assist in finding the Zardalu if they are still alive. Thus in either case, slave or nonslave, you cannot remain here with us."

"Thanks, At." Nenda stepped forward and nodded to the Cecropian. "Couldn't have put it better myself." He turned to J'merlia and Kallik. "So that's the deal. We all go back in there now. You tell Speaker-Between and the others that you're ready to go. Right?"

Kallik and J'merlia exchanged a brief flurry of clicks and whistles.

"Yes, Mas—" Kallik caught herself before the word was fully out. "Yes, Louis Nenda. We are ready. J'merlia and I agree that we must return to the spiral arm with the others. We have no choice. We want to add only one thing. If ever you and Atvar H'sial need us, then you have to send only one word, *Come,* and we will hasten to your side."

The Hymenopt touched her black round head to the floor for a fraction of a second, then stood fully upright. She and J'merlia began to walk, without permission, from the chamber.

"And we will come *joyfully,* " she added.

"Joyfully," J'merlia repeated. "A human or a Cecropian may find this hard to understand—but there is no pleasure in *enforced* freedom."

CHAPTER 27

ALL SET.

But Birdie Kelly was going mad with frustration.

Everything had been ready for hours. The descending ramp to a new transportation vortex sat waiting in the next chamber, close enough for the airflow around the spinning singularity to be felt on skin and exoskeletons. Speaker-Between had assured the group that the system was prepared to receive them, with an assured safe destination. It would transfer to Midway Station, halfway between the planets of Quake and Opal; a perfect location from Birdie's point of view, since it was the last place in the spiral arm where the Zardalu were likely to have arrived.

But now, at the very last moment, everyone seemed to be having second thoughts about going at all.

"If I had one more opportunity to *reason* with Speaker-Between, I feel sure I could persuade him of the unsound basis for the Builders' plan." That was Steven Graves, talking

with Hans Rebka. Julius, unable to handle the idea of leaving
Louis Nenda and Atvar H'sial to their uncertain fate, had
abandoned the field to his interior mnemonic twin. Steven
had been making the most of his opportunity.

"It stands to reason," he went on, "that many races working *cooperatively* would have more chance of helping the
Builders to solve *The Problem* than any species working
alone. Humans and Cecropians should be engaged in a joint
effort, not fighting each other to decide who will assist the
Builders."

"It stands to *your* reason," Rebka countered. Like Birdie
he was itching to be on his way, though for different reasons.
He was still seeing nightmares in midnight blue returning to
dominate the spiral arm. He wanted to follow the trail before
it was too cold. "You know that the Builders have a completely different worldview from any species we have ever
met. And Speaker-Between is a Builder construct. You could
argue with him for a million years—he has that much time—
and you'd never persuade him to abandon two hundred million years of Builder prejudice. Give up, Steven, and tackle
a problem we may be able to solve. Ask yourself where the
Zardalu went, and what they are doing."

On that crucial question, Speaker-Between had been too
vague for comfort. The best after-the-fact analysis showed
that the Zardalu transition had been completed to an end
point on a Builder artifact, probably in the old Zardalu Communion territories. It did not indicate which one, or offer any
idea of what might have happened next.

Darya Lang was proving just as reluctant to leave.

"I know *someone* has to go back home and worry about the
Zardalu." She was examining a series of incomprehensible
structures that lined the chamber, an array of fluted glass
columns with turbulent green liquid running through them.
"But if I leave, who is going to study things like *this?* I've
spent my whole working life seeking the Builders. Now that
I've run them down, it makes no sense to leave. Once I go I
may never have an opportunity to come back."

"Of course you will." Louis Nenda seemed as keen as
anyone to speed the others' departure. He took her by the arm

and began to lead her in the direction of the vortex ramp. Ahead of him, Atvar H'sial was shepherding J'merlia and Kallik in the same direction.

"You heard what Speaker-Between says," Nenda continued. "The transport-system entry point on Glister won't be closed. You can go there and return here whenever you like. And when you go to Glister next time you'll be a lot better prepared. *And* you can have a good look at the wild Phages, too."

He reached his arm around Darya and deliberately stroked her hip. "Better go, sweetie, before I change my mind about lettin' you run off with Rebka."

She quietly removed herself from his arm and stared down at him from her six-inch height advantage. "Louis Nenda, I swore when I first met you that if you ever laid a lecherous finger on me, I'd bat your brains out. Now you've done it, and I can't bring myself to flatten you. You've changed, haven't you? Since you went to Glister? You touched my hip just to annoy me."

"Naw." The bloodshot eyes flicked up to meet her face, then went straight back to stare at her midriff. "I didn't do it *just* to annoy you. And it isn't a change just since Glister." His hoarse voice became even gruffer than usual, and he reached out to take her hand. "It happened before that. On Opal, when we first met."

He seemed ready to say more, but Speaker-Between appeared again, drifting up the tunnel that led to the vortex. He seemed oblivious to the strong gravity field, and to the swirling air around his silver body.

"The time is right," the creaky voice said. "The system is ready for planned transitions. However, the trip is much easier on individuals if they pass through singly. Who will be first?"

Everyone stared at each other, until Hans Rebka stepped forward. "I guess I will. I'm ready."

One by one, the others formed into single file behind him: Birdie Kelly, followed by J'merlia, Kallik, and Julius Graves. Darya Lang came last of all, still staring around her at the mysterious works of the Builders. Beside the line, awkwardly, as though unsure of their own role in the others' departure, stood Atvar H'sial and Louis Nenda.

"You may proceed." Speaker-Between drifted to the back of the group.

"Thanks." Rebka turned to look at the others, one by one. "I don't think this is a time for speeches, so I'll just say, see you there, and I know we're lucky to be on our way home." His eye caught Louis Nenda's. "And I wish you were coming with us. Tell Atvar H'sial, we owe both of you our special thanks. Tell her I don't know what you two did back on Quake, but so far as I'm concerned, what you did *here*, to get rid of the Zardalu, and the sacrifice you are making now, by staying, more than cancels that out. I hope I'll see you again, back in the spiral arm."

Nenda waved his hand dismissively. "Ah, we don't need thanks. Me and At, we'll manage. You go ahead, Captain. And good luck."

Rebka nodded and stepped onto the descending ramp of the tunnel. The others watched him walk forward, leaning far back to keep his balance. His hair and clothes began to blow wildly about him, and his pace slowed. Twenty meters along he paused. They heard his voice echoing through to them, oddly distorted.

"This is the point of no return. A couple more meters and I'll have no choice but to go." He turned and waved. *"Meet you at the other end. Safe trip everybody, and bon voyage."*

He took two slow steps, and then a new force gripped him. He tumbled forward down the ramp. There was an audible gasp, a *whomp* of displaced air, and a shiver in the outline of the tunnel walls.

The others peered down toward the spinning singularity. Rebka was gone.

"You may proceed," Speaker-Between said.

"Yeah," Birdie Kelly said softly. "I may. But I may not." He was clutching the rough sphere of E. C. Tally's brain to his chest like a holy relic. "Come on, Birdie. You've been saying for weeks that you want to go home. So let's do it. Feet, get moving."

As Louis Nenda patted him on the shoulder Birdie took a

first hesitant step along the tunnel. The whole line followed, like a slow processional.

"One by one," Speaker-Between cautioned.

Birdic was muttering to himself as he walked forward. Halfway along the tunnel he reached some decision and started to run. He shouted as he hit the transition zone, and again there was the rush of displaced air.

J'merlia and Kallik tried to pause by Louis Nenda and Atvar H'sial, but the Cecropian waved them on.

"That's right," Nenda said. "Keep moving, Kallik, don't hold up the line. And don't worry about us. We'll fight things out here between us. Get on back to the spiral arm."

"As you command. Farewell, beloved Master." The rear-facing eyes in the Hymenopt's dark head watched Nenda all the way, to the point where she was taken by the vortex field. Kallik vanished in silence, followed a few seconds later by a shivering J'merlia.

Julius Graves refused to be hurried. He paused in front of Louis Nenda and shook his hand. "Good luck. If you do succeed in returning, you can be sure of one thing. Whatever you did at Summertide on Quake, the charges against you and Atvar H'sial will be dropped. Please make sure that she knows, too."

"Appreciate it, Councilor." Nenda shook Graves's hand vigorously. "I'll tell her. And don't worry about us. We'll get by."

"You are a very brave man." The misty-blue eyes stared sightless into Nenda's dark ones. "You make me proud to be a human. And if I were a Cecropian, I would be just as proud." Graves touched his hand to Atvar H'sial's foreclaw and stepped onto the ramp.

In seconds he was gone. Darya Lang stood alone with Louis Nenda and Atvar H'sial.

She took Nenda by the hand. "I agree with Julius Graves. I don't care if you *were* a criminal before you came to Opal, it's what you are like *now* that counts. People *do* change, don't they?"

He shrugged. "I guess they do—when they have a reason to. And mebbe I had a good reason."

"The Zardalu?"

"Naw." He refused to meet her eyes, and his voice was gentle. "Nothin' so exotic. A simple reason. You know what they say, the love of a good woman, an' all that stuff . . . but you should be going, and I shouldn't be talking this way."

"Why not?"

"Because I'm nothin'. You've got a good thing going with Captain Rebka, and you're a lot righter for him than you ever could be for somebody like me. I come up the hard way. I'm loud, an' I'm coarse, an' I don't know how to talk to women, never did."

"I'd say you're doing just fine."

"Well, this isn't the time an' place for it. Go now. But maybe if I ever get back to the spiral arm—"

"You'll come right to Sentinel Gate, and look for me." Darya turned to nod to Atvar H'sial. "I want to say good luck to her, too, but that's stupid. I know only one of you can win, and I hope it's you, Louis. I have to go now—before I make a complete fool of myself. The rest of them will be waiting at the other end. I mustn't stay longer."

She reached out to take his face between her hands, leaned down, and kissed him on the lips. "Thanks, for everything. And don't think of this as good-bye. We'll meet again, I just know we will."

"Hope so." Nenda reached out and patted her again on the curve of her hip. He grinned. "This sure feels like unfinished business. Take care of yourself, Darya. And stay sassy."

She walked away from him along the ramp, turning to smile and wave as she went. There was a moment when she stood motionless, with the vortex blowing her hair into a cloudy chaos around her head. Then she took one more step and spun away down to the singularity. There was the usual explosion of displaced air. She did not cry out.

Nenda and Atvar H'sial stood staring after her.

"It is finished," Speaker-Between said from behind them. "I will receive confirmation when they reach their destination. And now—for you it begins. You must continue, human and Cecropian, until the selection process is complete."

"Sure thing. You're just gonna leave us to it, then?"

"I am. I see no need for my presence. I will check periodically to ascertain the situation, just as I did when your group expelled the Zardalu."

Speaker-Between was sinking steadily into the floor. The tail and lower part of his body had already vanished.

"Hold on a minute." Nenda reached out to grab the flowerlike head. "Suppose that *we* want to contact *you?*"

"Until one of you triumphs over the other, there can be no reason for me to talk to you. A warning: Do not seek to escape using the transportation system. You will not be accepted by it. In case of need, however, I will tell you a way to reach me. Activate one of the stasis tanks. That fact will be drawn to my attention . . ." The stem was sinking, until only the head itself was left. It nodded, at floor level. "This is farewell—to *one* of you. I do not expect to see both of you again."

Speaker-Between disappeared. Atvar H'sial and Louis Nenda stared at each other for a full minute.

"Has he gone?" The pheromonal message diffused across to Nenda.

"I think so. Give it a few more seconds, though." And then, when another half minute had passed, he said, "We oughta start right now, but we haven't had a chance to talk for a while. What do you think?"

"I think that something new and unprecedented has happened to the iconoclastic Louis Nenda." The pheromones were full of mockery. "I did not understand your spoken interaction with the female, but I could monitor your body chemistry. There was *emotion* there—and genuine sentiment. A grave weakness, and one that may prove your undoing."

"No way." Nenda snorted. "You were reading me wrong, dead wrong. It's an old human saying: Always leave 'em hot, someday it may pay off. That's all I was doing."

"I was *not* reading you wrong, Louis Nenda. And I remain unpersuaded."

"Hey, you didn't hear *her*. She was all ready to change her mind and stay—I could see it in her eyes. I couldn't have that, her stickin' around and poking her nose in. I *had* to make her realize how noble I was, see, remainin' here like this, because then she couldn't stay, too, without making me look less like

Mr. Wonderful. Anyway, I don't want to talk about that. Let's drop it an' get right to the real stuff."

"One moment more. I may accept that you were not deceiving me concerning your feelings for the woman, Darya Lang—accept it *someday,* if not yet. But I know you were seeking to deceive me, and everyone else, on another matter."

"Deceive you? What are you talkin' about?"

"Please, Louis. I am not a larval form, or a human innocent. If I inspected the Zardalu and their equipment with ultrasonic signals, is it likely I would do any less for you? Let us discuss the contents of your satchel—the small one. Open it, if you please."

"Hey, I was goin' to show you anyway, soon as the rest was gone. You don't think I'd try an' keep it from you, do you? We both know that wouldn't work for more than a minute."

"I knew that you could not *succeed* in doing so. It is good to hear that you did not intend to try." Atvar H'sial turned the yellow trumpets of her hearing organs to Nenda as he crouched down to open the little satchel that accompanied him everywhere.

After a few moments a pale-apricot head peeped out.

Atvar H'sial released the chemical equivalent of a sigh. "Louis Nenda, I *knew* of this, minutes after the last adult Zardalu vanished into the vortex. Where did you get it?"

"Little bugger bit me, when I was hiding inside Holder." Nenda peered into the satchel, careful to keep clear of the young Zardalu's questing beak. "Greedy little devil, that's for sure—eaten every last scrap of food I stuck in there."

"But you did not have to take and hide it. What act of folly is this, to keep in your possession a member of the spiral arm's most dangerous life-form? It can be of no use to you in the struggle here."

"Well, you don't seem too upset. Look at it this way. If the other Zardalu are all *alive,* then one more won't make a bit of difference. An' if the others are all *dead,* one surviving specimen would be absolutely priceless to anybody who got back home. Think of it, At."

"I did think of it—long since." The Cecropian reached out a forelimb and picked up the infant Zardalu. It wriggled furiously in her grasp. "And I agreed with you; otherwise I would have made my own thoughts known." She watched the writhing orange form. "It is alive, and obviously healthy. Apparently the Zardalu idea that their young need meat in order to thrive has no validity."

"Or maybe with no meat they grow up less vicious. That'd be nice. So you agree—I should keep it?"

"At least for a while." Atvar H'sial placed the little Zardalu down on the ground, close to Nenda's feet. "But let me give you a solemn warning. The Zardalu were the galaxy's most feared species. There must have been good reason for that, and our small victory over a few bewildered and desperate specimens does nothing to gainsay it. Remember, in a couple of years this infant will be big enough to tear you apart and eat you."

"Mebbe. I'm not worried. Hell, if I can't control a *baby*, I oughta be ashamed of myself."

"It will not *remain* a baby. And perhaps you *will* be ashamed of yourself—if you live so long. But now . . ." Atvar H'sial crouched close to Louis Nenda. Her emotional intensity had heightened, in subtle waves of chemicals. "Now the time for conversation has ended, and the time for action is here. There is a battle to be fought. Are you ready to put your new plaything to one side and begin the conflict?"

CHAPTER 28

"I MUST REITERATE to you the *great importance* of this matter." The speaker paused, and his eyes glared out of the screen. "And although it pains me to add this, I must remind you of your failure to honor your *commitment* and *promises.*"

Darya Lang wriggled in her wicker chair and stared at Professor Merada's recorded image with a mixture of disbelief and irritation. The video signal had been sent skipping across the Bose Communications Network, bearing its MOST URGENT—IMMEDIATE ACTION insignia and her full name and title. Within minutes of her final descent from Midway Station and her arrival at the surface of Opal, the video in her room had been flashing for attention.

"*Forty standard days,*" the speaker went on. "The fifth edition of the *Universal Artifact Catalog* is due for final compilation in just forty standard days! It cannot be completed without your assistance. As you well know, I told you of my great concern and worry when you announced your intention to travel to the Phemus Circle and observe the event you described as *Summertide.* If my cautionary words at the time were less strong than they should have been, it was only that I had your reassurance and *personal promise* that the journey would not affect your schedule for delivery of materials. It is imperative that the Catalog appear on time." The full mouth pursed in disapproval. "And if your material does not reach me in twenty days, at the very latest, it will be *too late.* The consequences of that will be most severe. I intend to—"

Darya turned off the sound.

Hans Rebka had entered the room as the words *personal promise* were spoken. He was carrying a sheaf of messages. He shook his head, sighed, and dropped into a chair at Darya's side.

"Half an hour we've been back on Opal," he said, "And look at these. Dozens of 'em. From Shipping Control: 'Please explain the failure of the Zardalu Communion ship, the *Have-It-All,* to file a flight plan before leaving the Dobelle system.' From Port Authority: 'Define current location and status of the freighter *Incomparable.*' From Transient Control and Emigration: 'Provide the present location of the Cecropian, Atvar H'sial'—hell, I just wish I *could* provide that."

Darya gestured at the screen in front of her. "I have the same sort of problem. Look at him! What are you going to do?"

"Dump the lot on poor old Birdie. You know the worst thing about all this? Everything has changed, yet I'm supposed to take all this bureaucratic nonsense *seriously.*"

"No, it hasn't." Darya pointed at the screen again, where Professor Merada was still in full spate and shaking his finger out at her. "Hasn't changed, I mean. Three months ago, that message would have had me weeping. I'd have been totally *appalled* at the idea that I was missing a publication date. Now?" She shrugged. "So I miss a deadline by a couple of weeks. I'll get the work done, and we'll still publish on time. You see things differently after you've traveled sixty thousand light-years and had a fight with the Zardalu. *Everything* hasn't changed, Hans. Everything else is just the same—*we've* changed."

"Well, everything *will* change, unless people start taking us more seriously." Rebka slapped the sheaf of papers onto the low table in front of him. "Julius Graves sent a message straight to the Alliance Council from Midway Station, telling what happened to us and warning about the Zardalu. He just received a reply. Know what they did? Ordered him back to Miranda, for psychological examination. And he's a councilor!"

"Is he going?"

"He is. He has to. But he's madder than hell. He's taking Tally's brain to be reembodied, and I'm going with them. Between the three of us, maybe the Alliance will start to believe what we say."

"The *four* of us. I know." Darya held up her hand. "I told you I had to get back to Sentinel Gate and catch up on my work. But I'm going with you anyway. All that"—she jerked her thumb at the irate face of Professor Merada—"is like a shadow world. *Studying* the Builders was all right, when there was no alternative. But we've been beyond the shadows. The-One-Who-Waits and Speaker-Between are real. The Builders are real. The Zardalu are real. We have to make other people *believe* that. And then I have to go back to Glister—and try again."

"Try again, and bring some *proof.* When you go to Glister, I go, too. The whole spiral arm has to know what we know." Rebka shook his head in frustration. "All that effort, and we came back completely empty-handed. No Builder technology, no proof that we went anywhere, nothing but our word about the Zardalu—even the tip of one tentacle would have made all the difference. We went farther than anyone has ever been, and we came back with *nothing.*"

"That's not true." Darya stood up, moved behind him, and started to massage the tight muscles of his shoulders. "We came out of it with *us.* You and me."

Rebka sighed and leaned back in his chair. "You're right. We're here. That's the only good piece. You know, I remember looking across at you when the Zardalu came along the tunnel leading to the vortex, and thinking that it was probably the last sight of Darya I'd ever have. I didn't like that idea at all. And thank God it wasn't true. We were unbelievably lucky, all of us."

"*Most* of us," Darya said quietly. "Not everyone."

The mood changed. They both went silent.

It was dusk on Opal, and the clouds had briefly opened. Without speaking, the two of them turned in unison to look up. They knew the direction. Out *that* way, thirty thousand light-years distant, floated the invisible enormity of Serenity. And somewhere within that great structure, lonelier and farther from home than any human or Cecropian had ever been, Louis Nenda and Atvar H'sial were locked in a final life-and-death struggle. No matter what happened, the logic of the Builders decreed that only one of them would win.

I can't help hoping that the one is Louis, Darya said to herself. And I know that Hans would be outraged if he ever found out I feel this way, but I pray that someday Louis will find a way to return.

Do you hear me, Louis Nenda? She stared upward, projecting her thought beyond the stars, beyond the galaxy. *Listen now. Come back. Come back safe.*

She felt it so strongly—surely he would read her emotions. Unless . . . The idea crept in like a wave of cold: unless Louis was dead already.

But that suggestion was . . . intolerable.

Darya brought her eyes down to the screen, to lose herself in the comforting warmth of Professor Merada's indignation.

EPILOGUE

"TELL ME, LOUIS Nenda." The pheromonal message was filled with quiet satisfaction. Outside the port, the convoluted structure of Serenity stretched away in endless arching spirals.

"Tell me this. Do humans have a word to describe the actions of two beings who are convinced that between them they can oppose and defeat an entire civilization, one that is hundreds of millions of years old and of huge technological powers?"

"Sure. We wouldn't be humans if we didn't. In fact, we have lots of 'em, with all shades of meaning. Fancy words, like *hubris,* or plain ones like *chutzpah* and *balls.* "

"I am delighted to hear that. Cecropians are the same. We have more than one expression for what we are proposing to do, but the most commonly used is *Fore-ordained by the Great Creator.* Shall we proceed?"

"Just one second." Nenda reached down to his feet. The

infant Zardalu had bitten a chunk off the leather toe of his boot, spat it out, and was ready for another go. He pulled a lump of hard cheesy material from his pouch and placed it where the hard bill could bite into it. "There. Try that, little feller."

The Zardalu began to eat. Nenda stood up again and stared out of the port at the alien abundance of the artifact.

"It's not just *a* fortune out there, At. It's *the* fortune. The biggest one ever. And there's millions more cubic kilometers of stuff we can't even see from here. Once we work it so the Builders and Speaker-Between do what *we* want *them* to do, an' not the other way round, we'll be sittin' on the ultimate jackpot."

"Indeed we will. And potentially, it is all ours."

"Hell, you can drop that *potentially.*" Nenda glared at Atvar H'sial. "I don't like to hear no negative thinking. I'm tellin' you, we're a ravin' shoo-in certainty. Like Graves said when he left, it makes you proud to be a human or a Cecropian. You have to feel kind of sorry for The-One-Who-Waits an' Speaker-Between an' all the rest of the Builders."

"With reason. Against us, they do not stand a chance."

"Not a prayer. They'll never even know what hit 'em."

Louis Nenda brushed his greasy hair away from his forehead, wiped his dirty hands on his pants, and stood tall.

"All right, let's go get 'em. Poor devils. Supposed to be smart, been around five hundred million years—and *still* don't know that guys like you and me always win."

ABOUT THE AUTHOR

Charles Sheffield is Chief Scientist of Earth Satellite Corporation. He is a past president of the Science Fiction Writers of America and of the American Astronautical Society, a Fellow of the American Association for the Advancement of Science, and a Distinguished Lecturer of the American Institute of Aeronautics and Astronautics. Born and educated in England, he holds bachelor's and master's degrees in mathematics and a doctorate in theoretical physics (general relativity and gravitation). He is the author of eleven novels, seventy short stories, and three nonfiction books on space. He now lives in Silver Spring, Maryland.